TOBY
THE RANCHER

DONNIE COLLINS

TATE PUBLISHING
AND ENTERPRISES, LLC

Toby the Rancher
Copyright © 2016 by Donnie Collins. All rights reserved.

No part of this publication may be reproduced, stored in a retrieval system or transmitted in any way by any means, electronic, mechanical, photocopy, recording or otherwise without the prior permission of the author except as provided by USA copyright law.

This novel is a work of fiction. Names, descriptions, entities, and incidents included in the story are products of the author's imagination. Any resemblance to actual persons, events, and entities is entirely coincidental.

The opinions expressed by the author are not necessarily those of Tate Publishing, LLC.

Published by Tate Publishing & Enterprises, LLC
127 E. Trade Center Terrace | Mustang, Oklahoma 73064 USA
1.888.361.9473 | www.tatepublishing.com

Tate Publishing is committed to excellence in the publishing industry. The company reflects the philosophy established by the founders, based on Psalm 68:11,

"The Lord gave the word and great was the company of those who published it."

Book design copyright © 2016 by Tate Publishing, LLC. All rights reserved.
Cover design by Maria Louella Mancao
Interior design by Manolito Bastasa

Published in the United States of America
ISBN: 978-1-68207-229-5
Fiction / Westerns
15.10.22

1

Toby Parker was an out-of-work cowboy. He had been without work for about a month. He could have had a job, but he wanted to work with his best friend, Pudge, his horse. Toby was a loner, a trait that was driven mainly by his childhood of bouncing between foster homes. He had been adopted by Jeb Parker and had a great life with his dad until his death, when Toby was eighteen years old. Toby had relegated back to being a loner. He could interact well with people but found most to be selfish and insincere, so he found himself migrating to enjoying the company of his pony. Toby had been working his way back from Utah to Texas. He had heard that there were several ranches in East Texas, albeit they were smaller than the one he had previously worked on in New Mexico.

Toby was heading toward Dallas/Fort Worth and decided he would stop and spend some time at the Fort Worth Stock Show and Rodeo. He figured he would enjoy it and might get lucky and find an opening for a job. Toby pulled into town the day before the rodeo was set to begin. He found a motel in the vicinity and set out to find a place to board Pudge for a few days. He knew he needed to find a job fairly quickly. He had money saved up, but it was starting to dwindle down to a level he wasn't comfortable with.

He found a horse-boarding barn and set Pudge up before he headed to the stockyards. He brushed Pudge and told him he would be back to see him that evening. Toby had heard a lot about the Fort Worth stockyards and was looking forward to experiencing them firsthand.

He found a parking spot and noticed a hat shop and decided to venture in and take a look. Toby hadn't planned on buying a hat, but he walked out with a new Resistol felt hat on his head. He took his old hat back to his truck before he headed to the Cowtown Coliseum where the rodeo was being held. He found a door that was open and asked a guy working if he could just take a look around. The guy agreed, and Toby went wandering through the corrals and looking at the rodeo stock in the pens.

Toby was scratching a bull on the head through the fence when he heard a guy say, "Pardner, that ain't real smart."

Toby turned to look at the guy and asked, "Why's that? He seems to like it."

"Yeah, until he decides to take your arm off," the guy said.

Toby glanced back at the bull. "He must be a bad one coming out of the gate." He stuck out his hand to the stranger. "Name's Toby Parker."

The stranger shook his hand. "Lane Carter is mine. Good to meet you. How'd you get in?"

Toby told Lane about the worker letting him in to look around.

"This bull is called Malo, which is Spanish for *mean*," Lane said.

"Has he hurt many cowboys?" Toby asked.

"He's never been ridden and has put the last three that tried in the hospital," Lane said.

"The rodeo clowns not keep him off the riders?"

"He hurt them by throwing them so high in the air," Lane responded. "He hasn't gotten anyone after they came off."

Toby shook his head. "Wow, can't wait to see him work."

"You in the rodeo?"

"Nah, just passing through town and decided to stop and see the rodeo, and see if a job opening might avail itself."

Toby the Rancher

"Enjoy, and good luck on the job."

Lane walked off, and Toby kept looking around. He made it through all the corrals and walked back over to take another look at Malo before he headed out the door. He marveled at how muscular the bull was and was excited to see the rodeo. He headed for the door, and as he reached for it, he heard Lane holler, "Hey, Toby."

Toby stopped and turned around and saw Lane walking quickly toward him with an older guy by his side. They reached Toby, and Lane asked, "Have you ever worked a rodeo?"

"Been in a few and in a Range Roundup, but only as a participant," Toby said.

"This is Ed Miles," Lane said. "He helps run this shindig, and he's had a couple of pickup men fall out on him. You seem to know your stuff, and I wondered if you might be interested since you are looking for work."

Ed Miles and Toby shook hands.

"Think you might want to give it a go?" Ed asked. "We could furnish a horse. The pay is $200 a night."

"I have my horse boarded, so I wouldn't need one," Toby said. "And I would definitely be interested."

Ed told Toby when to arrive and where to go, and they parted ways so Toby could go get Pudge and move him to the coliseum corrals.

Toby was happy. He was going to get to work on Pudge and get to see the rodeo firsthand. Two hundred dollars a night for three weeks would be great money to help him build his savings back up, plus he wouldn't have to pay for boarding Pudge.

Toby picked up Pudge and headed to the stockyards. He pulled in and backed up to the door and got out and went into the walk through door. He asked a man he saw where he could find Ed Miles. The guy called Ed on a walkie-talkie, and Ed showed up in short fashion.

Ed told the guy to open the door, and he showed Toby where to stable Pudge. Toby led Pudge out of the trailer, and Ed said, "That's a fine-looking horse."

"Thank you," Toby said. "We've been together a good while."

"I don't guess you'd be interested in entering any of the events, would you?" Ed asked.

Toby shut the gate on Pudge's pen. "I figured it was too late to enter."

"Nah, we have a couple of openings," Ed said. "One in saddle bronc riding and another in steer wrestling."

"Can I compete and work too?"

"Absolutely," Ed said.

"Where do I sign up?" Toby asked.

Ed walked Toby up to the office, and Toby completed the form and paid his entry fee. The prize money would be good if he was lucky enough to win the events. If not, it kept him sharp, anyway. Ed told Toby he would see him in the morning, and Toby walked back to check on Pudge. He fed and watered him and brushed him down good. He was talking to Pudge while he brushed him when he heard someone say, "Does he ever answer you?"

Toby turned to see a girl looking at him and smiling. She had light brown hair and was very pretty. Toby was a little embarrassed and said, "He tells me what to wear each day."

She laughed. "Are you going to be in the rodeo? I don't recall ever seeing you around."

"Yeah, in a couple of events," he said. "I'm working as a pickup man."

She started to leave but turned and said, "Sorry, I just made fun and didn't introduce myself. My name is Bethany Squires. I'm entered in the barrel racing."

"Pleased to meet you," Toby said. "They call me Toby Parker."

She smiled. "See you later, Toby Parker."

Toby tipped his new Resistol, and she walked away. Toby left Pudge and walked to his truck to park his trailer and go eat a bite somewhere before going to the motel. He saw a café that looked inviting, and he parked and walked in. He was waiting to be seated when he heard, "You following me, Toby Parker?"

Toby turned to see Bethany sitting in a booth with another girl and two guys. Toby got bashful and said, "Nah, just lucky."

The waitress came and told him to follow her, so Toby nodded at Bethany and walked the other direction. Where he sat, he couldn't see the booth she was in, so he didn't pay them any mind. He ordered his supper and looked at a paper he'd picked up. He finished eating and paid the waitress and headed for the door.

The group with Bethany was still there, and one of the guys saw Toby and said, "I hear you're in the rodeo?"

"Yeah, just a couple of events," Toby said. "Mainly working as a pickup."

"What events you entered?" the other guy asked.

"Saddle bronc and steer wrestling," Toby answered.

Bethany laughed. "Those are your events, aren't they, Kip?"

The first guy who spoke apparently was Kip, because he angrily said, "Yes, they are. I don't lose."

"Y'all have a good evening," Toby said, and he walked out the door. He got in his truck and drove to the motel.

"Looks like that guy won't like losing," Toby said to himself.

He pulled into the motel and settled in for the night. He was excited to be back working, and especially in the saddle, starting tomorrow. He drifted off to sleep while reading the Bible.

2

Toby woke up at around 6:00 a.m. He had gotten in a bad habit of sleeping later since he was unemployed. He was aggravated at himself for sleeping that late. He didn't have anywhere to be this morning but just didn't want to waste any part of the day. He decided to go eat at around 8:00 a.m. He had liked the food and the general atmosphere of the small cafe he had eaten supper at, so he went back to it for breakfast.

Toby ordered three eggs over easy, with ham, bacon, toast, orange juice, and his staple, coffee. He sat reading the paper about the stock show and rodeo and ate his breakfast. He had finished his breakfast and was drinking another cup of coffee when a couple of girls walked by and sat down at the booth in front of him. He glanced at the one facing him. She was a brunette, and wearing a cowboy hat. The one with her back to him also had on a hat and had light brown hair.

The brunette caught his eye, and he tipped his hat at her as he started to stand up to leave. Toby had talked some to the waitress, and as she saw him leaving, she said, "Good luck in the rodeo."

Toby nodded and touched the front of his hat and walked to the register. The word *rodeo* had perked up the two girls' ears, and they turned to watch Toby. He paid and turned to head to the door when he heard, "You *are* following me, aren't you?"

He looked and saw that the girl with her back to him had been Bethany Squires, from last night. Toby grinned and just tipped his hat and walked out. He got to the truck and thought that she sure seemed to like embarrassing him. He drove back to the motel to get ready to go to the stock show. He parked his truck where he felt it would be good to set all day and walked to the coliseum to take care of Pudge. He showed the card they had given him, and he headed for Pudge's stall. He fed and watered Pudge and was checking all his gear when he heard someone say, "That's too much horse for you."

Toby looked up to see the guy called Kip from the café, the one who had said he was in the events Toby was entered in.

"You sure you know which side to even get on a horse?" Kip continued. "Just because you have a nice, pretty hat doesn't mean you're a cowboy."

Toby was too quick to respond. "And just because you can put together a coherent sentence doesn't prove you have a brain."

The other guy that was with Kip in the café' said, "Come on, Kip. Leave him alone, and let's take care of our stock."

Kip glared at Toby, and Toby looked back at him with as much disdain as Kip was. The guy pulled on Kip's arm, and Kip turned and walked away.

"That idiot is going to be trouble before we get out of here," Toby told Pudge. "Always seems to be one."

Toby finished prepping his gear and headed for the door. As he started out, he ran into Bethany and the brunette. Toby said, "Pardon me," and held the door open for them.

"Why, thank you, Toby Parker," Bethany said. "By the way, this is Wendy Logan, and she thinks you're good-looking."

Wendy punched Bethany on the arm and shoved her through the door. Toby let the door shut and just shook his head.

He headed to the expo center to see some livestock. He spent the rest of the day kicking around, looking at cattle and hogs and watching them in the show ring. He decided to walk back through the first cattle barn because he had seen a bull he was very impressed with and wanted to take another look. He was standing and looking at the bull when a man said, "What do you think of him, young man?"

Toby glanced at the man and saw he was a man about sixty years old, and about Toby's height and build. "He's a very fine animal."

"Thank you," the man said. "I've been breeding for years to get my bulls to look like this. I'm very proud of him."

"I can understand why."

The man stuck out his hand. "The name's Hank Parker."

Toby kind of chuckled, and Hank asked, "What's funny?"

"Sorry," Toby said. "Didn't mean to laugh, but my name is Toby Parker."

Hank let out a deep laugh. "We'll, if that don't beat all. My dad's name is Toby Parker, although he has passed on now. Where you from?"

"I'm from Pennsylvania."

"Don't think we have any family up north."

"I really don't know where the family tree leads."

"Anyway, you have a great name, and you know livestock," Hank said. "You're a true Parker in my book."

Toby grinned. "Well, thank you, sir."

Toby and Hank stood and talked for nearly an hour, mainly about livestock and how Hank had built up his herd genetics. Toby looked at his watch and saw that it was getting close to the time for him to get back over to the coliseum. "Hank, I sure have enjoyed talking with you, but I'm going to have to get moving. I'm entered in and working the rodeo, and it's about time to show up."

"The rodeo?" Hank said. "That's cool. The missus and I are coming to the rodeo tonight. Can't wait to see you perform. I know you're a cowboy, but where do you work?"

"Been out of work," Toby said. "Heading to East Texas to see if I can find a job on a ranch. Took this job to help build savings back up."

"I see."

"Reckon I better run." Toby stuck out his hand to shake Hank's. He headed for the door and the coliseum. He was anxious to get lined out for the night.

Toby was surprised at the number of people already there when he walked in. He headed for Pudge's stall and began to get his spurs on and put the halter on Pudge. He was looking around to see if Ed Miles was there but couldn't spot him. He did see Lane Carter and walked over to talk to him.

"Howdy," Lane said as he saw Toby walking up.

"Howdy," Toby responded. "Do you know who or where I find out when and where I am supposed to be tonight?"

"Ed should be along shortly," Lane said. "You have time, so no need to worry."

"Much obliged." Toby said, and walked back to Pudge's stall.

Toby had been pleasantly surprised by Lane. He was six feet three, blond, and looked like he was put together very well. Toby figured the ladies found Lane very good looking. The typical guy to be stuck on themselves and not give folks the time of day. Lane wasn't like that at all.

Toby was messing with his gear when Ed walked up and said, "Evening, Toby."

Toby looked up. "Evening."

Ed proceeded to tell Toby where he needed to be and when. Toby would ride in the opening ceremony with everyone else. Toby was excited and happy to be back working with Pudge. It had only been a few weeks, but it had seemed like a lot longer. He would be not only working the arena but also participating in the saddle bronc riding tonight. He was getting Pudge ready to lead out when Kip walked up.

Kip held out his hand. "Just wanted you to meet the guy that is going to beat your pants off tonight. Kip Walker."

"Good luck," Toby said. "They call me Toby Parker."

Kip scoffed and walked off.

They sure grow 'em big in Texas, Toby thought. Lane was big, and this guy was bigger.

Toby mounted up and started for the arena entry. He had Pudge at a slow walk when Bethany and Wendy rode up on either side. He looked at Wendy and said, "I don't believe we have officially met. I'm Toby Parker."

"Wendy Logan."

Toby commented on her horse and asked if she was a barrel racer.

"Yes," Wendy said. "I was last year's winner."

"I look forward to watching you," Toby said.

"Hello," Bethany said. "I'm still over here, and I was second last year."

Toby decided to have some fun. He turned and said, "Oh, sorry, Bethany. I forgot you had ridden up. Only second? I prefer winners."

Bethany looked at him and said, "Well, you won't be one. Kip will kick your rear in the arena." She rode off.

Wendy laughed. "You played her well. I better catch up."

Toby tipped his hat as Wendy rode off. He got in line and was amazed at how large the crowd was. He had been in several rodeos but never with a crowd this large. He bent down and reached and patted Pudge on the neck. "A lot of people are going to get to see the best cow pony in Texas."

Pudge shook his head like he understood and agreed. Toby grinned. He felt as good as he had in a long time at that moment. An older man rode up beside Toby as they were going in two abreast. Toby introduced himself and found out the man's name was Jose Gomez. He was a calf roper and had won last year.

The procession started, and it was fun to ride in and have the music playing and the crowd cheering. After it ended, Toby stayed in the arena to begin working. The events started, and Pudge showed real quick what kind of horse he was. He handled every situation well, and as Toby left the arena to get ready for the saddle bronc ride, he had several comments and compliments on Pudge as he rode by. He put Pudge in the stall and got himself together to head up for the event to start.

He passed by Ed Miles, who said, "Toby, that's quite a horse you have. You two work great together. Good luck in bronc riding."

"Thank you, sir," Toby replied.

He waited by the fence and watched the other riders. He was the last to go. He figured it was because he was the last one to enter. He looked around the arena and spotted Hank Parker. Hank was looking at him, so Toby waved. Hank returned the wave.

"Waving at a girl?"

Toby turned to see Lane standing beside him. "Nah, a guy I met over at the stock show."

They watched Kip Walker ride. He was good and scored an 89, the highest score yet.

"Do you know him?" Toby asked.

"Just enough to know I don't like him," Lane said. "He is a loudmouth and a bully."

"Guess I read him right."

There was one more rider before Toby was up, so he headed for the chute. Lane patted him on the back and wished him luck. Toby was mounting when Kip pulled up on the fence and said, "Don't get hurt, pretty boy."

Toby ignored him and concentrated on getting ready for the ride. The gate opened, and the bronc jumped out. The horse was good, and Toby had to have the best ride he had ever had just to stay on. He had no idea how he had done. It had been a long time since he had ridden for a score. He was just happy he had ridden the full time. He dismounted and left the arena and waited for his score.

Some cowboys were patting him on the back and saying, "Nice ride." He caught a glimpse of Kip and the guy who had been with Kip. Kip didn't look happy.

The announcer came on the PA and said, "That ride by Toby Parker ends the first round of the bronc riding, with a score of 90, which gives him the lead going to the second round."

The crowd cheered, and several folks congratulated Toby as he headed back to get Pudge to work the arena for the rest of the evening. He reached the stall and was tightening the cinch on Pudge's saddle when Kip walked up and said, "You're a punk, and you got lucky tonight. You won't be so lucky next time."

Toby looked at him. "Get out of my face."

"Or what?" Kip said.

"Or else you will be disqualified." Ed Miles had walked up. "I warned you about your behavior. Now get out of here."

Kip turned and left without a word.

"Watch your back with that one," Ed said. "He is an idiot."

Toby nodded and climbed into the saddle to head to the arena.

The rest of the night went well, and the first night of the rodeo came to a close. Toby was taking care of Pudge when he heard someone say, "Nice ride, Toby."

Toby thought he recognized the voice, and he turned to see Hank Parker and a lady. "Thank you, sir."

"Toby, this is my better half, Sadie," Hank said.

"How do you do, ma'am?" Toby said.

"I sure enjoyed the rodeo," she said.

Toby grinned at her, and Hank said, "We'd like to buy you supper, if you haven't eaten yet."

"I'd be honored," Toby said.

Hank told Toby where to meet them, and they left. Toby finished tending Pudge and headed to his truck.

3

Toby pulled up at the restaurant where Hank had said they would meet him. It was a steak house, and Toby had a hankering for a good steak. He walked in, and the hostess greeted him, and then he heard Hank say, "Over here, Toby."

Toby walked over and noticed another couple at the table. Hank stood up and said, "Let me make some introductions so everyone knows each other. Toby, this is our daughter, Patty, and her husband, Carl Matthews. Carl and Patty, this is Toby Parker."

Carl stood up and shook Toby's hand. "Good ride tonight. You look like you have been on a horse for a while."

"Thank you," Toby said. "Been riding one since I was twelve. My dad got me started."

"Let's order some food," Hank said.

They ordered and ate and talked for over an hour. The Parkers were interested in Toby's life story, and Toby found out that Hank and Sadie had two daughters. Carl and Patty had two kids, but they weren't at the stock show. Carl was a veterinarian, and Patty was a schoolteacher. Their other daughter, Debbie, and her husband and three kids lived in Abilene.

Toby enjoyed himself and was very comfortable with them. He decided he better get to the motel, so he said, "Well, folks, I guess I better head to the motel to clean up some. I imagine I've added a little more flavor to your supper than you wanted."

"Didn't notice at all," Carl said.

They all laughed.

Toby tried to pay for his meal, but they wouldn't let him. "I sure have enjoyed this," He said. "Maybe I'll see you tomorrow."

"We enjoyed it too," Hank said. "It is very refreshing to find a young man with a head on his shoulders these days."

Toby put his hat on and tipped it to all of them and left the restaurant. He slept well that night after a good, hot shower. He woke up and was at the café for breakfast by 6:30 a.m. He took his time eating and reading the paper. He got up to leave the restaurant and saw some folks who had participated last night. He tipped his hat to them, and they nodded at him, and he left the café. He headed over to see Pudge and take care of him.

Toby was sitting on a box and watching Pudge eat when two cowboys walked up. One of the guys started talking. "We just wanted to let you know Kip Walker is doing a lot of talking about how he is going to beat you down in every way. Personally, after watching you ride last night, I don't think he can beat you, but he is a cheap shot artist, so watch your back. We can't stand him."

"Thanks, guys," Toby said. "But why has he decided he wants to beat me so? I hardly know anything about the guy."

"Because Bethany has shown an interest in you," the smaller one said. "She doesn't like him, but he tries to claim ownership anytime she is around. He fights someone at every rodeo they both participate in."

"I've said ten words to that girl, and she initiated it," Toby said. "Oh well, if he is ignorant, there isn't much I can do but be ready. Thanks again."

The guys walked off, and Toby asked Pudge, "Pudge ole buddy, why do I keep getting in these messes? I don't think I go around looking for trouble. If I am, let me know." He patted Pudge and sat back down on the box. He worked and made his seat comfortable and decided he might just hang out there most of the day. He had a new *Farm & Ranch Living* magazine and had picked up a *High Plains Journal* and wanted to look at and read both of them.

He had been sitting there for about two hours when Ed Miles walked up.

"You just hanging out with your horse?" Ed asked.

"Yeah," Toby said. "I thought I might head back over to the stock show a little later, but just takin 'er easy for a while."

"Just wanted to tell you nice job on last night," Ed said. "Looked like you had been doing pickup duties for a long time."

"Thanks. I appreciate the opportunity to earn some money."

Ed left, and Toby decided to mosey over to the show barn and see what was going on. He climbed up on the bleachers to watch the cattle show. He was trying to get a feel for what the judge was looking for and hadn't paid any attention to anyone around him. His concentration was broken when two people sat down next to him so close they bumped him. He turned and saw Bethany and Wendy.

"Hello, Toby Parker," Bethany said.

"Hey," Toby responded.

"So what are you doing here? I thought you were a rodeo cowboy."

"Nope, just riding and working in this one since it worked out."

"Where you from?" Wendy asked.

"Pennsylvania," Toby answered.

"That where you are going back to after you're done here?" Bethany asked.

"Nope," he said. "East Texas."

"Why not west Texas?" Wendy asked.

"Been there, done that," Toby said. "Want a new terrain."

"Well, that's okay," Bethany said. "We both attend East Texas University, so we'll be over there with you."

They both seemed giddy, but Toby brought their spirits down quickly. "Look, I don't know what's going on with you and Kip Walker, but I don't want to be in the middle of it. Good day, ladies." He got up and left them sitting there.

Toby decided to go back to the motel for a while, but he noticed a bulletin board with all kinds of ads on it. Most of them were livestock or horses for sale, or stud service. He was hoping to find some "Help wanted" ads but didn't notice any.

"You looking to buy another horse or some cattle?"

Toby turned to see Hank Parker. "Hello, Hank. Nah, just thought there might be some 'Help wanted' ads here."

"I guess I thought you had a job lined up," Hank said. "I must not have listened very well."

"That's okay," Toby said. "Don't worry about it."

"Where you heading?" Hank asked.

"Not sure," Toby responded. "Just to East Texas and then look around."

"You looking for anything particular or just a ranch job?"

"I just hope to find somewhere that I can work and do some of it on horseback, and be around good folks," Toby said. "I don't expect to get rich. I just enjoy the work, and as long as I have enough to live on, I'm good."

"Well, that's not a difficult list of requirements to fulfill," Hank said.

"I have found it a little more difficult than you might think. Maybe I'm expecting too much out of people."

"So it's the good-folks part that keeps you searching."

"Yep," Toby said, kind of embarrassed.

"Nothing wrong with that," Hank said. "Especially in a job that has some potential hazards. You have to know who has your back."

As he finished talking, Sadie Parker walked up and said, "Hank, they're waiting on us to go to the motel to freshen up."

"Sorry, ma'am," Toby said. "I kind of held him up."

Sadie looked at Toby and said, smiling, "Nice try, Toby, but I know my husband, and I have an idea it was the other way around. By the way, dispense with the ma'am stuff. I'm Sadie."

They laughed. Hank and Sadie walked off in one direction, and Toby went the other.

Toby spent the rest of the afternoon in the motel room and actually took a nap. He hadn't done that in forever and felt guilty when he woke up. He looked at the clock quickly, afraid he had overslept and would be late for the rodeo. He was relieved to see he had over an hour until the time he needed to be there, so he started getting ready.

Toby walked into the door, and he saw things were in mass chaos. It looked like a tornado had hit inside the barn. He stopped a guy and asked what had happened, and the guy said the bulls had gotten out somehow and had wrecked the place. Toby was worried about Pudge and started trotting to get to him. He was thankful when he saw that Pudge was okay. He saw Ed and walked over and asked if he could do anything to help.

"Nah, I think we're in as good of a shape as we can be right now," Ed said. "We'll reassess the damage and figure out what to do after tonight's performance. I will say that horse of yours is something. He didn't even budge during all the ruckus."

Toby was glad to hear Pudge hadn't been bothered by the bulls. He saddled Pudge and got ready to head into the arena. He had his work cut out for him when the events started. He and Pudge had to really work to help cowboys during the events since the animals were still rattled and several had trouble with them.

It was time for Toby to get ready for his first round of steer wrestling, so he headed back to the stall to tighten the cinch and make sure he had what he needed.

"Good luck, Mr. Hateful." It was Bethany.

He looked at her and said, "Thanks. I'll need it." He didn't intend to give her any more time or attention and had his back to her.

"You ready to get your butt kicked?"

Toby turned to see Kip standing by Bethany. Toby didn't say a word. He climbed up on Pudge and backed him right at Kip and

Bethany and rode to the arena entrance. It wasn't long until Kip came riding by and glared at him. Toby thought to himself that Kip may be so aggravated with him that it might take his mind off what he needed to do and give Toby a better chance to win. The prize money would be nice.

The event started, and again Toby was last to go. It came time for him, and the leading time was 5.5 seconds. Kip was in third with a 6.2. It was a decent bunch of cowboys, and Toby would have to be sharp to place. He bent down and patted Pudge on the side of the neck and said, "Get me close as quick as you can, and I'll try to do my part." He straightened and rode into the area beside the chute so the rope barrier could be put up.

The chute door tripped, and the steer bolted, and Pudge hit the rope at the perfect time. He was right beside the steer in no time at all, and the hazer was behind. Toby knew he had to go now or the steer would veer. He left the saddle and landed on the neck and grabbed the horns and was twisting as he hit the ground. The steer came down quickly.

The ride was done. He felt good, but was it as good as he thought? He heard the crowd and looked up at the time. It read 3.3 seconds! He couldn't believe his eyes, but he was happy. He walked to Pudge, mounted up, and rode out the gate. He headed back to the stall to put his things up. He was ready to mount up when he caught a glimpse of Lane walking over.

"Nice job, Toby," Lane said. "They haven't had a time like that here in a long time. Folks appreciate it."

"Pudge gets most of the credit," Toby said.

"He does seem to be quite a horse," Lane said. "I have to get ready. Catch you later."

Toby rode back to the arena to get back to work. Bethany and Wendy were on their horses, getting ready to ride in the barrel racing. They rode over to congratulate Toby, and Kip came riding up and rammed his horse between Pudge and Bethany's horse. Her horse got spooked and jumped back and knocked a guy down who was walking by.

"Are you some kind of idiot?" Toby yelled at Kip. He jumped off Pudge and ran to grab the reins of Bethany's horse to help calm it down.

Bethany dismounted and played the distressed damsel, putting her head on Toby's shoulder. Toby knew it wasn't good, but what could he do at that point?

"I will meet you outside after this is over tonight," Kip said.

"My pleasure," Toby said.

Kip rode off quickly.

Toby turned to Bethany. "All right, your horse seems ready to go."

Bethany mounted back up, and Wendy went in for her run.

The rest of the evening went off fairly well. Toby wrapped things up with Pudge and was getting ready to leave when Hank and Sadie walked up.

"Evening, folks," Toby said.

"You sure took that steer down in fine fashion," Hank said. "Worked the arena well too. Everything seemed a bit nervous."

Toby told them about the bulls getting out and pointed out some of the areas they had messed up.

"You feel like eating," Hank said. "We would enjoy your company."

"I would, but there is a guy here that has gotten a burr under his saddle for me, and I'm figuring he's going to start something outside," Toby said. "I don't want any trouble, but this guy seems bent on it."

"What's his beef with you?" Sadie asked.

"I don't even know the guy," Toby said. "He has a fancy on this girl, and she has been talking to me, and he wants to fight about it."

"A girl, huh?" Sadie said, smiling.

Toby grinned. "Trust me, I'm not interested. He just can't accept that."

"We'll walk out with you, and maybe he'll decide to leave it alone," Hank said. "At least for tonight."

"You sure?" Toby asked.

"Yep," Hank said.

They walked to the door and headed outside. They hadn't gone a hundred feet when Kip came running up with two other guys.

"I figured you would wimp out, sissy," Kip said.

"Kip, you need to back off," Toby said. "We're heading to eat and don't want any trouble."

Hank and Sadie held back a couple of steps.

"Well, that's too bad," Kip said.

Toby noticed people were gathering around. Apparently, Kip had been talking. The crowd was egging him on now, and Kip was bouncing around, so Toby turned slightly to tell Hank and Sadie, "Sorry, doesn't look like he is going to let—"

Toby was stopped in midsentence when he caught a glimpse of a punch coming in from the side.

4

Toby was able to dodge his head backward and bring his left arm up at the same time to knock Kip's arm up in the air after the failed sucker punch. Toby quickly shifted his feet, twisted, and drove his right fist into Kip's ribs left open by knocking his arm up above his head. That punch took the wind out of Kip and hurt him, and he stumbled back.

Kip wasn't smart enough to let it end, though. He started forward and started to swing, but Toby caught him with a left jab on the chin to stand him up and a right roundhouse to knock him cold. Kip wilted like a dead flower. Toby looked and saw a bystander holding a bottle of water. He took it from them and poured the water on Kip's face, and he started coming around. Toby looked at the two guys with Kip and said, "Get him up and take care of him since you're his backup."

They started helping him up, and Toby watched them before turning to Hank and Sadie. "I am sorry that you had to be a part of this."

Hank was grinning. "Don't apologize. You were forced into it."

"Yeah, it just brings back memories to Hank of forty years ago," Sadie said.

Toby kind of smiled and said, "My truck's over there." He pointed the way to his truck.

They started that way, parting the crowd. They got into the truck, and Toby drove to where Hank said they were parked. Hank and Sadie climbed out, and Hank said, "We'll meet you at the same steak house."

Toby, figuring the night was ruined for them, asked, "Are you sure?"

"Absolutely," Sadie answered.

Toby's spirits picked up. It would help him forget the fight.

They had a good supper and talked about several things, but the fight didn't come up, which pleased Toby. They finished their meal, and Hank asked Toby, "Do you have a pie preference?"

"Dad got me hooked on apple pie when I was twelve, and it has always been my favorite," Toby said.

Hank ordered each of them a piece of pie and coffee.

"Toby, you say East Texas is where you are heading, but do you have a specific location?" Hank asked.

"Nah," Toby said. "I figured I would head to Longview and branch out from there. It seems to be a spot on the map that might be a good start."

"That would be a good starting point," Hank said. "What about Nacogdoches?"

"Don't know anything about it," Toby said. "Are there ranches there?"

"Small ones," Hank said. "Not like West Texas or New Mexico, but the land is so much better. You don't need thousands of acres to raise livestock."

"Sounds like a place to look, for sure," Toby said. "Where you folks from exactly?"

Sadie smiled. "Hank, quit beating around the bush."

Hank laughed. "Okay. Toby, we live outside of Nacogdoches. It just so happens we are looking for a ranch hand. I've hired two in the last six months and let both go, because they were lazy and didn't do the job. We can't pay much but would be more than pleased if you would consider coming to work for us."

Toby was surprised at the offer. He never expected anything like this. Before Toby could respond, Hank continued, "We own nearly a section of land and lease another eight hundred acres, and it has good grass and plenty of trees. We do have some blueberries we raise, and Sadie cans and sells. You already know that we run around two hundred momma cows and they are all registered stock. We have a mobile home for the hired hand, and all utilities are paid."

"Sounds like a sweet place," Toby said. "I'd be honored to work for y'all."

"Fantastic," Hank said. "I never expected to come to the stock show and come home with a new ranch hand. I used to be able to handle the place myself for a good period of time if I didn't have a ranch hand, but at sixty, I'm slowing down."

"I imagine you can still work us younger guys into the ground," Toby said.

"He still tries and pays the price for a few days afterwards," Sadie said.

"So neither of your daughters or sons-in-law help out on the place?" Toby asked.

"Nah," Hank responded. "Carl as a vet is as close to as anyone comes to working with the ranch. Not even any of our grandkids want to help out."

"Hank, you know Kali would like to but she is still in college," Sadie corrected him. She looked at Toby. "She is Carl and Patty's daughter and our oldest grandchild."

Toby nodded his understanding of what she had said.

"Does $2,000 a month sound okay for your wages?" Hank asked.

"With a house and utilities furnished, it sounds more than fair," Toby said.

Hank stuck out his hand. "Welcome aboard."

Toby shook his hand and felt like a load was lifted off his shoulders. He had found a job, and for a couple he dearly liked and enjoyed being around.

They got up to leave, and once outside the restaurant, Hank asked, "How long are you working here?"

"They said three weeks when I was hired on," Toby said.

Hank grimaced and said, "Doggone, I was looking forward to having good help working the heifers I'm getting ready to put with the bull. Well, I guess I can do it one more time myself."

Toby felt bad but noticed Hank was smiling.

"Sure look forward to working with you," Hank said.

They shook hands, and Sadie hugged Toby like he had never had a mother do. Toby got into his truck and just sat there a while after Hank and Sadie had left. Were things really as good as they seemed? He almost felt like he wasn't supposed to feel this relaxed and happy.

He drove to the motel and slept like a baby all night and woke up at 6:00 a.m., ready to go. Toby wasn't real hungry but stopped by the café for some good coffee while he read the paper. Two guys walked up to his table, and Toby recognized them from the rodeo.

"We just wanted to tell you how much we enjoyed watching Kip get his tail whipped," one of them said. "Watch your back, though. He is a jerk and will play dirty."

"His kind usually do," Toby said. "Thanks for the warning, though."

They left, and Toby went back to his paper. They hadn't told him anything he hadn't already thought of, unfortunately. Toby finished the paper and headed to the coliseum to see Pudge. Toby fed and watered Pudge and was brushing him down when Ed Miles walked up.

"Morning, Toby," Ed said.

"Mornin'," Toby responded.

"Toby, I need to talk to you," Ed said. "The two guys you replaced as a pickup man have gotten well and came back wanting their positions. They are under contract, so I have to work them. I hate it, because I know you were counting on the money."

The news rocked Toby a little, but he thought a minute and said, "I understand, Ed. Maybe I can get lucky and win my two events tonight and get the prize money."

"From what I've seen, I think you stand a very good chance of that." Ed shook Toby's hand and thanked him for the work he had done and walked off.

Toby had said the right thing, but he was counting on the money, and now he was pondering his next move. He finished up with Pudge and said, "I'll see ya a little later, ole buddy." He headed for the door.

Toby needed some new gloves for the bronc ride and started walking toward the shops. He needed to win tonight to bring in the prize money and help fill the void in his account. He went into the first shop he thought would have the gloves he needed and bought a pair. He came out and saw a café and thought he would stop in and have a cup of coffee. He walked in and was starting to go for a booth when he heard his name. He stopped and looked behind him to see Carl and Patty Matthews. He walked over and said, "Hello. I didn't know you were still in town."

"We weren't," Carl said. "We went home and then came back this morning. Hank is so proud of his bull, so we wanted to come back and support him during the show. I think the whole family is coming in."

"That is great," Toby said. "What time does he show?"

"It starts at two o'clock," Patty said.

"I'll have to be there to see how he does," Toby said. "That is quite a bull he has. Maybe I'll see you there."

Toby walked to his booth and ordered some coffee. Toby heard the door of the café open and looked up to see some people walk up to Carl and Patty's table. They shook hands and hugged, and Toby surmised from how the lady looked that she must be Hank and Sadie's other daughter. Her husband and three kids—two girls and a boy—were with her. Toby went ahead ordered a piece of apple pie when he saw it on the menu. He guessed that would be one thing that he would always do and remember the times he had spent with his dad.

The group at the Matthews table was laughing and having a good time. Toby hadn't noticed more people had joined them. The waitress was filling his coffee cup again, and he glanced toward their table and saw the additional people. They were two girls who looked to be in their late teens to their early twenties and a guy about the same age. He turned back to thank the waitress.

He was taking a drink of coffee when he heard a voice he recognized. He looked over and saw that Hank and Sadie had come in to join the group. Toby smiled to himself as they all seemed to be having a good time enjoying each other's company. He finished his coffee and decided to head back to the motel room and hang out. He paid the waitress and got up to head to the door. He was reaching for the door when Hank spotted him and hollered, "Toby, come here. I want you to meet the family."

Toby stopped and walked over to the table. He took his hat off and said, "Hello."

"This is Toby Parker," Hank started. "He is going to be our new ranch hand when he finishes up with the rodeo. Toby, you've met Carl and Patty. This is our other daughter, Debbie, her husband, Albert Grissom, and their kids—Jackie, Susie, and Tim. Over here are Carl and Patty's two daughters, Kali and Carla. This is Drew Fisher, Kali's boyfriend. There will be a test to see if you remember them all when you start to work."

Everyone laughed.

"I didn't know Toby was coming to work for you," Carl said. He looked at Toby. "Why didn't you say something earlier?"

That kind of rubbed Toby wrong, and he said, "I didn't think it was my place to tell you."

Hank smiled. "And you are correct, Toby. Carl, you are out of line."

"It's nice to meet you all," Toby said. "I best be moving along."

"Where are you heading?" Hank asked.

Toby the Rancher

"Back to the motel to hang out. Plan to come watch you show. I would like to talk to you later, if I could."

"Let's walk outside and talk now," Hank said.

They headed for the door, and once outside, Toby said, "Ed Miles caught me this morning and said the two guys that were sick and I was replacing are coming back to work, so I am free after tonight. I didn't know when you wanted me to start."

"That's great," Hank said. "We are heading home tomorrow. You can follow us and get started."

"That's great," Toby said. "See you later."

They shook hands and parted ways.

Toby was a little puzzled by Carl's reaction and even more by Hank shutting him down. He decided to just slough it off and forget it. Toby watched the movie *No Time for Sergeants* back at the motel room and then got ready to go back to the stock show and then to the rodeo. Toby walked into the show barn at 1:55 p.m. and found a place to sit that seemed to have a good vantage point. He was looking at a brochure he had picked up and didn't notice Hank's entire family coming up to sit down by him.

"Do you mind if we join you?"

Toby looked up to see Sadie standing by him. "Not at all," he said.

They all sat down beside and in front of him. Tim came up and sat on the other side of Toby. Toby spoke to him, and it opened a floodgate. Tim told him he was eight years old and that they lived in Abilene. He asked Toby questions about the rodeo. He seemed in awe with Toby being a cowboy. Toby noticed Tim had boots, jeans, and a Western shirt on.

"Timmy, you need to stop talking Toby's ear off," Sadie said. "Your grandad is coming in the arena now."

They all watched closely as Hank led the bull he called Boss around the ring. There were 102 bulls in the class.

Tim started talking again. "Toby, do you have a horse?"

"Yes, I do," Toby said.

"What is its name?" Tim asked.

"Pudge," Toby answered.

Tim started laughing and said, "That's a funny name."

Toby smiled. He had watched Hank and Boss while he was talking.

"Timothy, come down here and sit and leave him alone," Debbie said.

Toby smiled. "He is fine. I don't mind the questions. I was probably the same way."

Debbie let Tim stay there, and it kept Tim quiet for a while.

Boss won the class, and Hank was beaming as he led him out. They all got up to go meet Hank at his stall. Toby helped Sadie down the last bleacher and heard, "Wow, good-looking and a gentleman."

Toby turned to see Carla walking by, along with Kali and Drew. He turned his attention back to Sadie as she was saying, "I am so happy for Hank. He has been trying to get his breeding to this point for several years."

"He sure looked happy," Toby said.

They all walked back to see Hank.

"That was round 1," Hank said. "I have two more to go. It would be great to win Grand Champion."

They were talking about it, and Toby slipped off and headed to the coliseum. He wanted to check on Pudge and make sure he was okay. He brushed Pudge and spent some time with him. He headed back over to the show barn, and Hank was showing when he walked in, so he just stood off to the side and watched it. He could see good enough. Hank won that event too and was up for Grand Champion next. Toby just stood where he was, and ten minutes later, Hank led Boss back in competing for Grand. He won Grand Champion of the Show.

Toby saw the family stand up and cheer when they gave Hank his trophy. Hank saw Toby standing where he was and grinned at him and motioned him over. Toby met Hank coming out of the ring and said, "Congratulations."

Toby the Rancher

"Thank you," Hank said. "Now you need to win tonight so we can take trophies back to Nacogdoches."

"I'll do my best," Toby said.

"I have no doubt," Hank said. "See you later."

Toby left and went to get ready for the bronc riding.

5

Toby got a cup of coffee on the way back to the coliseum and was sitting with Pudge, enjoying it, when Lane walked up. "Toby, I heard Ed had to cut your time short. I sure hate it, and I have heard that from a lot of cowboys. They like the way you worked the arena."

"I appreciate it," Toby said. "It is probably for the best, though. I have a job that I need to go ahead and start down around Nacogdoches."

"That's cool," Lane said. "Still hate to see you go. You're up twice tonight, aren't you?"

"Yeah. I could sure use the prize money, but I know I have an *X* on my back with all the other guys."

"Yeah, they don't take very well to new guys coming in and upstaging them. Good luck."

They shook hands, and Lane walked off. Toby sat back down and sipped at his coffee. He was running the last few days through his mind. He remembered he had left his chaps in the truck, so he got up and headed out to his truck. He was on the way back when he ran into the Parker family. They were looking around Cowtown and doing some shopping.

"Hello, folks," Toby said.

Toby the Rancher

"Toby, save me," Hank said. "They are dragging me around, shopping and spending money."

"Very funny, Dad," Debbie said.

"Yeah, this was his idea," Sadie said.

"Toby, where can I get a hat like yours?" Tim said.

Toby glanced at Tim's parents to see how they were reacting before he answered, "There are several stores with hats. You just have to find one that fits your head."

"I want some of them too," Tim said, pointing at Toby's chaps.

"Tim, I have got some old ones that maybe we can make them into chaps that will fit you," Toby said. "I'll work on that and send them to you."

Tim was excited. Toby glanced at Albert and Debbie, and they both mouthed, "Thank you."

"Y'all have fun," Toby said. "I need to get ready."

"We are finished shopping," Hank said. "We are heading to meet Patty's girls and get to our seats to watch the rodeo. Good luck."

"Thanks," Toby said. "I'll need it."

They parted ways, and Toby went to the stall and started getting his gear on. He was a little early but wanted to be ready and get his mind focused. He got Pudge saddled up so they could ride in the opening. He led Pudge to the arena and was standing, looking ahead, when he noticed Kip in front of him looking back. Toby just stared at him, so Kip looked away. Toby thought to himself that he was glad he would be leaving after tonight. He didn't want any more fights.

"You look like you are ready to ride. Chaps and all." Bethany had ridden up beside him.

Toby looked and saw her and Wendy, and said, "Bronc riding is coming up pretty quick."

"Aren't you working as pickup?" Wendy asked.

"Nah," Toby responded. "The regulars came back. I'm doing my two events tonight, and then I am out of here."

◆ 35 ◆

"You're kidding," Bethany said.

"Nope," Toby said as he went around and mounted up.

"Oh no," Bethany said. "Where are you going? I want to stay in contact."

Toby thought for moment because he wasn't sure he wanted to stay in contact but didn't want to be mean or rude. "Somewhere down around Nacogdoches. Not sure of the address or anything yet." He was hoping that would deter the two of them, but Wendy asked, "What's your phone number?"

Crud, Toby thought to himself, but he gave them his number. They both had it in their phone in no time at all.

"Here we go," he said, and the line of horses and people started into the arena. When the opening parade was done, Toby put Pudge in his stall and walked back to the arena to watch while he waited for the saddle bronc riding to begin. Different people walked up and talked with Toby as he watched the events. He really didn't pay much mind to anyone as he was focused on the ride coming up.

They called for the bronc riders, and Toby headed to the chutes. He would be last to go again, but he wanted to be over by the action. As he was walking through, he heard a little kid call out his name, and he looked to see Tim standing up and hollering. The rest of the family was there on the first three rows. Toby tipped his hat and walked on through.

The bronc riding started, and the first three got thrown off. The next guy got a 78, which raised the bar for the rest. More rides brought more scores and more thrown cowboys. The 78 was still the leading score, and Kip was up. He had glared at Toby throughout the whole event. It was clear Kip's head wasn't on his upcoming ride.

Kip's ride started, and he was thrown off in the first three seconds. Toby didn't even look at him once he was thrown. He was focusing on his bronc and ride. The horse he had drawn was tough, from what he had heard. He knew he would have to fight like he never had to stay on. Toby was ready and nodded for the gate to open.

The horse bolted from the chute in one powerful jump and twist. Toby tightened and strained every muscle he had to hold on. It jumped again, what felt like twelve feet in the air, and then hit the ground and spun and jumped again. Toby was riding it, but it was taking everything he had. He was trying to read the animal's head, but he figured out the horse must not be from where he was because he couldn't understand what it was saying. He just had to hold tight and ride.

The horse kept jumping and spinning, and the eight seconds seemed like eight minutes. He heard the buzzer and worked to get off. The pickups helped him off and clear, and he was glad that it was over. He was walking out of the gate when he heard the announcer say, "Folks, you just saw the first time a cowboy has stayed on Ole Jumper. He has thrown over seventy-five cowboys up to now. Toby Parker's score is 85, and he wins the saddle bronc riding with the best score on both rides."

Some other cowboys pushed Toby back out in the ring for the people to acknowledge. Toby was embarrassed, but he waved and turned to each side of the arena, waving, and then headed for the gate. He just wanted to get out of the limelight and get back to Pudge at that point. He went around the long way to get to his stall and to avoid having to stop and talk to folks.

He was brushing and talking to Pudge when Bethany walked up and said, "Nice ride, cowboy. You have them talking around the coliseum. They think you should try Malo."

"Not hardly," Toby said. "I have never ridden a bull in my life, and I ain't about to start with him."

"I bet you could do it."

"Thanks for the confidence, but I need to start work tomorrow and not be in the hospital somewhere," Toby responded laughingly.

Wendy walked up to them, and Bethany asked, "You want to go eat with us after the rodeo tonight?"

"I appreciate the offer, but most of the crowd you run with don't seem to like me," Toby said. "I don't enjoy being around people like that."

"It would just be us two," Wendy said.

Toby thought for a minute and said, "Okay. Since this will be the last night I see you."

"Great," they said in unison and then walked off, giggling to each other.

Toby wondered if they were setting him up for something. He hoped not. He didn't want any hassles tonight. He said to Pudge, "Ole buddy, I may have just made a tactical error there. Let's hope not."

Pudge acted like he understood and shook his head. Toby laughed.

It was time for the steer wrestling, and Toby led Pudge up to the arena. He rode over to the chute area and sat on Pudge and watched the other contestants. Kip was in the lead with a very good time of 3.8 seconds when it came time for Toby to go and end the session and event. Toby had beaten that time the first round, but everything clicked perfectly. Could he expect that again? He hoped so but doubted it. He backed Pudge up to the fence and waited for the steer to break. The gate opened and the steer broke, and Pudge bolted without Toby having to do anything. Pudge was on the steer almost before Toby was ready. He eyed the horns and was off and pulling the steer down quickly. The steer hit the ground, and Toby was confident he was at least in the money, even if he didn't win. He looked around to see the time and saw that they had finished in 3.4 seconds.

The announcer was saying that Toby had won the event and what a night it was for the newcomer. Toby mounted and waved to the crowd, and Pudge bowed his head. The crowd laughed, and the announcer said, "That is a quite a cowboy and horse."

Toby rode out and headed to the stall. He was finished and had won both events, so the prize money would help build his

Toby the Rancher

savings back up. Toby wanted to eventually buy his own ranch. He knew he had a long ways to go but hoped to save up and make it a reality someday. He was unsaddling Pudge and brushing him down when Kip walked up.

"Dude, you beat my tail off in more ways than one," Kip said. "I just wanted to say that I have no hard feelings."

Toby looked at him. "Thanks, Kip. I never intended to cause anyone any trouble."

Kip nodded and walked off. Toby hoped Kip was sincere, but he was always leery of people who reacted the way Kip did.

Toby was ready to leave. Bethany and Wendy walked up, and Wendy asked, "You ready to go?"

"Yeah," he said. "Where we going?"

They said the name of the same steak house he had been to with Hank and Sadie, so he knew the food was good. As they walked out, Bethany asked, "Can we just ride with you?"

"Yeah, that's fine," Toby said. "Climb in."

They got to the restaurant and went in and got a table. They were ordering and talking when Hank and his crew came in. Hank spotted Toby and walked over to talk. "Young man, you put on a good show tonight. I have no doubts you can handle anything my ranch will throw at you."

"Thank you, Hank," Toby said. "Things just fell into place."

"Nonsense," Hank said. "You were good."

"I enjoyed this rodeo more than I ever have before," Sadie said. Toby smiled. "Thanks."

They walked off to their table, with the others following. Kali and Carla both seemed to be sneering at Toby and the girls. Drew gave a huffy laugh as he walked by. Wendy said, "It appears those three don't approve of you or your company. Who are they?"

"They are Hank's granddaughters, and one of their boy-friends," Toby said. "But I don't even know them."

Their food was served, and they started eating. Toby actually enjoyed talking with Bethany and Wendy. They finished their meal and got up to leave.

◆ 39 ◆

"I need to find out what time we are leaving in the morning," Toby said. "I'll be right back." He walked over to ask Hank and didn't notice anyone walking through the door.

"What time are you planning on leaving tomorrow?" he asked Hank.

"I want to be on the road by 7:00 a.m.," Hank said.

Before Toby could respond, Carla asked, "You think you'll be able to get up that early after your evening with those two?"

Toby started to speak, but then Drew said, "Looks like someone is beating your time, bud."

Toby glanced back to see that Kip and two others had walked in and were talking to the two girls. He turned back and looked at Hank and said, "I'll be ready and waiting in the coliseum parking lot."

"Sounds good," Hank said.

Toby turned without acknowledging the others who had spoken. He walked over to where the group was and noticed they were agitated in their talking. "What's going on?"

Kip looked at him. "Is this how you repay me?"

"Repay you for what, and what am I doing?" Toby asked.

"My apology," Kip said. "Dating Bethany."

"I'm not dating anyone," Toby said. "We just came to eat. I am leaving in the morning and won't see them again."

Kip just looked at Toby.

"Well, that's not true," Wendy said. "You'll see me again. You can count on that."

Bethany started to speak, but Kip interrupted her, saying, "Let's step outside."

"I'm not fighting you," Toby said. "Just get over it. You can take the girls to their truck." He walked out and eased toward his truck. He heard the door open hard but just kept walking to the truck. One of the guys with Kip ran around in between him and his truck to stop him. Kip and the other guy caught up to him, and they circled him.

"This is stupid," Toby said. "There is no reason to fight over a girl that is toying with you."

"Hey," Bethany blurted out.

"Don't insult her," Kip said. "I'll pound you worse."

Hank came walking up and said, "Young man, he already gave you one butt whipping. You want another?"

"Stay out of this, old man," one of the other guys said.

Toby noticed Carl, Albert, and Drew were with Hank.

"You guys joining him?" Kip asked.

"No," Carl said. "We just don't want it to happen."

"Drew, get in there and help Toby," Hank said.

"I don't even know him, and he probably caused it," Drew said.

"He didn't do anything to cause this, you wimp," Wendy said.

Toby had turned to face Kip, and the guy who had run in front of him shoved him, and Kip started to swing. The push had actually helped Toby as it put him to Kip's right, which made Kip's punch hit air. Toby caught Kip's right arm with his and locked them together at the shoulder and then kicked Kip's feet out from under him and slammed him down on his back. Toby came up to see if one of the others was going to do anything.

Just then a police car pulled in. The police officers got out, and one of them said, "What is going on here?"

Everybody froze and just stared at the cops.

"Nothing, Officer," Toby said. "We're just contemplating a country flash dance."

"Well, break it up, and get out of the parking lot," the officer said.

"Yes, sir," Toby said, and he headed to his truck. He tipped his hat to Hank, and Wendy climbed in his truck.

"Bethany isn't coming," she said. "She is mad about what you said."

"Suits me," Toby said. "It is very obvious what she is doing."

"Uh-huh," Wendy said.

Toby dropped Wendy off at her truck.

"I'll call you when I get back to school," Wendy said.

Toby gave a brief nod and drove off. He was glad the police officers had shown up when they did. He hoped he could get out of Fort Worth without any more trouble.

He made it to the motel and fell asleep saying his prayer.

6

TOBY WAS AWAKE and ready to go by 5:00 a.m. He was anxious to get started and find out more about where he would be living and working. He sat and drank a cup of coffee before he loaded up. He was thinking about the events of the last few days. He was excited about the job and working for Hank, but he was trying to keep it all in perspective. Some of the things, like Carl's comments and how Carl and Patty's daughters and Drew acted and responded, had Toby a little puzzled. He didn't know how close Drew was to the family, so he had to consider it as a potential issue until he knew more. He had learned in his short life to go into anything with both eyes wide open, and that was how he would handle this even though it seemed like a great opportunity and fit for him.

He finished his coffee, loaded up, and headed out to get his trailer. He hooked his trailer up and pulled around to load up Pudge. He got the feed in the trailer feeder for Pudge and loaded him and the gear up. He looked at his watch, and it was 6:00 a.m. He pulled out to the edge of the parking lot and walked over to a café to get a cup of coffee to go. He was walking back when he saw Hank pulling up to his trailer, so Toby walked over to help him hook up.

Hank saw Toby and hollered out, "Good morning." He turned to Sadie. "I told you this lad was a good one for us."

Hank backed up to the trailer, and Toby hooked it and raised the jack. He hopped into the back of the truck to ride to the barn. Hank and Sadie got out when they reached the barn.

"Did you sleep well?" Sadie asked. "You had quite an evening."

"Yes, ma'am, I did," Toby said.

They walked to where the livestock was. They had four head to load up: one bull, one cow, and two steers. The bull had won Grand Champion, and the others had all was champion of their class. Hank led the bull, and Toby led the cow to the trailer. They went back, and both led a steer, and then they loaded the gear. They were closing up the trailer when Carl and Patty pulled up with the girls and Drew following them.

Carl stepped out of his truck. "I thought you wanted to start loading at 6:30?"

"I did," Hank said. "But Toby was already here getting his horse, so he hooked me up, and we got them loaded."

Carl just glanced at Toby and asked, "Are you ready to leave?"

"Let's chase some white lines," Hank said.

Toby started walking to his truck, and Carl stopped and said, "Hop in, and we'll drop you off."

Toby climbed into the backseat.

"Good morning," Patty said. "Didn't get to congratulate you last night. You did very well."

"Thank you," Toby responded. "I appreciate it."

They were at Toby's truck, and he got out and said, "Much obliged."

He checked on Pudge and fired up his truck and pulled in line, bringing up the rear of the four-vehicle convoy. They traveled a little over an hour and pulled into a café. Hank pulled into the truck parking area, and Toby followed him since he had a trailer. The other two vehicles parked in front of the building.

Hank got out and asked Toby, "You hungry?"

"Yes, sir," Toby said. "I always enjoy my breakfast."

"This place has some of the best food you have ever eaten," Sadie said. "We've stopped here for years."

Toby the Rancher

They walked in and saw where the others were sitting, and walked over and sat down. They looked at the menus and ordered before anyone really started any conversation.

"Toby, are you sore today?" Sadie asked.

"A little," Toby said, smiling.

"I figured you would be," she continued. "Both of those events seemed very strenuous."

"Yeah," Hank said. "But you can tell by looking that he is fairly well put together."

Toby was embarrassed, and was glad the waitress showed up with the coffee and water.

Patty started the talk after the drinks were sat down. "Toby, I have to ask, what was the fight about?"

Toby was getting uncomfortable. He thought for a little bit and said, "It was all a misunderstanding."

"A likely story from someone dodging a question," Carla chirped in from the other end.

Toby turned and looked at her with a look that let her know she had just stepped over the line. Her eyes got big, and she looked down at her drink.

"It was a misunderstanding, because Kip had it in his head that I was trying to move in on this girl," Toby said. "The strange thing about it is the girl doesn't like him. He wouldn't listen to reason." He had said more than he wanted to, but he hoped it would bring the subject to a close.

"I imagine the fact you beat him in both events didn't help matters," Carl said.

Toby was surprised Carl had noticed.

"The crazy thing about it is Toby whipped his tail the other night," Hank said. "He is a slow learner." He turned to Toby. "I do have a question, though. Where did the thought of a country flash mob dance come from?"

Toby grinned. "I'm not sure. It just popped in my head."

"I thought it was a weird thing to say," Drew said.

◆ 45 ◆

Toby totally ignored him and asked Hank, "Are we gonna start working the heifers in the morning?"

"Nah," Hank replied. "I want to show you around first so you can get a feel for the place. You can use this afternoon to get settled in."

"Sounds good," Toby said.

The food arrived, and everyone started eating. Toby was about halfway though his meal when he looked at Sadie and said, "This is good food."

She smiled. "I knew you would like it."

"Do I need to get groceries on the way, or can I go to town once we get there?" Toby asked Hank.

"You can go to town," Hank answered. "If you don't mind, Sadie may ride with you to pick us up some things since we have been gone."

"That would be good," Toby said.

"They have a good supply of Pop-Tarts and TV dinners," Carla piped in.

Toby ignored her and motioned to the waitress for more coffee. He drank his coffee while the others talked, and then he got up and told Hank he was going out to check on Pudge and the cattle. He paid and walked out and headed to the truck. He gave Pudge some water and checked the cattle. They were all chewing their cud, so Toby knew they were content. He closed up the trailer and got to his truck as Hank and Sadie walked up.

"Ready to go?" Hank asked.

"Yep," he replied. "We're burning daylight."

The convoy pulled out and rolled all the way to the ranch without any more stops. Toby enjoyed the scenery and looked forward to living and working in the area, from what he could see. Hank put on his blinker, so Toby did the same. Toby noticed the other two vehicles didn't, and they went straight when Hank and Toby turned.

They must live closer to or in town, Toby thought.

They drove two miles, and Toby spotted the ranch. It looked nice. They pulled into the drive, and Toby assessed the operation quickly. They had two big barns and a few smaller buildings. He noticed sheds for the cattle in the pastures he could see and was impressed with the corral system.

Hank stopped and walked back and said, "Toby, unload Pudge and pick any stall you want in the barn on the left. You can park your trailer in line with the others, and I'll get the key to open the mobile home for you."

"Okie doke," Toby said, and drove over to the barn. He unloaded and Pudge and led him into the barn and found a stall he liked and tied Pudge up. "Well, ole buddy, this is your new home. Hopefully, it will work out to be our home until we can get our own place." He got Pudge some water and patted him. "I'll be back a little later."

He went and unhooked the trailer and pulled over to the parking spot in front of the mobile home. He grabbed his suitcase and went inside. The mobile home was nice and homey. He hadn't had a place like this since his dad had passed away. He pinched himself because it all seemed too good to be true at this point. He went back outside to get the rest of his stuff and was putting it all away when he heard Hank say, "Knock, knock."

"Hello." Toby walked toward the living room and saw Hank and Sadie.

"What do you think?" Hank said.

"This is great," Toby said.

"If you need anything, let me know," Sadie said. "Are you ready to go to town?"

"Yes, ma'am," Toby said.

Toby drove Sadie to town so both could get some groceries. When they walked in, they both grabbed a shopping cart and headed in different directions. Toby was going down each aisle since he didn't know the store, and as he came to the end of one, he overheard Sadie say, "Hello, Kali."

"Hi, Grandma," Kali said.

"You shopping for your parents or to take to college?" Sadie asked.

"For Mom," Kali said. "I'm surprised you are already here."

"Toby needed to come and get some groceries, so I hitched a ride to get some things we needed," Sadie said.

"Grandma, I don't understand why Grandad hired him," Kali said. "He had told Drew he could work for him during the summer. I guess that went out the window since he found the cowboy."

"Honey, it is still three months until your summer vacation, and your grandad is not a young man," Sadie said. "He needs help now, and Toby seems to be a good young man and able to do anything with horses and cattle. If he needs more help in the summer, I am sure he will hire Drew. As far as being a cowboy, your grandad is a cowboy too. You don't like cowboys?"

"No, I don't have anything against cowboys," Kali said. "In fact, they are sexy. It's just that this one seems to have moved right in like he was family. It makes us all wonder what he is up to."

"You are all barking up the wrong tree," Sadie said. "Your grandad did the pursuing and hiring. Toby didn't ask for a job. I need to finish my shopping. I'll talk to you later. Bye, sweetheart."

Toby went ahead and circled the end of the row and nearly ran into Kali. He said, "Sorry," and tipped his hat to her. She smiled and went on.

Sadie looked back and watched the encounter. She smiled to herself and thought, *Sexy, huh.*

Toby the Rancher

Toby finished shopping about the same time Sadie did, and they checked out and headed to the ranch. He pulled in and saw Hank walking to the barn. Toby jumped out and helped carry Sadie's groceries in and then ran to the barn to see if Hank needed help.

"Get your groceries put away," Hank said. "You start to work tomorrow."

"Yes, sir," Toby said. He walked to his truck to get his groceries. He spent the evening sitting on his porch, drinking coffee.

7

Toby woke up at 5:00 a.m. and fixed himself breakfast. He went and checked on Pudge and fed and watered him and then sat on his porch waiting for Hank. Hank walked out at 7:00 a.m. and saw Toby sitting and waiting. He smiled. "You look like you are ready to go. Have breakfast yet?"

"Yes, sir, and took care of Pudge," Toby said.

Hank walked over to Toby's porch. "The heifers we need to work this morning are in the south pasture. There are thirty-two of them. You think you and Pudge can bring them in, or do I need to saddle up?"

"Not knowing the lay of the land makes it a little uncertain, but I figure we can bring them in."

"I'll get things ready here then."

Toby walked to the barn and saddled Pudge and headed out to the south pasture. He liked the land he saw—some rolling hills and good trees. He wanted to see more of the country, and would do that when he was off. Toby opened the gate to the south pasture and rode in to see where the heifers were. He found a group of them and again was surprised at how good they looked. Hank sure had some nice-looking cattle. He counted them and came up with thirty-one. He recounted twice more and still only got thirty-one. Where was the other heifer?

Toby rode off to check every nook and cranny of the pasture. He spotted a dark spot and rode over. It was the heifer, and her head was hung in between two trees. She was down and weak. He could tell from the ground that she had been fighting it for a good while. Being weak might help him get her out because she was a good-size heifer, and if she was fighting against him, he would have trouble turning her head to free her up.

He walked up slowly to the heifer so he wouldn't spook her and make her start fighting to get out again. She was scared of him but was worn out completely. Toby took hold of her nose and top knot and slowly started twisting her head. She started trying to fight against him, so he grabbed it more forcefully, but her pulling away from him wedged her head into the trees. He couldn't lift and turn her head like he needed to free her.

He decided he was going to have to try and use Pudge. He walked him over and took his rope and put it around the heifer's head and then tied it on the saddle horn. "Pudge, ole buddy, when I say pull, you need to pull quick and hold her."

Toby was afraid the heifer might go down pulling against Pudge and then he knew he couldn't lift her head, so he would have to go get the tractor, and she might choke in the meantime. Toby got ready to grab her head and twist. "Pull, Pudge."

Pudge pulled and brought the heifer's head about four inches from the trees she was wedged against. Toby grabbed her nose and top knot and twisted with all his might. He hollered, "Come forward, Pudge!"

The heifer pulled back and out of her predicament. She just stood there wobbling and dazed. Toby walked around the tree and slowly removed the rope from around her neck. He walked back to Pudge and said, "Nice job," and patted him on the neck. He mounted up and rolled up his rope. He watched the heifer, and she didn't seem strong enough yet to walk to the corrals, so he decided to leave her and take the others on in. He figured he would ride back and get her once the rest were penned up.

He drove the thirty-one heifers toward the house. He was pushing them into the pen when Hank walked out of the barn and said, "I was starting to get worried that they were causing you trouble."

Toby relayed the situation with the heifer, and Hank said, "Nice work. Sounds like she may have been dead if we had stayed at the fair another day."

Toby shut the gate and said, "I'll ride back now and bring her in slowly, unless you want me to wait."

"Let's leave her until we finish with these," Hank said. "She will have more time to recoup, and she may start drifting in if she realizes the rest are gone. You leave the gate open?"

"Yes, sir," Toby said.

"Okeydoke," Hank said.

They got everything ready and discussed how they would work them through and then started with the first one. They moved through the first twenty with ease.

Sadie walked out to see how it was going. "You look like you are close to being finished already."

"We're moving right along," Hank said. "This young man knows how to handle cattle. Makes a big difference." He told Sadie about the heifer and what Toby had done.

She just looked at Toby and smiled. "I will get a pot of coffee started so it will be ready when you are finished." She walked back into the house.

They went on through nine more head and only had two left when Carl pulled in. He got out and walked over to where they were. "Must have gotten a late start."

Hank looked at him and said, "How do you figure?"

"You only have two head done by this time of morning," Carl said.

Hank started laughing and said, "We only like two head."

"You must have started at 6:00," Carl said.

"Nope," Hank replied. "About 8:00, by the time Toby drove them in."

Toby got the next-to-the-last heifer in the squeeze chute and grabbed the syringe and filled it with the wormer.

"I only count thirty-one," Carl said. "I thought you said you had thirty-two to put with the bulls?"

Hank told Carl about the heifer Toby had found in the tree.

"Well, Toby sounds like a jack-of-all-trades," Carl said.

"If you have time, Carl, you might check the heifer out for me to see if she is okay," Hank said.

"I have to go check on a cow I did a C-section on before we left for Fort Worth," Carl said. "I'll stop back by, and maybe your hand can have her up by then."

"Sounds good," Hank said.

Toby had listened to all the conversation while he worked. He couldn't figure Carl out. He seemed to smart off about Toby every chance he got. Toby thought he might just ask Hank if he was stepping into something he didn't know about taking this job.

They finished the last heifer and walked to the front porch of Hank and Sadie's house to have a cup of coffee. Sadie brought out a bear claw for each of them too.

Toby broke the silence. "These heifers are good size for fifteen months old."

"They are two years old," Hank said. "When I started and couldn't afford to wait and feed them longer, I put them with the bull to calve at two years old. After we got going, I started pushing it back. Now I try to make sure they calve by three. I have found they calve easier and actually seem to make better mama cows."

"That makes sense," Toby said. "I knew they looked larger than what I was used to for heifers ready to breed." He took a drink of coffee. "Hank, judging from his comments, Carl seems to have a problem with me. I'm not getting in the middle of something with some history, am I? I don't need any more of that."

Toby hadn't noticed that Sadie had walked out of the house.

"You are very perceptive," she said.

"I hired Carl's younger brother as a favor to Carl," Hank said. "He was no good, but I told him I would give him a try. He turned out to be lazy, and even took some of my tools and sold them, so I fired him rather than press charges. Carl got upset, and we had words. It was tense for a while, but Patty finally got through to him. I imagine he wants anybody I hire to fail so his brother won't look so bad."

"Well, that explains it," Toby said.

"Don't let it bother you," Hank said. "You just do your job, and you will be fine."

"Now that I know the story, it won't bother me," Toby replied. "I just have to watch myself and make sure I don't pop off to him when he makes comments."

"If he can't take it, he needs to keep his comments to himself," Sadie said.

"I better go feed the heifers and then go check on the other one." Toby got up and walked off the porch.

"Carl is wasting his time on this one," Hank told Sadie. "He is a keeper."

Sadie agreed, and Hank got up to follow Toby.

It had been a while since Toby had driven a tractor, and he had never driven a Case tractor. He was trying to get a feel for all the controls when Hank walked up.

"Trying to figure the controls out," Toby said.

"You'll get it," Hank said. He stepped up on the step and pointed out what each control was, and Toby fired it up, and Hank stepped down. Toby fed the three round bales of hay and pulled in to park it.

"Looks like you figured it out pretty quick," Hank said.

Toby the Rancher

"Yeah, it all made sense once you showed me," Toby said. "I'm going after the heifer."

"Okay. Holler if you need help."

Toby was mounted, and as he rode off he said, "Will do." He headed for the spot where he had left the heifer, hoping she was not still there. He was hoping she would be walking and even grazing by now, but he rounded a grove of trees and saw her lying down. He rode up to her fast, hoping it would spook her to her feet. She just looked at Pudge and lay there. Toby dismounted and walked up to her and slapped her on the hind haunches. She flinched but didn't try to get up, so he walked around and jumped at her head. She turned slowly, not like a cow that was spooked, but she did start getting up. She got to her feet after some effort and was a little wobbly.

Toby didn't want to push her but figured she might get stronger as she walked, so he mounted up and let Pudge do the driving of the heifer. They walked right beside her, and she kept moving at a steady pace. His phone rang, and it was Hank.

"Having any luck?"

"Yeah, bringing her in slowly," Toby replied.

"Okay. See you when you get here."

Pudge kept walking with his head right on the heifer's hip, so she kept moving ahead. They reached the corral, and Hank and Carl came walking out.

"Took you long enough," Carl popped off. "I have other things to do."

Toby didn't like it and didn't hold back. "She is weak, and pushing her wouldn't have done anything but make her go down. You aren't the only one that knows something about cattle. You need to get the burr out from under your saddle where I'm concerned. I don't answer to you, hoss."

Carl looked stunned and didn't have any comeback.

Hank was smiling. "Let's see if we can get her in the chute."

Toby walked the heifer in, and they shut the head gate, and Carl checked her out.

◆ 55 ◆

"She looks okay," Carl said. "I think she just needs some time to get her strength built back up."

"I appreciate you checking her," Hank said.

Carl looked at Toby and walked to his truck and left. Toby let the heifer out and steered her into a pen by herself so she could be fed and watered and allowed to recoup before she was put back with the others or with the bull. He looked at Hank. "I am sorry if I was out of line."

"Don't give it another thought," Hank said. "He needed to hear that."

"You want me to drive the heifers back to the pasture?"

"Nah, let's feed them a couple of days and let this one get ready, and we'll drive them back out and take the bull to them."

Toby looked at the heifers. "Looks like you have two in heat right now."

"Sure does," Hank said. "Let's cut them out and put them with Boss since he is close. We will document those two and compare the calves when they are born."

Toby climbed onto Pudge and cut the heifers out quickly, and Hank opened the gate next to Boss's pen. After they finished, Hank said, "Let's eat, and then we'll take a ride and look the place and livestock over to give you a feel."

While they were eating, Toby's phone rang. He didn't recognize the number, so he answered it, and it was Wendy. He told her he was eating and would call her back.

"Is that your girlfriend?" Sadie asked.

"No, ma'am," Toby said. "I don't have a girlfriend. She is just someone I met at the rodeo."

"Was she with you in the restaurant?" she asked.

"Yes," he replied.

"She is very pretty."

"I suppose." Toby knew Wendy was pretty but didn't want Sadie or Hank to start bugging him about her. He hardly knew the girl.

He finished dinner and walked outside to call her. She wanted to tell him she had won the barrel racing. He congratulated her and said he better get back to work. He said he would call her later when he wasn't working. She was happy he said that, and they hung up.

Toby and Hank had a good ride, and Toby liked the area even more after he had seen the ranch. He tended the livestock and brushed and fed Pudge and went to cook his supper. He finished supper and took a cup of coffee out to the porch. He had just sat down when a truck came pulling up the driveway. He watched it and saw Carla and two girls and two guys get out in front of Hank and Sadie's. Carla looked over at Toby and waved, and he waved back. He could tell the girls were talking and the guys were looking. They went into the house, and Toby finished his cup and decided to call Wendy since he had told her he would.

They were talking about the happenings of the rodeo and about the heifer Toby had found trapped in the tree when Carla and the two girls walked up to him.

"Hey, Toby, watcha doin?" Carla said.

Toby nodded at her and showed her the phone, but Wendy said, "Well, sounds like you work fast. One day, and you already have girls calling on you. I better let you go. Bye." She hung up.

Toby just shook his head and put the phone in his pocket.

"Sorry," Carla said. "Didn't notice you were on the phone."

"That's okay," Toby said. "What's up?"

"These are my friends, Mindy and Debbie, and they wanted to meet a rodeo hero."

Toby laughed. "Hello, girls. I'm happy to meet you, but I am far from a rodeo hero."

"You won both events," Carla said.

"Just lucky," Toby said.

"We gotta go," Carla said. "See you later."

They got into the car and drove off.

"That girl is hyper," Toby said to himself. Then he remembered Wendy and thought to himself, *Why are they so darn dramatic?*

He went in and got another cup of coffee and watched TV the rest of the evening. He hit the sack at around 10:30 p.m. He read the Bible for a while and said his prayers. He was asleep shortly thereafter.

8

Toby was up early and had breakfast cooked by 6:00 a.m. He sat on the porch to eat it. The weather was cold, but it felt good this morning. As crazy as it seemed, he looked forward to the day and fixing the fence he and Hank had spotted in disrepair on their ride yesterday. He would get the feeding done then load up the gear and head for the fence. It was on the back side of Hank's place.

Toby finished his breakfast and got things cleaned up and was in the barn by 6:30 a.m. He fed and watered Pudge so he would be ready to go and then started feeding the bulls that were penned around the barn. He loaded six sacks of cubes on the Kawasaki MULE and went to feed the heifers they had worked yesterday. They still had some hay, but Hank wanted to give them a boost with some cubes.

Toby noticed three more heifers in standing heat while he was feeding, and he thought he needed to let Hank know. He pulled back into the barn as Hank came walking out of the house.

"You do like to start early, don't you?" Hank said, smiling.

"Yeah," Toby replied. "Been that way since I was knee-high to a grasshopper."

"Nice, crisp morning," Hank said.

"I had my breakfast on the front porch."

"Sadie saw you and said we should just go eat with you."
They both laughed.

"There are three more heifers in heat this morning," Toby told Hank.

"Well, we might as well try to get some more Boss calves," Hank said.

"I'll cut them out once I get Pudge saddled," Toby said. "If you don't mind, I would like to use a packhorse with the fence materials and ride Pudge out to the fence."

"Suits me," Hank replied. "I have to go into town for a cattleman's board meeting this morning, so I will be out of pocket for a few hours."

"No problem," Toby said. He climbed into the saddle on Pudge to go cut out the heifers. He got the heifers into the pen next to Boss and then turned Boss in with them and went to load the packhorse. He headed out to go fix the fence. He was fixing the fence and was noticing a lot of the ground was messed up, even to the point of affecting the fence posts. He couldn't figure out what was causing it, but it was making a mess of things.

It took him a couple of hours to get the fence repaired, and he was loading up to go back to the barn when he noticed movement in a grove of trees. He didn't know what it was or even what to expect, because he didn't know what animals lived in this part of Texas. He finished loading up while keeping an eye on the grove of trees. He mounted up and walked Pudge toward the trees. He went ahead and pulled out his rifle in case he needed it. As he got close, he saw the movement again and saw that it was hogs. He didn't shoot. He had heard about wild hogs but didn't know much about them.

He headed back toward the barn and was surprised when he saw hogs in three different places on the way back. He unloaded the packhorse and then unsaddled Pudge and spent a while brushing him down. He finished and checked on Boss and the heifers. He put the first two heifers back in the pen with the herd and then walked to the mobile home. He was going up the steps when Hank pulled in, so Toby walked over to Hank's truck.

"How'd it go?" Hank asked.

"Got it all fixed," Toby said. "I did see a bunch of hogs, and they tore up the ground around some fence posts."

Hank jerked his head around and looked at Toby and said, "Are you kidding me? We haven't had hogs in a long time."

"I saw them in three different places, and it looked like a good bunch in each place. Can we kill them?"

"You bet we can. We will kill them, field dress them, and donate the meat. You a good shot?"

"Decent."

"Tomorrow is Saturday, so I will call Carl and Drew to come out and help us try to bring some down."

Toby wasn't crazy about hunting with those two but knew he had no say in the matter, so he kept quiet.

"I understand Drew is a good shot and a good hunter," Hank continued. "What have you hunted before, Toby?"

"I have hunted for deer, turkey, quail, dove, and pheasant," Toby said. "I have shot all of those and cougars, bears, and wolves to protect cattle and people."

Hank looked at him. "Dang, son, you must be better than decent. All the chores done for the day?"

"Yes, sir."

"Why don't you head to town and see if you can have some fun on Friday night?"

"I may go see what movie is showing."

"Sounds good. Have fun." Hank walked back to the house.

Toby took a shower and got ready to head into town. He was walking to his truck when Patty pulled up the drive. He waved to her, and she motioned for him to come over to her car. "Hello, Toby. Are you getting settled in?"

"A little more each day," Toby said.

"I was wanting to invite you over for supper tomorrow night with Dad and Mom."

Toby was kind of surprised as he had never been invited to anyone's family meal at their house. "I would be honored."

"Great," Patty said. "Just hop in with Dad because I am not very good at directions."

They laughed.

"Will do," Toby said. "Thank you."

Patty smiled at him and walked into the house, and he walked to his truck.

Toby pulled into town not knowing where the theater was or what was playing. He drove down the main drag and saw a sign to the mall and figured the theater might be around it. He drove to the mall, and sure enough, there was a six-screen cinema. He drove by the front, trying to see what was showing, and nearly jumped out of his seat when something hit his truck fender. He looked in his mirror and saw Carla and her friends. He stopped and rolled his window down and said, laughing, "That scared me out ten years of my life. I thought I had hit someone."

Carla and her friends laughed.

"What are you here to see?" Carla asked.

"Don't know," Toby said. "I was trying to see what was showing. What is supposed to be good?"

"We are going to see *Snitch*," Carla replied. "You want to join us?"

"I've seen the previews, and that looks good. Yeah, I'll park and catch up to you."

The girls were acting giddy when Toby walked up. There were about ten of them in a group. Toby walked up and got his ticket and walked toward Carla.

"Girls, this is Toby Parker," Carla said. "The cowboy Mindy and Debbie were telling you about."

Toby was all of a sudden wishing he had gone to another movie because having ten girls all looking at him and giggling was making him very uneasy. It was too late to back out now, so he tipped his hat at them and said, "Hello, ladies."

They all sighed, and he knew he had to be turning red. He looked at Carla and said, "I need some popcorn." He walked toward the door and didn't realize it until he opened the door to hold it for Carla, but all ten high school girls followed in single file.

Why didn't I stay home? he thought to himself.

He followed them in and walked to the refreshment counter and ordered popcorn and a bottle of water. He got his order and turned to see which door to go to, and all the girls were still standing there, and some guys were there too. They weren't giggling anymore.

Toby walked toward Carla. "I'm going to get a seat."

One of the guys, who stood about six feet four and looked to weigh about 240 pounds, said, "You get yourself a seat by yourself, cowboy."

"Well, I hadn't planned on sharing a seat with anyone, hoss," Toby said.

The girls laughed, and the guys—all six of them—got mad. Toby looked at Carla and started toward the door to get a seat. He went in and found a seat in the back and sat down and started eating his popcorn, and wondered why he couldn't do a simple thing like go to a movie without it turning into a brawl. What was he doing wrong?

He saw the gang of girls and guys come in. Carla, Mindy, and Debbie spotted him and headed his way. The rest of them sat down toward the front, which pleased Toby. He wasn't about to fight some high school kid and get himself thrown into jail.

The girls sat down, and Carla said, "I am sorry about Mike. He is a jerk most of the time. He is the star of the football team and thinks he is real tough."

Toby nodded. The movie previews started.

The movie was good, and as soon as the credits started rolling, Toby bid the girls adieu and headed down the steps to leave. He got in his truck and backed out and was starting to leave when Mike and the other guys stepped in front of his truck.

"Get out!" Mike hollered.

The girls came running up, and several more people started gathering around.

Toby rolled down his window. "This is all a misunderstanding. You need to just walk away, dude."

"I ain't going nowhere," Mike said.

Toby was too quick-witted for his own good at times. "Well, that's apparent with that kind of response. Good use of those double negatives, bud."

The crowd laughed, and Mike got even hotter under the collar.

"Walk away, dude," Toby repeated. "I'm not fighting some high school kid over a silly misunderstanding."

"I'm eighteen," Mike said.

"I don't care if you're twenty-two," Toby said. "You don't want to do this." He had a bad feeling that this wasn't going to just end, and his mind went into high gear trying to think of a solution. He wasn't afraid to fight, because he had never lost one. He just didn't want to fight a kid for no reason. He decided to try and get the guy to accept some other type of challenge to end this standoff.

"I'm not going to fight you," Toby said. "But I will lock knuckles with you, and we can see if you are tough as you think you are."

The crowd was cheering like it was a prizefight or something. Toby was getting really agitated. He glanced at the crowd and saw Carla, and standing beside her were Drew and Kali.

Great, he thought. *Hank will hear about this.*

"How does that work?" Mike said.

"I'll show you if you won't try to fight when I get out," Toby said.

"Okay."

Toby got out of his truck and had Mindy step up, since he had seen her in the front line. He had her hold out her hands, and he bent his fingers and stuck his knuckles between her fingers. "Once you get locked in, someone says go, and we squeeze. Whoever can squeeze harder and make the other one holler calf rope wins. It shows hand strength." He was hoping Mike would jump at it because Mike thought himself a stud.

"That sounds easy," Mike said. "Let's go."

Toby wasn't naive enough to believe Mike didn't have some strength, but he had been doing this since he was fourteen years old, when he and his dad used to play around doing it. "If we do this, it is over regardless of who wins. Agreed?"

Mike hesitated a minute and then said, "Agreed."

Now if he will just stick to his word, Toby thought.

The two of them squared off and locked knuckles.

"Mindy, say go," Toby said.

She waited a little while before she hollered, "Go!"

The squeeze was on. Just as Toby thought, Mike was strong. Toby knew he had his work cut out for him. He squeezed harder than he had ever had to, and Mike's face started getting red. Mike was squeezing, but Toby could feel him start to loosen a little, so he put another hard push on his squeeze and Mike started to pull back some and Toby stayed on it.

"I give," Mike said.

Toby let loose of him. "Good match. You *are* strong."

Mike seemed shocked, and his countenance changed. "Thanks, but you have a grip like a vise."

Toby stuck his hand out to shake Mike's. "No hard feelings."

Mike shook Toby's hand and turned and walked away. Toby opened his door and glanced in the direction he had seen Carla, Drew, and Kali, and they were all watching him. He started his truck. The crowd parted, and he pulled away.

"What a fiasco," he said to himself.

He stopped at a convenience store on the edge of town to get a cup of coffee, and as he walked out of the store, Drew and Kali pulled up. Toby tipped his hat at them and walked to his truck. They got out, and Drew said, "You seem to cause trouble everywhere you go."

Toby looked at him. "You seem to voice your opinion when you should keep your mouth shut." He tipped his hat to Kali and said, "Ma'am," and got in his truck and drove away. He drove to the ranch and went in and sat down to watch some TV and finish his coffee. He didn't go to sleep until around midnight.

9

Toby woke up at 5:00 a.m., aggravated with himself for being so preoccupied the night before that he didn't check on Pudge when he got back. He slipped on his jeans and boots and a hoodie and headed out to check on Pudge before he started breakfast.

As he got close to the barn, he heard a commotion and the horses acting upset. He walked in and flipped on the light and saw two hogs tearing into sacks of feed. He grabbed a shovel as the hogs started to run toward the door. He swung and hit the smaller one on the head and knocked it down. He grabbed a piece of rope and jumped on it and hog-tied it. He left it squealing and went to check things.

He went to Pudge first. Pudge was rattled but okay. Toby checked the other animals and was looking at the feed when Hank came into the barn.

"I started to ask what was going on, but I see from the hog tied here," Hank said. "The animals okay?"

"Yeah," Toby said. "Everything seems to be in good shape outside of the feed sacks."

"That's a lot of damage for one hog."

"There were two, but I couldn't get both with the shovel before the bigger one got away."

Hank started laughing and said, "You got this one with the shovel. Pretty impressive. Got it with the shovel, and hog-tied too."

Toby grinned. "I'll put this one in the trailer and get this mess cleaned up."

"Eat breakfast before you start cleaning up." Hank started walking out of the barn and started laughing and shaking his head.

Toby grinned again and was happy at how Hank was taking this mess. He picked up the hog and carried it to the stock trailer and took the rope off and let it loose in the trailer. He went back and checked on Pudge and the other animals again before he went to start breakfast. He was back out cleaning up the mess the hogs had made by 6:15 a.m. He had it cleaned up and was brushing Pudge when Hank walked in at about 7:00 a.m.

"You already have it done?" Hank asked.

"Yeah," Toby said. "It didn't take long." He said that even though it was a mess and he had to work to get it done.

"I was trying to get back out here and help."

"No problem."

There was a moment of silence. Toby broke it by saying, "What time are Carl and Drew supposed to be here?"

"Knowing those two, probably not before 9:00," Hank replied.

"You want me to drive the heifers back to the south pasture before we start?"

Hank seemed surprised by the question. "You think you can do that before they get here?"

"I believe so," Toby replied. "I can feed too." He started saddling Pudge, and Hank walked out to check on Boss and turn the heifer that been stuck in the tree back in with the herd. She was looking good and strong. Toby rode and opened the gate and got around the heifers and started working them toward the gate. A few of them tried to be cantankerous, but Pudge put on a cutting horse showcase, and the heifers didn't stand a chance. Toby and Pudge had them heading south to the pasture. He pushed them about a quarter mile and then doubled back to turn the two bulls out to join the heifers. He had the herd moving and out of sight in short fashion.

Hank had just sat and watched with admiration. "Those two are as good as any I have ever seen," he said to himself.

Toby and Pudge worked the herd from side to side and kept pushing the sides in to keep the bunch moving along. They reached the pasture, and Toby pushed them in and then shut the gate so he could ride the pasture to make sure everything looked okay with the fences and whatever else he might notice. He had checked all the fences and was standing on the stirrups, looking around, when he saw movement in a small grove of trees. He started walking Pudge closer and was reaching for his rifle when four hogs bolted out of the grove, heading to the woods.

Toby pulled his rifle and pulled it up to take aim. He had squeezed Pudge hard with his legs, which told Pudge to stop and stand still. Toby got the first one in his sights and pulled the trigger. The hog went down. He quickly aimed and fired on each of the others and had four hogs down in a matter of seconds. He rode up to them and dismounted to bleed them so the meat would stay good. He bled them and climbed back into the saddle to go get the MULE to haul them in.

As he rode into the barn, Hank came walking from the house and asked, "What were the shots I heard?"

"I shot four hogs," Toby responded. "I bled them and am going back to get them with the MULE, if that is okay."

"Absolutely. Shot four. Wow."

Toby was getting the MULE out, and Hank walked up and said, "I'll go with you to help load them."

"Okeydoke," Toby replied.

They pulled up to the hogs, and Hank said, "You pulled them all into a group, huh?"

"Nah, I just bled them where I shot them," Toby replied.

The hogs were all within twenty-five feet of each other.

"Man, that is some good shooting," Hank said.

Toby was amused but didn't say anything. He got out of the MULE and grabbed the first hog and lifted it up into bed of the MULE.

"I guess I better wake up and help you," Hank said.

They loaded the other three and headed back to the barn. They pulled into the barnyard and saw that Carl's truck and Drew's Toyota Prius were parked at the house. Toby backed the MULE into the barn, and he and Hank hung the four hogs up in the lean-to on the west side. They would let the hogs finish bleeding and then take them to town later, hopefully with others they were fixin' to go hunt. Toby pulled the MULE back out and was starting to get out when he noticed Mike Stine walking with Drew. He wondered what was up and if there was a connection that was going to cost him his job.

"Hello, Mike," Hank said.

"You guys ready to go hunt some hogs?" Carl was unloading his Polaris Ranger off his trailer.

Toby went to get Pudge and came walking him out. He glanced at Mike, who wouldn't look at him. Toby decided to walk over and break the ice. "Hello, Mike. I didn't expect to see you again so soon." He held out his hand.

Mike looked at him and then stuck out his hand. "Same here."

"You must have met Mike last night," Hank said. "He is Drew's cousin and is going to play for the Longhorns this fall."

"He may not play much this year, but he will before his four years are up," Carl said.

Toby the Rancher

"That's cool," Toby said.

Drew had been conspicuously quiet. The hog made a racket in the stock trailer, and Drew seemed a little spooked and asked, "What in the world was that?"

"That's a hog that Toby caught in the barn this morning tearing into the feed," Hank said.

"Did he bulldog it like a calf?" Carl said laughingly.

Toby glared at him. "No, I hit it in the head with a shovel."

Carl met Toby's eyes and saw Toby wasn't smiling. Carl looked away very quickly.

"Mike and I will ride in the MULE, and Carl and Drew can ride in the Ranger," Hank said.

"Is he riding his horse?" Drew asked.

Toby started to speak, but Hank answered, "Yes, he is. That is quite a horse. His rider ain't too shabby either."

Mike had walked to the MULE and looked in the back. "Where did all this blood come from?"

"Toby shot four hogs when he drove the heifers back to the south pasture," Hank said.

"With John Wayne around, you don't need the rest of us," Carl said.

Toby could tell by Hank's clenched jaw that Carl had gone too far with his remarks.

"Carl, I have had about all the childish remarks I am going to tolerate," Hank said. "You either accept the fact that your brother screwed up, because he is no good, or you quit coming around here except with Patty. Do I make myself clear?"

Patty, Kali, and Carla came pulling up into the drive as Hank finished speaking. Sadie had walked out and heard all that was said. She walked out to meet the car.

Hearing the car pull up gave Carl more of a backbone, and after a short silence, he said, "So you are going to take this kid who you just met and know nothing about over me? I have been in your family nearly twenty-five years."

Patty and the girls stopped in their tracks and were listening.

"Don't get involved," Sadie whispered to Patty. "This is between Carl and your dad."

Patty just looked at her mother and nodded. They stood and watched and listened.

"This has nothing to do with Toby, but yet you are making him the issue," Hank said. "He is doing his job and is good at it, and you don't like it. Your smart comments have been going on ever since Frank was fired, and I am tired of it and am not going to overlook them anymore."

Carl looked at Hank and then looked around some. "How can you say Toby isn't the issue when you gave him the job you promised to Drew?"

Hank was getting hotter by the minute. "You don't even know what you're talking about. I told him I would look to hire him if I needed some extra summer help. If he told you something different, then you need to question him." Hank looked at Drew as he finished talking.

Toby was over petting Pudge and staying out of the argument. Carl looked at Drew. "Is that true?"

Drew wouldn't look at him.

"There's your answer," Hank said. "I have hogs to hunt. Come or not. I don't really care at this point."

Toby mounted up and headed for the lane that led to the pastures. Hank and Mike were behind him on the MULE.

Carl and Drew didn't follow as Carl started in on Drew, and Patty and Kali stepped in and took up for him. Carl loaded up his Ranger and headed home.

"I would still like to go hog hunting, but I don't have a way now," Drew said.

"Maybe we can ride the horses," Kali said.

"What is this *we* stuff?" Patty said.

"With the way Grandad is acting, I want to be there if he jumps on Drew again," Kali said.

That statement hit Sadie wrong, and she snapped at Kali, "Young lady, you are out of line. Your grandad was fine until Carl smarted off about Toby again. He had all he could take."

Patty started to speak, but Sadie interrupted her. "Don't speak. Think. You will know I am right. It all started when Frank screwed up."

Silence gripped them all for a while after that.

"I'm sorry, Grandma," Kali finally said. "Drew can go on by himself."

"I'm going home," Drew said.

Kali snapped her head around and looked at him. "Do what?"

"I'm tired of all the drama around here, so I'm going home," he said.

"You caused part of the drama," Kali said. "Now you're leaving? Whatever."

Drew left, and they all went into the house.

Unaware of anything going on at the house, Toby was leading the others in the MULE to where he had spotted the hogs yesterday. He spotted movement in the brush and squeezed his legs on Pudge as he grabbed his rifle. He pulled up and saw the hog as he put it against his shoulder, he sighted and shot. The hog was down. He started to lower his gun and saw five more hogs burst out of the brush and head toward the trees. He sighted in and started shooting. He shot all five before the other two could get their guns up and ready to shoot. Six more down. He headed over to bleed the hogs.

"Holy cow, he can shoot," Mike said to Hank.

"Yes, he can," Hank said.

They pulled over to where Toby was bleeding them.

"Dude, that was sweet," Mike said.

"Thanks," Toby said. "Are they coming with the Ranger?"

"Don't know," Hank said.

"We don't have enough room to haul them all back, and we may get more," Toby said.

"I'll try to call," Mike said. He said to someone on the phone, "Where are you? Home! We needed your Ranger. I'll tell them." He hung up and turned to Toby and Hank. "Carl and Drew went home, so no Ranger."

"Well, I guess we best head back and get the old truck," Hank said.

"I'll hunt while you are gone," Toby said.

He rode off, and they headed back.

10

Toby had started to ask why they weren't taking some of the hogs back with them, but then he realized Hank was upset, so he left it alone. He rode toward another grove of trees, and as he approached, he saw two more hogs. One of them was huge. He guessed it to be over four hundred pounds. He watched it for a minute and was amazed at how much dirt it could root up in a short period of time. He took aim on it and put it down.

The smaller hog bolted toward the trees and was out of sight before Toby could take aim. He circled around the trees, keeping a watchful eye for any movement. He saw movement, but the color and size were wrong, and then a doe shot out of the trees. On her heels was the hog, so Toby fired quickly and was dead-on. He bled that one and then walked over to the big hog, leading Pudge. He was wondering how many more hogs were around. That was a total of thirteen caught or killed, and he hadn't had to look hard.

When Toby walked up on the big hog, he realized it was bigger than he thought. He wasn't sure how much it would weigh, but it was a large hunk of bacon. He wrestled it around for a little then decided to hook a rope to it and let Pudge turn it so it would bleed out better to save the meat. He didn't know if the meat would be good in a big hog but wanted to save it all, if possible. He had it turned and taken the rope off the hog and the saddle horn and was starting to roll it up when he heard noise in the brush. He was on the opposite side from his gun, so he was trying to think of what to do. He didn't know what it was but had enough dealing with wild animals to expect anything.

Toby started to put his foot on the stirrup. A huge hog bolted from the brush and was running straight at Pudge and him. Pudge jumped sideways, and Toby dropped the loop of the rope down. The hog had gotten spooked when Pudge jumped and changed direction, enough to give Toby a chance to rope it. He had the loop swinging and flying in an instant. He roped the hog and quickly ran around a tree to use it for leverage and tie the rope holding the hog.

It was a monster of a hog, considerably larger than the one he had shot. He had it roped now, but what in the world was he going to do with it? He decided he would try to use a small nylon rope he had in his saddlebag to rope its legs. It wasn't an ideal rope for that, but the hog was moving enough that he thought he might get lucky. It took four throws to catch it, but he roped the back two feet and pulled them until the hog went down. Once it did, he was on it like a duck on a June bug to get it hog-tied. The hog slung its head at him and nearly got him, but he was able to hog-tie it, and the hog quit fighting.

Toby heard a racket and saw the old truck bouncing along, the MULE and two horses following behind it. The figures looked like two girls, both with dark-brown hair, so he figured them to be Kali and Carla. He mounted up and rode over to them to help load the hogs.

Hank looked at Toby as he rode up and asked, "You get some more? We heard a couple of shots."

"Yeah, a couple over there, and I have a live one hog-tied," Toby replied.

"Why didn't you shoot it?" Mike asked.

"Didn't have my gun. I was off of Pudge, taking care of one of the hogs, when it started at us. All I had was a rope, so I roped it."

Hank burst out laughing. "Now that's a cowboy for you. Let's get these loaded up."

Toby looked at the girls who had been listening attentively. He tipped his hat to them and said, "Hello, ladies."

Carla grinned at him. "Hey, Toby."

Kali turned her head and didn't say anything.

Toby remembered Kali's talk with Sadie in the grocery store and figured she must be blaming him for the whole deal. He didn't let it bother him because he knew he hadn't done anything wrong.

He grabbed one of the smaller hogs and lifted it into the back of the truck. Hank and Mike were lifting another one in. Toby grabbed another hog.

"I'll help you," Carla said. She slipped down from the saddle and came over to grab the hog's back legs.

"Much obliged," Toby said.

They loaded two, and as they looked, they saw there was one more hog to load. They started toward it.

"Carla, let Mike and Toby load that," Hank said. "You don't need to lift with Mike here."

Carla looked at her Grandad, kind of aggravated, but she stepped back, and Mike and Toby lifted the hog into the truck.

"We can put the other two in the MULE, and we will have to come back for the live one," Hank said.

Toby didn't say anything, but he knew the big hog would fill the bed on the MULE by itself. It was that big.

Hank and Mike pulled up to the smaller hog, and Toby grabbed it and put it on top of the others in the truck.

"Why don't you put that one in the MULE?" Hank asked.

"They won't both fit in the MULE," Toby replied.

Hank looked at him with wide eyes. "Say what?" He turned to look into the trees but couldn't see the hog from where he was.

Toby started walking toward the trees, leading Pudge by the reins. When they got to the edge, Hank parked the truck and got out to walk in. Mike was driving the MULE, and the girls were off their horses, now walking too. They came around some trees where Hank could see the hogs, and he said, "Holy smokes. Those things are monsters. They could take Boss down."

"Those things are so big they are scary," Carla said.

Mike got out of the MULE. "Wow."

"Mike, let's see if we can get this thing loaded," Toby said. He grabbed the front legs, and Mike grabbed the back, and they got ready to lift.

"I can't do much, but I'll lift in the middle," Hank said.

"On three," Toby said. He counted three, and they lifted. The hog was heavy, but they got it loaded, and it filled the MULE bed completely with the head sticking up. Toby looked at the one he had hog-tied. "I reckon it will be okay until we get back."

"I'm sure it will," Hank said.

Toby started walking toward Pudge, and as he walked by Kali, she slipped putting her foot on the stirrup and started to fall. He caught her and lifted her back to her feet.

"Whoa there," Toby said.

Kali didn't even look at him. "Don't 'Whoa' me. I'm not a horse."

"Well, I sure am sorry, ma'am," he replied sarcastically.

Carla looked at Toby and laughed. "You can catch me anytime."

He grinned at her and grabbed the saddle horn and swung up into the saddle without using the stirrups. He noticed Kali was watching.

"Cowboy up," Carla said. "Let's race back."

Toby looked at Hank to see if he approved.

"Good luck, girl," Hank said. "Be careful."

Carla took off, and Toby and Pudge hesitated a little bit and then started after her. She was riding pretty good, so Toby pushed Pudge on up beside her and rode along with her, but she was trying to get her horse to go faster. She looked at Toby. He smiled, tipped his hat, and Pudge left Carla and her horse in his dust. They rode into the barnyard.

"That horse is fast," Carla said.

Toby the Rancher

"Pudge likes to run." Toby dismounted and got the ropes ready to hang the hogs.

Carla rode on up to the house. The others got to the barn, and Kali put her horse in the stall with the saddle still on it.

"That's okay," Toby said. "I'll take the saddle off."

"You're the hired help, so you should," Kali said.

Hank heard her. "Hold your horses, Kali. We don't act like that, and you need to take your own saddle off. You know that is the rule of riding around here."

Kali turned around and went back inside to take care of her horse.

They unloaded all the hogs, and Toby backed the truck up to the trailer to hook it up. Hank and Mike got in the truck, and Toby went to get Pudge. He grabbed a piece of rope to try and tie and hold the hog's head still while they loaded it. He caught up to Hank and Mike and was riding beside them when he spotted two hogs breaking across a meadow. He pulled his rifle and shot both before Hank or Mike even saw them.

"Jeez, boy, I don't guess you need any help getting rid of the hogs," Hank said.

"Just lucky," Toby responded.

"That shooting isn't luck," Mike said. "You are good with that rifle."

"Thanks," Toby said. "My dad taught me how to shoot when I was thirteen."

Hank and Mike went to the live hog while Toby went to make sure the other two didn't spoil. He rode to join the other two men and try to load the huge hog. "Let me see if I can get this loop around the top or bottom of its snout. If we can, Hank can control the head while Mike and I try to load it."

Toby put his foot on the hog's head and dropped the loop. He was able to get the top jaw, so Hank took the rope and pulled on it while Mike and Toby each got behind the back and started lifting. The hog was heavy and could still squirm, so they dropped it from about a foot up the first time.

"Let's try it with you in back and me underneath it," Toby said. "Maybe pushing against each other will help us lift."

They tried that and were able to get the hog lifted and loaded in the trailer.

"Jeez, I don't think lifting weights helped me with that," Mike said. "That sucker was heavy."

"He is the biggest I have ever seen," Hank said.

They loaded the other two hogs up, and Hank said, "Let's get some dinner. We'll take in what we have so far and then start again."

They rode into the barnyard. Patty, Carla, and Kali were walking out of the house to leave.

"Dad, we'll see you and Toby this evening!" Patty hollered.

"Okay!" Hank hollered back.

"Bye, Toby!" Carla hollered.

Toby waved to her and noticed Kali had a look of disgust on her face. He wasn't real eager about going tonight after what had happened this morning.

Sadie was on the front porch. "Dinner is ready."

They ate a good dinner of chicken fried steak, mashed potatoes and gravy, green beans, and homemade rolls. Toby was enjoying his coffee when Sadie brought out an apple pie. "I hope you boys like apple pie."

"That's my favorite pie," Toby said. He told them about his memory of his dad and sharing coffee and apple pie. He finished his pie and coffee. "I'll go and hook up my truck to the trailer so we can load the hogs. Do you want me to hook yours to the stock trailer?"

"Mike and I can do that," Hank said. "You don't need to do it all."

Toby hooked up his truck and had loaded five hogs by himself before Hank and Mike got his truck hooked up. They finished loading and headed out to town. The meat processor staff was surprised to see them pull in with so many hogs and was shocked at the size of the two big ones. Hank introduced Toby to him and called Toby a hog hunter extraordinaire. Toby was surprised to hear Mike agree. They were going to have to wait to bring in more hogs because they had filled up the cold locker and the meat-processing man couldn't handle any more. Hank hoped they had gotten the majority of them, if not all, and maybe the rest would leave.

Toby headed back to the ranch. Hank went to take Mike home since Mike had been left without a ride. Toby started feeding the livestock and cleaning up the stall where the hogs had been hanging. He was just about finished when his phone rang. He answered it without checking the number. It was Bethany, and she was in Nacogdoches and wanted to see him. He told her he was working and was invited to a dinner tonight.

Sadie walked in while he was talking and heard his conversation, so without Toby knowing it, she called Patty to see if Toby could bring a guest. Patty agreed, so Sadie walked back into the barn and had Toby stop talking while she told him he could bring Bethany to Carl and Patty's. Toby thanked Sadie even though he wasn't sure it was a good idea. He felt like he needed to spend some time with Bethany since she had come to town to see him. He and Bethany planned where and when to meet, and he finished cleaning the stall. He had everything taken care of and was walking to his quarters when Hank pulled in.

"I got sidetracked a little," he said.

Toby smiled. "Everything is taken care of, so I am going to get cleaned up, unless you have something else."

"Nope," Hank said. "Sounds good. We leave around 5:45."

"Okay."

Toby was ready and sitting on his porch when Hank and Sadie walked out of the house.

"I hear you have a date tonight," Hank said.

"I don't know if you would call it a date," Toby replied. "But she is in town, so I figured I should see her."

Hank laughed and got in his truck. Toby pulled in behind them, and they headed toward town. They stopped and picked up

Bethany. She got in the truck and leaned over and kissed Toby on the cheek.

This may have been a mistake, Toby thought. He wasn't interested in her, even though she was a good-looking cowgirl. She was too pushy for his liking.

They pulled up to Carl and Patty's. It looked like a very nice house, with a wraparound porch. Jeb's house had a wraparound porch, and Toby had spent many hours on it with his dad when he was growing up. Toby hoped to have one of his own in the future.

Hank rang the doorbell, and Carla opened the door. She was smiling. "Come on—"

She stopped in midsentence when she saw Bethany.

"Carla, this is Bethany," Toby quickly said. "You may remember her from the rodeo."

"No, I don't," Carla said.

"Me either," Kali chimed in.

Toby turned in that direction to see Kali and Drew sitting on the couch. They were both staring at him. Carla walked by and went to her bedroom. Toby thought about just leaving but figured he was already there, and it wouldn't be polite at that point. He was dreading the evening, though.

11

Toby felt uneasy sitting in the living room with Kali and Drew. Carl and Hank came walking in, and that helped lighten the atmosphere some until Carl opened his mouth. "Well, I hear the great white hunter had quite a day."

Everyone looked at Toby, and he got mad and nervous. He did the only thing he could think of to try and disarm Carl.

"Really?" Toby replied. "Where did you go hunting after you took your Ranger and went home?"

Hank burst out laughing. "Carl, when are you going to learn this young man is more than a match for you?"

Carl looked angry but then smiled and said, "Hank, I believe you are right. Toby, my apologies."

Toby nodded. "Thank you."

Carla came walking in as he said it and asked Bethany, "What was your name?"

"Bethany Squires."

Carla sat on the arm of the couch by Kali. "Did you win?"

"No. My friend Wendy Logan did."

Carla looked at Toby. "Is that the same Wendy you were talking to on the phone Thursday night?"

"Yes," Toby replied.

Carla smiled, thinking she was getting ready to stir up trouble.

"Wendy told me she was going to call you and tell you she won," Bethany said to Toby.

"Yep. She did." Toby glanced at Carla. Her smile had disappeared, and Kali was frowning too.

"Enough about Bethany and me," Toby said. "Drew, what did you do today?"

Drew glared at Toby. "Nothing."

"You sure missed a good time. Kali even joined in for a while."

Drew didn't say anything.

"I didn't enjoy it," Kali said.

"Hey, nobody twisted your arm to come out there," Toby said

"I did," Carla said. "Toby and I raced back. His horse is fast."

"He does like to run," Toby said.

Patty walked in. "Carl, if you will say the blessing, we are ready to eat."

Carl looked at Toby. "Toby, would you offer thanks?"

"I'd be honored to," Toby said.

They all stood behind their chairs in the dining room, and Toby led the prayer. They sat down to start eating, with Carl and Hank on the ends, Sadie sitting by Toby, and Patty by Bethany. Kali was directly across from Toby and Carla was across from Bethany. Drew sat across from Patty. Toby enjoyed the supper. It was Mexican food, and he always liked good Mexican food. There was idle chitchat while they ate but nothing that started any long dialogue. When they finished the meal, Patty brought in a chocolate cake and a peach cobbler.

"Wow, those look delicious," Toby said. He looked at Kali and Carla. "Can you girls cook like your grandma and mother?"

Neither girl answered. They just glared at Toby.

"I can't get either one of them interested in the kitchen," Patty said.

"Gonna be hard to catch a hubby if you can't cook," Toby said.

Kali looked mad, but Carla went on the offensive to try and divert the attention. She turned to Bethany and asked, "Can you cook, Bethany?"

"Yes," Bethany answered. "I enjoy cooking. I still have a ways to go on desserts, though."

"Desserts take time," Sadie said. "If you enjoy cooking, you'll get there."

Carla was striking out all the way around tonight. She looked down at her cake and took a bite. There was a moment of silence, and then Kali spoke up. "I disagree. You don't have to be able to cook to get a guy. You just need to take care of yourself and make yourself presentable."

"Ya think?" Toby said.

"Yes, I do," Kali answered. "Drew doesn't care that I don't cook much."

"You sure won't be able to have these types of get-togethers if you can't rustle up some good grub like Patty and Sadie," Toby said.

"You can order takeout and have a good meal," Drew spoke up.

Everyone looked at him like he had the plague.

"Yeah, okay," Toby said. "By the way, why are you sitting there by Carla and Carl when there is an empty seat by Kali?"

Everyone looked at Drew, and he got very nervous. He couldn't think of anything to say, so Toby helped out more. "Chalking up points with the future father-in-law, huh?"

"No, I'm not," Drew snapped back. "I picked this chair before I noticed where Carla and Kali were sitting."

"Sitting down before the ladies," Toby said. "That's not very gentleman-like."

Drew, Kali, and Carla were all looking at Toby like they could pinch his head off, so he laughed and said, "Just pulling your strings, Drew. Don't get upset."

Drew gave Toby an uppity-chin throw, and it was all Toby could do to leave that one alone. He ate the rest of his cobbler and drank another cup of coffee before he got up from the table. He and Hank were the last to get up. He walked to the kitchen and said, "That was an excellent meal. I sure do appreciate the invite."

"Thank you, and you are more than welcome," Patty replied. "We enjoyed having you."

"I hate to eat and run," Toby said. "But Bethany has a fairly long drive and doesn't need to be on the road late."

They said their good-byes, and Toby took Bethany to her truck. He hugged her good-bye, and she kissed him on the cheek again. He shut the door on her truck, and she rolled down the window and said, "I really can cook."

Toby smiled. "I never doubted you."

She drove off, and he headed to the ranch. He was running the evening through his mind and got very aggravated with himself. He couldn't believe he had been so vocal and mouthy. That wasn't like him, and he shouldn't have let his himself get irritated to the point of becoming something he wasn't.

"I bet Patty regrets asking me, and Hank and Sadie are probably disappointed," he said to himself.

Toby got to the ranch and went to the barn to see Pudge and talk to him. He spent over an hour with Pudge, brushing him and talking to him. Pudge was his oldest and dearest friend, and he enjoyed talking with him even though it was a one-sided conversation. He shut the door on the barn and was walking toward the mobile home when he noticed Hank and Sadie were home. He glanced at his watch, not realizing he had been in there so long. He got ready for bed and read the Bible and went to sleep after saying his prayer.

The next day, after waking up, he had breakfast cooked and eaten before 6:00 a.m. He sat and looked at a magazine for a while and then went out to take care of the morning feeding. He checked on Pudge and then fed the bulls and cows that were penned up. They had shut the barn door so hogs couldn't get in, but Toby didn't see any signs of hogs being around during the night. Maybe they had taken enough out that they weren't coming up around the barnyard now.

Toby finished up and went in to get ready for church. He was in the truck and heading to town by 8:30 a.m. so he could stop and get a newspaper. He met one of the men who showed him where to go for Bible class.

After class, he was walking in the auditorium when he saw Hank talking to a couple of guys. Toby was surprised as they hadn't talked about where they attended. Hank spotted Toby and walked over and shook Toby's hand. "Are you church of Christ?"

"Yes," Toby said. "Ever since my dad adopted me."

"That's great."

Toby walked on and took a seat near the back. He was flipping through the songbook when he looked up and saw Patty and Carl sitting down by Sadie, and Kali and Drew were walking down the aisle and looking at him.

"You going to let me in?"

Toby looked to his left to see Carla waiting to slip by him to sit down.

"Sure." He stood up to let her in.

"I am surprised to see you."

"Why's that?"

"I don't know. Guess I figured cowboys only attended cowboy church."

Toby just chuckled.

Services started, and when it was time, he walked to the front to place membership with the church. He had a lot of people shake his hand and meet him.

Carl walked up. "I have to be honest, I thought you were just here for show. I see I was wrong."

Toby just looked at him and walked on. *That guy has some issues.*

He made his way out of the building and decided he would drive around some out in the country to look the area over. He stopped at a convenience store to get a cup of coffee for the drive. He was walking back to his truck when Drew and Kali pulled up in Drew's Toyota Prius. Toby tipped his hat to Kali as she was on the side of the car next to him. He got in and started his truck and started to back out.

"Hey," he heard someone holler.

Toby turned back to see Mike standing in front of the store. Toby stopped, and Mike walked to his window and asked, "How's it going?"

"Good," Toby replied. "Just got out of church and going to take a drive."

"No hog hunting today?"

"I may run out later this afternoon to see if I can spot any."

Mike laughed. "If you spot them, they will be dead."

Toby laughed. "I'll talk to you later."

"See ya."

Toby started to turn and look behind him but noticed Drew and Kali had been watching them. He said to himself, "Bet that burst Drew's bubble. He probably wanted a fight."

Toby drove about ten miles looking around and started back in the direction of the ranch. He hoped he could work his way back without going to the highway. He drove six more miles and noticed a For Sale sign. He pulled over to see what the place looked like. It was 150 acres—a house, a barn, and corrals. The land he could see looked nice, but naturally, he couldn't see all of it. He wrote the name and number so he could call. He thought he might try to pull it up on the computer.

Toby wanted his own place. He had been saving money ever since he was thirteen, and with what his dad had left him, he had decent savings. He pulled away, excited. He hoped the house was not out of his price range and that it was all as nice as what he had seen from the road.

As he drove on to the ranch, he grew deep in thought. Was he rushing this? He had just got there less than a week ago. He had liked everything he had seen so far, and it felt like home. Maybe this was how a guy was supposed to feel when he found the right place in life. Especially someone like him who had bounced around most of his life.

He pulled up into the drive of the ranch and saw Bethany's truck sitting in front of his place. "What in the world?" he said to himself.

He pulled on up and got out, and she got out of her truck.

"What's going on?" Toby asked.

"Just waiting for you."

"I thought you were going back to school last night."

"I was but decided to get a motel room instead."

Toby walked up on the porch. "Come on in where it's warm."

Hank and Sadie had pulled in as they were talking. Toby waved at them as they walked up on the porch. Hank motioned him to come over, so Toby told Bethany, "Have a seat, and I'll be right back." He walked over.

"I have some pie you can have for your guest," Sadie said. "Are you two getting serious?"

"No, ma'am," Toby said.

"She is a beautiful girl."

"Yeah, she is easy on the eyes."

Hank had walked in, and laughed. "So that's how the young folks say it, huh? She drives a truck and wears Western clothes. Good combination."

"I developed a bad taste in my mouth about her with the dealings at the rodeo," Toby said. "The fights were because that guy liked her. She said she didn't like him and never had, but either he was a very slow learner or she played him. I'm not sure yet which it was, but that is keeping me at more than an arm's length away from her at this point."

"She seems pleasant," Sadie said.

"Yeah, she is very nice," Toby said.

Sadie handed him the pie. "Sounds like it could develop into something more."

Toby took the pie. "I don't know. Not going to rush anything. Thank you for the pie." He headed for the door and said to Hank, "I will ride out later and see if I can see any hogs."

"Okay, but it can wait until tomorrow," Hank said.

Toby nodded and shut the door behind him. He walked into the mobile home and showed Bethany the pie. "I'll whip up some dinner, and we have dessert."

"I'll help."

They both went to the kitchen and started dinner.

12

Toby had put a roast on to cook before he left for church so he could have it to eat on all week. He and Bethany fixed some ears of corn and bread, and after they had eaten, Toby pulled out a couple of the pieces of pie Sadie had given him. As he finished his pie, he said, "I need to ride out and see if there are any hogs still roaming around. I had told Hank I would."

"If you have another horse, I would like to ride along, if you don't mind," Bethany said.

"Not at all."

They changed their clothes and went to the barn to saddle up.

"Hello, Pudge," Bethany said.

"You remember his name, huh?"

"How could I forget, especially after y'all's performance at the rodeo?"

They finished tightening the cinches and mounted up and headed out to the southwest pasture.

Hank saw them ride out and told Sadie, "I guess he is taking her hog hunting."

"They make a cute couple," Sadie replied. "I sure wish Carla was closer to his age. He would be good for her."

"Grandma, you trying to pick your granddaughter's beaus?" Sadie smiled. "Doesn't hurt to wish."

"Guess not." Hank went back to reading his paper.

As they rode along, Toby noted to himself how well Bethany rode. He knew she could handle anything that might come up. He had no more than gotten that thought out of his head when he spotted a hog moving in some trees, but as he squeezed Pudge to stop and pulled his rifle up, he saw three hogs running straight at them. Luckily, Bethany had ridden past before she realized he was stopping, so she wasn't in harm's way.

Toby pulled up and dropped the first hog then the second. The third one was still coming, and Toby spurred Pudge to move to the right. It gave him a better angle and slowed the hog some. He shot and dropped it and glanced to make sure Bethany was okay. She came riding up as he moved slowly toward the trio.

"You okay?" Toby asked her.

"Yeah. That was crazy. I didn't know they were that aggressive."

"Neither did I." Toby slipped out of the saddle to bleed the three hogs. He finished and said, "There was at least one in those woods over there. That was what I was stopping to try and shoot." He started in that direction, and as he rounded the edge of the grove of trees, four hogs burst out and ran for a small canyon.

Toby pulled his rifle up and shot the first one and then the second, but as he lined up to shoot the third one, a shot rang out from behind him and dropped one of the hogs, so he switched his aim and dropped the fourth one. He turned to see Bethany with a rifle in her hands.

"Nice shot," he said. "I didn't know you could shoot."

"Thanks," she said. "I have been hunting since I was ten."

They rode over closer to the hogs. Toby dragged two of them to get them closer together then bled them. "We best go back and get the old truck to haul all seven of them."

They mounted up and took off, and Bethany started pushing her horse and looking back at Toby. He took the challenge and urged Pudge to go get them. Bethany could ride, but she was no match for Pudge and Toby. Toby and Pudge caught up to her and passed her, and Toby was taunting her as they were in the lead heading back to the barn.

They rode into the barn and started unsaddling.

"You won that one, but if I had my horse, I would have given you a run for your money," Bethany said.

Toby laughed.

"You laughing at me makes me want to go get my horse and come back and race."

"That wasn't me. It was Pudge."

Bethany laughed, and they walked out of the barn to get the truck. Toby popped the hood to check the oil on the old truck.

Hank walked up as Toby was closing it. "Heard some shots. You must have gotten more than the MULE can haul."

"Yeah, we have seven down," Toby said. "Bethany shot one of them."

Hank looked at her. "Nice job, young lady."

"Had the strangest thing happen, though," Toby said.

"How's that?" Hank asked.

Toby relayed the story about the three hogs charging at him and Pudge.

The story worried Hank. "If they are that aggressive, we may start losing more livestock and everyone will have to walk around armed."

"I hope we are about to get them all taken care of," Toby said.

"Me too," Hank said. "But I'm afraid they may be migrating this way and we may have problems for a while."

"We'll keep our eyes open," Toby said, and he pulled away to go get the seven hogs.

Bethany drove the truck while Toby loaded the hogs. He spotted another hog while he was riding in the back between the two groups of hogs and hollered for Bethany to stop. He shot the hog too, so they were going back in with eight hogs.

Once they got all the hogs hung up in the barn, Toby and Bethany went to the mobile home to clean up.

"I go to church at 6:00," Toby said.

"I'll go with you if you don't mind, and then I will leave from there," Bethany said.

"Sounds good."

They got in their separate trucks and headed to town. Toby decided to call the real estate agent on the way to town to try and find out some information on the ranch he had seen earlier. He found out the land was all good grass and trees. The house was two thousand square feet, with three bedrooms and two and a half baths. The barn was fifty by seventy-five feet, and there were several outbuildings and calf sheds. They were asking $575,000 for the place, and it had just gone on the market. They also had an option of taking all livestock and equipment for $700,000.

Toby had asked to see the place tomorrow afternoon. He felt sure he could work out some time around 2:00 p.m. He kind of hoped Hank would go with him to see the place. He would talk to Hank after church, and he hoped Hank wouldn't be upset. Toby intended to keep working for Hank even if he got the place. He had no doubt he could handle both jobs. He was excited about the possibility. He just hoped it worked out as he planned.

Toby arrived at the church building and went to Bethany's truck to walk in with her. Carla spotted them walking in and came over to sit with them. She asked Bethany, "I thought you went home. Where did you stay?"

"I stayed at the motel on Main Street," Bethany replied.

"What have you been doing today?"

"Hog hunting with Toby."

Carla looked agitated. "I was hunting with him yesterday. Don't you have school tomorrow? Kali and Drew went back to school this afternoon."

"I'm going back after church."

"Enough with the questions," Toby interrupted. "Services are about to start."

After church let out, Toby walked Bethany to her truck and told her he had enjoyed the day and for her to drive safely back to school. He hugged her, and she kissed him on the cheek again. She said she had a blast. She drove off, and Toby headed for his truck. He walked by Patty, and she said, "Toby, I didn't get a chance to talk to you this morning, but I was sure glad to see you here."

"Thank you, ma'am," Toby said as he tipped his hat and walked on to his truck.

Toby drove to the ranch and waited for Hank and Sadie to get home so he could talk to Hank. He was as nervous as he had ever been. Hank and Sadie pulled up into the drive and went into the house. He waited a few minutes before he walked over.

Hank opened the door and saw Toby and said, "What's up, Toby?"

"Hank, could I have a few minutes to talk to you about something?"

Hank looked puzzled but said, "Sure enough. Come on in."

"The coffee is on," Sadie said. "Should be ready in a minute."

They walked to the kitchen table and sat down.

"What's on your mind?" Hank asked.

Toby hesitated, looking for the words to start with. "Hank, I've had an idea of what I wanted out of life ever since my dad died. Actually, I had the idea before then. Dad and I were planning on trying to get a ranch, and then he passed away. I haven't lost that dream and have been working and saving every penny I could to hopefully buy one someday. I think I am ready to try and make that happen. I found a ranch today that seems to fit what I have dreamed about."

Hank and Sadie had listened without any change in expression. "You wanting to quit?" Hank asked. "Is that what you are leading up to?"

Sadie was standing back by the coffeepot. Toby could see her face, and he saw she got a sad look on her face.

"No, sir. I want to try and buy the ranch down the road but still work for you too."

"Which ranch?"

"The one about a mile south of here."

"The Glover place?" Sadie asked.

"Sounds like it," Hank said. "I didn't know it was for sale."

"I saw the sign on the way home from church and called about it on the way to church," Toby said.

"They must have decided to move to town since Bud has been sick," Sadie said. "That's a shame, since they are only in their thirties."

There was silence for a minute, and then Hank asked, "Are you sure you want to stay here in Nacogdoches?"

Toby was stunned. He wasn't expecting that kind of response from Hank. He didn't know what to say.

Hank continued, "Don't get me wrong. I would love to have you as a neighbor, but you haven't been here but a few days, and buying a ranch is a big decision. One that can tie you down or ruin you for the rest of your life if you decide to sell and don't come out financially."

Toby felt relieved. If that was all Hank meant, he knew how to respond to that. "I understand what you are saying, and yes, I am ready to live here the rest of my life. I have looked hard since I got here and liked everything I have seen—the land, the town, the church, and the people. It is a place I would like to put down my roots, and for me, that is saying a lot."

"Well, it sounds like you have that thought through," Hank said. "What about working both places if you get it? That is a lot of work."

"Yes, I know it would be," Toby said. "But work is all I have at this point. I don't have any family, and Pudge is all I have. It would also help me make the payments on the place."

"What about that young lady you spent the day with?" Sadie asked. "Are you thinking you need a place to start a family?"

"I am a long ways from that."

"She may not have that same thought."

Toby looked at Sadie and saw she was grinning. "I don't think of her that way at this point. Still too many questions in my mind about her and the antics I saw at the rodeo."

"Sadie, you need to leave the matchmaking to the young folks," Hank said. "Toby, if I might ask, how much are they asking for the Glover place?"

Toby told him the two prices.

"I'm not real sure about his livestock," Hank said. "I think he picked them up from several places, and there are different breeds. A fellow can make it work, but if he is looking at a lifelong venture, I believe one breed and improving that herd is more profitable."

"I appreciate your thoughts and value your opinion," Toby said. "That is why I wanted to ask you if you would go with me tomorrow to look the place over."

"I would be honored," Hank said. "What time are you going?"

"I think I can have everything done and be ready to go by 2:00."

"Sounds good."

Sadie poured both of them a cup of coffee and walked out into the living room.

"I don't mean to get in your business, but I don't want to see you get your hopes too high and then not be able to get the place," Hank said. "You said yourself all you have is your truck, trailer, and Pudge. Either amount is a large sum of money to have to borrow with very little collateral."

"I understand what you are saying and don't mind you asking at all," Toby said. "I feel like if I am asking you to be involved it is only fair to let you know where I stand. My dad got me my first loan when I was thirteen. I bought an old car to restore and put it on payments at the bank. I have had different loans ever since then and have a good credit rating. I also have $325,000 in savings. Dad left me the house and some money, and I have saved all the money I can."

"Sounds like Farm Credit will be more than happy to see you walk in."

"I sure hope so."

"Did you know the Glover place connects to our place?"

"I had no idea. I figured it was too far away."

"The land runs north more than south and meets up to our south boundary."

"That's cool," Toby said. He finished his coffee and said, "I best get out of here and leave you folks be. I have tied up your whole evening." He got up and headed toward the door.

"You are not a bother at all," Hank said. "It is great to see a young man with his head firmly planted on his shoulders."

"Thank you, and thank you, Sadie, for the coffee. You folks have a good night."

Toby closed the door and walked to the mobile home. He was so excited he couldn't go to sleep. He read a lot and watched TV, but his eyes would not get heavy. He finally laid down at about 1:30 a.m. and fell asleep at 2:00 a.m.

13

Toby was up and out of bed at 5:30 a.m. even though he hadn't gone to sleep until 2:00 a.m. He was so excited for the day to begin and move quickly that he couldn't even take time for his usual good breakfast. He put coffee on to brew and walked to the barn to check on Pudge and the hogs hanging up. It was cold this morning and ice was forming on all the water tanks, so he made sure he had busted the ice in all the tanks before he went back to drink a cup of coffee and eat a Pop-Tart. He was feeding before 7:00 a.m. and was nearly finished when Hank walked out of the house.

Hank walked up to him. "You must be a little anxious about something today."

Toby grinned. "I couldn't hardly sleep. I can't wait for two o'clock to get here."

Hank laughed. "I understand totally. It is a huge step."

"Do you want to take the hogs to town once I'm finished feeding?"

"Yeah, that would be good. Then we can stop by and get some supplements to put out in all the pens and pastures." Hank walked to the barn to take inventory of what he needed to get, and Toby continued feeding. When he finished, he backed the truck and trailer up to the barn and started loading the hogs. Hank had gone into the house to get his wallet and got back after Toby had four hogs loaded.

"You must have drunk a lot of coffee this morning," Hank said. "You are moving like your house a fire."

Toby smiled. "Adrenaline is pumping."

They got the hogs loaded and headed to town.

"I hope you don't mind doing all this work in bringing down these hogs and donating the meat," Hank said. "It would be a pretty good drop of money if we didn't donate it."

"Don't mind it at all," Toby said. "Hadn't even given it a thought, to be honest."

Hank smiled. "You can claim these today as donations on your taxes."

"Thanks. I'm sure that will help if I become a landowner."

They got the hogs unloaded and went to the co-op to get the supplements. Hank introduced Toby to the owner and the employees so they would be familiar with him as his hand and if he got his own place.

The owner, Joe Bassett, said, "You must be the one Mike Stine was telling me about when he came over to see my daughter yesterday. He said you were a crack shot."

"Yes, this is him," Hank said. "He can flat out shoot."

"Were you in the military?" Joe asked.

"No, sir," Toby said. "My dad taught me how to shoot."

"I see," Joe said. "Well, you may be able to hire out if you have time. Hogs are causing problems all over the area right now."

"That would be up to Hank," Toby said.

"We'll see how things go," Hank said.

Toby and Hank left and headed back to the ranch. Sadie had dinner ready by the time they had the trailer unloaded and unhooked. They sat down to eat, and Sadie said, "Patty called and said that Carla was home from school with a bug. Throwing up and running a fever. I told her I would go check on her and spend the afternoon with her."

"Sounds good," Hank said. "I am going with Toby to look at the Glover place."

Toby finished dinner and went out and put the supplements out to the pens around the barn. He would take them out to the pastures when he got back. He washed up and started his truck and pulled up to pick up Hank. He could hardly hold in his excitement. It had seemed like a week since he had seen the For Sale sign, and it had only been a day.

They drove down the road and pulled into the drive. Toby noted a couple of things he would like to change if he was able to buy the ranch. The real estate guy was already there, so they were able to get started looking immediately. They started with the house, and Toby was blown away. The house was immaculate, and he couldn't find one thing he didn't like about it. They looked at the barn, and it was nice. Whoever had built it knew what they were doing and what was needed in a barn. The stalls were well built and very functional.

After they looked at the sheds, they piled into Toby's truck to drive over the land. Although it was still winter, Toby could tell the grass was good and thick and there were good tree lines to provide shelter for the cattle. The fences were in good shape, and there were two nice corrals and working chutes in the pastures.

Toby was sold on the place but was trying to hold it in, even though he was about to burst. They hadn't talked price or specifics while they were viewing the property, but when they pulled back up to the house, Toby asked, "Do you think they are firm on their prices, or is there some room for negotiation?"

The agent, Harold Jones, said, "They do need to sell, but they have loans and mortgages to pay off. That doesn't mean they won't listen to offers, but they would need to be reasonable offers. I think you will find the property and the livestock and equipment will appraise out above the asking price."

Toby thanked Mr. Jones for his time and told him he would let him know something by noon Tuesday. Hank and Toby got in the truck to leave, and before he pulled out of the drive, Toby asked Hank, "What do you think?"

Hank grinned. "You have held it in good."

Toby laughed. "I am excited but curious, if you saw it as I did, or I am looking through rose-colored glasses."

"We are both looking through the same glasses, if that is the case, because I loved what I saw. If I were a young man looking to buy, I would sure take a run at it."

"I was thinking of offering $525,000, but do you think I should check with Farm Credit before I do? Is that too low an offer?"

Hank smiled. "Let me answer the first one. I think it would be a good idea to check with Farm Credit. In fact, let's take a right and head up there now. As far as the offer, all they can do is say yes or no. Are you not considering the equipment and livestock?"

"I did put a pencil to it for what I figured things were worth, and it is a decent deal," Toby replied. "My concern is the cattle. They are not in great shape and are a mixed herd. I would like to have a purebred herd. I know it would take a while, but that is what I have envisioned. I thought about trying to improve the condition of the herd and then sell them to start my herd, but with what I am putting into the place, I'm not sure I could afford the feed needed to get them to where they need to be. Am I being shortsighted?"

"You have thought everything through, and what you say makes sense," Hank said. "I would wonder if you could possibly set the loan up for semiannual payments. That way, you could use the money you make working for us to buy feed, and then when you sell the herd, pay it on the place and then start your herd slow, as you suggested. I would be willing to lease some of the pasture-land until you get your herd built up, as we always need grass."

The more Hank talked, the more Toby got excited. *Could this actually be happening?* he thought to himself. Would he be able to swing the loan?' It all seemed too good to be true. He kept expecting to wake up from a dream.

They talked all the way to town about the equipment and the different pastures that were fenced off. Toby turned into the parking lot of Farm Credit and parked. He sat there for a minute and took a deep breath and said, "Here goes nothing."

Hank laughed. "You may be surprised."

Once inside, Hank introduced Toby to Slade Hopkins, the loan officer. Toby went in with Slade while Hank sat out in the lobby. Slade knew the Glover place and knew it had gone up for sale. Toby briefly explained what he was thinking on purchasing everything and what he would do with the livestock if permitted.

Slade seemed to like his thought process. "Toby, you have thought things through and have a good plan of action in mind. We would just need to get a credit application completed and see if the debt ratio and credit score look good."

"Can I fill it out now?" Toby said.

Slade smiled. "Absolutely." He handed Toby an application.

Toby didn't have many bills, and all his loans had been paid off, so he was able to complete the application in short fashion. Toby handed the application to Slade and turned to walk out, and Slade said, "I will run this and give you a call shortly."

"Thank you," Toby said.

Toby and Hank got in the truck.

"What did he say?" Hank asked.

"He said my plan sounded good and he would run the credit app and let me know," Toby replied.

"Hopefully he will move quickly on it so you can decide what to do."

Toby pulled into a convenience store. "You want a cup of coffee? My treat."

"Sure. Just black, please."

Toby got their coffees, and they headed back to the ranch. Hank walked to the house, and Toby headed for the barn. He talked to Pudge a little and told him about the place, and then he loaded up the old truck with the supplements to take to the pastures. He couldn't take the MULE due to the weight and size of the protein blocks. He started to pull out and decided to stop and get his rifle in case he saw more hogs.

He headed to the northwest pasture first and put out the trace mineral block and a protein block and headed for the gate. He spotted a deer running like a scared jackrabbit and wondered what had spooked it. He got his answer when he saw a large hog come out after it.

Toby had stopped outside the gate, so he grabbed the gun and laid it across the hood and downed the hog. He drove over to it, watching to see if any others were around. He started to bleed the hog and got back in the truck and went to the other pastures.

The last one he entered was the pasture that bordered the land he was hoping to buy. He drove back to the fence and sat and looked at the land and dreamed. He decided he could put a gate at the west end to allow Hank's cattle to graze his place if he leased it to him, and he could ride Pudge to work by coming that way.

His daydreaming was interrupted by his phone ringing. He just knew it was Slade, but it wasn't. He didn't recognize the number, but he answered it anyway. "Hello?"

The lady on the other end asked, "Is this Toby Parker?"

"Yes, it is," he said. "Who am I speaking with?"

"My name is Carol Dobbs. I am Tom Gray's daughter."

Toby had worked with Tom. Tom had left and gone to be closer to his kids and grandkids. Toby thought a lot of Tom. "Yes, ma'am. How is Tom?"

"That is why I am calling."

Toby felt a cold chill go over his whole body.

She continued, "He has had a stroke and is in critical condition. He always talked a lot about the times you two had, and so I wanted to let you know."

Toby was in shock, but he struggled with his emotions. "What are the doctors saying?"

"They aren't saying a lot right now. They say a lot of it depends on him and his will to live."

"Where is he at?"

"He is in the hospital in Lubbock, Texas."

"Thank you for calling me. Please keep me informed."

Toby hung up and just sat there. He was remembering the times he and Tom had spent together, and his mind went back to that of his dad passing away. He started the truck and headed back toward the gate. He shut the gate and drove to the hog he had shot. He loaded it up and went into the barnyard. He had the hog unloaded and was pulling out of the barn when Hank walked out.

"Get another hog?" Hank asked.

"Yeah, it was chasing a deer." Toby paused a minute and then said, "I got a call that one of the few people I count as a friend has had a stroke and is in the hospital in Lubbock. I hate to ask since I haven't been here long, but could I head over there to see him?"

Hank didn't hesitate. "Absolutely. My only concern is will it jeopardize your opportunity to get the Glover place."

"Jeez," Toby said. "I had forgotten all about that since I got the call." He paused for a minute and then continued, "I guess maybe it wasn't meant to happen if it doesn't work out."

"Ah, I don't believe that," Hank said. "There may still be a way to work it out."

"We'll see if I get a call," Toby said. "I sure appreciate you letting me go and all your help in trying to get the place."

"Not a problem. Let me know if we can do anything else to help."

"I will. Thanks again."

Toby parked the truck and put everything in its place and went to take care of Pudge. "Pudge, ole buddy, our friend Tom is real sick. I am going to see him. Hank will take care of you while I'm gone." He petted and brushed Pudge before he headed to the mobile home to get ready to leave.

While he was in the shower, his phone rang. He saw he had a voice mail when he got out of the bathroom. He checked the missed-call log and saw it was from Slade. He was scared to listen to the message. Was it good or bad news? He hit the button to dial his voice mail and put the phone to his ear.

14

Toby was surprised by what Slade said in his message. Slade told him that it looked good for the $700,000 to include the livestock but not the loan for just the place. Toby was happy, but it took away any options he had on negotiating both prices. He called Slade back quickly to see what he needed to do and if it could be done before he left or by fax from Lubbock. Slade told Toby that he had what he needed at that point. Toby just needed to make his offer, and if the offer was accepted, Slade would go to work on Toby's loan.

Toby hung up, feeling better about the situation, but that turned quickly when he called Joe Bassett. Toby told Joe about his trip, but Joe told him he needed a signed offer in his hand to give to the Glovers. Apparently someone had made an offer. It hadn't been accepted yet, so Toby could still offer, but it added pressure on him since he didn't know what the other offer was. Joe agreed to meet Toby as he left town for Lubbock. Joe assured Toby they could do what would be needed after that by fax, as long as he wasn't gone for a long period.

Toby walked up to the house and knocked. Hank came to the door, and Toby said, "Just wanted to let you know I was leaving."

"Okay," Hank said. "You drive safely. We hope your friend recovers from his stroke."

"Thank you." Toby started to walk off the porch.

"Don't want to hold you up, but any word from Slade?" Hank asked.

Toby stopped and told Hank everything that he had discussed with Slade and Joe.

"If there is anything I can do to help in the process while you are gone, just let me know," Hank said.

"Thank you," Toby said as he walked to his truck.

He met Joe and signed the offer sheet showing that he wanted to purchase the place, livestock, and equipment for $660,000. Toby knew it was risky dropping the offer like that but hoped they would counter if they wanted to sell everything. It was his understanding the other offer was just for the place.

Toby finally pulled out heading to Lubbock at 7:15 p.m. He had five hundred miles to drive. He figured he would stop at a truck stop after midnight and catch a few winks so he wouldn't get too tired, and it would put him in there between 7:00 and 8:00 a.m.

He had been on the road for an hour when his phone rang. He answered it without looking since he was driving. "Hello?"

The person on the other end said, "Hello, Toby. This is Joe. I have already heard back from the Glovers' agent."

"Is that good or bad?"

"Well, they didn't accept your offer."

When Toby heard that, he felt like he had been hit in the gut.

"They did make a counteroffer of $675,000," Joe continued.

Toby was surprised, and very happy. "That sounds good to me. What do we do now?"

"If you want to accept it, then we need to get you to sign a contract."

Toby was concerned because he was afraid he couldn't get it signed quickly enough. "Joe, I want be able to get the contract signed until sometime tomorrow. Is that going to hinder the deal?"

"No, I don't think so. I will let them know you accept the counteroffer and what your situation is. I am confident they will be okay with not getting a signed contract until tomorrow."

"That sounds great. I will call you with the information on how to get the contract to me once I know where I'll be. Thanks for your help."

"Okay. Talk to you tomorrow."

They hung up, and Toby called Hank to tell him. Hank was very happy for Toby. Once they hung up, Toby felt like he could drive all night. His mind was running wild with plans he wanted to do with his "own" place. He had driven another two hours before he realized it. He was in Dallas and thankful the traffic was not heavy since it was 10:00 p.m. He stopped and got a cup of coffee and was back on the road within five minutes.

He had just started rolling again when his phone rang. He answered it, and it was Bethany. She called to see how his day went and to make idle chitchat. He told her what he was doing, and she told him she was sorry, and they hung up.

Toby was a little surprised she hung up, because he hadn't tried to get her off the phone. He decided it wasn't worth his time to think about it. He had enough on his mind already.

He made it through the metroplex and was out of the lights and driving into the black night. He had focused on getting through the cities but was now back to thinking about the place and his plans for it. He drove right on through and pulled into Lubbock at around 3:00 a.m. He found a motel and checked in and was asleep by 3:30 a.m.

Toby woke up at 6:30 a.m. and went to the office to see if they had a fax he could pay to use. They did, so he got the number and sent a text message to Joe so Joe could fax the contract over to him to sign. He went back to the room to shower and get ready to go eat breakfast and then to the hospital.

Toby was in the shower when it hit him. This was the first time he had left Pudge to the care of anyone else since he had gotten him. He had so much on his mind yesterday that he really didn't consider Pudge, and that bothered him. He couldn't do anything about it now, but he promised himself that it would never happen again. He grabbed a quick breakfast and made it to the hospital at 8:00 a.m. His phone rang as he pulled up, and it was Hank.

"Hello?"

"Toby, this is Hank. I just wanted to see if you had made it safely."

"Yeah, I made it in about 3:00."

"Wow. You drove straight through."

"Yeah, I was so excited about the place that I was wired and never got drowsy until I was about twenty miles out."

"I can certainly understand that. I'll let you go. I'm glad you made it."

"Thanks. I am walking in the hospital now."

Toby found out where to go and rode the elevator up to the third floor. The door opened, and there was a woman and a little girl waiting to get on the elevator.

"Pardon me." Toby stepped out and to the side to hold the door open so it wouldn't shut on them. The lady was starting to step into the elevator when she stopped and asked, "You wouldn't be Toby Parker, would you?"

The question surprised Toby, but he said, "Yes, ma'am."

She stepped back off the elevator. "Your voice sounded familiar, and seeing you with a hat made me think it must be you. I'm Carol, Tom's daughter."

Toby grinned. "You had me wondering if I was on a Wanted poster or something. Pleased to meet you."

She laughed. "You must have driven all night."

"Yes, ma'am. How is he doing?"

"Not showing any improvement. The doctors aren't saying much. We sure appreciate you coming."

"Tom and I spent a lot of time together and had some wild experiences," Toby said. "Not too many people I trust with my life, but Tom was one of the few."

"I'll show you where to go."

Carol led Toby down the halls to the ICU room Tom was in. She excused herself and left, and Toby opened the door to the room. He stepped inside the door and looked at Tom and stopped cold in his tracks. The feeling he had when he had found his dad slumped over at the kitchen table when he had died of a heart attack came rushing back. Toby couldn't move for a while. He just stared at Tom and at all the devices hooked up to him. He finally moved over to the bed, and tears filled his eyes as he looked at Tom lying there.

Toby took Tom's hand. "Tom, it's Toby. Carol called me, and I drove over to see you. I am in east Texas now. You've got to pull through this. You just got back close to your family." He had tears rolling down his cheeks. "We have battled too many things to let something like this stop you."

A nurse walked into the room, so Toby stepped away from the bed. Toby watched her to see what she was doing.

The nurse turned to look at him. "His vitals are looking better. He seems to be reacting to you. Keep talking to him."

"Yes, ma'am."

She walked out, and he walked back up to the bed and sat down on the stool. He started talking, telling Tom about how he and Pudge had been in the rodeo, about his new job, and about the place he was trying to buy. He sat there just talking and reminiscing of the time they had spent together, until Carol came back.

"Any change?" Carol asked.

"A nurse came in earlier and said his vitals were looking better."

"I wish Josh would hurry up and get here. He had to take his son to the doctor today, so he hasn't made it yet."

"I assume that is your brother? Tom always talked about his family but never mentioned names."

"Yes."

"I will step out and let y'all be with him."

"You're welcome to stay."

"I think I'll try and find a cup of coffee."

Carol told Toby where she thought some was, so he went to check it out. He had turned his phone off before he went into the room, so he turned it back on to see if he had any messages. He had a text from Joe telling him he would have the contract faxed over by noon. Toby decided to call Slade and tell him of the status of things with the contract and see if he needed to be doing anything else.

Slade was happy to hear they had agreed to the $675,000 and told Toby he would get started so he could get it to the underwriters. "I don't want to get your hopes too high, but it looks very good to me."

That put a grin on Toby's face, but as he hung up, he saw Carol come out of Tom's room and go to the nurses' station. His smile faded as he hurried down to her. He didn't say anything but was just listening as he walked up.

Toby heard good news. Tom had opened his eyes, and Carol had come out to tell them.

Carol looked at Toby. "Come on back in. I think you are what made him wake up."

Toby doubted that, but he was very happy Tom was showing improvement. He followed Carol and the nurse back into the room and stepped to the side so he could see Tom but be out of the way.

Tom's eyes met Toby's, and tears welled up in Tom's eyes. When Toby saw it, the tears started rolling down his cheeks again. Carol noticed both and said, "Toby, come on over here."

Toby walked over and took Tom's right hand. He could feel Tom try to squeeze it. He hoped that was good. He smiled. "I knew you were too much of a fighter to let this keep you down."

Tom's eyes brightened, and that made Carol start to cry. She turned and walked out of the room. Toby stayed with Tom for a while. He would talk some and watch Tom's reactions. He could tell Tom was hearing and understanding what he said.

The door opened, and Toby turned to see Carol and a man walk in. The man walked up beside the bed, and as he bent down to hug Tom, the man said, "Hello, Dad."

Toby saw tears in Tom's eyes again and decided he needed to get some air and dinner. He walked to the door and told Carol he would be back later.

Toby went to his truck and drove back to the motel to see if the contract had arrived. It was there, so he took it to the room, read and signed it, and went and faxed it back. He wanted it to happen quickly. He knew it probably wouldn't, but his part was going to be done as quickly as possible. He drove around some looking for a place to eat and found a small café. He ordered a chicken fry and the trimmings and a piece of apple pie.

When he finished his dinner, he drove back to the motel to try and take a nap. He had wound down and was starting to feel the effects of all that had happened in the last couple of days. He fell asleep around 12:30 p.m. and didn't wake up until 3:00 p.m. He hadn't planned on sleeping that long but knew he was tired.

Toby got around and pulled up at the hospital at 4:00 p.m.. He got to the room, and Carol introduced him to Josh. Carol and Josh both thanked Toby for coming, as the doctor had even said that his coming must have helped Tom. The doctor had said Tom needed to sleep, so Toby excused himself, saying, "Please call me if anything changes."

He went to the mall and bought a Randolph Scott movie and went back to the motel to watch it. He had brought his portable DVD player with him, in case the motel didn't have a DVD player in the room. After watching the movie, he tried to put numbers together on the payments of the place if it worked out and what the cattle would cost to get in shape and how much they would bring. It seemed like it would work, but he wanted to talk to Slade to see if he could only put $300,000 down and save $25,000 for expenses.

Toby went to sleep early and woke up at 5:00 a.m. He got ready and went to the café for breakfast. He decided to go on to the hospital even though it was only 6:45 a.m.

Toby walked into Tom's room. Tom was awake.

Toby walked over. "Good morning, sir."

Tom tried to speak and slurred, "Hi, Toby."

Hearing Tom not be able to talk ripped at Toby's heart, but the fact that Tom knew him showed Tom's mind was still sharp. That was a great sign. Toby talked to him and told him not to try to respond, but every once in a while, Tom would slur some words. Toby didn't know if Tom should be trying to speak or not, but then the nurse came in and saw them talking.

"The more Tom tries to talk, the better it is," she said. "That is the only way he will get back to his old self."

That pleased Toby, and from the look on Tom's face, Tom was happy too.

Carol and Josh showed up at around 8:00 a.m. They all sat in the room talking for a couple of hours. The nurses came in to move Tom out of ICU, so Toby went down to his truck to make some calls. He called Hank to see how things were going. Hank told him things were good and not to worry and to just enjoy the progress and company of his friend.

Toby called Slade about the down payment. Slade agreed that it was a good idea to keep some working capital on hand. Toby started to get out of the truck, and his phone rang. It was Bethany.

"Are you still in Lubbock?"

"Yep."

"How is your friend?"

"He is doing much better. Thanks for asking."

"That's good. When do you think you will be coming home?"

"I'm not sure at this point."

"Well, okay, be that way."

"Whoa," Toby said. "What is wrong with you? I'm not being any way. I answered your question the only way I know how to at this point. I don't know how he will progress. You need to lighten up."

"Okay. I have to go to class." And Bethany hung up.

Toby looked at his phone and shook his head. "Weird."

He went up to Tom's new room and spent a couple more hours with him. The doctor came in and said Tom was doing great and would start therapy tomorrow. Tom was happy but worried. Toby knew Tom was concerned about not being able to feel or move his left side. Tom went back to sleep, and Toby read a magazine while he slept. When Tom woke up, he looked at Toby and tried to say, "I 'preciate you comin' more than you know. You need go home take care thins."

Toby listened and said, "I am glad I came. And I am happy you are doing better. I can stay longer."

Tom shook his head. "No. You have job, home."

Josh and Carol had walked in and heard the conversation.

"Toby, you don't know how much we appreciate you coming," Carol said. "You being here has helped Dad more than anything else. We aren't trying to run you off, but you just started a new job and you're trying to buy a ranch. You need to be home. We will keep you updated."

Toby looked at Tom, and he was nodding what he could in agreement.

"When you get up and around and out of here, you need to come see me," Toby said. "Hopefully I will have my place and you can see it."

Tom tried to smile and nodded as tears welled up in his eyes. That nearly got Toby, so he bent over and hugged Tom. He walked over and hugged Carol and shook Josh's hand and walked out. He headed to his truck. He had mixed feelings, but Tom seemed to be on the road to recovery, and he did have a responsibility back home. Plus he missed Pudge.

Toby started his truck and drove to the motel. He knew they were charging him for the day, but he checked out and hit the road anyway, heading back to Nacogdoches. It was 2:00 p.m., so he should be home by 10:00 to 10:30 p.m. if all went well.

15

Toby was making good time and was debating whether to stop and eat or just grab some jerky at a Quik Stop and drive on. He drove through the metroplex without stopping and had decided to grab something quick when he spotted a café called the Round Up Café. He just had to turn in and check it out. He liked the looks from the outside as it looked like an old barn, with harnesses and sickle blades and other things hanging on the walls.

Toby opened the door and stepped in and was happy he had stopped. The place was decorated in Western style, just the way he hoped to do his home. He ordered his food, and as the waitress poured his coffee, he asked if they would mind if he took some pictures of the place. She went and asked the owner, and when she came back, she told him to take all he wanted. He wanted to use them to help him decorate if he got the Glover place. The house was already in Western style, and the way the café looked would make it homey for him.

Toby started taking some pictures and looking at things. An older couple asked what he was doing. He explained why he was taking the pictures, and they wished him luck with his place. His food arrived, so he sat down to eat. The food was as good as everything else about the place. He finished his meal and drank another cup of coffee and then paid out and took a few more pictures before leaving. He was about an hour down the road when Hank called.

"Hello, Hank."

"Hey, Toby, how are things going?"

"They are going good. Tom is out of danger and improving and has a bunch of rehab ahead of him. I am heading back. Tom insisted."

"Well, that all sounds good. What time will you be in?"

"Between 10:30 to 11:00."

"Drive carefully," Hank said, and they hung up.

Toby rolled on down the road. He stopped at about 9:00 p.m. and got a cup of coffee to drink as he drove. At 9:30 p.m., his phone rang. It was Bethany. He hesitated to answer it after the way she had been acting. He let it ring four times but decided to go ahead and answer.

He said, "You rang?"

She didn't answer for a while and then said, "Uh, yeah. What are you doing?"

"Driving back to the ranch."

The tone of her voice changed as she said, "Oh, really? You're through in Lubbock?"

"I don't know about through, but my friend is doing better, and I needed to get back to my job."

"I'm glad you are getting to go home."

"Why?"

Bethany paused for a minute and then said, "I—I just know you probably don't like hospitals."

"Me not liking hospitals has nothing to do with how you have been acting on the phone."

There was a dead silence for a while, and Toby said, "Hello?"

"I can't explain it."

"That's bull."

"I like you and didn't like the fact you were leaving and going to see other people."

"Bethany, I am not ready for any serious relationship. I have too much going on right now. We can be friends and see where it goes, but if that isn't enough for you, then maybe we need to say good-bye now."

Bethany waited for a while before she said, "I can live with that. At least you aren't looking elsewhere if you aren't ready, and that means I still have a chance."

Toby laughed. "You reasoned that out, didn't you?"

"Don't laugh at me," she said cheerfully.

"I'll talk to you tomorrow."

"Okay."

They hung up. Toby didn't spend any more time thinking about the conversation. His mind went back to what he was thinking on before the call. He was considering an intercom system in his barn to talk to Pudge. He knew people would think it weird, but he had missed Pudge the last two days. He was his best friend. He was thinking of how to make Pudge more comfortable. His mind ran through a lot of things, and before he knew it, he was pulling up into the drive at the ranch.

Toby unloaded his stuff and then went to the barn to see Pudge. He brushed him and talked to him about Tom and the Glover place. It was midnight when he finally walked out of the barn. He cleaned up and went to bed and fell asleep saying his prayer.

Toby was awake by 5:30 a.m. and had breakfast cooked and eaten before 6:15 a.m. He didn't know what the day held for him, but he was eager to face it. He headed to the barn and started feeding. He was finished feeding by the time Hank came out. Hank saw the livestock eating and said, "You must have gotten an early start."

"Yeah," Toby said. "Just woke up ready to go today. Not sure why."

"Maybe you'll get some good news today."

"That would be nice, but I'm not counting on it this quick. What's the plan today?"

"I have been considering building a corral in the far west pasture. It is difficult to treat or work the cattle that are in that patch, and I think a corral would make it easier for us."

"You talking a board corral?" Toby asked.

"Yeah," Hank said. "Fifty by fifty, with lanes around it and two chutes. One to load and one a squeeze chute."

"Do we have the material?"

"Not yet. Since you're through feeding, let's hook the trailer up and go in and drink a cup of coffee and figure out what we need before we head to town."

They calculated the posts and boards they would need and then headed to the lumberyard. On the way, Hank said, "By the time we get the corral built, the cows in that pasture should start calving. We didn't preg check them because we didn't have a corral there."

"I never have priced them, but are the portable corral systems very expensive?" Toby asked.

"They are expensive, but I have probably just been bullheaded not wanting to buy one," Hank said. "I like having corrals built. To me, it adds to your place, where the others are just an implement."

"I see."

Hank laughed. "That wasn't very convincing."

Toby laughed as well.

They arrived at the lumberyard and got all the boards and posts loaded for them, so Toby went out to strap them down while Hank was talking to a couple of guys he knew. As he tightened the last strap, Hank came walking out with one of the guys he had been talking to. "Toby, this is Ridge Stoddard. He has something he wants to ask you."

Toby stuck out his hand to shake Ridge's, and glanced down just in the nick of time to see Ridge's hand was all bent and crippled. He didn't squeeze hard, but he could tell Ridge tried to give a good, firm handshake. "Yes, sir. How can I help you?"

"I bought a horse that I got hoodwinked on," Ridge said. "It was supposed to have been saddle broke and had one hundred rides. I must be getting senile, because I would never have let this happen to me when I was younger. Anyway, she is far from being broke and ready for a kid to ride. I bought her for my youngest grandson. He is the only one that seems to like ranching, so I wanted to have a horse for him to ride with me when he comes out. I was wondering if I could pay you to break her for me."

Toby glanced at Hank, and Hank nodded his approval, so Toby said, "Sir, I'd be happy to help you if I can work it in with building this corral and my other chores."

"That sounds great," Ridge said. "It doesn't have to be done in the next week or two. I just hoped it could be done by spring break."

"Ridge, that is only three weeks away, I believe," Hank said.

"I will sure try to work it in to have it done by then," Toby said.

"We didn't talk pay yet," Ridge said.

"Just whatever it is worth to you," Toby said.

"Is $200 an insult?"

Toby grinned. "Not unless that horse is a widow-maker."

They all laughed, and Toby assured Ridge he would be over in a day or two to size the mare up. They left the lumberyard, and Hank pulled up to the café and said, "Let's have a cup and a bear claw."

Toby smiled. "If you insist."

Toby noticed Carl's truck as he and Hank walked in, and wondered if that was why Hank had stopped. He realized Hank hadn't seen the truck when Hank walked to a table on the opposite side of the café, never even looking Carl's way. Toby and Hank ordered and were eating their pastry and drinking their coffee when Carl walked up. "What brings you two to town?"

Hank looked up. "Well, hello, Carl. You just get here?"

"Nah, I was over there when you came in," Carl said. "I'm heading out to the Jones place to check on a cow. What are y'all doing?" He turned to Toby. "Toby, I thought you were gone to Lubbock?"

It was Hank who answered. "We are getting material to build a corral in the west pasture, and Toby got back last night."

"That will help," Carl said. "Last time was a joke when we tried to vaccinate some cows in that pasture."

Toby could tell that comment didn't sit well with Hank.

Carl continued, "I wondered why a guy would take off on a vacation in the first week of employment. Good thing you have a gracious boss."

That comment stung Toby. He was about to jab back, but Hank beat him to the punch. "Carl, you are letting your mouth override your backside again. Not that you're entitled to an explanation, but he had a good friend who had a massive stroke, so yeah, I wanted him to go."

Toby was glaring at Carl when Carl glanced at him.

"I wasn't trying to be insensitive," Carl said. "I have just been upset for the last couple of days."

"Why's that?" Hank asked. "Something wrong with the girls or the business?"

"No, they're fine," Carl answered. "I thought I had found a ranch to buy, but they accepted someone else's offer over mine."

Toby's ears perked up when he heard that, wondering if Carl was referring to the Glover place. He knew if it was, Carl would never like him. The Glover place apparently didn't register with Hank because he said, "Patty was out yesterday, and she didn't say anything about y'all trying to buy a ranch."

"You know I have talked about it for a long time," Carl said.

"Yeah, but I didn't know you had finally decided to act on it," Hank countered.

"This one was ideal and is right by your place."

Hank's eyes got a little wide. He glanced at Toby, and Toby was looking at him. Hank asked, "The Glover place?"

"Yes," Carl answered. "I thought we put in a good offer, but apparently, someone wanted to pay full price. Hopefully, they lose their tail on it and it will come up for sale again."

"I wouldn't count on that."

"Why's that?"

"I think the guy that outbid you can make a go of it. Don't you, Toby?"

"Sure hope so," Toby said.

Carl's head snapped around to look at Toby and sneered. "What?"

"Toby is the one that made the offer they accepted," Hank said.

Carl became furious. "You little punk. You don't even know how to run a ranch. You won't be able to get a loan at your age, so I will still get the ranch."

Toby grew furious. "Punk?"

Hank held up his hand to Toby as if to say, "Wait a minute," and said, "Carl, I wouldn't count on that, and it is probably best that you leave. We can talk later when you calm down."

Carl turned and walked out fast. The waitress walked up and said, "Something sure put a burr under Carl's saddle, didn't it."

"Yep," Hank said.

Toby and Hank finished their coffee and paid out and headed for the ranch.

"It doesn't look like Carl and I are ever going to get along," Toby said, "If I get the ranch, he will resent me from now on."

"Don't let that bother you," Hank said. "You didn't do anything wrong. He has talked about buying a ranch for years, and there have been plenty of opportunities to do it. He just wanted this one because he thinks it will give him a big spread when I am gone. He doesn't know that isn't going to happen."

Toby wondered what Hank meant but knew it was none of his business. "I just hate that I am causing issues with your family."

"You haven't caused anything. You have to take care of you."

They got back to the ranch. Toby took the truck and trailer and headed to the west pasture to unload the wood while Hank went into the house. He figured Hank was going to tell Sadie about the talk with Carl.

Toby spotted two hogs but didn't have his gun with him. He noted that he needed to keep his gun with him anytime he went to the pasture from then on. Once he got the wood unloaded, he headed back to get the tractor and posthole digger and the other tools so he could get started.

Hank walked up as he was getting ready to leave.

"I am going to get started, if it is okay with you," Toby said. "I thought I would take Pudge along so I can ride and check the cows in the other pastures before I come in."

"That sounds good," Hank said. "I will be out in a little while."

"Okay." Toby headed out with Pudge in tow.

Toby made good progress but was concerned that Hank never showed up. He didn't need the help but was worried that something was wrong. He mounted up at about 4:30 p.m. and headed to the other pastures to check the cattle. All the cows looked good, and so he hitched Pudge to the digger and headed back to the barnyard.

It was dark when he pulled in and noticed Carl's truck and Patty's car sitting in front of the house. He thought to himself that this didn't look good. He put the tractor up and fed and watered Pudge and brushed him down before heading to the mobile home. He had cleaned up and was cooking supper when someone knocked on the door. "Come in."

The door opened, and he glanced to see Carla walk in. "Hello."

"Hi."

"What's up with you?"

Carla walked over and sat down at his table. "Why did you knock Dad and Mom out of getting the ranch they wanted?"

Toby turned and looked at her. "You're not serious, are you? I didn't even know they were interested in it—or any other ranch, for that matter."

"That's not what Dad says."

"Well, that's the truth."

"Are you calling my dad a liar?"

"I didn't call your dad anything, but I think it best you go on back up to your grandad's house."

Carla looked at him and got up fast so fast the chair fell over. She stomped to the door and slammed it behind her. Toby worried about it for about five seconds then remembered he hadn't done anything wrong, so he finished fixing his supper. The bear claw had left him a while back, so he was hungry. He fixed chicken fried steak, mashed potatoes and gravy, green beans with bacon and onions, and biscuits. He intended to eat well and sit back and watch some TV and relax.

He was halfway through his supper when Carl came barging into the door and yelling, "What did you do to my daughter?"

Toby didn't get up but instead took another bite of steak and just looked at Carl as he chewed it.

"I asked you a question," Carl said in a loud voice.

Hank came in behind Carl, and Toby took a drink of coffee and said, "I didn't do a thing to your daughter, and I don't appreciate you barging in here uninvited."

Carl, still speaking loudly, asked, "Then why is she crying?"

Toby, still sitting at the table, said, "My guess is because you have put her in the middle of your lie."

Carl seethed. "You little punk."

"That's the second time today you have called me a punk," Toby warned. "I wouldn't do it again."

"Carl, let's get out of here and leave Toby alone," Hank said.

"Not until he apologizes for upsetting Carla," Carl said.

Hank looked at Toby. "What happened?"

Toby was aggravated by the entire mess, and Hank getting involved didn't please him at all. He sat there a minute and finally said, "She came in here accusing me of purposely knocking her dad and mom out of getting the Glover place. I told her that wasn't the truth, and she got upset, so I told her it would be best if she left, and she did. That was the extent of it."

"That's a lie," Carl said.

Toby stood up, and Hank got in front of Carl and pushed him out the door. Toby walked over and locked the door behind them.

He walked back over and sat down to eat, and someone started trying to open his door. Then they knocked, and he heard Hank say, "Toby."

Toby got up and walked over and opened the door and looked at Hank.

"I am sorry about all of this," Hank said.

"I am starting to wonder if this is going to work out," Toby said. "I'm growing very tired of your son-in-law, and I don't see a bright future."

"Please don't do anything rash."

Toby nodded. "I can't make any promises, because if he talks to me anymore like he has today, I will dot his eye, and you don't need that."

Hank looked at him. "Good night."

"Good night." Toby shut and locked the door. He finished his supper with his mind reeling. He decided to call Carol to check on Tom. Carol reported that Tom was still improving and was taking the rehab with a great attitude. That pleased Toby, and he sat and watched TV without worrying about Carl. He went to bed at about 11:00 p.m. and said a good long prayer before nodding off.

16

Toby woke up at 5:30 a.m. and lay in bed thinking about what had happened last night. He couldn't believe how something that had him so excited had turned sour so quick. He truly appreciated the relationship he had with Hank and Sadie, but would that relationship be shattered if he got the Glover place? The fact that Carl and Patty wanted it too sure had put Hank and Sadie in the middle. Should he back out of the deal so he could keep them as friends? If he did, would he lose his $1,000 earnest money? It was only money, but Toby hated to lose it. Having Hank in his corner was worth more than $1,000, though.

Toby rolled out of bed still thinking it through, and no closer to making a decision. He said out loud to himself, "I guess we'll see how things play out today and go from there."

He got dressed for the day and then cooked breakfast. He walked out on the porch at 6:30 a.m and felt the cold bite of the north wind. It was going to be a cold one today.

He went and took care of Pudge and told him all that had gone on last night, and then he completed all the feeding. He saddled Pudge and tied him to the posthole digger and started the tractor and headed out toward the corral he was building. He didn't look back toward the house, so he didn't see Hank come running out to try and catch him. He made it to the corral site and started in where he left off yesterday. He hoped to get all the posts set today, and then he could start putting up the boards tomorrow. It was a tall order working by himself, but he was going to give it a go.

Toby worked until 12:45 p.m. He took a break and rode Pudge back to the house to grab a bite. His mind had been running scenarios all morning, wondering how things were going to be after last night. He didn't know if he could afford the ranch if he wasn't working for Hank too. He knew the sale of the cattle would get him through the first year and then some, but he needed to buy a starter herd to get his ranch going. If he had to use all the funds he received from selling the cattle, he would have a ranch with no livestock, and that wouldn't last long. He had counted on leasing some land to Hank, but that may be out the window too.

Toby was climbing into the saddle when he heard Hank holler at him. He looked and saw Hank motioning for him to come over. Toby had a sick feeling in his stomach as he rode over to the house.

"You heading back to work on the corral?" Hank asked.

"Yes, sir," Toby answered. "Trying to get all the posts set today."

"I'll be out to help you in a just a minute. I have been on the phone with some guys wanting to buy some calves out of Boss. If we can get them started off good when they are born, it will bring in some good money."

"That should help the ledger. I'll see you when you get out there." Toby turned Pudge and rode out of the barnyard.

He walked over to the next post he was going to put in the ground and noticed the ground was all torn up around it. He quickly started surveying as far as he could see, and sure enough, he spotted two hogs about two hundred yards out.

Toby ran and jumped on Pudge and took off in the direction of the hogs. He pulled his gun when he was a hundred yards out. He swung Pudge and stopped him at fifty yards. He sighted in each hog and made good kill shots. He took care of the hogs and hoped Hank could take them back if he came out as he said he would. He rode back to the corral and dropped a post in a hole and put the level on it. He was tamping dirt when Hank pulled up.

Hank got out. "What was the shooting?"

"Two hogs out there about two hundred yards. They had been rooting while I was gone and messed up a hole over there."

"Let's go load them up, and I'll take them on to town."

Toby went and loaded up the hogs, and Hank left to go to town. Toby finished setting all the posts and mounted Pudge to go check the pastures. He didn't find any problems, so he was back to the tractor and heading in by 4:45 p.m. He pulled into the barnyard at 5:15 p.m. and started unhooking the posthole digger from the tractor. He didn't notice that Sadie had come outside and was walking toward him. As he climbed up onto the tractor, he saw Sadie and said, "Hello."

"Hello, Toby. I was wondering if you wanted to eat supper with us. I fixed up a big pot of stew since it was colder today, and there is no way Hank and I can eat it all."

"Stew sure sounds good. I'd be honored."

"We'll eat at 6:30."

"See you then." Toby tipped his hat to her. In the back of his mind, he couldn't help but wonder if there was an agenda to the invite. He parked the tractor and walked Pudge to the barn. He fed, watered, and brushed him down and then starting feeding the livestock that needed to be fed twice a day. He heard Hank pull up and expected him to come into the barn, but Hank didn't. Toby was a little surprised at the lack of involvement from Hank yesterday afternoon and today. He didn't want to speculate, but it seemed he had changed since the news of Carl trying to buy the Glover place.

Toby went to clean up after he had finished his chores, and remembered he had forgotten to call Bethany like he told her he would. He had a brief conversation with her since she had a party to go to, but she was very happy he had called. He called Carol to check on Tom, and it sounded like Tom was making progress every day, which was the kind of news Toby needed to hear to lift his spirits. He walked over to Hank and Sadie's at 6:30 p.m. and knocked on the door, ready for whatever the evening would bring.

Just as Hank opened the door, Toby's phone rang. He said, "Excuse me," to Hank and answered the phone. He was going to stay on the porch, but Hank motioned him in and whispered, "It's too cold out there."

"Hello?" Toby said.

"Sorry to be calling so late, Toby."

Toby recognized the voice. It was Slade Hopkins. "That's okay, Slade."

Hank's ears perked up when he heard Slade's name.

"I was out of town today at a meeting, and when I got back a little while ago, I saw where your loan had already been approved," Slade said. "I decided to call and make your weekend."

"Are you kidding me?" Toby exclaimed. "That is great news. Thanks for calling. I guess I'll let the real estate agent know now?"

"Yeah. They will set the closing date and get all the required paperwork done."

"Thanks again, Slade."

"Glad to help. I'll be talking to you."

Toby hung up with a grin that stretched from ear to ear.

"I guess that was a good-news call?" Hank said.

Toby's grin went away as he just realized he had probably ruined supper. He turned to look at Hank, and saw Hank was grinning. "Yeah, I got the loan."

Hank stuck out his hand to shake Toby's. "Congratulations."

Sadie had walked into the room. "Supper is ready, neighbor."

Toby looked at her, and he saw she was smiling. He grinned. "It smells great."

They sat down, and Hank said the blessing, and they started eating. As they ate, Hank said, "Toby, I am sure sorry that you and Carl and Patty decided to go for the same place. I know Carl hasn't made it easy for you, and this just adds fuel to the fire."

Toby was looking at him as he talked, and Hank paused and took a bite of stew. After he swallowed, he continued, "I know yesterday, and especially last night, were not pleasant, and Carl was out of line. However, Sadie and I want you to know that we are happy for you and realize this is all Carl's problem. You have done nothing wrong."

"That is right," Sadie said. "You have handled all this quite well for a young man."

Toby was happy to hear what he was hearing but weighed his words as he replied, "I sure didn't want to cause any problems with your family. I have never had a family, so I know how important a family can be."

Sadie asked, "You have never had a family?"

"Just foster families, and none of them for any length of time. When my dad adopted me, he was all that was left of his family. It was great having a dad, but then he passed away, and so did my family."

"I had no idea," Sadie said. "You have sure turned into a fine young man despite your circumstances."

"I owe it all to my dad. I was headed the wrong way when he adopted me, and he showed me the right way."

Sadie smiled, and Hank said, "Family means a lot to us, but Carl has always been a wild card. He tends to let his mouth get in the way. We have learned how to deal with it for Patty and the girls' sake. He is a good man. Just too volatile at times. Unfortunately, Carla takes after him."

"I understand," Toby said. "I just wish we weren't both wanting the place. Working for you and living next door will constantly rub it in."

"I found another ranch on the other side of town that is for sale," Hank said. "It is a lot like the Glover place. We are hoping they will like and want it."

Hank not helping him out today made sense now. Toby didn't comment. He just kept eating stew. They finished supper and sat and drank coffee and ate a piece of apple pie.

"I guess we can start planning how we will work the two places now that it looks like you are getting it," Hank said.

"Yeah, I have been running things through my head continually," Toby said.

"I bet you have."

"I thought I would put a gate on the north fence between us so we could move cattle and equipment and I can ride Pudge to work. Does that make sense to you?"

"That sounds like a great idea. We'll plan on it. We can talk lease amounts when you actually get the place, and we can look it over better."

"Sounds like a plan." Toby turned to Sadie. "Sadie, supper was great. Thanks for the company."

He got up to head to the door. Hank and Sadie both told him they enjoyed it and he was welcome.

Toby walked to the barn to see Pudge and tell him about the night and that he was going to have his own barn before long. He was sitting down, talking to Pudge, when he heard a car pull up into the drive. He heard one door closing and got up and walked to the door to see who it was. It was Carla, and she was on his porch, knocking on his door.

Toby heard Hank call out, "Carla, what are you doing here?"

Carla looked back at her grandad and said, "I want to talk to Toby."

Toby walked out of the barn and shut the door. Hank walked back inside. Toby walked toward his porch and asked, "Talk about what?"

"Last night," Carla said.

Toby saw movement in the car. There were two other girls inside. He walked up on the porch and opened the door. "Come in."

Once inside and with the door shut, he looked at Carla and said, "I'm listening."

"I wanted to apologize," Carla said. "I was wrong last night. Mom explained what happened. I was just upset because Dad was upset. I took it out on you."

"I wish we hadn't both wanted the same place," Toby said. "I hope it doesn't make your dad dislike me forever."

"He won't."

"Thanks for the apology. Your friends are going to get cold out there."

"Yeah, I better go. Bye."

Toby shut the door behind her. He sat down to watch TV. "This has been two interesting nights," he said to himself.

He went to bed at around 11:00 p.m. and woke up early. He cooked and ate breakfast and then went out and checked on Pudge and fed until the sun came up. It was a cold morning, so he started his truck and let it run while he was feeding the feeder hogs that Hank had bought to raise up and butcher for the freezer. Once he finished feeding, he went and got in his truck and started backing out.

Hank had walked out of the house, and Toby rolled down his window. "Everything is fed. I'm going to take a drive. I'll be back shortly."

Hank grinned because he knew where Toby was going. "Take your time. I know you are anxious."

Toby grinned and rolled his window back up. Hank was right. Toby wanted to drive down and look at the Glover place. He was so excited about owning it. He hoped the closing date wasn't too far off. He drove by slowly, looking everything over, and then turned around and started slowly back. As he reached the drive, he saw a man walking toward the barn. He stopped and thought for a minute and then decided to pull in and talk to him. Toby pulled up the drive and drove to the barn where he had seen the man walking. He got out and walked to the door.

The man looked up from the feed sack he was opening and asked, "Can I help you?"

"I hope you don't mind me stopping in," Toby said. "I am trying to buy your place and saw you out and hoped I could see things again."

The man stood up and walked toward Toby and held out his hand. "I am Bud Glover. You are more than welcome to stop by and look at things."

Toby shook Bud's hand. "Toby Parker is my name. It is sure good to meet you."

"Same here. I am sure glad you want to buy it all. I just don't feel up to trying to hold a dispersal sale. I have been in and out of the hospital with heart problems, and from what the doctors tell me, the rest of my life will be pretty consumed with doctors and hospitals. I love this ranch and ranch life, but sometimes, things just don't work out."

"I am sure sorry to hear that. You have a very nice place, and I know you have put in a lot of work to get it that way."

"Thank you. The wife and I have put in considerable time. We both wanted a ranch, but now it is a dream that will fade. I almost think it would have been better to never have realized the dream."

"I understand, but hopefully you can get some peace from the memories, and if I am lucky to get it purchased, you are more than welcome to stop by anytime."

Bud had started carrying sacks of feed to load on a trailer that was hooked to his tractor, and he got winded and leaned up against the wall in the hallway of the barn.

"Let me help," Toby said. "How many do you need loaded?"

"Thanks. Four more."

Toby grabbed two sacks and walked to the trailer and then grabbed the last two and loaded them.

"I vaguely remember when I could do that," Bud said.

Toby felt bad, but he looked at Bud and saw he was smiling, so Toby smiled too.

"Just look around, and I'll answer any questions you have when I get back from feeding," Bud said.

"I'd be happy to go help you feed."

"That would be greatly appreciated. I still need to load some hay."

Toby walked behind the tractor as Bud drove it to the hay barn. Toby loaded eight bales of grass hay, and then he sat on the trailer as they headed to the pasture. He had his head on a swivel, taking full advantage of the opportunity to see the land, buildings, equipment, and livestock. He noted that the two bulls looked better than he remembered and was glad to see they apparently had good genetics. That might help his decision to keep a few head rather than sell them all and start over.

They reached the pasture where Bud wanted to feed, and Toby unloaded the sacks of feed and poured them in the feeder, then opened the bales of hay when Bud pulled alongside the hay bunks. They headed back to the barnyard, and when they arrived, Bud asked if there was anything in particular Toby wanted to see.

"Going with you and letting me see things helped a bunch," Toby said. "I do appreciate you allowing me to ride along."

"You don't know how much I appreciate the help," Bud responded.

"Glad I could help."

They shook hands, and Toby walked to his truck. He grabbed his phone and called Hank and asked him if he had a problem with him helping Bud until he saw if the sale went through. Toby thought it would give a good indication of how well it would work when he bought the place and still worked for Hank. Hank agreed to it, because he knew how bad Bud needed the help, and it would show them if their plan would work.

Toby left his truck running and got back out and walked to the barn to talk to Bud. Bud saw him and asked, "Think of something?"

"Nah. I talked to Hank, and he is agreeable to letting me help you with your daily chores until the place sells, either to me or someone else. Is that okay with you?"

Bud's eyes welled up with tears. "That would be fantastic. I am so grateful to you and Hank."

They discussed the best time of day for Toby to come over, and Bud took him up to meet his wife and tell her about the help. Her name was Roberta Glover.

"You are a godsend," Roberta said. "I have been so worried about Bud. Thank you so much."

Toby tipped his hat to them and walked to his truck. He felt good. He would be able to help, and it would be a bonus getting to know the place in case he was successful in buying it. He turned in and started up the drive. He saw Bethany's truck sitting in front of the mobile home. He parked beside it but didn't see her in the truck. He got out, and he saw she was walking out of the house with Sadie saying, "Just bring your things in and use our spare bedroom."

What? Toby thought.

Bethany walked up grinning at him and said, "Can't you speak?"

"Sorry, I am just surprised."

"I hated that I couldn't talk last night, but I had offered my truck to go to the party in, and they were all waiting on me. I wanted to come and see you."

"I didn't give it a second thought. Do you not have any homework?"

"Yes. I brought it, and planned on working it in over the weekend. I was going to spend as much time as possible with you and then stay at the motel in town. However, Sadie invited me to stay with them so I could save money and be close to you. They are super people."

"Aren't they, though," Toby said rhetorically.

He started walking toward the front door. "Come on in out of the cold."

Toby put on a pot of coffee and made some hot chocolate for Bethany. They talked over the events of the week for about an hour, and then she said, "I best go get my stuff put in the house. I'll see you later."

"Okay," he said.

After she walked out, he said to himself, "So much for just doing what I wanted to this weekend." He decided to go tell Hank he was heading over to Ridge Stoddard's to get a look at the mare, and maybe start trying to break her.

Hank agreed with Toby going on over. Toby got his gear and headed over to Ridge's place. He was turning into the drive when his phone rang. It was Bethany. "Where did you go?"

"I am supposed to break a horse for a guy, so I came over to start."

"I would have liked to have gone along."

"Sorry. I thought you were going to do homework."

"I guess I will. See you when you get back."

"Yep. You will." Toby hung up and killed his truck by the barn. He got out, and Ridge walked out of the barn, followed by a boy who looked to be about twelve to thirteen years old and a girl who caught Toby's eye. Something about her kept him wanting to stare. His stare was broken by Ridge saying, "Hello, Toby. How are you today?"

"Doing well," Toby said. "Thought I would come over and get started on that mare."

"That sounds great. This is the young man that will ride the horse. My grandson, Jake Stoddard, and this is his sister, Jessie."

Toby shook Jake's hand and tipped his hat to Jessie. She smiled, and he stumbled as he started to walk. Why was she having this effect on him? He was already uncomfortable.

"Grandad, are you sure he can ride?" Jessie said. "He nearly tripped over his own feet."

Toby looked back at her. She grinned at him, and he ran into the gate. He recovered quickly by saying, "I am trying to make the horse overconfident."

They all laughed, but Toby didn't like being unsure of himself like this.

"Grandad, I will come back and get him when I get my laundry finished," Jessie said. "I brought a carload home from school."

"Okay," Ridge said.

Jessie looked at Toby. "It was nice to meet you."

Toby nodded. "Same here." He watched her walk to the car and then looked back at his chaps.

"I think somebody likes the way my sister looks," Jake said sarcastically.

Ridge laughed. "He has good taste."

Toby was embarrassed. He was ready to get to the mare. He walked into the pen with her and started talking to her and getting her used to him. He spent the next two hours getting her used to the blanket and then the saddle. He was ready to try and ride her. Just as he put his foot on the stirrup, he heard a car pulling up, and it broke his concentration.

17

Toby hesitated when he heard the car pull up. He fought the urge to look but decided to glance over his shoulder and see if it was Jessie. He was surprised when he saw it was Kali. He wondered why she was there but focused back on the mare and climbed up on the saddle. The mare jumped and started bucking, and Toby squeezed his legs and held on tight. He rode her to a standstill. They were cheering, but Toby knew she had just lost the battle, and the war wasn't over. He nudged her to walk, and she started in again but not as aggressively as before. He rode her until she started walking around the corral. He dismounted and tied her up, leaving the saddle on her for a while.

Toby walked out of the gate and looked over at Ridge and the others for the first time. He saw Kali and Jessie both standing there, watching. All of a sudden, he got real nervous again.

"One thing for sure, you can ride," Ridge said.

"That was great," Jake said. "I hope I can do that someday."

"You will, if you learn how to cowboy the way Toby can," Ridge told him.

Toby was nervous. Ridge and Jake were praising him, and Kali and Jessie were staring at him. He was almost frozen, including verbally. He finally got his words together to speak. "Jake, it just takes a lot of practice. You can do it." He hesitated a minute then said, "Hello, Kali." He was curious how she would act since the situation with the Glover place.

"Hi, Toby," Kali said. "I had forgotten how well you ride."

"Where did you see him ride before?" Jessie asked.

"At the Fort Worth rodeo," Kali responded. "He won the bronc riding."

Jessie looked at Toby. "So you really are a cowboy and don't just wear the clothes."

"I suppose," Toby said sheepishly.

Jessie laughed. "Kali, let's go in the house where it is warm and we can talk."

Toby watched them walk to the house.

"Why don't you take a picture?" Jake said. "It will last longer."

Ridge laughed. "Leave him be, Jake."

Toby looked at Jake and just shook his head. He knew Jake was right, and he couldn't figure why he was so taken with Jessie.

He turned to Ridge. "Ridge, I better get on back and take care of some things. I will come back over and work with her some more to make sure she is ready by spring break."

"Sounds good," Ridge said. "I sure appreciate your help."

Toby headed back to the ranch. He was driving and thinking about how goofy he had acted around Jessie and Kali. He was aggravated with himself. He pulled into the drive and saw Bethany's truck and realized he had forgotten she was there.

"Whoops," he said to himself.

He parked the truck and went and put his chaps up and then walked to the barn to see Pudge. He was talking to Pudge when Bethany walked into the barn.

"I wish you would talk to me that way," she said jokingly.

Toby smiled. "I don't have to worry about him talking back. You get your homework finished?"

"Yes, I did," Bethany answered. "You were gone a long time."

"I was making progress with the horse, so I wanted to stick with it until she would let me walk her around the corral."

"So are you free the rest of the day?"

Toby the Rancher

"Yeah, what's left of it."

"Let's go see a movie."

"What's showing that's any good?" Toby asked.

"I think *A Good Day to Die Hard* looks pretty good," Bethany said.

"That sounds pretty good. Let me finish checking things out in here, and I'll get ready."

Bethany walked out, and Toby finished up his chores and then went and got ready to go. He stepped out on the porch, and Bethany bolted out the front door of the house. She covered the hundred feet to the truck before Toby did the twenty feet he had to go.

"We better hurry, or we will miss the movie," Bethany said.

"They have different showtimes," Toby said. "When does it start?"

"I don't know."

He looked at her, puzzled, and then just shook his head and started the truck. They pulled up to the movie theater. Toby saw Mike Stine walking across the parking lot, so he rolled down his window and said, "Hey, you look like a guy that I saw chasing hogs last week."

Mike laughed. "Hey, Toby. What's been going on?"

"Not much."

"See you inside."

Toby parked the truck, and Bethany asked, "Who was that?"

Toby told her the story of how he became acquainted with Mike.

"He looks like he could handle himself," Bethany said.

Toby looked at her. "Down, girl. He is only seventeen."

"Is that the only reason, or are you jealous?"

"That's the only reason." Toby didn't like what she had said about Mike. It made him think of the mess with Kip Walker at the rodeo, and he wondered how much of that Bethany had played. He hoped he was wrong, but he hadn't been able to shake the thought.

They got out of the truck and started walking toward the theater, and a truck acted like it was going to run over them. Toby stepped aside and saw that it was Jessie and Kali as it passed by. They were both smiling at him.

"Who is that?" Bethany asked.

"The granddaughter of the guy I am breaking the horse for, and Kali, Hank's granddaughter," Toby said. "You know her."

"Yeah, I remember her. Where is her boyfriend?"

"Don't know."

Toby bought the tickets and they were walking to the door when Jessie hollered and said, "Hey, wait for us. We'll join you."

Toby started getting nervous. Having three girls with him had trouble written all over it, and Jessie was doing the talking. Bethany walked on through the door, but he waited for Kali and Jessie to get their tickets and join him.

"We aren't intruding on a romantic evening, are we?" Jessie asked.

"Not at all," Toby replied. "We are just friends."

The four of them walked into the theater room where the *Die Hard* movie was showing, and Toby found where he wanted to sit. He started in, and Kali came right in behind him. As he sat down in the middle, Jessie came in from the other side, so now he had Kali and Jessie on each side of him and Bethany on the other side of Kali.

Toby felt like he was sweating. He figured Bethany was hot, and he was already nervous around Jessie, and now Kali and she were sitting close. For the first time in a long time, he felt like he was in a situation he couldn't control. He decided he needed to just slide down in the seat and get comfortable to watch the movie.

Jessie leaned over. "You did say she was just a friend."

Toby looked at her, and they were face-to-face. He gulped. *Dang, she is hot.* "That's right." He turned to Kali and asked, "Where is Drew?"

Kali looked at him. She didn't look happy. "He stayed at school."

Jessie started laughing, and then Kali did too.

"Did I miss the joke?" Toby asked.

Jessie said laughingly, "She left without him, and he had to stay."

"Ohhh," Toby said. He didn't figure he wanted to get into that.

Bethany had been listening, and she said, "He is probably having fun at school without you."

Kali and Jessie glared at her. Toby stood up. "I want a Coke. Anyone need anything?"

Nobody said anything.

Toby was glad to be out of that. The movie was starting when he returned, so he just sat down in an empty seat on the first row. When the movie was over, he was out first and waited in the lobby for Bethany to come out. She walked out with Jessie and Kali right behind her.

"Where did you go?" Bethany said. "We came to the movies together."

"It had started when I came back, so I sat in an empty seat I could see," Toby said.

Bethany headed for the door, and Jessie said, "We'll, I was looking forward to watching a movie with you. Maybe some other time, when your friend isn't along."

Toby looked at her and tipped his hat as he turned to walk out the door. He and Bethany got in the truck, and Toby asked, "Where do you want to eat?"

She looked straight ahead. "I want to go back to the ranch so I can pack and leave."

"What are you talking about? We watched the movie. That is why we came."

"You just don't get it."

"I get it better than you think. Your deal with Mike before the movie was just like with Kip Walker. I have an idea you played that whole deal up between him and me at the rodeo."

Bethany started to speak and then didn't.

"You can't deny it." He sat there for a minute and then said, "I still like spending time with you, as a friend."

She was quiet and then said, "I'm not sure if that will work."

"Let's give it the weekend and then you can decide if you want to come back."

Bethany shook her head, and Toby backed out and headed to the restaurant to eat. The meal was quiet and the drive home as well. He dropped her off in front of the house before he pulled into his parking spot. He was in bed and asleep within thirty minutes of getting home.

He woke up at 5:30 a.m. and had breakfast and was out feeding by 6:15 a.m. He had to finish and then go to the Glovers to help there before church. He was talking to Pudge when he heard a vehicle start. He walked out the door to see Bethany backing up to the porch. Her bags were on the porch.

Toby walked over to her truck. "Where you going?"

She was startled and spun around and said, "I didn't know you were up."

"I am. Where are you going?"

"Going back to school. You were clear it wasn't going to work with us."

"That isn't what I said, but if that is how you wanted to take it, then so be it."

"Well, good-bye." Bethany got in and drove off.

Toby felt bad that she felt she had to leave, but still, he didn't have feelings for her. He went back to his feeding and figured he would send her a text and see if she made it safely. He finished the feeding and drove to the Glovers to do the feeding there.

Bud came out, and Toby could tell he didn't feel well. "Bud, I can do this. Why don't you stay in where it is warm?"

"Are you sure?" Bud asked.

"Absolutely."

Bud went back in, and Toby did the feeding. He was in hog heaven, because by all intents and purposes, he was feeding his livestock. He finished up and hurried home to get ready for church. He sent Bethany a text asking if she made it safely. She responded yes, and that was all she said. He decided to let it go and go on to church. He headed back to the ranch after church and worked on the corral the rest of the afternoon. He made it to the evening services after it had started, so he slipped in and sat at the back. He was out before anyone else, and he headed back home.

Toby hadn't talked to anyone since Bud this morning. He had a quiet day and went to see Pudge when he got home. He spent about an hour in the barn and then went in and fixed a bite to eat for supper and sat and watched *Big Jake*.

He was up early on Monday morning. He finished feeding both Hank's and Bud's livestock and was working on the corral before 9:30 a.m. He hoped to finish it up tomorrow. At noon, he stopped working on the corral and rode the pastures to check on the cattle. He hadn't seen any hogs for a couple of days, so he was hoping they were gone. Everything looked good in all the pastures, and he was back working on the corral when Hank came pulling up.

"I haven't seen you for a couple of days," Hank said. "Why did Bethany leave early?"

"Some things happened that made her mad, and she left." Toby didn't want to say any more, and Hank didn't need to know any more.

"The corral is looking great," Hank said. "I had no idea you were this far along."

"I worked on it yesterday too. I just checked all the pastures, and all the livestock were good."

"That's good. Thanks." Hank put on his gloves and started helping Toby.

Toby was glad. It made leveling and nailing the boards easier with two. They worked until just before dark, and Toby was riding Pudge back when his phone rang. He answered it.

It was Slade. "Toby, I have good news. You were approved for the loan. They also asked that it close quickly so Bud can get out from under his loan and get to town."

"That is great. When you say quick, how quick?"

"Joe and their agent will set it up, but they are asking for no more than two weeks out. You might call Joe and tell him and he can work on it."

"Thank you. I will."

Toby called Joe and told him, and Joe said they had the paperwork all in good shape, so setting it in ten days should work. Toby rode into the barnyard after dark.

Hank was in the barn. "I was getting worried."

Toby told him about the call. Hank grinned and shook Toby's hand and congratulated him. Toby was glad to see Hank's reaction, knowing the Carl factor was still in play.

He spent the evening checking his accounts and making sure all his ducks were in a row. He was planning on how to get the items he had stored in Pennsylvania down there as well. His phone rang at about 9:45 p.m., and he didn't recognize the number.

"Hello?"

"Hello, Toby. This is Kali."

"Hey, Kali. What's up?"

"You seemed preoccupied in church yesterday morning. I hope Jessie and I didn't ruin your evening Saturday night."

"Not at all, but I do appreciate you calling to check. I guess y'all made it back to college okay?"

"Yeah. Jessie is coming over so we can study for a test."

"Good luck."

They hung up. Toby thought about Kali's call for a little bit and then realized he needed to call Carol and check on Tom. He called. Carol was happy he did, and told him not to worry about the time. Tom was still making good progress and was walking now. Toby promised to call Tom tomorrow with his good news.

He went to bed with a hundred plans running through his head.

Five o'clock in the morning came with Toby already awake and staring at the ceiling and thinking about all that needed to happen in the next couple of weeks and how his life was going to change with him owning a ranch. He had thought and dreamed about it, but now that it seemed to be a reality, it was overwhelming him a little bit.

He got up and had breakfast and was feeding before 6:00 a.m. It was another cold morning, and it was clear the livestock were not enjoying the cold. Boss just stood and snorted when Toby fed him. Pudge even seemed a little out of character this morning. Toby rubbed Pudge and brushed him and then was on his way to Bud's by 7:15 a.m. He finished feeding Bud's livestock and saddled Pudge and rode out to work on the corral.

Hank had talked about building a loading chute off one of the lanes they were building, so Toby started laying out the plans for it. The next three days were spent in the same routine: feeding, building corral, and checking on the herds in the outlying pastures.

He awoke on Friday morning to a cold rain, and according to the weatherman, it was going to hang around all day. Toby fed at both places and got back to his abode wet and cold. It took him a good while to get warmed up. He was drinking a cup of coffee when Hank knocked on the door.

Toby hollered, "Come in."

Hank opened the door and walked in and looked at Toby wrapped up in a blanket drinking coffee, and he grinned. "I bet you were nearly frozen when you got back."

"I felt like an iceberg."

"You want to run to Longview with me or just hang around here and stay warm?"

Toby figured Hank wanted him to go or he wouldn't have asked, so he said, "I'll go with you."

"Great. I'm going to pick up a new squeeze chute for the corral you built. By the way, that loading chute you built will work good."

Toby got ready, and he and Hank left for Longview. They talked about various things on the trip, but it always seemed to come back to Toby buying his own place. Hank seemed as happy for Toby as Toby felt his own dad would have been.

They arrived in Longview. Toby looked around the store and tried to visualize if he would need any of the panels or feeders.

Hank walked up. "We will have some room on the trailer if you think you will need some panels."

"I was contemplating that," Toby said. "I think a dozen of these Powder River panels would work well, and they seem built to last."

"Your call, but we have room."

Toby calculated the price on his tablet, which he had in his pocket, and decided he had the funds to purchase them, so he bought twelve panels and a calf creep feeder. When they got back to the ranch, Hank said, "We can leave your panels and feeder on the trailer until you close next Friday."

"Thank you," Toby said. "That will work. When do you want to unload the chute?"

"We can let it stop raining. Maybe tomorrow. Enjoy the rest of the day staying dry and warm."

"I appreciate it, but I best go check the pastures."

"You may get stuck. You will need to take the MULE."

"I'll take Pudge. We are used to riding in this kind weather."

"I bet you are." Hank smiled and walked to the house.

Toby got his slicker on and saddled Pudge, and they headed out. There were two cows in one pen off by themselves, so he drove them back over with the rest of the herd. All the rest were good, so he was back in about an hour and a half. He rubbed Pudge down and fed and watered him and then made sure everything else was good in the barn before he went in for the evening.

Toby made a pot of coffee and sat down to call Tom. Tom sounded good, and they talked for nearly an hour. Tom promised he would come and see Toby's ranch once he was able to drive and be out of rehab.

Toby had asked Hank if he could bring Ridge's mare over so he could work it some each day. Hank had agreed, so Toby called Ridge, and he told Toby he would bring the mare over in the morning.

Toby spent the evening watching *Cheyenne* on his DVD. Watching old episodes always made him feel close to his dad, since he was the one who got him started on liking *Cheyenne*. He slept well and woke up hoping to see stars when he looked out. It had quit raining, but the sky was still cloud covered. He made breakfast and took care of Hank's feeding and then headed to Bud's.

Toby took time after feeding to decide what changes he wanted to make in the barn. It was well built, but he wanted some more and different stalls and a tack room/office. He headed back to Hank's, and as he turned into the drive, he saw that Ridge was already there with the horse. Toby pulled up and parked and looked into the trailer at the mare. He heard people coming out of Hank's house, talking. He stepped back and saw Hank, Ridge, Jake, and Jessie.

"Oh, crud," he said to himself. He didn't like being nervous, and Jessie made him feel that way.

They all walked out to where Toby was.

"Seem to take you longer than usual," Hank said. "Any trouble at Bud's?"

"Nah," Toby replied. "Just drawing up some plans."

"Hello, Toby," Ridge said. "Plans for what?"

"Toby is buying Bud Glover's place," Hank said. "Close next Friday."

"That is great," Ridge said. "So you are here to stay, huh?"

Toby glanced at Jessie. She was smiling. He spoke to Jake and said, "You okay with leaving your horse with me?"

"Heck, yeah," Jake said.

They all laughed.

"You cold?" Toby asked Jessie.

"Yes," she said. "It is colder than I thought it would be."

Toby walked over to his truck. He got a jacket and handed it to Jessie. "This should help."

"Thank you," she said.

"Jessie thinks Toby is a stud," Jake said.

Hank and Ridge laughed. Jessie turned and punched Jake on the arm. For some reason, Jake saying that made Toby even more nervous. He went to open the trailer gate. He led the mare out and led her to the barn and put her in a stall. "I'll start with her right after dinner, and I'll work her every day. That way, she will be ready for Jake to live on next week during spring break."

Jake was grinning from ear to ear.

"That sounds good," Ridge said. "Let me know if you need anything."

"Will do," Toby said. His phone started ringing, so he answered it. It was Joe Bassett, the real estate agent. Toby excused himself and walked to the house to talk to Joe. Joe told him that everything was set for the closing, what the cashier's check needed to be written for, and what time to be there.

Toby hung up and sat and thought for a minute. He was still in awe of the fact he was getting close to being a ranch owner. He heard a truck start and walked to the door and saw Ridge's truck and trailer pull down the drive. He walked out on the porch, and Hank was walking his way with his jacket.

"Here is the jacket you let Jessie wear," Hank said. "She said to tell you thank you."

"Okay, thanks," Toby said. "I guess I will get started working with Belle." Belle was the name of the mare.

Toby spent the next three hours working with Belle and was very pleased with how she was progressing. He decided to take her along with Pudge and him as they checked the pastures. They were gone a little over an hour, and Belle was leading good when they returned. He spent the rest of the day and evening piddling in the barn and watching TV. He read the Bible and was asleep by 10:00 p.m.

Toby woke up at 4:30 a.m. He fixed coffee and figured up his finances again. He had done it every day for the last two weeks, but he just wanted to be certain he hadn't forgotten a possible expense that would put him in jeopardy right off the bat. He knew things could always come up, but he wanted that to be the unknown, not the overlooked.

He decided to fix some pancakes and eat and was feeding before 6:00 a.m. He finished Hank's and headed to Bud's. He fed the stock in the corrals around the barnyard and then headed out on the four-wheeler to check the pastures. He counted the cows in the last pasture and came up one short. He started driving around the pasture, looking and checking the fences as he went. He noted that he was going to have to put some work in to tighten the fences once he got on the place.

Toby rode into a grove of trees and stopped the four-wheeler. He got off and walked through the thick brush and spotted the cow. She was lying down and trying to calve. He walked up to check her, and she looked like she had been trying for a good while. There was only one leg out, and he knew the calf wasn't in the right position to come out. He walked up easy to the cow, trying to see if she would let him get close enough to help. The cow didn't try to get up, which told him she was tired and had been at it a while. He was afraid the calf was already dead but hoped it wasn't since it only had one leg and the nose showing.

He started to work on the calf, trying to push it back so he could try and find the other leg. He found it, and it was turned all the way back. He worked for a good while, trying to get the leg freed up and pointing in the right direction. He was excited when he felt the calf moving, so he knew he still had a chance of saving it. He got the leg pulled around and both legs in the birth canal correctly, but he knew he needed to try and get the calf out as quickly as possible for the good of both the cow and calf.

Toby realized he had a problem. He didn't have any rope to tie on to the legs to pull. He thought about it for a minute and debated whether he should go back for rope or not. He didn't want to wait that long, and he made a promise to himself to never get in this fix again. He decided to take his belt off and try to use it. He hooked it to the calf's legs and started pulling. He was able to get it pulled after some strong pulls, and was surprised at how big a calf it was.

The calf was not breathing well, so he rubbed it vigorously and pumped its front leg. He got it breathing better and ready to try and get up on its feet. He made the cow get on her feet, and she started cleaning the calf. He watched them a little while longer and realized he had just pulled his own calf come Friday. He got on the four-wheeler and headed back to the barn.

Bud came walking out and asked, "Have problems?"

Toby told him about the calf and what he had to do to pull it and save it.

"That is a problem I have been having," Bud said. "The bull is throwing entirely too-large of calves. I have had to pull several and have lost three. I just haven't had the energy to do anything about it."

"I appreciate you telling me. I will need to make a change."

"Yes, sir. Sorry."

"Not a problem. I better get going so I can make it to church. I'll come back this afternoon and check on the cow and calf."

Toby looked at the clock in his truck and saw that he was already late for class. He would have to hurry to make worship.

He walked in ten minutes late and sat down in the first empty pew he spotted. He didn't look around for a while, and then as they sat down after singing a song, he looked down the pew and saw Drew, Kali, and Carla. He nodded at Kali and Carla as they were looking at him.

As soon as services were over, he headed out the door to head back to the ranch. He wanted to get back and check on the cow and calf. He started his truck and started to back out. Carla walked up and hit his window. He stopped and rolled it down and asked, "What's up?"

"Why were you late?" Carla asked. "Where are you going so quick? Got Bethany out at the ranch?"

Toby looked at her and said, "See ya." He noticed Kali and Drew standing off to the side behind her, and Kali was smiling. He tipped his hat to her as he pulled away.

He made it to Bud's and took off on the four-wheeler. He was happy to see the cow and calf were doing good. He headed back to eat a bite and work with Belle some more. He pulled up into the drive right behind Hank and Sadie. Hank walked over as Toby got out and said, "I saw you weren't back from Bud's when we left and you were late to worship. You have trouble this morning?"

Toby told him about the cow and calf.

Hank laughed. "You definitely think quick."

"The problem is, Bud said he has been having all kinds of trouble with large calves," Toby said. "I need to change out the bull. I will still have one but hoped to have two. Plus, I don't know how many are bred to that bull that still may have trouble."

"I understand your concern. The first thing to do will be to get the bull away from the cows to keep it from breeding anymore. Why don't you come on over for dinner with us?"

"Are you sure?" Toby asked. "I don't want to impose."

"Sadie told me to ask."

"Okay, I'll be over. Thank you."

Toby got cleaned up and walked out the door and saw that Carl and his family had come for dinner too. He hesitated a bit but decided it best to go face them and see how it would go. He knocked on the door, and Carla let him in. "Maybe now you will answer my questions."

He looked at her and walked on in without saying a word.

Kali laughed. "Carla, I think you have your answer. It's none of your business."

Toby walked over to Carl, nodded, and shook his hand without saying anything.

"How is the loan going for the ranch?" Carl asked.

Hank answered before Toby could. "He closes on it this Friday."

Carl looked at Toby and said, "Congratulations."

"Thank you," Toby said.

Sadie called everyone to the table.

"Sit here." Kali pointed to the chair between her and her mother.

Toby hadn't realized Drew wasn't there. "Where's Drew?"

"He has to study, so he didn't come," Kali said.

Toby sat down, and Carla said, "Kali, what are you doing? Just because you and Drew have been fighting, you are hitting on Toby?"

Toby began to feel a little weird.

"I'm not hitting on him," Kali said.

"Yet," Carla said.

"Let's say the blessing," Hank said.

19

Hank said the blessing and then said, "Let's eat."

Everyone started filling their plates. This pleased Toby, because he didn't like the way the conversation was going with the girls. There was general talk during dinner, and Kali talked to Toby some, mainly asking him questions about himself and why he liked being a cowboy so much. He answered all her questions but was a little curious about her line of questioning.

They finished eating, and Sadie brought out two pies and said, "Today we are having Toby's favorite. Apple pie." She smiled at Toby.

Toby smiled and nodded his agreement. "Outstanding."

"Why is that your favorite?" Kali asked.

Toby told her about his dad and how they always ate apple pie and drank coffee.

"That's cool," Kali said.

"Guess I'm a prophetess," Carla said.

Toby wondered what she was talking about but noticed Kali glaring at Carla.

"Carla, quit trying to cause trouble," Patty said.

"The meal was great, and I sure appreciate it," Toby said. "But if you will excuse me, I need to go work with Ridge's mare."

Toby put on his chaps and spurs and was saddling the mare when he heard a vehicle pull up into the drive. He couldn't see the drive, so he didn't give it any thought. He rode Belle for nearly an hour and a half, stopping and starting and basically teaching her to follow the rider's instructions. He finished working with Belle and was walking her back to her stall when he noticed Drew's car as he came around the corner.

Must have studied quick, he thought to himself.

He fed Belle and brushed her down and then saddled Pudge to take a ride to check the cattle in the pastures. He started out of the barn as a car started, so he glanced to see who it was. It was Drew, and he was leaving. Drew drove forward and took a wide turn that brought him too close to Pudge and Toby. Pudge jumped back, and Toby started off the saddle. Drew had taken such a wide circle he couldn't make the turn without stopping and backing up.

Toby grabbed the car's door handle as Drew started to back up and yanked the door open.

"Hey, what are you doing?" Drew said.

Toby reached in to get the keys, and Drew fell away, like he thought Toby was going to hit him. Toby threw the car in park and killed it and took the keys. As he came out, he grabbed Drew and brought him out with him.

Carla had seen what was happening and ran back into the house, yelling, "Dad, Grandad, y'all better get out here!"

Hank and Carl got to the porch in time to see Toby yank Drew out his car. They took off running to get to Toby.

Toby shoved Drew up against the car and asked loudly, "Are you out of your mind?"

Drew looked scared and didn't say a word.

Toby continued, "You could have hit Pudge, and there was no reason to get anywhere near us."

Drew saw Carl and Hank coming and got a little courage and said, "You were in the way."

Carl got there first. He grabbed Toby's arm and asked, "What's going on here?"

Toby jerked away from Carl. "Don't ever grab me."

Hank was there by then and said, "Everyone, calm down. What brought this on?"

Carl was staring a hole through Toby, and Toby said, "Save the stare, man. It's weak."

Sadie, Patty, Kali, and Carla were on the porch, watching. Toby looked at Hank and asked, "You see anything odd about where this car is?"

Hank looked around and asked, "Why is it all the way up here?"

"Exactly," Toby said. "That is what I was trying to find out here. He nearly hit Pudge and me, and from the look on his face, it seemed intentional."

Hank looked at Drew and said, "I would hope your argument with Kali wouldn't cause you to do something stupid like that."

"Oh now, come on, Hank," Carl said. "You really believe Drew could do something like that? You have known him a lot longer than you have this guy."

Hank looked at Carl and, pointing back to where Drew was parked, said, "Maybe you can explain why he took this route to leave when a blind monkey could have turned around back there and left." He looked at Drew. "What do you have to say for yourself, young man?"

Drew just looked at Hank and didn't say a word.

"I think we have our answer," Hank said. "You best get in your car and leave, and don't come back here until you are ready to apologize to everyone." He looked at Toby and asked, "Everything okay with you and Pudge?"

"Yeah," Toby said. "I'm going to check the pastures."

"Okay," Hank said.

Carl had walked away toward the women but turned around and said to Toby, "You stay away from my daughters."

"Carl," Patty said. "What are you doing?"

Carl turned to her. "He is too disrespectful to his elders to have anything to do with my girls. He likes to fight too much."

Toby just looked at Carl and shook his head. He grabbed the saddle horn and swung up into the saddle. He looked at Kali, and he could tell she was upset, so he rode toward the porch and said, "I'm sorry, Kali." He turned Pudge and rode off.

"Sorry for what?" Carl asked.

Hank had walked up to the porch and said, "Carl, you just keep stepping in it, don't you?"

"We're leaving," Carl said.

"You go," Patty said. "I will come with the girls later."

They walked into the house, and Carl left.

Toby rode to the first pasture, wondering what had caused Drew to act like that. He had come to expect Carl to act out at every opportunity he had. He spent the next hour checking the pastures and rode back into the barnyard as Patty and the girls walked out to leave. He noticed Carl's truck was gone. Kali stopped and looked at Toby and kind of waved. He tipped his hat to her and rode into the barn. He was taking care of Pudge when Hank came walking in. Toby knew he was there to talk.

"You got a minute to talk?" Hank asked.

"Yeah, but I have a pot of coffee on in the trailer, and it was cold out there," Toby said. "Can we go in and talk over a cup?"

"Absolutely."

They walked to the trailer, and Toby poured them each a cup of coffee. They sat down at the table.

"What would you have done to Drew if we hadn't got out there?" Hank asked.

"I wasn't going to hurt him," Toby said. "I was just trying to get his attention and scare him to realize what he done was foolish."

"I think you scared him."

"What happened in the house to make him do that?"

"Kali and him have been fighting, and your name came up in the fight, I guess, and he stormed out."

"My name," Toby repeated. "How would my name come up in their argument?"

"I think we have Carla to thank for that."

Toby just looked ahead and shook his head.

"I am a little curious about how you reacted when Carl grabbed your arm," Hank said.

Toby thought a minute and fought his aggravation of having to answer the question. "Hank, I apologize for that. I am trying to handle my childhood and grow out of it. I was grabbed a lot and physically abused in two different foster home situations, and I just don't like anyone to grab me like that."

"I'm sorry. I understand."

"When you grab someone like that, you will always inflame a situation."

"Yeah, I guess that is true."

"I am sorry to be causing trouble with your family," Toby said. "Maybe when I get moved to my place, it will get better, even though I'll still be working here."

"Toby, you are not causing us trouble," Hank said. "We have had some volatility in our family ever since Carl came into it. He just seems to want conflict."

"I guess we best get ready for church."

Hank looked at his watch. "I reckon so."

Toby sat at the back of the auditorium and left as soon as services were over so he wouldn't run into Carl. He didn't want to stir anything up. He spent half an hour with Pudge when he got back to the ranch. He spent the rest of the night watching TV.

The next day, Monday, he got started by 6:00 a.m. and got to Bud's by 7:15 a.m. While he was in the barn getting the feed ready, he couldn't stop thinking about the fact he would be living there this weekend. Granted, he didn't have any furniture, but he had been on a trail drive before, so living in a bare house would be easier than that. He could have had his things in storage in Pennsylvania hauled down, but he just didn't want to jump the gun on things. He still didn't feel real confident about the place, and guessed he wouldn't until he had signed for it and had the keys in hand.

Toby checked on the new cow and calf. They were both doing well, so he headed back to Hank's and saddled Pudge and headed to the corral to finish it up.

He spent the next two days working on the corral and fixing corrals around the barn. Boss had nearly shoved his fence down just by rubbing on it. While eating dinner, Toby decided to go ahead and call and get the ball rolling on getting his things hauled down. He walked to the house after he finished dinner and knocked on the door.

Hank answered the door. "Hey, Toby, what's up?"

"Hank, we are getting low on feed."

"Why don't you hook on to the trailer and go to town and get a ton of 20 percent cubes."

"Okay. What about calf feed?"

"Get some of it too."

Hank didn't seem like himself, and Toby hadn't seen him since Sunday, so he asked, "Hank, are you okay?"

"Toby, I'm sorry," Hank said. "Sadie is very sick. It hit her Sunday night, and she is not doing well."

"What does the doctor say?"

"Pneumonia," Hank replied.

"Jeez. I hope she gets to doing better. Don't worry about anything on the ranch. I'll take care of it. Do you need anything from town?"

"I know everything is in good hands, and that takes a load off." Hank paused. "I do need to pick up a prescription at the pharmacy. If you could do that for me, it would be a big help."

"Absolutely," Toby said. "And if you think of anything else, give me a call."

He hooked the trailer to his truck and headed to town. He couldn't get Sadie off his mind. She was the closest thing to a grandma he had ever had and was what he had imagined one to be like. He knew Hank was worried, so she must be very ill.

Toby got the feed bought and then stopped to get the prescription. They wouldn't let him have it, so he had them dial Hank's home number, but there was no answer. He was worried, so he grabbed his cell phone to call. He didn't get an answer, so he left a message about the prescription. He was going to stop and look at some televisions, but he decided to get on back in case he needed to come back or help Hank with Sadie.

He met the ambulance about halfway back to the ranch, and Hank was behind it in his truck. Toby didn't know what to do. He wanted to turn and follow, but he knew he needed to take the feed and get it unloaded. He decided to go unload the feed as quickly as he could and then head back to town to the hospital. He took his hat off and prayed for Sadie the rest of the way to the ranch.

He unloaded the sixty sacks of feed in record time and got the trailer unhooked and took off for the hospital. He hoped he didn't get a ticket, because he was speeding all the way. He walked into the emergency room entrance and saw Hank sitting with his head in his hands and looked to be crying.

Toby's heart sank. What had happened?

20

Toby walked over and laid his hand on Hank's shoulder. Hank looked up and started crying harder. Toby didn't know what to say. He didn't know what to ask, so he just sat down beside Hank and waited.

Hank regained his composure. "She took a turn for the worse. They don't know if she will make it or not." He paused for a minute. "How did you know we were here?"

Toby told him about trying to call and then meeting the ambulance and Hank on the way back.

"Thank you for coming," Hank said.

They sat there for about ten minutes before Patty came rushing in. Hank stood up, and they hugged.

"Dad, what happened?" Patty asked. "I thought she was getting better."

"I did too," Hank said. "Then all of a sudden, she started having a horrible time breathing."

"What are they saying?"

Hank paused. "They don't know if she will make it."

Toby could tell Patty was shaken but was trying to be strong for her dad. "Dad, you know Mom is a fighter. She isn't going to give up that easy." She looked at Toby. "Hello, Toby. Thanks for being here."

Toby nodded. "Yes, ma'am."

They sat there in silence, waiting for some news. Carl and Carla showed up thirty minutes after Patty. Around forty-five minutes went by before a nurse came out to get Hank. He was trying to ask her questions as they walked through the doors, but she wasn't offering any answers.

Patty looked at Carl. "Her not answering Dad's questions worries me."

"I know, but let's not read anything into it," Carl said.

Patty went back after another thirty minutes, and then Carl and Carla went back shortly thereafter. Hank came walking out, and he looked very sad. Toby waited for Hank to say something.

Hank sat down. "She looks so bad, and all those machines hooked up to her are scary."

"Did the doctor say anything?" Toby asked.

"He said it would be touch and go for the next eight hours."

"Hank, I am so sorry," Toby said. "I know she will pull through."

They sat there until Carl and Carla came back out. Toby stood up and said to Hank, "I am going to go and check on things. Don't worry about anything at home. I will take care of it."

Hank stood up and grabbed Toby and hugged him. "Thank you, Toby."

Toby nodded and tipped his hat to Carl and Carla and walked out.

Once he was out the door, Carl said, "He acts like he is really doing something. I believe it is his job to take care of things."

Hank's head snapped up, and he looked at Carl. "Carl, shut your mouth. I am tired of you and your poison that you spew out. If that is all you have on your mind, you need to leave now."

At this, Carl looked like a whipped dog, and Carla's mouth dropped wide open. She was shocked at her grandad, but as she thought about it, she realized why Hank had acted as he did.

"I am sorry," Carl finally said. "This isn't the time or place."

"There isn't a time or place for that crud," Hank said. "It is pure jealousy, and you need to grow up. Now be quiet and leave me alone."

Toby was worried as he drove home. He hoped it wasn't selfishness that was causing him to hope Sadie pulled out of it. He knew things could possibly change with Hank if he lost Sadie, and would it affect his job?

He wrestled with this thought all the way to the ranch and while he took care of the chores. He talked it out to Pudge, and when he walked into the mobile home, he was at peace with himself as he knew he only wanted Sadie to get well because he thought so much of her and Hank.

Toby called Carla's cell phone at around 9:30 p.m. to see if there had been any change or news.

"Hello?" Carla said.

"Carla, this is Toby. How is your grandma?"

"Here, I'll let you talk to Kali."

"Hello?" Kali said.

"Kali, this is Toby. I was just trying to check on your grandma."

"She has improved a little. They said she is far from being out of the woods yet, though."

"It's good to hear she made some improvement. She will keep fighting. I didn't know you had come back."

"I couldn't concentrate at school, so I came home," Kali said.

"I'll let you go. Please let me know if anything changes."

She agreed she would, and they hung up. Toby didn't know why Carla didn't just answer his question and instead handed the phone to Kali. He sloughed it off as her just being a kid.

The next day, Toby woke up at 5:00 a.m., wondering how Sadie was. He was hoping that no news overnight meant she hadn't taken a turn for the worse. He fixed breakfast and went about his morning chores at both places. He decided to ride Belle to check on the cattle in the pastures. She did good, so he was feeling good about Jake being able to handle her.

Toby called Ridge and asked him if he could bring Jake over later to ride her with Toby riding beside him on Pudge. Ridge agreed to get Jake over there right after school.

Toby went in to eat a late dinner and called Hank to check on Sadie. Hank told him that Sadie was doing much better but was still in the intensive care unit. Toby assured Hank that everything was okay at home and not to worry. He went out and saddled Pudge and Belle so they would be ready when Ridge and Jake arrived.

Toby sat and talked to Pudge about the fact they would have their very own place after tomorrow. He heard a vehicle pulling up into the drive, so he walked out of the barn to see if it was Ridge. Jake was grinning from ear to ear when he stepped out of the truck.

Toby asked him, "You ready to take a ride?"

Jake responded, "You bet I am."

Toby helped him up in the saddle. He climbed on Pudge, and they started walking away from the barn. Jake did well riding, and Belle acted good. They rode for about an hour, and then Toby had Jake unsaddle Belle when they returned.

"You have to be able to saddle and unsaddle your horse to ride it," Toby said.

"But I am too small to lift the saddle on her," Jake said.

"You can get help lifting, but the cinching down and unsaddling are yours."

"Yes, sir."

Toby glanced at Ridge. He was smiling at Jake, so Toby knew Ridge approved.

"What time do you want me to come and get her tomorrow?" Ridge asked.

"Why don't I bring her home as I go to my closing tomorrow?" Toby said.

"Are you sure?"

"Jessie won't be there, Toby," Jake joined in.

Toby looked at him. "On second thought, maybe you need to put the saddle on her back yourself."

Ridge laughed. "We'll see you tomorrow." He and Jake walked to the truck and left.

Toby put Belle up and climbed back up on Pudge, and they went for a ride. He checked fences and then rode to the back side where his place would join Hank's. He decided he would put a gate in as soon as he started living there. That way, he could ride Pudge to work without getting on the road.

He rode back into the barn and put Pudge away for the day. He was walking to the trailer when his phone rang. "Hello?"

Slade was on the other end. "Hello, Toby. You ready for tomorrow?"

"I am going to get the cashier's check in the morning, but ready other than that."

"Good deal. It has been a pleasure working with you. Good luck, and call if you need anything."

"Thank you," Toby said, and they hung up.

Toby fixed supper and sat down to watch TV. He heard a knock at the door and opened it to see Kali standing on his porch. "Kali, has something happened with your grandma?"

"No, I just needed to get out and away," Kali said. "The waiting is horrible. I hoped I could come and hang out with you."

"Sure. Come on in."

He was watching a rodeo, and Kali said she wanted to watch it. They sat and watched it for two hours without saying much. When the rodeo show ended, Kali said, "Grandad tells me you have a big day tomorrow."

"Yeah, I close on the Glover place tomorrow. I am sure sorry for the trouble it caused your dad and mom."

"Don't worry about it. Mom was perfectly fine with not getting it. Dad can buy another ranch if he wants one."

"I just hope he doesn't hold a grudge."

Kali looked at him differently. "And why is that, Mr. Toby Parker?"

Toby got uncomfortable real quick. He didn't know how to respond. Was Kali thinking he meant he wanted to date her? Even though she was hot, he never had even thought about her since it seemed she and Drew had been going together since high school. He decided he would play along and see how she responded, so he said, "Well, I might need his blessing."

Kali seemed to get uncomfortable. "I guess I better get going." She got up and walked to the door, and Toby got up and followed her. She opened the door to step out, and Toby said, "Sorry. I didn't mean to make you uncomfortable."

"It's not you. I am just confused about everything right now." Kali walked to her car and left.

Toby felt like a heel for putting her in a position to feel like she needed to leave. "I need to focus on my ranch and helping Hank and forget everything else," he said to himself. "Less problems that way."

He watched the news and the *American Rancher* on the Rural Channel and went to bed. He read the Bible for a while and prayed for Hank and Sadie and for himself to handle tomorrow okay, and then he went to sleep.

Toby woke up at 4:30 a.m. and was out of bed and eating breakfast by 5:00 a.m. He was so excited he did the feeding faster than he ever had. He realized how fast he had done it and said, "Well, crud. Now I just have to wait longer. Come on, Toby, get it together."

He saddled Pudge to ride out to the pastures and spent over an hour and saw another hog. This time, it was on the Glovers' place, so he would have to start ridding his place for hogs. He was aggravated with himself that he hadn't hunted them for Bud so they could have benefited from the money brought when they sold them. He decided to hook up to the trailer and load Belle and head on over to Ridge's.

He turned into Ridge's and had to maneuver around a truck sitting in the way. Ridge came walking out and opened the gate to the stall for Belle. Toby opened the trailer gate and led Belle out and started to the barn.

"So is she ready for my brother to ride?" Jessie asked. She had walked out of the house, and Toby hadn't noticed.

He turned to answer her and saw a guy walking with her. "I think she is ready for Cowboy Jake."

"That's good," Jessie said. "Toby, this is Rob Evans, my boyfriend."

Toby was disappointed but stopped with Belle and stuck out his hand and shook Rob's. "Pleased to meet you."

"I felt like I needed to come and meet you and see what all the fuss is about," Rob said. "Jessie and Kali have done nothing but talk about Toby the cowboy for the last few weeks."

"Not sure what that means, but hope you don't get bored watching me."

Toby led Belle into the stall and took her halter off. He shut the gate, and Ridge handed him two-hundred-dollar bills. "Money well spent. I sure do appreciate it."

"I enjoyed it," Toby said. "It was fun working with Belle, and even more fun watching the excitement in Jake." He paused and put the money in his wallet. "I best get moving. I want to stop by the hospital before I go to the bank."

Jessie and Rob had stopped outside the barn. Toby saw them as he walked out and said, "Good to see you, Jessie, and to meet you Rob."

"We'll see you during the week," Jessie said.

"Yeah, I am staying," Rob said. "Small town and farm living should be good for some laughs."

Toby didn't comment but walked on to his trailer. He shut the gate and then went to the truck to leave. He pulled out of the drive and headed to town. He thought about Rob and said, "What a jerk. Oh well, I guess she wasn't my type if she likes that."

Toby parked across the street and walked over to the hospital. He asked what room Sadie was in and was pleased to hear she was out of the ICU. That must mean she was still improving. He stepped off the elevator and saw Debbie. He walked up to her and said, "Hi, Debbie."

She looked up from what she was doing. "Hello, Toby. How are you?"

"I'm okay," he replied. "How is Sadie?"

"She is improving all the time, but it is slow," Debbie said. "Dad is wanting her well in a couple of days, and it just isn't going to happen."

"Can she have visitors?"

"Yes. Go on in."

Toby lightly knocked on the door and then stuck his head in, and Hank said, "Come on in, Toby."

He walked in, and Sadie's eyes opened. She seemed to smile through all the tubes and things she had in her mouth and up her nose. Toby walked over and took her hand. "It sure is good to see you."

Hank said, "She is doing much better, but the doc said it may be weeks before she is back to being her old self."

"It will be good to see her back to her old self," Toby said.

"Sit down," Hank said. "Are you in town for your closing?"

Toby told him about the progress Belle had made and of taking her home and heading to the bank and then the closing.

"When you planning on moving in?" Hank asked.

"Well, my stuff probably won't be here until the middle to latter part of next week, so I probably won't start living there until then, if that is okay."

"Of course that is okay. You take your time, and stay as long as you want."

Toby stayed awhile and talked about Sadie's progress. Then he excused himself so he could get to the bank for his cashier's check. He told Debbie good-bye and waited for the elevator to come. The elevator door opened, and out came the rest of the Parker and Grissom clans.

Tim saw Toby and said, "Hey, Toby, is that your horse trailer out there?"

Toby grinned at him. "Yeah, it is. How you been, Tim?"

Tim turned to his dad and asked, "Can I go with Toby?"

"No," Albert, Tim's dad, said. "You are here to see your grandma."

Tim looked rejected. "Oh yeah. Bye, Toby."

"I'll see you later, Tim," Toby said.

That seemed to perk Tim back up. Toby nodded and tipped his hat to the four girls and stepped on the elevator, totally ignoring Carl.

He made it to the bank and got the cashier's check. He had an hour until closing, so he stopped at the café for coffee and pie. He was just about through with his pie when he looked up and saw Jessie and Rob walk through the door. He hoped they wouldn't see him, but Jessie spotted him and walked over.

"Care for some company?" she asked.

"Sure," Toby replied. "But I have to leave in fifteen minutes."

"Got a hot date with a horse?" Rob piped up.

Toby looked up at him but didn't respond.

"I think I touched a nerve," Rob said.

Jessie felt the tension and tried to help out. "Is Bethany coming down this weekend?"

"Nah," Toby said. "I'm gonna go. Y'all enjoy your meal."

As Toby slid out of the booth, Rob said, "Don't go away mad. I was just joking."

Toby stopped and turned around. "Pardner, it's best you stop while you are ahead. You don't know me well enough to joke with me." He was angry and looked it, and Rob's smile went away fast. He tried to stare at Toby, but Toby was too intimidating with his look, and Rob looked down.

Toby looked at Jessie. "I'm sorry." He walked out.

Toby got to his truck and was aggravated with himself that he let what Rob had said get to him. He knew it was because of Jessie, but he should have just let it go. He pulled out of the parking lot and drove to the office where the closing was taking place.

The closing went off without a hitch, and Toby walked out of the office as a homeowner and landowner. It felt as good as he thought it would. He drove straight to his ranch to take it all in as the owner. He spent two hours looking around at things and getting a better feel for what he needed to do. He turned into Hank's drive and saw Bethany's truck sitting in front of the mobile home.

"What in the world," Toby said as he pulled up into the drive.

Toby pulled up past the mobile home and backed his trailer into the line of equipment. He pulled back around to the drive to park his truck. He killed his truck and, out of the corner of his eye, saw Bethany's truck door open. He got out, and she said, "Hello, Toby. You have to take Pudge somewhere?"

"Nah. I brought the mare I was breaking over here to work with and took it home today."

He started walking to the porch then stopped and asked, "What are you doing here? I haven't heard a word from you since you left mad."

"I know. I have felt bad about how I left and wanted to see you before I go home for spring break."

Toby opened the door, and they walked inside.

"I don't think you have any idea what you want at this point," he said. "That is what keeps me unsettled about you. There doesn't appear to be any sincerity in what you do."

Bethany looked hurt. "I listened to what you said when I was here before. It seemed mean at first, but the more I thought about it, I started to see what you were saying. I hope we can still be friends and maybe even more some day."

"Time will tell. When you leaving for home?"

"I was hoping in the morning. I hoped Hank and Sadie would allow me to stay tonight."

"They aren't home. Sadie is very sick in the hospital with pneumonia, and Hank is there with her."

"Oh no. Is she going to be okay?"

"It was touch and go for a while, but she is making some progress now."

"You think I could see her?" Bethany asked. "They have been so nice to me every time I have seen them."

"I don't see why not," Toby said.

"I better go, before it gets too late. What room is she in?"

"I'll go with you. I'd like to talk to Hank."

Bethany seemed plum giddy as she replied, "That sounds great."

Toby drove, and Bethany followed in her truck. They didn't talk as they walked to Sadie's room. Toby was surprised they didn't see any of the family in the waiting room as they came off the elevator. He lightly knocked on the door, and they walked on in.

Hank was looking to see who was coming in, and when he saw them, he said, "Hello, Toby. Why, it's Bethany. It is good to see you, girl."

Sadie was awake and was kind of smiling. Bethany walked over and bent down and hugged her. Then she walked around and hugged Hank.

"Has the doctor been in since I was here earlier?" Toby asked.

"No, but his assistant came in, and she is steadily improving," Hank replied. "Still not sure how long she will be in here."

They sat in silence awhile, and then Hank asked, "Toby, do you have a ranch now?"

Toby grinned. "Yes, sir."

"That grin tells me everything. I am so happy for you."

"You bought a ranch?" Bethany asked.

"I thought you knew I was trying."

"Nope. Don't think I had heard that."

Toby was sure she did and wondered if it was a typical Bethany ploy. He decided to let it go. "I am eager to get started doing things over there."

"I can imagine. Just be careful to not overwork yourself," Hank said.

Toby said, laughing, "I think I could go on adrenaline for at least a month."

"That's probably true," Hank said.

Toby stood up. "We need to get out of here and let y'all rest."

"Where are you staying, Bethany?"

"I am heading home for spring break," Bethany answered.

"Tonight?" Hank asked.

"Yeah, I may stop along the way."

"That's silly. You can spend the night in our house and leave in the morning."

She planned and played that to her advantage, Toby thought. He didn't like it.

"Are you sure?" Bethany asked.

"Yes, I'm sure," Hank said.

She hugged Hank and Sadie again, and she and Toby left.

"You can head on back," Toby said. "I am going to the grocery store for a couple of items.

Bethany hesitated but said, "Okay."

Toby started his truck and left. He was going down the aisles of the store when he looked up and saw Bethany walking toward him.

"I thought you were going to the ranch."

"I started to but figured I'd come and help you."

"Thanks, but I'm not getting enough to need help."

"I'll just tag along. Might be fun."

Toby shook his head and walked on.

They headed toward the ranch when he was finished, but he turned and went to his place to put the dry goods he had bought. Bethany didn't notice where he turned, so she turned around and started looking for him. Toby finished putting things up and drove on to Hank's. He was surprised when he turned into the drive that Bethany's truck wasn't there. He parked and got his phone to call her.

"Toby?" she answered.

"Yeah," he said. "Where are you?"

"I don't know. I'm lost."

"How in the world can you get lost coming here? You have been here enough times, and it is easy to find."

"I turned around and tried to find you."

Toby was angry now. "Why?"

"I don't know."

"Give me an idea of what you see so I can try to figure out where you are."

Bethany told him what she was seeing, and he said, "That sounds like Ridge's place. I don't know how you got there. Hang tight, and I will be there directly."

He turned down the road that led to Ridge's, and sure enough, she was sitting on the side of the road. He pulled up beside her and said, "Follow me." He took off, and she followed him back to Hank's.

She got out and said, "Thank you."

"No problem. I have to go take care of Pudge."

Bethany knew he was aggravated, so she said, "Okay. I'll go in the house."

Toby was in the barn for about thirty minutes, and then he walked to the mobile home. He shut the door and put his hat and coat up and was taking off his boots when Bethany knocked.

"Come in," he said.

She walked in. "You want to watch a movie?"

"It's already 9:30. What time you leaving in the morning?"

"Just whenever I get up."

"I guess we can watch one. What did you have in mind?"

"I was thinking *Rio Bravo*. I like Walter Brennan in it."

"Okay. I haven't watched that one in a while. You want some popcorn?"

"That would be great."

Toby fixed the popcorn and fixed himself some coffee and sat down to watch the movie. Bethany went to the restroom and came back and sat nearly on his side of the couch. There was about six inches between them.

"This isn't a scary show," Toby said.

Bethany looked at him, smiling. "Would you protect me if it were?"

"I doubt you scare easy."

She laughed and pulled her feet up under her, the act which nearly put her up next to him.

She isn't going to quit, Toby thought.

They watched the movie, and when it was over, Toby said, "I have a lot to do tomorrow. I best hit the hay." He walked her to the door and asked, "You want me to walk with you to the house?"

"Would you?" Bethany said. "That would be cool."

He slipped his boots on and walked her to the porch. "Good night." He started to hug her, but she had other ideas. When he leaned in to hug her, she maneuvered a kiss on the lips.

It surprised him, but he didn't embarrass her.

"Well, I had to try," she said.

"What does that mean?" he asked.

"I could tell you didn't want the kiss."

"I don't know much about kissing. I have had very little experience."

"Are you serious? A cowboy that looks like you hasn't been kissed a lot?"

"Nope," Toby said. He walked off the porch.

Toby went straight to bed, and as he laid his head on the pillow, he found himself thinking about what Bethany did and what she had said. He had never had a girlfriend, and he really didn't know why. He just never had met anyone whom he really wanted to call his girlfriend. Was Bethany the one? He really didn't think so, or at least not yet. He really thought Jessie or Kali would be more to his type of girl. Oh well, it was time to go to sleep.

Toby woke up early and was out feeding forty-five minutes later. He finished feeding Hank's and headed over to feed his cattle. He took his time feeding his because he was looking each bull, cow, and calf over. He spotted damage that hogs were causing and even saw three hogs, so he decided to go get Pudge and his rifle and do some hog hunting.

He got back to Hank's and hooked up his trailer. He loaded Pudge and pulled out without Bethany ever showing herself. He was surprised she wasn't already gone, but he had too much to do than spend time trying to figure out what she might be doing.

He pulled into his drive and saw two hogs running around the barn. He parked and unloaded Pudge and saddled him as quick as he could. He loaded his rifle and mounted up and headed toward the first pasture. He had barely started out when he spotted a hog. He pulled up and shot it as he rode.

He spent the next three hours hunting, killing, and field dressing nine hogs. He put Pudge in a stable, loaded the hogs in his trailer, and took them to town. He hoped the meat-packer plant was open. Sure enough, it was, so he had $1,200 in his pocket when he left. The money would come in handy buying feed for his cattle. He went back and loaded Pudge and headed back to Hank's to go check his outer pastures. He turned into the drive and was very surprised to see Bethany's truck still sitting in front of the house. He parked and unloaded Pudge and was climbing on the saddle when Bethany walked out and hollered, "Where have you been all day?"

Toby looked at her and didn't respond. She walked over to him and asked again, "Where have you been?"

Toby responded with a question, "What are you still doing here?"

Bethany stopped in her tracks. "Are you mad that I am here?"

"No. Just curious."

"I am staying for a few days. I talked to Hank and Sadie, and they agreed you would need some help with your new house. They said I could stay here."

Toby didn't quite know how to respond. The help would be nice, but he felt like he should have had some say in it. However, he couldn't be mad at Hank and Sadie, so he might as well just roll with it.

"I am going to run the pastures," he said. "You want to come along?"

"Yes."

Toby dismounted to get her a horse and saddle. They mounted up and were riding out of the barnyard when Hank's truck started pulling up into the drive behind them. Toby told Bethany to hold up, and he watched to see if Hank needed anything. He saw Kali get out of the passenger side of the truck. Toby left Bethany and rode back to talk to Kali. "Is everything okay?"

"Yeah," Kali said. "We just came to check on things and get Grandad some clothes. What is she doing here?"

Hank shut his door and saved Toby from having to respond. "Hello, Toby. What's up?"

"Heading out to check the pastures," Toby said. "Need me to do anything for you before I go?"

"You mean before *y'all* go," Kali said.

Toby looked at her and said, "I'll talk to you later." He tipped his hat to her and rode back to Bethany.

They took off at a gallop, and Bethany looked back and waved. Toby saw it out of the corner of his eye and wondered why she did it. He would ask her later.

22

Toby dismounted to open the gate in the first pasture, and as he walked back to Pudge, he asked Bethany, "What was the purpose of turning back and waving to Kali?"

Bethany smiled. "It's a girl thing."

"I don't what that means, but I know you didn't do it for a nice reason."

"Why are you upset? Doesn't she have a boyfriend?"

"It was childish."

Toby kicked Pudge, and they rode through the gate, leaving Bethany there. She spurred her horse on and rode up beside him, but Toby didn't acknowledge her. He was aggravated but wasn't sure if it was because Bethany did it to Kali or just the fact that she did it. It seemed like the typical Bethany, which was what had been his problem with her from the git-go.

Neither one talked as they checked all the pastures. They rode back into the barnyard, and Toby noticed Hank and Kali were gone.

"I'll unsaddle the horses," he said, hoping Bethany would go on into Hank's house.

She dismounted and started walking toward the house, and Toby led the horses into the barn. He spent about thirty minutes taking care of Pudge. He headed to the mobile home and went in to change coats before he headed over to his place. He got in his truck and drove off as Bethany walked out the door. He didn't notice her, but he wasn't looking either.

Bethany ran inside to get her keys to follow Toby, but by the time she got rolling, she didn't know where he was. She figured he had gone to town or to the hospital, so she decided to go check.

Toby pulled into the barn and shut the doors to help keep some of the cold out. He had promised Pudge a nice stall, and noticed there was ample wood that came along with the place to complete it the way he had envisioned. He was planning on having Pudge's stall totally enclosed, like his own tack room. The stall he was converting was oversized, so he could make a tack area for all the items he used for Pudge. The stall was on the south end, so it would be away from the north wind, but he still planned on insulating at least the ceiling.

Toby realized most would consider him foolish for doing this, but he really didn't care. Pudge was all the family he had, and he was going to take care of him. Pudge had taken care of him many times in the past when they gotten in a pickle.

Bethany didn't even look for Toby's truck when she arrived at the hospital. She went up to the room and walked in without knocking.

Hank, Patty, Debbie, and Kali were sitting in the room, and all looked at Bethany with some disgust.

"Bethany, what are you doing back here?" Hank asked.

"And alone," Kali added.

Bethany didn't speak, and Kali sensed what was up. "Oh, she is looking for Toby and thought he was here. Isn't that right, Bethany?"

Embarrassed, Bethany spun around and headed back out the door.

"Kali, that wasn't necessary," Patty said.

"Mom, you don't know the whole story," Kali said.

"She is a nice girl but seems a little mixed up at times," Hank said.

Bethany debated between heading on home and going back to Hank's. She decided on the latter, since it was too late and she would have to drive all night. She sat by the window, waiting and watching for Toby.

Toby made considerable progress on building the private stall for Pudge. He had built a line shack with Tom when they had worked together, and the experience was coming in handy. He saw it was nearly 10:00 p.m., and so he shut down for the evening and headed back to Hank's.

When he stepped out of the truck, Bethany was walking toward him.

"Where did you go?" she asked. "It has been lonely around here."

"I went to work on things at my place."

"Really? I would have loved to have seen your place and help you."

"I didn't figure you wanted to build a stall."

"Never done that before, but I would like to try."

"Maybe you can go over next time. Good night. See you in the morning." Toby turned to walk to the house.

She hesitated then said, "Good night."

Toby got ready for bed, read the Bible, and went to sleep. He was up early and had breakfast finished and was feeding by 6:00 a.m. It had warmed up a little from yesterday, and seemed like it was going to be a good day. He had everything fed at both places and was back by 8:00 a.m. He got ready for church and walked over to see if Bethany was ready to go with him. She opened the door in her pajamas and saw Toby was dressed in starched Wranglers and a pretty George Strait shirt.

"Wow, you look pretty," Bethany said.

"Why aren't you ready to go?" Toby asked.

"Go where?"

"To church."

"I don't go much and wasn't going this morning."

Toby looked at her and said, "Well, that is disappointing." He turned and walked off the porch to his truck and drove off to attend church services.

Bethany could tell by the look on his face that she had just about cooked her goose with him. She ran into the house and started getting ready. She made it to worship service after Bible class was over.

Toby was sitting by himself. Alfred, Debbie, and their kids came in and sat down in front of him.

Tim turned around and asked, "Toby, can I sit with you?"

"It's okay with me if it is okay with your folks," Toby said.

Tim got up and came back to Toby's pew, grinning from ear to ear.

"If it is okay with your dad and mom, you can go with me this afternoon to work on some fence," Toby said. "We can ride the horses out to do it."

"Dad and Mom, can I go with Toby?" Tim asked.

"Yes," Albert said. "We'll talk about it when we get out."

Tim was showing Toby his pocketknife, and Toby saw a girl's legs and boots scoot in by Tim. He looked up to see Bethany. He nodded to her, and as he turned his head back toward the front, his eye caught Kali turning around from two rows up, looking at him. He acted like he didn't notice it.

When services were over, they stood to walk out, and Bethany asked, "Who is this handsome young man?"

"I'm Tim, Hank's grandson," Tim said.

"And our son, thank you very much," Debbie said.

"Oh yeah," Tim said. "That's my parents and sisters."

"So you are related to Kali," Bethany said.

"Yep."

Toby pushed by her, because he was tired of the talk. He walked with Alfred and Debbie, and they discussed Tim. They told him they would be staying at Hank and Sadie's tonight, so they would be there when Toby got finished. Debbie got some clothes from the car for Tim to change and handed them to Toby.

Toby started to his truck with Tim in tow, and Bethany came walking up and asked, "Where are we eating?"

"We are going to get a burger at McDonald's and get on out to work," Toby said.

"Oh," Bethany said. "Well, I think I will go to a restaurant."

"Enjoy," Toby said. He got into the truck and drove off.

Kali was watching curiously, and Drew asked, "What are you looking at?"
"He left her standing in the middle of the parking lot."
"So what?"
"Nothing."

Toby and Tim got their food in the drive-thru and ate on the way to the ranch. They changed clothes, and Toby saddled Pudge and a pony for Tim and loaded the tools needed for putting in a wire gate. They enjoyed the ride to the back corner of Hank's and started working on the gate.

"Where will this gate go to?" Tim asked.

"That is my land on the other side of the fence, so I am putting in a gate to be able to ride Pudge to and from work each day when I move."

"You are moving?"

Toby explained to Tim how he had bought the ranch and how he was still going to be working for Tim's grandad. Tim seemed okay with Toby's explanation. Toby wondered if there had been a gate at this location before, because the gate and brace posts were already in place. He worked and got the gate put up and ready for use.

When Toby was finished, he asked Tim if he wanted to ride and see his place. Tim was more than ready to go see it. Toby shut the new gate behind them, and they started riding to the barnyard.

Bethany had returned and spent the afternoon looking out toward the pasture. She knew she had blown the day by not being ready this morning. She hoped to have a good night and the rest of the time she was there.

Toby rode up to the barn with Tim siding him. He dismounted and opened the barn door and led Pudge and Tim's pony inside. He tied Tim's pony up and then opened the door to Pudge's personal stall. Pudge seemed to like it, and Tim was blown away by it. "I could sleep out here."

"Maybe we can sometime," Toby said.

They went and looked in the house and at some of the cattle. Tim acted like it was his. He was grinning the entire afternoon.

"You want to help me finish up on the stall, or are you ready to go back?" Toby asked.

"You bet I'll help," Tim said.

They worked for over three hours and completed all they could with the materials they had. Toby would have to go to the lumberyard tomorrow for insulation and door hardware. They put the tools away and closed everything up and were mounting up when they heard a vehicle pulling up into the drive. Toby figured it was Bethany, but as he turned, he saw it was someone he didn't recognize.

The car turned around and left without stopping. It gave Toby an uneasy feeling, so he rode down to the end of the driveway and closed the gate and locked it.

"Who was that?" Tim asked.

"I don't know, but they didn't need to pull all the way up the drive to turn around. Seemed suspicious." Toby looked at Tim and saw that Tim seemed a little scared. "Hey, don't worry about it. You ready to race back to the gate?" He wanted to try and get Tim's mind off the event.

Tim laughed. "You are gonna lose."

Toby let Tim get to the gate first, and Tim was beaming. "I beat you and Pudge!" he shouted.

Toby smiled. "You sure did." He dismounted to open the gate. He closed the gate behind them and started toward the house. Toby spotted something that bothered him, so he took off quickly to his left to check it. Tim turned and followed slowly. Toby had Pudge come to a stop, and he pulled out his rifle.

It was a pack of wolves. There must have been ten to twelve wolves running together. They weren't as big as what he had dealt with in western New Mexico, but they were a lot larger than coyotes. He watched them to see how they were acting, and he grabbed his phone and called Hank.

"Hello?" Hank answered.

"Hank, I am sorry to bother you, but I am looking at a pack of wolves."

"Say what? On my land?"

"Yessir. Do you want me to see if I can shoot some? I am hesitant because Tim is with me. I can take him back and come back out and see if they are still around."

"Please do, but be careful."

Toby motioned for Tim to follow, and Toby headed for the house as fast as he could without losing Tim or putting him at risk of falling off the pony. They rode into the barnyard and up in front of the house. Toby saw Alfred and Debbie's car, so he told Tim to go into the house and he would be back in a while. He took the pony and tied it up in the barn and said, "Let's go, Pudge." He grabbed the saddle horn and swung into the saddle as Pudge bolted toward the pasture.

Toby didn't know it, but Tim, his sisters, and Bethany had walked out on the porch to see what was going on. They all saw Toby take off like that.

"Whoa, that was impressive," Bethany said.
"It sure was," Tim said. "I'm going to ride like that someday."
His sisters said almost in unison, "Yeah, sure, Timmie."
"Don't call me that, and you just wait and see." Tim stormed into the house with his boots clanking on the floor.

Toby rode hard to get back to where he had spotted the wolves. There was still enough sunlight to see. He spotted them and rode closer than he had before. He had his rifle pulled out and ready. The wolves were eating on something but had it mauled so bad Toby couldn't tell what it was. He hoped it wasn't one of Hank's cows or calves.

As he rode closer, some of the wolves noticed him and turned to face him, growling. Toby counted about ten of them facing him, and the others were still involved in eating. He was trying to decide what to do when the wolves helped him make up his mind. One of them darted out of the pack at him, and he pulled up and shot it. Two more had started, and he shot both of them.

The others were all growling now, and he didn't want to wait to see how they would charge, so he picked off two in the middle, hoping it would deter some of the others. It worked, but four of them still acted like they wanted him and Pudge. He started shooting and downed all five as they bolted toward them. He had ten down, and the other ten were heading for the woods.

Toby decided to see if he could chase them and make them keep running well out of the area. Two of them decided to turn and try to fight, and Toby pulled up and put them down as well. He couldn't see any more once he shot those two, so he roped the feet of those he had shot and dragged them back to where the others were.

The air was clear, and Tim had walked back out in the porch and heard the first shots. He ran into the house, hollering, "I heard shots."

The others all ran out to the porch and heard all the shots.

"Holy cow, it sounds like World War III," Albert said.

They all stood watching for Toby to ride in.

Toby piled all the wolves up so he could bury them. He would go get the tractor and use the loader to dig the hole. He was out of daylight, so he pushed Pudge to get back. He rode into the barnyard and into the barn, and all of them started to the barn.

Tim ran ahead, and as Toby entered the barn, he asked, "What were all the shots?"

Toby was dismounting and leading Pudge into the stall. He walked out of the stall as all the others walked into the barn. "Tim, I was shooting wolves."

The whole group exclaimed at the same time, "Wolves?"

"I didn't think they had wolves over here," Albert said.

"Don't think it is common," Toby said.

"How many did you shoot?" Bethany asked.

Hank pulled up in his truck, and he and Kali got out. Hank walked around the front of the truck and asked, "Did you get any of them?"

"Yeah," Toby said. "I got twelve of 'em."

"Twelve?" Kali repeated.

Bethany looked at her and said, "Yeah, twelve."

"Bethany, you didn't know how many," Toby said.

Kali looked at Bethany, smiled, and shook her head, as if to say, "Na, na, na, na, na, nah."

"I'm going to take the tractor out and dig a hole to bury them," Toby said.

"I'll follow you," Hank said. "I want to see them."

Toby the Rancher

Tim and Kali got in with Hank and waited for Toby to get the tractor. Toby led them out to the wolves, with Hank close behind. Toby decided to grab his pistol and take it with him since it would be awkward to carry the rifle on the tractor. He started working on the hole while Hank, Kali, and Tim got out of the truck to look at the wolves. He was digging it deep and not paying attention to what the others were doing when he heard a scream over the tractor motor. He slammed the clutch and brake and spun his head to see what had happened. He saw four eyes in the darkness looking at Kali and Tim. Hank had walked over to look at the hole and left the two of them behind.

23

Toby threw the tractor out of gear. Luckily, the loader was on the ground, so the tractor wouldn't roll. He put his right hand on the fender and used it to spring out of the seat and over the fender and tire to the ground.

Hank had looked to see what Toby was doing because he knew he couldn't get back to Kali and Tim quick enough. He saw Toby flying over the fender and tire and felt some relief.

Toby was pulling his pistol as he was landing on the ground and had it pointed at the eyes as he ran toward Kali and Tim. When he was still about ten feet away, the eyes started charging them. Kali and Tim were frozen stiff with fear but managed to just grab each other.

Toby kept running and started shooting. He shot six times although he saw the two wolves go down on his first three shots. He was scared that Kali and Tim were in danger, and he wanted to make sure the wolves were dead. He ran on up to Kali and Tim, and both of them grabbed onto him and squeezed for dear life.

Albert had stepped out on the porch and heard the shots. He was worried about Tim and all of them, so he started walking to his car.

Debbie walked out and saw him and asked, "Where are you going?"

"I heard more shots," he said. "I am going to check on Tim."

"You can't make it out there in the car. Give them some time."

"Okay." Albert started walking slowly back toward the porch while still looking toward the pasture.

Toby was trying to console Kali and Tim when Hank got to them. They both kept holding on to Toby. Hank just patted them and told them it was okay.

"Hank, why don't you take them on back and I'll get the wolves buried," Toby said.

"Sounds good," Hank said. "Let's go, kids."

Kali and Tim finally let go of Toby and walked to the truck. Toby felt bad that they were so shaken up. He hoped it didn't keep Tim from enjoying being out and about in the future. He finished burying the wolves and headed back toward the house.

Albert was at the truck when Hank opened the door. "What was the shooting?" he asked. "Is everyone okay?"

"They are shook up, but will be okay," Hank said.

They both turned to see who was pulling up into the drive. It was Jessie and Rob. Albert turned back to check on Tim, and by now, everyone was out of the house and close to the truck. Debbie was helping Kali and Tim out of the truck, because she could tell they had both been crying. She didn't ask them questions but just hugged each one as they got out.

Albert asked again, "Hank, what happened out there?"

Hank looked at him and then at Kali and Tim. "Let's get the kids in the house."

Debbie agreed and, with an arm around each of them, walked into the house. Once they were in the house, Hank looked at Albert, knowing the others were listening. "We ran into some trouble. Toby was using the bucket to dig a hole to bury the wolves in, and I had walked around to the other side of it to see how he was coming. Kali and Tim were still standing over by the dead wolves and looked up, and four eyes were staring at them from the dark. They screamed loud enough that Toby heard them over the tractor engine. He jumped off the tractor and pulled his pistol and shot the two wolves as they charged toward the kids. I couldn't get there fast enough to help. Luckily, Toby was so quick thinking and a good shot."

"I knew they shouldn't have gone," Albert said.

"Yeah, sure," Hank said. He walked to the barn to see if Toby was coming. Albert walked to the house, but everyone else followed Hank.

"Where is Toby?" Jessie asked.

Bethany looked at her. "He's working. What do you think?"

Jessie ignored her.

"He had to finish burying the wolves," Hank said.

"How long does it take to bury a couple of wolves?" Rob asked sarcastically.

Bethany laughed. "Probably holding a memorial service."

She and Rob were the only two who laughed.

"How many wolves were there?" Jessie asked. "I didn't know wolves were around here."

"There were twelve dead before the two that came at us," Kali said as she walked up.

Jessie hugged her. "Are you okay?"

"Yeah," Kali said. "Didn't know I could be so scared."

"That's not the way to impress Toby," Bethany said.
"You should know, since you haven't impressed him yet," Kali said.
"Girls," Hank said. "Now is not the time."
Tim walked up and said, "There comes Toby."
They all looked and saw the lights of the tractor in the distance.

Toby drove into the barnyard and was surprised to see everyone outside waiting for him. He was really surprised to see Jessie and Rob. He parked the tractor and walked toward the barn.
"Any more trouble?" Hank asked.
"Nah," Toby replied. "I got them covered by over a foot of dirt."
"Okay," Hank said. "That should help keep other animals from digging."
Albert came walking up and said, "Toby, I wanted to thank you for saving Tim and Kali's life."
"It scared me," Toby said. "I was afraid I couldn't get the tractor stopped and get off in time to help them."
"And I thought you rode a horse," Rob said.
Toby stopped and turned to look at Rob. "I am in no mood to deal with your smart mouth. If you can't be quiet, stay away from me."
Rob bristled, but when he saw no one seemed to be on his side, he didn't respond.
Toby looked at Kali and Tim. "Are you guys okay?"
They both nodded that they were.
Toby walked into the barn to take care of Pudge, and the whole crew followed him. He unsaddled him and started brushing him.
"No wonder a girl can't get anywhere with Toby," Bethany said. "He is too crazy about his horse."
Rob had a short memory and said, "I bet it gives wet kisses."

"So that's why he hasn't kissed any girls," Bethany said.

Toby stopped brushing. "Bethany and Rob, leave the barn now, or I will physically throw you out." He looked at Jessie. "I'm sorry, but I will not tolerate that crud."

"No problem," Jessie said. "He *is* out of line."

"Well, I guess it is time for me to head home," Bethany said. She walked out toward the door, but Rob stood still.

Toby looked at him, and Rob said, "You aren't man enough to throw me out."

"Young man, you need to leave," Hank said.

"No, I won't," Rob said.

"This is—" Hank started to speak.

Toby grabbed Rob and shoved him toward the door. Rob tried to turn around, but Toby grabbed him by the seat of the pants and the collar of his jacket and pushed him to and out of the door. "Don't come back." He turned to walk back into the barn.

Rob turned, and Hank stepped in front of him and said, "Leave. Now!"

"Jessie, come on," Rob said.

"You go on," Jessie said. "I will catch a ride with Kali."

"I'm heading home then."

"Probably a good idea."

They walked back into the barn. Toby finished with Pudge and helped Tim with his pony, and then they all walked out of the barn.

Kali looked and said, "They are sure taking their time."

Bethany and Rob were standing by her truck, talking. Toby started to walk that way, and they got in their vehicles and drove off. He walked back to the group and said, "I think I will go in and eat a bite."

"Yeah, I need to get back to the hospital," Hank said.

"Toby, can we join you?" Jessie asked.

Toby started getting nervous. Kali and Jessie wanting to spend time with him made him uncomfortable. He liked it but wasn't sure how to act. "Sure. Not sure what I have for supper."

"I'm not hungry," Kali said.

Jessie agreed, and they walked to the trailer.

As Toby walked off, he turned to Tim and said, "Tim, I will see you in the morning."

Tim grinned. "Okay. See ya."

Once inside the mobile home, Toby asked, "Y'all want anything to drink?"

"I'll take a cup of coffee when it's ready," Jessie said.

Toby smiled. "That's my kind of girl."

"I'll take one too," Kali said.

They sat and talked and watched TV for a couple of hours, and then the girls got ready to leave.

"I have to ask," Jessie said. "Did the fact that Rob is larger than you and a good athlete worry you at all?"

Toby started to speak, but Kali said, "Why would it? You should see him jump on the back of horse from a standstill."

"I'd like to sometime," Jessie said.

They left, and Toby got ready for bed. He knew he was probably going to have a full week.

Toby had breakfast cooked and eaten before 5:30 a.m., and was walking out the door to feed. He spent the next three hours feeding at Hank's and his place, and then he started working on Pudge's stall. He worked until noon and nailed the last nail to finish it and then headed back to Hank's to eat dinner. He had just sat down to eat when his phone rang. It was the moving company, and they were only about fifteen minutes out. They had gotten there two days sooner than Toby anticipated. He had to get a move on the get a better idea where to put the furniture and other items.

He gobbled his sandwich down and was heading out the door when he saw Kali pulling up into the drive. She waved big, and he waved as he got in his truck. He started it up, and she came walking over, so he rolled down the window.

"Where you going?" Kali asked.

"Got to get to my place and get ready for my furniture," Toby said. "It is getting here in a little bit, and it's a couple of days sooner than I was expecting."

He tipped his hat and drove off. He was excited about getting his things to get his house set up and to start living there, but really, he wasn't ready since he had expected to have a couple more days. Oh well, he would have to buckle down and get everything done. He unlocked his gate and pulled up into the drive. As he got out of his truck, he heard the sound of a car and looked to see Kali pulling up.

She parked over by the barn and got out and asked, "Could you use some help?"

Toby grinned. "You have no idea. Thanks for coming."

"I called Jessie, and she is coming over too."

Toby was both nervous and excited. He was glad to have their help but was nervous about letting people see his things. They were antiques mostly, and although he loved them, he figured most wouldn't. His dad had left most of it to him, and he wouldn't part with them.

"I best get everything unlocked and the garage doors opened," he said.

He was opening the second garage door when he noticed the truck start turning into his drive. Kali was standing by him and asked, "You have enough for two trucks?"

"One is probably my household items and the other is my vehicles."

"Vehicles?"

Toby turned and looked at her, grinning. "Yes, vehicles."

"What kind, and how many?"

"You'll just have to wait and see."

Kali looked at him. She saw Toby was grinning, so she said, "Okay, Smarty."

The van with the furniture got backed up to the house, and the men started unloading. Toby was telling them where to put things, and Kali started unpacking boxes. Jessie showed up and started helping Kali unpack things. Toby was enjoying having them around to help. He told them to put the things where they thought they needed to go and he would be happy with it.

He walked into the kitchen, and Jessie said, "Kali tells me you have a trailer full of vehicles out there. How many?"

"I forget."

The two girls laughed and kept on working. Toby started putting tools in the barn as they were unloaded from the truck. He was walking out of the barn to get another load when he noticed a car driving slowly by on the road. He stopped and watched it and noticed it was the same car that had pulled up the drive Sunday.

Toby decided to go follow the car and see if they would stop. He jumped into his truck and headed down the drive. He started catching up to the car, and it took off.

Toby got up to 90 mph following them, but they had to be going well over 100 mph because they pulled away. He turned around and thought about what they were doing on his way back. He parked his truck and heard the truck start up to pull away from the house. It was empty. It meant everything was in the house or barn.

He walked into the house, and Kali and Jessie were still working like little beavers.

"Where did you go?" Kali asked.

Toby told them about the car and what it had done the last two days.

"My dad said there had been some robberies around in the last three to four weeks," Jessie said. "The law can't seem to catch them."

"Well, that's all I need," Toby said.

"My uncle is the sheriff," Kali said. "I hope he can catch them. You might want to see if they have a description of the car."

"That is a good idea," Toby said. "I'll give him a call."

The truck with the vehicles pulled up into the drive. The guy driving it started unlocking the doors, and the girls ran to the back to see what was coming off.

"You're going to be disappointed," Toby said.

The doors opened. He looked at them, and both of their mouths dropped open.

24

"I don't know what that is, but I have never seen a car shine so much," Kali said.

"It's a Corvette, isn't it?" Jessie asked.

"Very good," Toby replied.

"My dad loves Corvettes," Jessie said. "He has an old one, but it isn't that pretty."

The mover pulled the car out. He got out and said, "Man, this is one sweet ride. It's a '67 Stingray, isn't it?"

"Yeah," Toby responded. "It was my dad's. I have tried to keep it as perfect as he had it."

The guy looked at the car and shook his head as he walked back to the truck.

"Okay, I don't know cars," Kali said. "Exactly what is it, other than a gorgeous red?"

"It is a '67 Corvette Stingray," Toby said.

"Isn't it worth quite a bit of money?" Jessie asked.

"Yeah, but I would never sell it," Toby said.

"I can understand that, since it was your dad's," Kali said.

They heard the next car start up, and it rattled the sides of the van trailer. Kali stepped up to see what it was. "Another pretty car."

Toby grinned as his '66 Chevy Malibu SS pulled out of the van. Jessie saw his grin. "Why the grin?"

"Dad and I fixed it up," Toby said. "I never lost a race in it."

"That blue paint looks a foot deep," Kali said.

The guy got out of the car. He looked at Toby and back at the car and shook his head and smiled as he walked back into the van.

"I see what is going in your garage," Kali said.

"I sure was happy to see the oversized garage attached to the house," Toby said.

The last vehicle started in the moving van, and it sounded loud too.

"You like loud cars, don't you?" Jessie asked.

"The van makes it sound louder," Toby said.

"I like loud pipes," Kali said.

Toby looked at her. "Loud pipes?"

"Yes," Kali said. "Grandad always had them on his truck until this last one."

"A truck," Jessie said.

"Yep. I fixed that one up after Dad passed away. He always wanted a '72 Chevy truck with a short wide bed, so I found one and did it in his honor," Toby said.

"It is very sharp," Jessie said. "That blue and white looks great together."

"Which one do I get to drive back to school next week?" Kali asked.

Toby looked straight ahead. "Whichever one you want to, but if you scratch it, I will take your firstborn."

They all laughed, and Toby went to drive the 'Vette into the garage. He pulled both cars into the garage and shut the doors. He turned and looked at the pickup and asked, "You girls hungry? I'll buy for helping me."

They both said they were, so he said, "Hop in the '72, and we'll run to town."

Jessie and Kali climbed in, and Toby fired it up. He revved up the engine a little to show off and then drove to the end of the drive. He stopped to shut and lock the gate. He didn't know what

Toby the Rancher

was up with the car that had been driving around, but he wasn't taking any chances.

He drove slowly to the highway, and when he turned onto the highway, Jessie asked, "Will this thing run?"

Toby didn't respond. He started normally, and when he got to 40 mph, he floored it. The girls' heads hit the rear glass, and he kept them there until he hit 120 mph. He let off and started slowing down.

"Holy cow," Kali said. "That was scary but fun. I haven't ever been in a car going that fast that quick."

"I guess I got my answer," Jessie said. "Jeez."

Toby laughed and drove within the speed limit to town. They had a late dinner and then drove back to his place. Toby let them out to get their cars and put the '72 in the barn and covered it up. He got in his dually truck and drove to Hank's to get his things from the mobile home. He took them back and unloaded them and put them in the house and headed back to get Pudge. He led Pudge out of the trailer and into his new stall. "Welcome home, boy. We are going to be here a long time. I hope you like your stall."

Toby fed and brushed Pudge before he went to the house. He looked things over to see if anything seemed to need his immediate attention. The girls had everything in good-enough shape, so he headed back to the truck to go back to Hank's to take care of some more chores. He needed to clean some stalls and wash out the feed troughs.

He worked for a couple of hours. When he walked out of the barn, he saw the same car sitting at the end of the drive. When he spotted it, he started toward his truck, and the car took off. He walked on to his truck and went home.

He was actually excited about cooking his first meal in his own house. He got things organized to his liking in his kitchen and started supper. He decided he better call Hank to let him know he was staying at his place now.

Hank told Toby he appreciated the call, but he was taking Sadie home tonight. Toby felt better about moving out and staying at his house, and even better that Sadie was doing well enough to go home. He finished supper and went to hook up his television and DVD player. He decided to watch a movie, but as he sat down, he remembered he wanted to tell Tom he was moved in, and see how he was doing.

He talked to Tom for over an hour, and he hung up feeling good about Tom. Tom was sounding like his old self. Toby walked outside to go check on Pudge in his new stall. It was starting to mist. He trotted to the barn and opened the door and turned on the light. He saw the cover was half off his '72.

Toby stopped in his tracks and started looking around to see if anything else looked off-kilter. He didn't see anything, and opened Pudge's door to check on him. He was petting Pudge when he noticed where it looked like Pudge had reared up and hit the wall with his front hooves.

"What's wrong, boy?" Toby said. "Was someone in the barn?"

Pudge snorted and seemed agitated.

"So somebody was looking at my truck. I wonder if they might still be here." Toby grabbed a pitchfork and walked around the barn, looking. He didn't find anyone but did see some footprints. He looked outside the barn and saw more footprints before the rain. He went back in and calmed Pudge down some more and then turned everything off and walked down and shut and locked his front gate.

He tried to watch a movie, but he couldn't concentrate on it. He was wondering who had gone into his barn and why. He also was thinking about all that he hoped to do with his place.

He read the Bible and said his prayer and went to bed. He lay in bed for an hour before he finally dozed off at about midnight.

Toby only slept about five hours and had breakfast cooked and eaten before 6:00 a.m. He decided to take care of his livestock first and then ride Pudge over to Hank's to take care of Hank's livestock. He enjoyed the ride over, and after finishing the chores, he went in and talked with Hank and Sadie for over an hour. He rode back home and on the way checked all the livestock in the pastures. Two of them needed more hay, so he would head back over before dark to feed hay.

He stayed busy the rest of the day doing things around his place. Kali dropped by to see how it was going. He asked her in for a cup of coffee, and she gladly accepted. He poured her a cup and set it down, and Kali asked, "Have you heard from Bethany?"

"Nope, and don't expect to either," he said.

"You must not know that her and Rob got together after they left here the other day. They are seeing each other now."

"Good for them. From what I saw, they deserve each other."

Kali laughed. "I believe you are right."

"I haven't seen Drew around," Toby commented.

"I don't know if you will. One of us has changed, and I'm not sure which one, but we just don't seem to mesh anymore."

"I'm sorry. I thought y'all had been a couple for a long while."

"We have dated since we were juniors in high school."

"Over five years?"

"Yeah, but we have broken up a bunch throughout that time."

"Oh, I see."

They sat quietly for a minute, and then Toby said, "I'm sorry I don't have something to go with the coffee. I want to try a pie in the new oven, but haven't yet."

"I can cook," Kali said. "Why don't I fix one while you do what you need to? I'll leave it on the counter when I leave for Grandad and Grandma's."

"That would be great. Thank you."

Toby mounted up and rode out to check all his fences. He spent the better part of two hours riding fences and looking at each head of cattle. He noticed he had three cows springing heavy, so he decided he would drive them to the barn so he could keep an eye on them while they calved. Once he had the cows penned up, he went in to check the house and saw the pie

Kali had left him. He locked up and walked down and shut the front gate. He got to the barn and mounted up and headed for Hank's place.

Toby went through the gate, and as he was closing it, he noticed what looked like a wolf. He knew he hadn't gotten them all, so he jumped on Pudge and took off. It was dusk, so he couldn't see very far, and he lost the sight of the wolf. He rode on to Hank's, keeping an eye out for any more wolves. He didn't see any wolves, but as he came up to the barn, he saw the car he had been seeing in the area. He rode Pudge into the barn and dismounted. He tied Pudge up and started to walk out of the barn. He stopped short when he saw two guys carrying the TV and DVD player out of the mobile home. He watched them load it up, and when they had them in the car, they pulled pistols out of the jacket pockets.

"This ain't good," Toby said to himself.

He stepped back away from the door and dialed 911, and then he got his rifle and pistol from his scabbard and saddlebag. He walked to the back door of the barn and slipped out and moved in the shadows to the back of the house. He had called 911, but those guys having guns made him very uneasy. Did they plan on using them, or were they just for effect? He needed to know.

Toby made it to the back door and looked in through the window and counted three men. He could see that they had Hank, Sadie, and Kali lying facedown on the floor. He decided to try the door, and to his surprise, it was unlocked. He slowly opened the door, and it didn't make a sound. He slipped through the door and pushed it closed, and turned the knob to latch it. He moved over in the darkness against the wall to listen.

One of the guys said, "We have gotten enough things to make this a great haul."

Another asked, "Are we going to let them live?"

The last one said, "No, we aren't. The old man has been too mouthy for my liking, and I don't want witnesses."

"Who does it, and who gets it first?" the first one asked.

The last one, who seemed to be the leader, said, "We'll decide after we have some fun with this pretty girl. Take her to the bedroom."

Toby knew he had to act and not wait, so he started trying to figure out how to do it without jeopardizing Hank's, Sadie's, or Kali's lives.

One of the guys reached down and grabbed Kali and lifted her to her feet, while the other one kept his foot on Hank's back. As they started dragging Kali to the bedroom, Sadie raised her head and said, "Please don't."

The leader kicked her in the head.

Toby had seen all he could take. He set his rifle down and grabbed his pistol and stepped out and said, "Hold it, guys."

The leader spun around to shoot, and Toby shot him between the eyes. One of the others had turned to shoot, and Toby dove to his left and shot the guy in the chest.

The last one put Kali in front of him and held his gun to her head. "Put your gun down, or I will shoot her."

Toby debated with himself on what to do. He was confident he could shoot the guy, but he only had a three-inch window past Kali. If the man moved Kali at all, Toby might hit her.

"Put it down, or she is dead!" the guy screamed.

He had barely gotten the words out when Toby shot and dropped him. The guy fell as Kali just stood there, trembling and crying. Toby ran to her and grabbed her and held her. She was sobbing badly, and he helped her to the couch so he could help Hank and Sadie. He untied Hank, and Hank untied Sadie while Toby held Kali. Sadie was conscious but had a huge bump on her forehead.

"Grandma, are you okay?" Hank asked.

"Yes." Sadie looked up at Toby. "Thank you, Toby."

Toby nodded at her. He was still holding Kali.

"Are you okay, dear?" Sadie asked Kali.

Kali was so shaken up she just nodded yes and didn't speak.

"Let's get you to the couch, Grandma," Hank said.

Toby got up and helped Hank get Sadie up and on the couch. Sadie immediately started hugging and holding Kali.

Hank looked at Toby and shook his hand. "You saved our lives, son. You are a godsend."

Sirens were heard getting close, and the cars pulled up the drive. Hank walked to the door to let the police in. He assured them things were under control. The police walked in and saw the three dead guys. They looked at Toby.

"Did you have to kill them?" one of the officers asked.

"They didn't give me any choice," Toby said.

"The court will decide that," the officer said.

Toby was stunned. Were they going to arrest him?

25

Toby realized the officer had his gun pointed at him.

"Face the wall with your arms above your head," the officer said.

Hank had gone to Sadie and Kali and was checking on Sadie's health condition and trying help Kali calm down. He hadn't heard the dialogue between Toby and the officer over Kali's sobbing and the other officers' talking while checking the bodies of the robbers. He looked around and saw Toby against the wall being searched.

Hank jumped off the couch and walked over. "What is going on here?"

"He killed three men," the officer said. "We are taking him in."

"He killed them because he had to," Hank said.

Another officer walked over to listen. The one frisking Toby said, "Nine-one-one had been called. We were on the way. We don't even know that they were dangerous."

"It's a known fact that you county guys don't typically respond very fast," Hank said. "That is why a new sheriff was just elected."

The officer didn't like what Hank said but didn't do anything but glare at him.

"Why don't you just slow down and try to listen and figure out what happened here?" Hank said. "My granddaughter is very upset, and I just brought my wife home from the hospital. They don't need you guys acting like we're the criminals." He walked back over to Sadie.

"Have him sit in the chair until we review this," the other officer said.

Luckily, the front door opened, and the county sheriff walked in.

"I'm glad you are here, James," Hank said. He had known James Dearing a long time and had unofficially campaigned for him to be elected sheriff.

James walked over to Hank and shook his hand. "Is your family okay?"

"Very shook up, but we will make it," Hank replied.

Sheriff Dearing bent down to talk to Kali. "Are you okay, Kali?"

Toby remembered that Kali had said the sheriff was her uncle. Once the sheriff had talked with Kali, he looked at Toby and asked, "Is he one of them?"

"Absolutely not," Hank said. "He works for me, and he saved our lives, and your deputies are treating him like a criminal."

"How so?" James asked.

"Putting him up against the wall and frisking him and telling him the courts will decide if he is innocent."

James looked around the room and then walked over and talked to each deputy. He walked back over to Hank. "Let's talk in the kitchen if Sadie and Kali are okay."

Hank got up and walked with him and a deputy.

Toby had been quiet and just listening and observing what was going on. He was concerned about Kali and Sadie. He knew the kick in the head Sadie had taken may have hurt her, but she was taking care of Kali. He looked at the deputy and asked, "Can someone take a look at Mrs. Parker? She just got out of the hospital for pneumonia, and took a hard kick to the forehead by one of them."

The deputy looked at Toby and then at Sadie and walked over to her. He checked her out. He found her fever had returned, and she was glassy-eyed. She had a concussion. Her forehead had a huge bump on it. The deputy told Sadie to lie down and looked at Toby and said, "Come and help her," nodding at Kali.

Toby went over and knelt down by Kali, but she wouldn't let him hug her. He just stayed by her and didn't say a word.

Meanwhile, Hank and James were discussing what had happened. Hank explained how the men had burst through the door when he went to open it and how they had them on the floor at gunpoint. He explained the kick to Sadie's head and what they were planning for Kali.

"You are very lucky he was here," James said.

Hank and James came walking out of the kitchen.

"It is apparent this young man's action saved these folks," James said. "Leave him be. Let's get this wrapped up and these bodies out as quick as possible."

Toby stood up. "Hank, we can go to my place while they take care of this."

"That would be great," Hank replied. He noticed Sadie lying down. He rushed over to her and asked what was wrong. The deputy told him, and he knelt down by her and talked with her. Toby went out to get Hank's truck pulled up so they could get in it. He helped Sadie while Hank helped Kali into the truck, and Toby drove to his place. He helped them all into the house and apologized for not having the house more comfortable.

"This is fine," Hank said. "You actually have it better than I thought you would this quickly after getting your goods."

"I have Kali and Jessie to thank for that," Toby said. "They helped me a lot." He looked at Kali as he was saying it. She didn't even acknowledge he had said her name.

"Hank, have you called Carl and Patty, and Albert and Debbie?" Toby asked.

"No, I haven't," Hank said. "And I better get that done."

Hank called them while Toby was putting on a pot of coffee and fixing some tea.

Toby walked back into the living room and said, "I am going to take my truck and go get Pudge and ride him back home. Y'all make yourselves at home. I put coffee and tea on if you want something to drink. I'll be back in thirty to forty minutes."

He walked out and got into his truck and headed to Hank's. He was concerned about Kali. He knew she was scared about tonight, but two big frights in a few days may have messed her up. He pulled up and got out and started walking to the barn, but he remembered he had left his rifle in the house, so he walked to the house. He walked through the door, and the deputy asked, "What are you doing back here?"

"I came to get my horse, but remembered I left my rifle in the breakfast nook," Toby said.

"Your rifle?" the deputy replied. "You were really planning on some killing, weren't you?"

"I didn't know what was going on inside, so I just brought both guns."

"If you don't live here, how is it you had two firearms with you?"

Sheriff Dearing walked out of the kitchen and stood, listening.

"I always carry my rifle and pistol when I am riding out checking the cows," Toby said. "I have had too many situations with wolves, cougars, and hogs to not carry them."

"Cougars?" Sheriff Dearing said. "There aren't any cougars around here."

"I worked in New Mexico, and they had them there," Toby said.

"We don't have wolves either," the deputy said.

Toby the Rancher

Toby had walked to where his rifle was, and he picked it up. "I killed a dozen a couple of days ago, so I'd say we do."

The deputy started to argue, but the sheriff said, "I had heard we had some wolves in the area. How are Hank and Sadie? How is Kali?"

"Still very shook up." Toby said. He walked out and got Pudge and headed out through the pastures. He spotted something moving in the darkness and swung his flashlight in that direction. It was another wolf. He pulled his rifle and tried to take aim with the light. The wolf had stopped and was growling at Pudge. Toby got his aim to where he felt good about it and squeezed the trigger. The wolf dropped. Toby hooked a rope to it and dragged it off to a gully, figuring he would bury it in the morning.

He rode to the gate and went through and rode on to his barn. He noticed several vehicles parked at his house when he rode up but didn't try to figure out who they belonged to. He put Pudge up and walked out of the barn to see flashing lights. He saw that it was a police car, and several people were on his porch.

Toby walked toward them with his rifle in his hand, and the deputy pulled out his gun and pointed it at him, and yelled, "Drop your weapon!"

Toby stopped. "What is going on?"

Another police car pulled up the drive.

"I said drop your weapon," the deputy repeated.

Sheriff Dearing got out of his car and hollered, "Stand down, Mac."

"He has a gun," the deputy said.

The sheriff walked over to Toby. "Why do you have the rifle?"

"I was taking it to the house," Toby said. "I don't leave it in the barn overnight."

The sheriff looked at the deputy, and the deputy lowered his pistol and turned away.

"We heard shooting in the pasture," the sheriff said. "What was it?"

Hank had walked over by Toby, and Toby said, "I saw a wolf and shot it."

The deputy spouted off, "Then where is it?"

Toby looked at him and started to speak, but the sheriff spoke, "It would seem that you would bring it in if you shot a wolf."

"We bury them," Hank said. "We don't bring them in."

"Then that shows he poached a deer," the deputy said. "He didn't have time to bury it."

"If I shot a deer, I wouldn't have had time to field dress it either," Toby said.

"Did you bury it?" the sheriff asked.

"No, I didn't have a shovel," Toby said. "I dragged it over in a wash until morning." He looked at the deputy. "I'll be happy to take you out and show it to you."

The deputy walked to his car and left.

"Sorry to bother you with this in light of what went on tonight," Sheriff Dearing said. "Hank, we are still working at your house."

"Not a problem," Hank said. "Toby said we could stay here." James waved to Carl and said, "I hope Kali is okay."

"Thanks," Carl replied. "Tell my sis hello."

James got in his car and left.

Toby and Hank stood and watched until he left.

"That deputy sure seems bent on pinning something on you," Hank said.

Toby nodded. "I hope I don't ever see him again."

They walked toward the porch, and Carl said, "You are always stirring things up, aren't you, Toby?"

Toby looked at him and walked on up the porch and into the house.

Carl followed him in and continued, "You need to stay away from my daughter. You have nearly got her killed twice."

"What?" Toby asked as he stopped and turned around.

Hank walked in and said, "Carl, you need to take a walk. You are not thinking straight."

"I'm not going anywhere until my family is ready," Carl said. "This guy just attracts trouble, and you won't accept that."

"You are in my house," Toby said. "Do not come in here and start throwing around wild accusations. You can stay for Kali, but only if you are quiet." He turned to walk to his bedroom.

"Don't try to tell me what to do," Carl said.

Toby walked on and shut the door behind him. He heard talking going on in the living room. He changed his clothes and washed up. He heard a car start as he opened his bedroom door. He walked into the living room and saw Patty, Debbie, and Albert there with Hank and Sadie. Carl and Kali had left.

"I apologize for not speaking when I came in," Toby said. "Can I get anything for any of you?"

"We are fine, Toby," Albert said. "But thanks."

Toby looked at Sadie and asked, "How are you doing?"

Sadie smiled. "I'm okay, sweetie."

"Thanks to you," Hank said.

Toby looked at Patty and asked, "How is Kali?"

"Not good," Patty said. "I wanted to make sure Mom is okay, but I need to get home to her. I do apologize for Carl's behavior. He is upset and took it out on you."

Toby ignored what she said about Carl. "I know she has had two bad incidents. I hope she will be okay."

He walked into the kitchen and sat down at the table with a cup of coffee. He hadn't allowed himself to think about what had happened, but it hit him like a ton of bricks, sitting there. He had killed three men. He didn't know how to deal with that. He felt more than justified in his actions, but he had taken three lives. He had to live with that, but would it haunt him? He sure hoped not.

Debbie and Patty both walked into the kitchen and thanked him for saving their parents and Kali.

"I am just glad I was there to help," Toby said.

They left. Toby helped Hank and Sadie to their bedroom, and he sat down to drink a cup of coffee and eat a piece of the pie

Kali had made. He went to bed at midnight and finally dozed off at 1:15 a.m. He was up at 5:00 a.m. and got ready and went on out and tended to his stock. He came back in at around 6:45 a.m. and started breakfast.

Hank and Sadie came in at about the time he got everything ready. They sat and ate without anyone saying much. When they finished, Toby started cleaning up the dishes.

"Let me do that," Sadie said.

"No, ma'am," Toby said. "You are my guest."

She sat down, and he finished them.

"Y'all stay here as long as you need," Toby said. "I am heading over to your place to feed, and bury the wolf."

Toby went out and saddled Pudge and rode out. He stopped on the way and buried the wolf. He rode and checked the pastures and saw that two of the herds were low on hay, so he needed to get hay out there to them. He rode into the barnyard and saw a deputy car sitting just up the drive. He led Pudge in the barn and tied him up and got the tractor key to start feeding hay to the pastures. He started the tractor, and the deputy came driving up and got out.

"What are you doing?" he asked.

"Feeding the livestock," Toby said.

"Okay," the deputy said. "Just didn't see you come up."

Toby finished the feeding and headed home. He got back and started doing some odds and ends. He walked out of the barn and saw Patty's car pull up. Toby was happy to see Kali with her. Patty waved at him, but Kali never looked his way. He was worried. Did she blame him, or had she retreated into a shell?

Jessie came pulling in as Patty and Kali reached the porch. She waved at Toby and then went into the house. Toby went back to work and was nailing some boards when he heard, "Hey, good-looking."

He turned and saw Jessie in the barn door.

"How are you?" she asked.

"I'm okay. Just worried about Hank and Sadie, and especially Kali."

"Kali seems okay this morning."

"That's good." But Toby didn't buy it. She wouldn't even look his way.

"We are going to go ahead and head back to school early," Jessie said. "I just wanted to say bye."

"Thank you," Toby said. "Drive safe."

Jessie hugged his neck, and they walked out. Kali was loading her stuff into the car and never looked in Toby's direction. They drove off, leaving Toby scratching his head.

26

Toby walked to the house, and as he walked up on the porch, Hank, Sadie, and Patty were walking out the door.

"Toby, we appreciate your hospitality," Hank said. "But it is time to go home."

"You're welcome, and you are welcome to stay longer if needed," Toby answered.

"Sadie wants to get home and get her house in order. Did you see the girls leave for college?" Hank said.

"Yeah," Toby said. "Jessie came out to the barn and saw me and told me they were going back early."

"Kali felt like it would help her to get back in a routine," Patty said.

"School is out, so there is no routine," Sadie said. "Carl just wanted her away from Toby."

"Mother!" Patty exclaimed. "That's not true."

"Patty, you know it is, and this young man has done nothing wrong," Sadie countered. "In fact, he has done everything right where she is concerned."

"All right, ladies," Hank said. "Let's stop arguing and get going."

"Everything is good on your ranch," Toby said.

"Thank you," Hank said. "See you later."

Toby the Rancher

Toby watched them get in the vehicles and waved as they drove off. He walked into the house to get a cup of coffee and a piece of pie. Toby thought about last night and Kali while he ate his pie. He decided the best thing he could do was stay busy, and he had enough plans to do that. He got the supplies he needed and strapped them on the back of the saddle to go check and fix some fence.

When he rode into the far pasture, he saw that a cow was calving and was surprised. She hadn't bagged up at all, but he hoped she would come to her milk once the calf was born. He started working on a fence that was close enough to the cow for him to keep an eye on her. Luckily, she had the calf with no problem.

Toby finished tightening the stretch of fence he was working on and rode over to see his new calf. It was a bull, and he had decided he would try banding the new bull calves rather than castrating them later. The problem was that he didn't have any bands or a tool to put them on. He needed feed, so he fixed one more fence and then headed to town to get feed, ear tags, and bands. He shut and locked everything and headed into town. He went into the feed store and bought the things he needed and then stopped at a convenience store to get a cup of coffee. When he walked out of the store, the deputy sheriff who had given him a hard time after the shooting was standing behind his truck.

"Afternoon, Deputy," Toby said.

"Start your vehicle," the deputy said. "I need to check it out."

"What's the problem?"

"Just start it up."

Toby was getting agitated but knew it was best to go along for now. He started his truck.

"Rev up the engine," the deputy said.

Toby gave it some gas and then let off.

"More!" the deputy said.

Toby figured the deputy was looking for anything to get him, but he couldn't avoid what he asked. He revved the truck up some more and then killed it.

"Your exhaust is illegal," the deputy said.

"I beg to differ, Barney," Toby said. "I have had them checked in four states, and they have passed every time."

"This is Texas, and not some other state. They aren't legal here."

"Texas is one of the states I had it checked in, Barney."

The deputy didn't speak for a minute and then said, "Well, you better keep it down, or I will write you up."

"Yes, sir, Barney, sir."

The deputy started to walk to his car and then turned and said, "By the way, my name isn't Barney. You call me Officer from now on."

Toby smiled. "Okay, Officer, but Barney fits."

The deputy got in his car and Toby in his truck, and they drove off their separate ways. Toby was thinking about the deputy and wondering why he seemed to take such an interest in him when all others said he was in the right with his actions. He drove back home and unloaded the feed and then rode out to band the new calf. The calf was spirited and didn't stand and wait for Toby to get it, so he got his rope loose, mounted Pudge, and caught the calf. Toby roped it and tied it so he could band it. The momma cow was not real happy about the calf being bothered and especially tied down. Luckily, Toby had loosened the rope, and Pudge stayed between the cow and Toby.

Toby smiled and shook his head. "We've been together a good while, and you still continue to amaze me. Thank you, my friend."

Toby rode back to the barn and put Pudge in his stall. He brushed, fed, and watered Pudge. He decided to text Jessie and see how Kali was doing.

Jessie responded that Kali was still shook up. Jessie hoped Kali would get better when school started.

"Did you hear that Bethany and Rob are an item now?" she added.

"No, I didn't," Toby responded. "I'm sorry."

"I'm not," Jessie texted back. "They deserve each other. I have my eye on someone else, anyway."

Toby the Rancher

"Okay," Toby sent back. "Good luck with that. Please keep me updated on Kali. I feel responsible to a degree."

He decided to run down to Hank's and check on everything before he called it a day. He pulled into the drive and saw Albert and Debbie's car in front of the house. With everything that had happened this week, he had forgotten that Tim was in town. He felt bad, because he had promised to do more with him.

Toby pulled to the barn and checked all the livestock and feed. He noted they would need more feed by Monday. He pulled his truck back to the house and left it running while he walked up to see how Sadie was doing. Tim opened the door when Toby knocked and said with a grin, "Hello, Toby."

"Hello, Tim. How you doing, bud?"

"Bored."

"Poor baby," Debbie said. "So mistreated."

"Everything okay, Toby?" Hank asked.

"Yeah," Toby said. "We will need feed Monday. I just wanted to see how Sadie was doing."

"I'm doing fine," Sadie said. "How are you?"

Toby smiled. "Doing well, ma'am."

"Toby, can I go with you?" Tim asked.

"Tim, you are out of line," Albert said.

"That is up to your parents," Toby told Tim. "You are more than welcome to come with me."

"That really helps Toby," Albert said.

"I'm sorry," Toby said. "I just wanted Tim to know he was welcome at my house."

"Can I spend the night?" Tim asked.

"Timothy, you need to slow down," Debbie said.

Nobody said anything for a while, then Toby said, "It's okay with me, if it is with you folks."

Debbie and Albert looked at each other. Both shrugged.

"Okay," Debbie said. "But you had better be good, and careful."

Tim jumped up and down from excitement.

"You don't have any pajamas," Debbie said.

"I can let him sleep in one of my shirts," Toby said.

Toby and Tim left and made it home right before dark. Tim wanted to see Pudge, so they went out and spent some time with him. Toby told Tim about the calf and what Pudge did to protect Toby from the cow. Tim was wide-eyed listening to the story. They went into the house and had supper and spent the rest of the evening watching movies.

The next day, Toby was up early. He sat and drank coffee until 6:00 a.m. He was thinking over the last few days and planning what he needed to get done today.

Tim came walking into the kitchen and broke Toby's train of thought.

Toby turned and said, "Good mornin'. You ready for some breakfast?"

Tim grinned. "Yes, sir."

"Do you like pancakes?"

"Yep."

"Pancakes it is then."

Toby fixed Tim two big pancakes, an egg, and bacon. Tim ate every bite of it. They finished breakfast and went to the barn to start the chores. Toby saddled Pudge and climbed on and looked at Tim. He was down in the mouth because he didn't have a horse.

Tim started to sit down on a bale of hay but brightened up when Toby said, "There's a stirrup. Climb on up."

Tim climbed on behind Toby, and they went and checked the cattle and new baby calf. Toby spotted a coyote and was able to shoot it before it could get away. He decided to try and find some guard donkeys to put with his cattle to protect the calves at least.

They rode back up to the barn at about 8:30 a.m. Albert and Debbie pulled up to the front gate. Toby rode down to open the gate for them. Tim climbed down and unlocked and opened the gate and started walking toward the house. Toby noticed Tim's mood had changed, and figured Tim didn't like seeing his parents come this early.

Albert pulled to the house, and Toby dismounted and tied Pudge up to a tree limb. "Mornin', Albert."

"Good morning," Albert said. "We have come to get Tim so we can head home."

Toby never figured they were leaving for home. Tim must have known. Tim walked up and hugged Toby around the waist. "Bye, Toby. I had a great time."

Toby's eyes welled up. "I had a great time too. Maybe you can come back during the summer and we can do it again."

Debbie was standing outside the car too. Toby glanced at her, and she said, "Thank you for everything. Please continue to look out for Dad and Mom."

Toby replied, "It will be my pleasure."

Albert shook Toby's hand, and they loaded up and drove off. Toby looked at Pudge. "I don't like those kinds of good-byes, pard. Let me drink a cup, and then we'll head over to Hank's."

He finished his coffee and walked out of the house, and saw a deputy sheriff car sitting at the end of his drive. He climbed up and rode toward the pasture and over to Hank's place. He wondered what the car was doing there but didn't give it much thought. He figured it was just a patrol after what had happened. He rode and checked all the cattle in the pastures before he rode to Hank's barn. He noticed Hank had two new calves. He was feeding the bulls and horses when Hank walked into the barn.

"Good morning, Toby," Hank greeted.

"Good mornin'," Toby replied. "You have two new calves in the middle pasture this morning."

"That's good," Hank said. "I sure hope all the wolves are gone."

"Yeah, me too," Hank said. "I did shoot a coyote this morning that was hanging around my new calf." He told Hank about the calf and how Pudge had protected him.

"I never cease to be amazed by both you and your horse," Hank said.

"Thank you." Toby poured a bucket of feed and then said, "I think I am going to try and find some guard donkeys. You ever use any?"

"No, but I would like to have some if you find more than you need."

Toby agreed to look, and he mounted up and headed back to his place. He rode into his barn and put Pudge in his stall, and when he walked out of the barn, the deputy sheriff car was in front of his house. He didn't know what to think, but he walked back into the barn and got his pistol out of his saddlebag and stuck it in his belt under his jacket. He walked up to the house and saw no one was in the car. He looked up and saw his front door was open. He knew he had locked it, so he backed off and stood on the side of the house and called Hank to tell him what was going on. Hank told him he would be right over.

Toby walked back to the barn to wait for Hank. He stood where he could see the house, and he never saw the deputy come out. Hank came pulling in rather fast and slammed on his brakes. Toby walked toward the house as Hank piled out.

The deputy came running out of the house with his gun drawn. He looked at Hank and said, "I thought you were the other one."

"Who, me?" Toby hollered.

The deputy spun and shot at Toby. Luckily, Toby dove behind a tree when the deputy spun around his way with the gun.

"Are you out of your mind?" Hank yelled.

Toby was crouched behind the tree, and the deputy had turned back toward Hank. Toby pointed his gun and hollered, "Drop your weapon."

The deputy realized he was cooked, and stopped. He lowered his gun and dropped it to the ground.

Toby walked out from behind the tree, and Hank said, "You better sit down on the porch, Deputy."

They heard a siren, and the sheriff came pulling in. He jumped out of the car and asked, "What in the world is going on here?"

Toby the Rancher

Hank proceeded to tell him what had gone down. James turned to his deputy and asked, "What do you have to say?"

The deputy just stared at the ground.

Toby walked up on the porch and looked at the door facing he had busted by kicking it in. James walked up and looked at it and then looked at Toby and said, "I don't know what to say. This is the most ridiculous thing I have ever seen."

Toby glanced at the house and said, "That may match it."

The sheriff looked in and saw that the deputy had trashed Toby's house.

Toby walked in and went through his house. He walked back out on the porch and said, "You better get him out of here before I decide going to jail would be worth beating him to a pulp."

"I know you are upset, but you need to calm down," James said.

Toby looked at James with contempt in his eyes, and James said, "All right, I'll put him in the car."

Another deputy came pulling up into the drive as James was putting the deputy in the backseat. The new deputy got out and asked James what was going on. James relayed the events, and the deputy said, "I did find out that one of the guys that was shot at the Parkers was his cousin."

James's head jerked around. "Why wasn't I told about that?"

"I just found out last night," the deputy said.

"You do realize this was attempted murder," Hank said.

"You are out of your mind," the deputy said. "All he did was bust his place up."

"You need to be quiet," James said. "You don't know all that went on."

"James, I am losing confidence in your staff real fast," Hank said.

The deputy spun around and said, "Old man, I'll kick your rear."

Toby jumped off the porch. "Just try it."

"Settle down," James told his deputy. He looked at Hank and Toby. "You two get up on the porch."

"Before you get hurt," the deputy spouted off.

Toby was walking back to the porch and stopped in his tracks and turned around. Hank took hold of Toby's arm and pulled him toward the steps. "Let it go, son. There are other ways to deal with that."

The deputy came storming toward the porch, yelling, "Old man, you have a big mouth."

James tried to stop the deputy, but the deputy shoved James down and was pulling his pistol when Toby dove off the porch and knocked the deputy off his feet. The deputy started to point his gun at Toby, but Toby kicked it out of the deputy's hand. They hadn't noticed that he had opened the door of James's car and the other deputy had gotten out. James had broken his arm when he had fallen over the landscape timbers. He was trying to get up, but the bone was sticking out of his forearm.

"Toby, look out," Hank hollered.

The deputy who had gotten out do the car was running toward him. Toby jumped back and kicked the deputy in the stomach as he got to him. The other deputy had gotten to his feet and squared off with Toby and said, "I'm going to enjoy this."

"You must enjoy getting whipped," Toby said.

The deputy swung, and Toby blocked it and nailed him with a right cross. He turned to block another punch from the first deputy and punched him hard in the stomach. The two blows to the stomach caused the deputy to start throwing up, so Toby turned back to the other deputy and proceeded to give him a boxing lesson. He beat on him like a punching bag until the deputy dropped and couldn't get back up.

Toby walked over and helped James to his feet.

"You handle yourself well," James said.

Hank walked up to them. "James, I called an ambulance, and now I'm calling the Texas Rangers to get your deputies."

"I don't know what to say," James said. "I will probably be the shortest-termed sheriff in history."

"You inherited these bums," Hank said. "People can't hold that against you. You can get your own deputies now."

The ambulance came and got James, but it was over an hour before the Rangers arrived. They heard what went on and looked at Toby's house. They loaded the deputies up and left.

Hank looked at Toby. "I am so sorry for all that has happened. I will help you get everything fixed."

"You don't have to do that," Toby said.

"All of this happened because you saved us, so yes, I do need to help."

"Thank you for coming and helping today. I guess I better clean some of the mess up before I go look for donkeys."

"I'll help you," Hank said.

"You need to be there for Sadie," Toby said. "I can get this."

"Momma is stronger than both of us. She is back going strong."

"She is a jewel."

They cleaned up some, and then Toby hooked on the trailer and headed to Ridge's, and Hank headed home.

27

Toby pulled into Ridge's drive and was surprised to see Jessie's car sitting there. He couldn't help but wonder what was going on. Ridge was in the barn and came walking out to meet Toby. As Toby stepped out of his truck, Ridge said, "Hello, Toby. What brings you by?"

Toby replied, "I am looking for some guard donkeys and wondered if you might know anyone that has some for sale."

"It just so happens my neighbor has some. You want to run over there?"

"Yes, sir."

They both climbed into Toby's truck. As he backed up to turn around, Jessie came walking out of the house. She heard the truck and looked their way and was surprised to see Toby. He could tell she wasn't expecting to see him. He stopped and rolled the window down. "I didn't know you were coming back."

She hesitated and then said, "Kali decided she wanted to see her mom and grandparents."

"How is she doing?"

"Still struggling."

"Maybe I'll see her."

"I don't think she wants to see you."

That stunned Toby. He didn't know what to say. He just nodded at Jessie and pulled away.

Ridge could tell that the statement bothered Toby. "Son, don't let that bother you. You have nothing to be sorry about. She will come around."

Toby didn't speak. He just looked straight ahead and drove. They pulled in and parked at the house of Ridge's neighbor, and Toby was impressed with the barn and corrals. He had never driven that direction before, and so he hadn't seen it. "Wow, what a nice place."

Ridge laughed. "Yeah. He had some money to start, and he has done well. He is a very nice guy, and hasn't let the money change him."

"Where did he get his money?"

"From his wife's family. She was an only child, and her parents both died young, leaving her a fortune."

"What is his name?" Toby asked.

"Ryder Weber," Ridge replied as they walked to the barn.

"Hello, Ridge," someone said as Toby and Ridge walked into the barn.

"Hello, Ryder," Ridge said. "What you got going on?"

"Have a mare foaling," Ryder replied. "She is carrying the embryo of our top stallion and mare, so we are giving her special attention."

"Is that the stallion you lost?"

"Yep. That is why we have four embryos in four of our lesser mares. What brings you by, and who is the cowboy with you?"

"This is Toby Parker, and he is looking for some guard donkeys," Ridge said. "I told him you might have some."

"Are you the one working for Hank Parker?" Ryder asked Toby.

"Yes, sir," Toby replied.

"It's good to meet you. Hank speaks highly of you."

"Thank you. You have a nice place."

"Thanks. You ride much?"

"All the time. Why?"

"He is the one that broke the mare I bought for Jake," Ridge chimed in. "He knows his stuff."

"That's good," Ryder said. "You interested in some work?"

"Not sure at this point," Toby replied. "Helping run two ranches right now."

"Hank's and whose?"

"Mine."

"You have a ranch around here?"

"I just bought the Glover place."

"That's good," Ryder said. "So you are running your own place and helping Hank on his? You probably don't need any extra work, do you?"

"It keeps me busy, but what kind of work are you talking about?"

"I need to bring in my cattle and vaccinate them."

"How long do you think it would take?"

"Usually four to five days minimum."

Toby was surprised. "How many head do you have?"

"Close to a thousand."

"Wow."

Ryder laughed. "You'll get there one day. Starting as young as you are and not afraid of work."

"Don't know 'bout that, but I appreciate the thought," Toby said. "I would like to try and help you. Not sure I could give you the amount of time you need, though."

"If you are as good as Ridge says, I'll take whatever you can offer," Ryder said. "Can't find good help anymore. Especially part-time help that knows horses and cattle."

"When you wanting to start?" Toby asked.

"In the morning," Ryder said.

Toby thought for a minute and then said, "I can probably be here by 10:00 at the latest."

"Sounds good."

"Now the reason we are here."

Ryder and Ridge started laughing, and Ryder asked, "What was the reason you came?"

"I was needing to buy some guard donkeys," Toby replied.

"I think we can help you out. How many you need?"

Toby smiled. "We need four. How much are they?"

"Fifty dollars a piece," Ryder said. "And if you want them, we can work it out of your wages, if you like."

"That would be great," Toby said. "I'll pick them up tomorrow afternoon, if that is okay."

"That'll work."

Toby and Ridge started for the truck, and Ryder said, "You can ride one of my horses."

"I would rather ride mine, if you don't mind," Toby replied.

"No problem, if that is what you wish," Ryder said.

Toby drove Ridge home and thanked him for taking him to Ryder's. He headed back to Hank's to talk to him about the donkeys and the job with Ryder. He pulled up into the drive and saw Jessie's car. He started to turn around but decided to just drive on to the barn. He went in and did some make busy work, trying to wait and see if Kali and Jessie would leave. He didn't notice Jessie walking in. She walked up behind him and said, "Toby, I'm sorry."

Toby jumped from being caught off guard. He turned toward her. "For what?"

"For being so short and hateful when I said Kali didn't want to see you."

"Don't worry about it. I just hope she can put it all behind her."

Hank walked in, and Jessie said, "I better get back to the house."

"Any luck on the donkeys?" Hank asked Toby.

"Yeah," Toby said. "I got us four from Ryder Weber."

"I don't know why I didn't think of him. He has quite a place, doesn't he?"

"Yes, sir. He asked me to help with his roundup. I hope you don't mind if I help part-time."

"Not all at. I know you need the money, and I have no doubt you will take care of things correctly."

"Okay, thanks. Please let me know if you feel I'm slacking off."

Toby started to walk to his truck, and Hank said, "Toby, son, I don't know what to tell you about Kali. Her dad is filling her head with wrong thoughts, and you seem to be the brunt of them."

"Don't worry about it," Toby said. "I figure it must be telling me to stick to my own business."

"I know you two were getting close, and nothing could please Sadie and I more."

"I'm sorry." Toby walked to his truck and left. He took care of Pudge and went to the house to fix supper. He ate supper and decided to watch some *Cheyenne*. He knew it would keep his mind off the trouble of the week. He couldn't believe how a week that seemed to start so good had gone totally upside down by the end.

He watched four episodes of *Cheyenne* and fell asleep on the couch.

He woke up at 4:30 a.m. and decided to get his day going. He finished breakfast and had Pudge saddled by 5:45 a.m. He fed all his cattle and then hooked onto his horse trailer so he could take Pudge and bring the donkeys home. He rode over to Hank's and had his feeding done and pastures checked, and he was back at his place by 8:30 a.m. He went in and drank his last cup in his pot and then headed to Ryder's.

Toby pulled in at 9:00 a.m., and Ryder was just leading his horse out of the barn. Toby pulled up and asked Ryder where he needed to park. Ryder led his horse over while Toby was unloading Pudge.

Ryder looked Pudge over while Toby was checking the cinch. "That is a good-looking horse. Where did you get him?"

"I got him when I lived in Pennsylvania," Toby replied. "I bought him while I was in high school."

"Have you worked cattle with him much?" Ryder asked.

Toby smiled. "A whole bunch."

The other three hands had gathered around with their horses, and one of the guys, named Gavin Small, said, "I recognize you. You won the bulldogging and bronc riding in Fort Worth."

Ryder was looking at Gavin as Gavin spoke, and then he turned back to Toby and asked, "Is that right?"

Toby nodded. "Yeah, I needed the money."

They all laughed and, Gavin said, "You may have just needed the money, but from what I saw, you can definitely cowboy up."

"Sounds good," Ryder said. "Let me get Sam, and we'll be on our way."

Toby got everything ready and stepped into the stirrup and swung into the saddle. He started to pull on the reins to turn Pudge around when he heard a girl's voice say, "I'm ready, Daddy."

Toby glanced over his shoulder to see a girl in jeans, chaps, a jacket, a hat, and boots with spurs.

She looks the part, he thought.

"Sam, come over here and meet Toby," Ryder said.

Sam walked over, and Toby leaned down from the saddle to shake her hand. "Pleased to meet you, ma'am."

Sam grinned. "Wow, a cowboy gentleman. That takes my breath away."

Toby laughed.

"Seriously, it is nice to meet you," Sam said. "Looking forward to seeing you work. Heard a lot about you."

"Not sure what to think about that," Toby said.

"Jessie speaks highly."

Toby tipped his hat to Sam and rode to join the other hands. She was cute but didn't worry about trying to show it. She was dressed for work.

I like her already. He caught himself smiling.

Ryder rode up beside him. "We will go to the closest pasture first. I want to see how everyone works before we start trying to bring in the difficult herds."

Toby wondered what Ryder meant by difficult but didn't give it a lot of thought. He noticed a horse siding him and looked to his right to see Sam's horse's head even with his leg. She moved on up beside him and rode looking straight ahead.

They reached the first pasture gate, and one of the hands got off to open it. As they started through, Sam said, "We have eighty-three head in the pasture."

Toby was impressed. She knew what was going on with the ranch. They all rode out and spotted the cows and started gathering them up. Toby spotted something over in the trees and rode over to check it out. Sam saw him going that way and watched to see if he needed help. There were four head, and they didn't want to leave the area. Toby and Pudge put on a show moving them out with the others.

When they reached the herd, Ryder said, "Nice work. I see why you wanted your own mount."

"That was almost as good as Blue and me could have done," Sam said.

Toby looked over at her. She was smiling, and winked at him.

"I hope to see that," Toby said.

"You will, big boy," Sam said. "You will."

The cows moved on out of the pasture and up to the corral. When they had them penned, Ryder said, "We will start working these while Sam, Toby, and Joe go get pasture number 2."

"Sounds good," Sam said. She wheeled Blue around and took off.

Toby and Joe rode to catch up to her, and Joe said, "Slow down, girl. This old man likes to sit in my saddle, not bounce around on it."

Toby knew Joe looked like an older fellow but didn't know how old.

"Joe, your seventy-year-old bones are stronger than mine!" Sam hollered, laughing.

Toby wondered, Was Joe really seventy, or was Sam just shooting a number out?

They rode on to the second pasture, and Toby got off and opened the gate. He grabbed the saddle horn and swung into the saddle without using the stirrup, and Joe said, "There was a time I could do that, sonny."

"I doubt that," Sam said.

"Didn't your dad teach you to respect your elders?" Joe said.

Toby chuckled and rode toward some cattle he saw. Sam caught up to him, and they begin moving the cattle toward the gate. "How many should we have?"

"One hundred two in this one," Sam replied.

They tried counting, and all three of them kept coming up one short.

"I'll go check the rest of the pasture," Toby said. He rode off to look while Sam and Joe kept the herd moving. He rode into a patch of woods and spotted the heifer. She was in a pickle. Somehow, she had gotten in a washed-out gully and couldn't get up. From the looks of the ground around the gully and her tired condition, she had been trying for a good while.

Toby didn't figure he could get her out by himself, so he turned Pudge around and rode to catch up with Sam. He relayed what he had found, and Sam grabbed her phone. He listened as she spoke. "Dad, we have a problem. There's a heifer down in a wash. Could you send one of the guys out to help Joe bring the herd in? And I'll go with Toby to try and get her up." She hung up the phone. "Let's go." She took off for the trees.

Toby spurred Pudge, and he ran up beside Sam. She smiled and kicked Blue, and she started going faster.

"Show her how to run, Pudge," Toby said.

They pulled up beside her and went on past with ease. He slowed to ride up to the heifer. They got there and sat on the horses, looking at the heifer and contemplating what to do.

"Man, that horse can run," Sam said.

"Yeah, he doesn't like to lose," Toby replied.

"And I have an idea neither does the rider."

Toby laughed. "Ya got that right. What do you figure we need to do here?"

"Not sure. Any ideas?"

Toby explained that he thought taking both horses and tying the ropes on the saddle horns and having both horses pull while he tried to help from the rear was their best option. Sam could have the reins and help the horses know to pull.

"Let's give it a go," Sam said.

They worked for a while but finally got the heifer out. She was very weak and wobbly, so they didn't want to push her. They sat and watched her for a while, and then Toby said, "Let's see if she can walk over to the water. I'm sure she needs a drink."

They were watching her drink and try to stand.

"Are you of kin to the Parkers?" Sam asked.

"Nope," Toby said. "Just the same name."

"Where you from?"

"Pennsylvania."

"A Pennsylvania cowboy. I doubt there are a lot of them. How did you become one?"

"My dad loved Westerns and got me hooked. I loved watching *Cheyenne*."

"I love that show too. He was a true cowboy gentleman."

"Yup. Where do you go to school?"

"I graduated college last year with a degree in farm and ranch management." Sam paused and then asked, "How did you wind up in Texas?"

"Last year, I was working in New Mexico," Toby said. "That played out, so I came this way to try and find a ranch job."

"Your folks still live up there?"

"Nah. My dad passed away about six years ago."

"And your mom?"

Toby hesitated. "Dad's wife had already passed away when he adopted me."

Sam's head jerked sideways to look at him. She waited a minute and then said, "I'm adopted too."

Toby looked at her. "Seriously?"

"Yep," Sam said. "When I was nine years old. How old were you?"

"I was twelve."

They talked a little bit more about their childhood similarities, and then Toby said, "She looks like she can go now. Want to try it?"

"Yeah, let's give it a go."

They started moving the cow toward the gate so they could get her in and move to another pasture. They reached the corral, and Ryder asked, "How is she doing?"

"She is getting her strength back," Sam said.

"How did you get her out?" he asked.

"Toby tied both ropes around her neck, and I had both horses pulling on her as he pushed her from behind."

Ryder looked at Toby. "Nice work. I think we have all we can do today. Let's work on these and push them back to their pastures."

Toby and Sam dismounted. Toby started working the corral and moving cows into the lane while Sam helped her dad with the vaccinations. They finished up at around 4:15 p.m. Toby and Joe moved the herd to the new pasture and then rode back into the barnyard.

Toby dismounted and walked Pudge to the trailer to load him up.

"Toby, come and get a beer," Ryder hollered.

"No thanks," Toby replied. "I don't drink." He loaded Pudge and walked over to talk to Ryder. "I guess I'll get going. I need to check things at home and Hank's before it gets too late."

Sam walked up behind him. "Leaving already, cowboy?"

Toby turned to her. "Yes, ma'am. It was nice meeting you and working with you."

"Same here," Sam said. "You want a soda before you go?"

"Nah," he said. "I hear my coffeepot calling me."

They all bid Toby farewell, and he headed home. He decided to go to Hank's first and check on things since he had Pudge saddled in the trailer if he needed him. He pulled up into the drive and saw cars sitting at the house. He pulled on past them and parked by the barn. He was checking the feed and water when Hank walked in and asked, "How did it go at Ryder's?"

"Pretty good," Toby replied. "Got about two hundred head taken care of today."

"You didn't need to come back and check on things here," Hank said. "I could have done it."

"I need to earn my pay. Besides, you have enough to deal with right now."

"I guess I'll get back in for supper. I wish I could invite you, but I'm afraid it would cause issues. I am sorry."

"Don't worry about it," Toby replied. "I need to get on home, anyway. I'll see you tomorrow."

When he got home, he took care of things in the barn and put Pudge up for the day. He went and started making a sandwich for supper, and his phone rang. He answered it.

It was Sam. "I got your number from Jessie. I hope you don't mind."

"Nah, that's fine," Toby replied. "What's up?"

"I wanted to call and tell you what time we were starting in the morning. Dad said we would head out about 9:00."

"I won't be able to be there until I get out of church. That should put me there around noon."

"Dad isn't going to like that."

"I'm sorry, but that is how it is. If he doesn't want me to come then or continue helping, just let me know."

"Okay, I will tell him."

Toby figured he was through working for the Webers. He was eating his sandwich and looking at a magazine when his phone rang again. "Hello?"

"Toby, this is Sheriff James Dearing."

"Yes, sir," Toby replied. "How can I help you?"

"I just wanted to call and tell you that we won't need your testimony. The DA said that mine would be enough to lock the two deputies up for a good while."

"That's good. I appreciate you calling. How is your arm?"

"It hurts some, but the surgery and pins they put in should help it to work fine in a few months."

"That's good. Sheriff, I have another call coming in."

"I'll catch you later," James said, and hung up.

Toby answered the call and heard Sam say, "Dad said that would be fine. You're too good with horses and cattle to not use."

"Okay. I will see you tomorrow around noon." Toby hung up and thought about the call from the sheriff. He was very glad he could put that incident behind him, or at least that part of it. The killing of three people still weighed on his mind. He knew he did what he had to, but it was something he would always remember.

He watched some television and then went out to see Pudge. He spent around thirty minutes talking to Pudge and brushing him. He closed up the barn and went in and decided to hit the hay a little early. He felt tired and said his prayer and was asleep before 10:00 p.m. He didn't sleep well, waking up four or five times during the night.

Toby got up at 5:30 a.m. and cooked breakfast. He only ate about half of what he usually did and went out to start feeding and checking on the cattle. He fed and checked both places and felt like it took forever to get it done. He looked at his watch when he put Pudge back in his room and saw it was only 8:45 a.m. He just knew it was close to 10:00 a.m. the way it seemed feeding had taken so long. He took a shower and got ready for church.

He walked into the church building and sat over in the corner opposite where he usually sat. He didn't want to make anyone feel uncomfortable. He watched Kali walk in, and she seemed happy, which pleased him. His eyes grew heavy, and he dozed off during the preaching. He was embarrassed when he woke up, hoping no one had noticed. It was the first time he had ever done that. He didn't feel real good but was aggravated with himself for falling asleep.

As soon as the closing prayer was said, he was out the door and headed for home to get changed and load up Pudge. He grabbed an apple and some jerky for lunch, although he really wasn't hungry. He drank a cup of coffee on the way over and didn't eat anything. He unloaded Pudge and was putting the saddle on when Sam rode in. "Dad wanted me to come and see if you were here. We need some help on the pasture we are in now."

Toby asked, "What's the problem?"

"It's a group of heifers that Dad bought, and they are very high-strung," Sam replied as they rode out of the barnyard.

They rode through the pasture gate, and Toby saw cattle running everywhere. He pulled at the reins and brought Pudge to a stop. Sam rode on a ways and then turned around and rode back to him. "What are you doing?"

"They are already running, and if we just go riding in, we may spook them more," Toby said. "We need to figure out the path of least resistance, so to speak."

"That makes sense. Any ideas?"

Toby's stomach felt very queasy, but he fought it off and said, "I think if we walk along the west fence we can get around them without adding to the agitation."

Toby the Rancher

They started their horses walking slowly and were able to get to the back side of the cattle without any incident. Once they were behind them and Toby watched how the others were running them, he said, "We'll never get them out like this, and if we do, they will just scatter once they are outside the fence."

"How do we work them then?" Sam asked.

"Don't you have a portable corral system?" Toby asked.

"No," Sam said. "We have never needed one."

Toby thought for a minute. "I hope you can borrow one from someone. I don't see us working these without one."

Ryder came riding up. "You two pay to watch the show? Get busy and help get these heifers rounded up."

"Toby doesn't think we can ever get them worked without a portable corral here in the pasture," Sam said.

Ryder looked at Toby. "I didn't hire you for your thinking. I thought you could cowboy up. Now is when I need it."

Toby got aggravated. "I'll chase cows all day long for you if that is what you want, and that is exactly what we will do if you persist in trying to get these heifers to the corrals at the barn."

"That is what I want," Ryder said.

Toby nodded and then said as he rode off, "The thinking comes free of charge."

Toby was mad, but he knew Ryder was upset because the heifers were causing so much trouble, so he let it go.

After Toby had ridden off, Sam said, "Dad, he was just trying to help. I think he is right."

Ryder looked at her but didn't speak. He rode off toward the herd.

Sam spurred her horse and followed.

Toby reached the heifers and started Pudge to working. They were cutting singles back to the herd, and as fast as they would cut one back, another would bust out on the other side. Toby decided to try roping one and see if it would settle the rest down.

He rode to the left of the herd and roped the biggest heifer and started pulling her out. She fought, but Pudge was too strong, and she lightened up and started following while still trying to break away every little bit. He got her over a hundred feet from the herd, and some of the heifers started coming after her. They weren't calm by any stretch, but they were just bucking and jumping all around her and following along.

Toby was feeling light-headed but was working to stay focused on what he was doing to help Pudge and not hinder him. The other riders had followed in behind, pushing the others along with the herd. Toby didn't know how long this would work, but he was going to fight it as long as it did. He knew it was tough on Pudge, but he knew his ole friend was up to it. He made it to the gate, and when the heifers went through the gate, they started scattering, just as he had feared.

Toby maintained his grip on the roped heifer, hoping it would pique the others' curiosity and bring the other heifers back. The roped heifer was fighting more, but Pudge was staying the course. The farther Toby got from the gate, the more the heifers started taking notice and working back to them. He eventually got the heifer to the lot and jumped off the saddle and tied her up. He rode out to help bring the others into the corral. They were close but wanting to spread. They worked to keep them moving in the gate, and Toby just held on and let Pudge work. He was getting so weak he could barely hold on.

Once they finally got all the heifers into the pen, Toby just sat in the saddle. He had never felt so bad and weak.

Sam walked over. "Nice work. I would never have thought of doing that."

Ryder had followed her and echoed her comments. He looked at Toby and asked, "Are you okay? You look like a ghost."

"I feel horrible," Toby said. "I have never felt so weak."

"We are going to let these heifers sit overnight and see if they settle down," Ryder said. He turned to his daughter. "Sam, follow him home to make sure he makes it."

Toby got Pudge loaded and headed for home. It felt like a fifty-mile trip. He pulled out by the barn and unloaded Pudge. Sam helped him unsaddle and fed and watered Pudge. She helped Toby into the house and set about fixing Toby some coffee and soup.

Toby was lying on the couch and had his eyes closed when he felt Sam's hand on his forehead. He opened his eyes and caught a glimpse of Jessie at the door. Jessie turned and walked off the porch, and Toby tried to get up.

"What are you doing?" Sam asked.

"I need to catch Jessie," Toby said.

Sam turned and looked but didn't see anything. She got up and walked to the door. She saw Jessie, and she went out and caught her.

"Jessie, where you going?" Sam hollered after Jessie.

Jessie turned around and looked at Sam. "To school."

"Why did you stop by and not knock on the door?"

Jessie hesitated. "I didn't want to intrude."

Sam laughed. "Intrude? On what? Toby is sick, and I am helping him since he is so weak."

"Oh," Jessie said. "I—I didn't know what—"

"We'll talk later," Sam said. "You two better come on in before he goes to sleep."

"Okay," Jessie said. She motioned for Kali to get out of the car. Kali shook her head no, so Jessie went inside the house by herself.

Toby heard the door and opened his eyes to see who was coming in, and was pleased to see Sam had caught Jessie.

"You look bad, cowboy," Jessie said.

"Why, thank you," Toby said, smiling.

"I thought he was going to fall off Pudge," Sam said. "He was so white when we got the heifers penned up."

Jessie looked at Sam and asked, "So Toby is working with you?"

Sam smiled at her. "Yes, and he was a lifesaver today. We had a bunch of heifers I don't think we would have gotten up without him."

"Interesting," Jessie said.

Toby had closed his eyes again but opened them when he heard Jessie say that. "What's interesting?"

Jessie realized she had let it slip out and tried to cover it up by saying, "Oh, just figured that would have been interesting to watch that."

Sam laughed. "Yeah, right." She got up and walked into the kitchen.

"What's up?" Toby asked Jessie.

"Kali and I just wanted to stop by and see you before we headed back to school," Jessie said.

Toby raised his head and looked around for Kali. "Where is she?"

"I guess she got scared when I came back so quick and Samantha came out."

"That's disappointing."

"I know. I hope a week at school gets her going again."

Sam walked out of the kitchen with a cup of coffee. "She'll milk it as long as anyone lets her."

Toby the Rancher

"Shut up!" Jessie said.

"You are her friend, and I get that," Sam said. "But you also know she is a big baby."

Toby just listened. When Sam first spoke, it had bothered him, but as he listened, he started realizing there was apparently history and Sam didn't care for Kali.

Jessie looked at Toby. "You are not saying anything."

"I don't know what to say," Toby said. "That is between y'all, and I really don't feel like getting into an argument."

Jessie stood up. "Good-bye. Hope you feel better." She turned and walked out, and Sam shut the door behind her.

"Samantha," Toby said.

Sam turned and looked at him. "Yes, dear?"

"I really don't feel like it, but I need to know what that was all about."

29

Sam walked over and sat down. "Which part are you talking about?"

"I gather you and Kali don't get along," Toby said.

"You gather right."

"Why?"

Sam looked at him. "It is a long story, and you really had to be there the last seven to eight years to really get it."

"Give me the condensed version."

"She uses people," Sam said. "She backstabs her so-called friends if it helps her with guys. She is just not the kind of girl I like to associate with, and as I said, it goes a ways back."

Toby was feeling bad. Sam felt of his forehead and said, "You are burning up. Let's take your temp."

She got the thermometer and put it in his mouth. She walked to the kitchen to get the soup she had put on, and when she got back, she checked the thermometer. Her eyes widened. "Wow. A 104.7. You need to take some medicine to try and bring that down. I'll see if I can find some. Try to sit up and eat some of this soup."

Toby tried to raise himself up but began to chill and shake. He laid back down and tried to wrap himself in the blanket.

Sam got up. "I am going to try and get your fireplace going to warm you up."

Toby just curled up, shivering and trying to get himself warm. It wasn't long until Sam had the fire raging and putting out some good heat. It was warming the room up, but Toby was still shaking.

"Let's see if we can get into this chair in front of the fireplace," Sam said.

Toby got up with her help and moved to the chair. The fire was helping him to warm up.

"I need to get back and take care of my chores," she said. "Is there anyone I can call to have check on you before I get back?"

Toby asked her to let Hank know he wouldn't be able to check Hank's livestock today.

Toby fell asleep and didn't know when Sam left. He woke up at 9:00 p.m., and he was burning up and freezing at the same time. He ached badly, but he got up and added more wood to the fireplace and got it going again. Then he went and put on an extra sweatshirt and got another blanket to try and stay warm. He took some medicine for his fever and was back asleep by 9:30 p.m.

When he woke up, it was daylight outside, and he still felt bad. He looked at his watch and saw that it was 8:00 a.m. He lay there, taking stock on how he felt and what he needed to do. His phone ringing interrupted his thoughts. He reached for his phone and saw that it was Hank. "Hello?"

"That hello answers my question," Hank said. "You sound horrible."

"I'll try to get going to get things taken care of this morning," Toby said.

"No, you won't," Hank said. "I will take care of mine and yours this morning. You take care of yourself."

"I'm sorry for this, but thank you for understanding."

"Nothing to be sorry for."

They hung up. Toby felt bad because he couldn't do what he was supposed to do, but he was thankful that Hank was able and willing to help out. He started to doze off and heard the doorbell. He got up and made it to the door and saw Sadie standing on the porch. He opened the door and said, "Hello, Sadie. What are you doing here? You don't need to get sick."

"I am fine," Sadie said. "You just get back in bed—or on the couch, as I see—and I'll take care of things."

Toby didn't argue because he felt like he could fall over at any time. He got back to the couch, and Sadie felt his head. "My land, you are burning up."

She got the thermometer and washed it and gave it to Toby. She went to get him a drink as she waited for the temperature to read. She got back and checked the thermometer and said, "One hundred five. I'm not sure we don't need to get you to the doctor."

"I'll be all right," Toby said.

"If your fever isn't down by noon, you are going to the doctor."

"It's just the flu, isn't it?"

"People die from the flu."

Toby didn't feel up to arguing and just closed his eyes to go to sleep. He slept until noon, and Sadie woke him up, feeling his forehead.

"You are still very hot," she said. "Let's take your temp. If it is still above 101, you are going to the doctor." She checked the thermometer, and it showed 102.7. She called Hank. "Come on over. We need to get him to the doctor. He is still running nearly 103 after taking medicine." She hung up and turned to Toby. "Let's get a jacket on you and get you ready to go."

Toby could see there was no use arguing. "Yes, ma'am."

"You sound and look so weak. I hope we haven't waited too long."

Hank arrived and came in to help Toby to the truck.

"Hank, how was Pudge this morning?" Toby asked. "I didn't get a chance to take care of him right yesterday after he worked so hard."

"Pudge is good," Hank said. "He will be better if you get well and get back with him."

Toby felt content. He knew Hank appreciated the feelings he had for Pudge and would take good care of him.

Toby the Rancher

They left for town, and Toby's phone rang. Sadie answered it and talked to the person calling. She hung up and said, "That was Samantha Weber checking on you. She said she hoped you got to feeling better."

"I sure wish her and Kali were still friends like they were in high school," Hank said. "I always enjoyed having Sam around."

Sadie said, "I really don't know what happened, but Kali just says they are too different to be friends any longer."

Toby was fighting dozing off because he wanted to listen to what Hank and Sadie were saying.

"I guess it is possible for people to develop different interests and not be friends anymore," Hank said. "Sure seemed to happen quickly, though."

"Yeah," Sadie said. "I don't know if it was over a guy or something like that. Suffice it to say, they don't care for each other."

They arrived at the doctor's office and got Toby inside. The doctor checked Toby out and said, "Young man, you have a very bad case of the flu. If you don't take it easy and get more fluids in you, your next visit to town will be to the hospital."

They started back home, and Sadie said, "Toby, you are going to stay in our guest bedroom until you get back on your feet."

Toby started to argue, but she said, "I don't want to hear any lip on the matter."

Toby didn't say anything else.

"I can take care of things for a few days," Hank said.

They got to Hank and Sadie's and got Toby to bed.

Toby was sick and flat worn out. Except for an occasional trip to the bathroom, he stayed in bed asleep for the next three days. He didn't speak to anyone nor had he any idea what was going on outside the walls of that bedroom. He had never been so sick in his life.

On Friday morning, at about 5:30 a.m., Toby woke up and found he was feeling better than he had in nearly a week. He got up and took a shower and went to the kitchen to start coffee. He didn't know where things were, but he was hungry, so he searched until he found everything to make a good country breakfast for them. He cooked eggs, bacon, sausage, pancakes, biscuits and gravy, and hash browns.

Sadie walked into the kitchen at 6:30 a.m. "I take it you are feeling better. Breakfast smells great."

"Yeah," Toby said. "It is like a switch turned, and I feel good and hungry."

Hank walked in and said, "I'm hungry too. Let's eat."

They sat down. Hank said the blessing.

Toby ate like he hadn't eaten in a month. "I have been out of it all week. Is everything going okay?"

"No problems at all," Hank said.

"Sam called twice a day to check on you," Sadie said.

"She showed up and helped with the feeding of your livestock yesterday afternoon," Hank said.

"I can't thank y'all enough for the help," Toby said.

"That is what friends and Christians do for each other," Sadie said. "Besides, look what all you have done for us."

Toby smiled and finished breakfast. He washed the dishes after arguing—and winning the argument—with Sadie. Once he was finished, he grabbed his things and headed home. His first stop was not the house but instead was Pudge's stall room.

Pudge was excited to see Toby, and Toby spent the next hour brushing and talking to him. He was walking out of the barn when Sam turned into the drive. She got out of her truck and hugged Toby's neck. "I am so glad to see you back on your feet again."

"It feels good to be active and out of bed," Toby said. "I have never been that sick before and hope I never am again."

"How is Pudge?"

"He is good. Seemed excited to see me."

"I'm sure he was. I have never seen anyone as close to their horse as you are. It's very cool."

Toby smiled. "Did y'all get your roundup completed?"

"Not yet," Sam said. "It seems things went wrong about the time you got sick, and we haven't been able to bring any others in. Dad hopes you can be ready to help again real soon."

"I hope so too," Toby said. "I'll have to see how my stamina is as I work the next couple of days."

"Do you think you will feel up to it, and would you want to go to the Cattlemen's Association dinner tonight with me?"

"I feel good now. As long as I don't have a relapse, I'd be happy to go. Sounds interesting."

"Great," Sam said. "I'll call you later to see how you are feeling. We need to be there by 7:00 p.m."

"Okay," Toby said. "I'll drive and pick you up at 6:30."

"I hope you go." Sam hugged his neck, got into her truck, and left.

Toby walked into the house to sit down for a minute and make a pot of coffee.

30

Toby sat in the chair at the kitchen table and dozed off. He woke up when his head nodded, and he jerked and spilled his coffee. It was going to take some time to get his stamina back. He cleaned up the coffee and headed out to the barn to take care of some things. He was cleaning out Pudge's stall when Hank pulled up. He walked in and said, "You are going to overdo it and make yourself have a relapse."

"I just can't sit still," Toby said. "I need be doing something."

"I understand," Hank said. "Just don't try to do too much."

"I won't. I am going with Samantha to the Cattlemen's dinner, so I will need to go take a shower in a little while."

"I'm glad she asked you. I hadn't even thought of it since you had been sick. It will be good for you to meet other cattlemen in the area."

"I didn't ask her, but how should I dress?" Toby asked.

"Wranglers are fine." Hank responded.

"Sounds good."

Hank got in his truck and left. Toby finished Pudge's stall room and then took the cover off the '72 pickup. He figured he would drive it tonight. He headed into the house to start getting ready. He sat down on the couch for a while before getting in the shower. He knew he had been sick, but he was frustrated at how

Toby the Rancher

quick he was tiring out. He made himself get up and get to the shower. It felt good and helped revive him some. He put on his starched Wranglers and cobalt blue shirt and his black elephant-skin boots, and black hat. He locked everything up and headed for the Weber place to pick up Sam.

The old truck was running good, so he opened it up when he hit the highway. He had missed driving it, and it felt good. He pulled into the Webers', and Ryder was standing out by their Denali. The windows on Toby's truck were tinted, so Ryder couldn't tell who was driving it, and he didn't know the truck. He started walking toward Toby's truck.

Toby opened the door and started out. Ryder stopped and looked his truck over and said, "That is one sweet ride. Sam will love riding in that."

Toby grinned. "Thank you."

"How are you feeling?" Ryder asked.

"Better, but still feel weak."

"I don't doubt that, as sick as I heard you were. We'll see you up there."

They drove off as Toby walked to the door. He rang the doorbell, and Sam opened the door. He knew she was good-looking, but cleaned up and in a Western-style dress, she was a knockout.

"Hello," Toby said. "You look great."

Sam looked at Toby and said, "Thank you, and you clean up good too. In fact, you look like a model from a Western-wear catalog."

"Oh, bull," Toby said. "You ready?"

Sam walked out and saw his truck. "Wow, that is beautiful. Where did you get it?"

"It is mine," Toby said.

"This just gets better all the time."

"What does that mean?"

"I am going out with a cowboy model in a slick truck. It just doesn't get any better than that for a date."

Toby started to say it wasn't a date but decided to just let it slide. He smiled and said, "We better get going, or we will be late." He opened her door for her, and when she saw the tuck-and-roll upholstery, she stopped and smiled and shook her head. She slid in the seat and looked at Toby and grinned. He just gave her a smirky smile and shook his head as he shut the door. He never dreamed a girl would be taken back by his truck.

Toby went around and got in and started it, and the 400 hp ripped through the headers. The pipes sounded good.

"I have goose bumps all over," Sam said.

Toby laughed and backed out and headed toward town. They drove to the convention center and saw Hank and Sadie getting out of their truck as they pulled in. They waited for Toby and Sam to get out, and Hank said, "Hello, kids."

"Hello, Samantha," Sadie said. "You look pretty tonight. In fact, y'all make a very good-looking couple. Toby, how are you feeling?"

Toby ignored the statement and answered, "I am feeling good. Just wear down pretty quickly. How are you feeling?"

Sadie replied, smiling, "I'm bouncing back."

They walked into the common area between the meeting rooms and spotted the table for one to register. They signed in and walked in, with Hank speaking to several people and introducing Toby to them. Toby was hearing so many names he wasn't able to remember them all.

They found a table to sit at. Toby glanced at the program and noticed Carl was the guest speaker.

I wonder how he will act if he sees me here, he thought.

Hank and Sadie were talking to people they knew, and Sam had walked over to another table to greet some people. She came walking back with two girls in tow. Toby stood up, and she said, "This is Kathy and Gwen. We went to school together. Girls, this is the guy I have been telling you about."

Toby shook their hands. "I'm glad to meet you, ladies." He noticed some guys walking up behind them.

"These guys are their husbands, Jimbo and Harry," Sam said. "They ranch with their dads."

Toby shook their hands. "Guys."

Toby the Rancher

"Aren't you the one that bought the Glover place?" Harry asked.

Toby responded that he was, and Harry said, "Dad and I thought about trying to get it so Gwen and I could live there and we could expand our operation. We decided we had enough to deal with right now. It can be a nice place."

"Yeah, it needs some work," Toby said. "Mr. Glover wasn't able to take care of things after he got sick."

"Isn't that the place Carl Matthews was complaining about not getting when we ran into him at the café a while back?" Jimbo asked.

"Yep, it is," Harry said. "I wouldn't lose any sleep over it, though."

"Thanks," Toby said. "I wasn't going to."

Harry laughed. "Somehow I knew that."

"Might not want to be so cocky since you are sitting with his in-laws," Jimbo said.

"Pleasure meeting you guys," Toby said. "I don't think I caught your last names, or did you say them?"

"Mine is Stuart and Jimbo's is Carter," Harry said. "What was yours again?"

Toby replied, "Parker."

"Isn't that convenient?" Jimbo said. "Have the same name as the in-laws of the guy you bought your place out from under."

Kathy pulled on Jimbo's arm. "It's time to sit down."

Toby stared him down, and Jimbo turned and walked to his table.

"Sorry, man," Harry said. "He was out of line."

"Yeah, he was." Toby nodded at Harry as he sat down.

Hank had heard Jimbo, and he said to Toby, "Don't let that idiot ruin your evening. He has always been a loudmouth, just like his dad. Harry and his dad are good guys."

Sam reached over and squeezed Toby's hand. "I'm sorry. I shouldn't have brought them over."

"Don't worry about it," Toby said. "You didn't do anything wrong. You can't control others' idiotic actions."

251

Toby glanced at Sadie, and she smiled at him and said, "You handled it well. Forty years ago, Hank would have punched him in the nose."

Hank laughed. "You know, she is right."

The president of the Cattlemen's Association went to the podium to have the prayer led for the food. Once it was done, they started serving at the tables. Toby was looking at some literature on the table and not paying attention to what was going on in the room when he heard, "Who is this guy?"

He looked up and saw a guy standing by Sam, looking at him.

"It's none of your business," Sam said.

The guy kept staring at Toby. "Who are you?"

Toby glanced at Sam and then Hank and Sadie. He didn't like the look on any of their faces. He looked back at the guy and said, "Why don't you go sit down and let us enjoy our supper?"

The guy started to speak, but Hank said, "That's right, Stone. Everyone wants to eat. Please go on back to your table."

Stone glared back at Toby and then turned and walked away.

Toby looked at Sam. "Okay, what's the story?"

Sam hesitated and then said, "I went out with him for a while. He was crazy, so I broke it off. He still thinks we have a chance. I have told him a number of times there is no way."

Toby just shook his head and took a bite of salad.

"What?" Sam asked.

"I have to agree with her," Hank said. "He is not very stable."

"I just wonder what I am doing wrong that I always seem to run into crazies," Toby said.

"You need to get married and settle down, and things will improve," Sadie said.

Toby looked at her with a puzzled look on his face. "I'm sorry, ma'am, but how in the world would that help?"

"Then all the guys wouldn't feel threatened by this new, single, good-looking cowboy that just rode in."

"She makes sense," Hank said.

Toby looked down and ate another bite of salad. When he finished chewing it, he said, "That settles it then. I will find me a mail-order-bride company and order me one." He took another bite of salad.

"Now, Toby, there are plenty of nice, pretty young ladies around here," Sadie said. "You are sitting next to one."

"Seems they always have too much local history," Toby said. "Might be good to get one that nobody knows. Anyway, let's eat." He wanted the topic changed and hoped that would do it.

They ate, and as they finished, Carl was introduced. He gave a talk on some new veterinarian procedures. It was interesting to Toby, and he thought Carl did a good job presenting it.

Once Carl was finished, they had people who were attending for the first time stand up, which Toby didn't like. He didn't like that kind of attention. He had to say his name and a brief background. He said as little as he thought he could to get by with.

He sat back down, and Sam said, "Good job."

Toby smirked. "I doubt that. I was too nervous."

"It didn't show," Sadie said.

Toby noticed Hank was gone and then heard Hank's voice over the speaker system. He was talking about the wolves that had been on his place, and he said, "Toby Parker, who you just heard from, killed over a dozen of them. We need to all keep our eyes open and be ready in case more have migrated this way."

Hank ended his talk and came back to the table.

Once the meeting was over, several people came up to meet Toby and talk to him about the wolves. Toby was as uncomfortable as he had ever been. He didn't like crowds and sure didn't like all the attention he was getting. He saw an opening, and he was out the door and headed to the truck to wait on Sam. He opened the door to walk out, and he heard someone say, "Running away like a scared jackrabbit. Figures. Big sissy."

Toby turned to see Stone coming toward him.

31

Toby stood where he was, halfway out the door and with his hand on the door. Stone was not slowing down.

"Stone, what are you doing?" Sam hollered from behind.

Toby never shied away from a fight, but being sick all week didn't leave him feeling like he could stand up to a fight. As Stone reached Toby, Stone swung with his right hand, and Toby slammed the door shut into his fist to block the punch. The fight ended as soon as it started, as the blow to the door broke Stone's hand.

Stone grabbed his hand and yelled, "You broke my hand, you…"

Toby just looked at him, shut the other door, and walked to his truck.

Sam reached Stone and started trying to help him with his hand. She looked outside and saw Toby walking to the truck. She looked back at Stone and opened the door and walked out of the building.

Stone looked up. "You're leaving me like this?"

Toby the Rancher

Sam turned. "It was your fault, and I don't owe you anything." She walked to the truck and got in and looked at Toby. "Well, that was fun."

Toby smiled. "A bundle of laughs."

He looked back at the doors and saw other people there with Stone and all of them looking toward his truck. "I guess it would be safe to say this isn't over with your boyfriend."

"He isn't my boyfriend," Sam said. "Never was. I dated him a few times and realized how crazy he was, so I started turning him down when he would ask me out. He seemed to think there was something between us."

Toby started the truck and backed out of the parking spot and started to the exit.

"I feel like drinking a shake," Sam said. "How about you?"

"Sounds good," Toby said. "Where do you want to go?"

"Sonic has a good cookies-and-cream shake."

"Haven't had one of those in a while."

Toby drove to the Sonic and turned in and drove around the store before parking in the last spot next to the street. Toby noticed everyone was watching them pull around the parking lot, and he knew it was his truck. He smiled inside because he enjoyed driving his classics.

"Well, your truck definitely got some attention," Sam said.

"Yeah, seems to," Toby said.

"Go ahead and smile and quit holding it in. The truck is sweet."

Toby grinned. "What do you want?"

"Cookies-and-cream shake."

"They don't have that. They have an Oreo blizzard."

"Are you sure?" Sam leaned over by Toby to look at the menu. "Well, I must have them and Braum's confused. Chocolate shake will work."

Toby laughed at her and rolled down his window and pushed the button to order. He was waiting for them to respond to take his order when he heard someone say, "Hey, Toby, that is one nice truck."

255

He looked to see Mike Stine walking over. "Hey, Mike, how you doing?"

Mike walked on up just as the person spoke wanting Toby's order, so he ordered two chocolate shakes and then looked at Mike.

"Where did you get this?" Mike asked.

"I have had it a good while," Toby said. "It was stored in Pennsylvania, so I brought it down when I bought my place."

"This is bad," Mike said. "You want to let me drive it to prom?"

Toby laughed. "I don't know about that."

Mike smiled. "If you change your mind, let me know. I'll catch you later." He started walking off, and Toby asked, "When is the prom?"

Mike stopped and turned around. "In two weeks."

"Call me, and we'll talk," Toby said.

Mike was excited and said, "You got it." He went over to start talking to the other guys hanging out.

"You really going to let him use it?" Sam asked.

"Maybe," Toby said. "It's only a truck. I think he will take care of it."

Sam was looking around and said, "Well, lookie there. If isn't Miss Prima Donna."

"Who?"

"Kali Matthews."

Toby looked and saw Kali but didn't say anything.

"And there is Jessie, protecting her as usual," Sam said.

"I still don't understand your resentment of her."

"It is probably a girl thing, but there is history, and that is all I can say about it."

"Okay. It's none of my business, anyway. Just makes it weird for me knowing both of you."

"Here comes Jessie."

Toby looked, and Jessie was walking their way. He rolled down the window as she walked up.

"I thought I recognized this truck," Jessie said. She saw Sam in the truck and that she was dressed up. "Hello, Sam. Out on a date?"

"Hey, Jessie," Sam said. "Yes, we are."

Toby glanced at Sam. She was grinning, and then he was looking back at Jessie when she spoke. "Well, that's a rarity. I didn't think you dated anymore since you and Stone broke up."

"You can't break up if you aren't a couple, and we weren't," Sam said.

Toby looked at Jessie. She was smiling, so he knew she was needling Sam.

Sam continued, "Speaking of breaking something, Toby broke Stone's hand tonight."

Jessie looked at Toby. "You fought over her?"

Toby noted a tone in her voice, so he weighed his response before he spoke. "There wasn't a fight. He ran into a door with his hand."

Some other people started gathering around and looking at Toby's truck and were asking Jessie who Toby was. Toby noticed Kali was still over at the table by herself. This wasn't the place to ask Jessie anything about Kali, so he just answered questions the people were asking about his truck. They started dispersing, and Jessie said, "I will let y'all get on with your date. You look sharp, Toby. Sam, you look nice too. See ya."

Jessie walked away, and Toby caught Kali's eye looking his way. He nodded at her, and she turned her head. The shakes showed up, and Toby started the truck to let the heater run to take the chill off in the truck.

When Jessie got back, Kali asked, "What are they doing?"

"I guess they are on a date," Jessie replied. "Both are dressed up."

"Really?"

"Yes. If you like the guy, you better stop avoiding him."

"You like him too."

"I told you I would not interfere. If you don't hurry, though, all bets are off."

Kali looked at Jessie and got back in the car.

Toby and Sam drank their shakes as they watched the people out of their cars, talking.

"I used to do this all the time," Sam said. "It seemed the thing to do, but now it doesn't interest me."

"I never have hung out like this, but they seem to be having fun," Toby said. "You ready to go?"

"You want to drag the strip a couple of times?"

"What is that?"

"Pull out to the right, and go down to the grain elevator, and turn around."

"Okay."

He turned right and started driving slow along with the traffic. He noticed it was all younger folks and they were checking his truck out as they passed them. He kind of liked dragging the strip and figured if he had the chance in high school it would have been real cool. The last time he pulled through Sonic, he caught Kali's eye again, and she smiled at him. He couldn't figure her out, and decided to slough it off.

"I'm ready to head on out," Toby said. "You okay with that?"

"Sure," Sam said. "You have been awfully quiet."

"Just taking it all in and thinking what it might have been like in high school."

She laughed. "It was a blast. I miss it, but we have to grow up."

"Yep, that is true."

"What did you think about the treatment Carl Matthews talked about?"

"It was interesting. I would like to try it if it isn't cost prohibitive."

"I know Dad will try it, especially if it will help calving and milk production."

They arrived at Sam's house. Toby got out and opened her door and walked her to the porch. She leaned in for a kiss, and Toby kissed her on the cheek.

"You can do better than that." Sam grabbed the back of his neck and pulled him in for a long, passionate kiss. When she finished, she said, "Let Kali top that."

"Good night," Toby said. "I will talk to you later."

"Good night," Sam said.

Toby walked to the truck and fired it up. He blew out the cobs on the way home and ran it up to 120 mph. He opened his gate and pulled in and then shut the gate behind him. He drove to the barn and parked the truck back where he had it in the hall. He would wait to cover it up in the morning after it had cooled off.

He went in Pudge's room. "How are you tonight, ole buddy? I had an eventful night. It was a little crazy." He brushed Pudge for a while and then just sat down on a stool he had in the room. "I just don't know why I always seem to run into guys wanting to fight. And then the girls are different than I thought too. I never dreamed it would be so hard to figure out what to do with my life when I started reaching my midtwenties."

Toby sat silent for a while, pondering his life. He dozed off and woke up three hours later still sitting on the stool and leaning back against the wall. He got up and turned on the heater he had put in the room. He got a horse blanket, wrapped it around him, sat back down, and went back to sleep. He slept until 6:15 a.m. He stood up and said, "I slept well, Pudger. How 'bout you? I may have to try this more often."

He patted Pudge and walked out and headed to the house. He changed clothes and started breakfast. He still wasn't feeling strong, but he wanted to eat a good breakfast and see if he could push himself through the day. He ate four eggs over easy, three pancakes, four patties of sausage, and six slices of bacon. He also had two pieces of toast to sop up the egg yolk, and four cups of coffee. He loved breakfast and hadn't had a big breakfast in a while, so he enjoyed every bite. He finished eating and cleaning up and walked back to the barn to start his chores.

Toby fed his cattle and was pleased to see he had two more new calves and both were bulls. Luckily, he had the bander in his saddlebag, and he roped and banded both calves. As he rode to Hank's, he thought about his loan and his herd. He was a little aggravated with himself that he had been preoccupied with other things and hadn't already put his plans down on paper to have a map to follow and a measuring stick to watch. He knew that he needed to get it worked up before the weekend was over. He checked the cattle in the outer pastures before he rode into the barnyard.

Hank walked out of the house and asked, "How are you feeling this morning?"

"Better," Toby said. "I slept well."

"I am sorry about Stone. He is a loose cannon and stirs up trouble everywhere he goes. That broken hand will slow him some."

"I didn't want to fight and figured that was the only way to stop it. He is a mixed-up bucko."

"How are your cattle looking?" Hank asked.

Toby told him about his calves and his plan he needed to work up.

"If you need any help, let me know," Hank said. "I might be able to help you avoid some of the pitfalls I found along the way."

"Thank you," Toby said. "I sure may."

He finished up the feeding and rode back to his place. He left Pudge tied up to the hitching post and went inside for a cup of coffee. He pulled his phone out to call Hank about a bull, and saw he had a message. He looked. It was from Kali, and it came last night. He opened it, and she said she wanted to talk to him if he wasn't too mad at her for avoiding him. He thought for a minute and decided to wait a while to respond. He had other things he needed to take care of first.

He called Hank and asked if he knew where he could try and buy a Beefmaster bull.

Hank told him that the best herd he knew of was in Weatherford, Texas. "Can I ask why you are wanting to go that route? I thought you liked my cattle."

"I do like your cattle," Toby responded. "But I figure it would be a disservice to both of us to have the same breed competing for buyers and other things."

"That makes sense. I should have thought of that. You are wise beyond your years, young man."

"I will try to find their number and let you know what they say."

Toby found the number on the Internet and called them. They had several young bulls that sounded like what he was looking for. He wanted a bull with Spartacus and Synergy bloodlines. He knew he would need to pay close to five thousand dollars for a bull with those bloodlines, but he wanted to build a special herd.

He mounted Pudge and headed out to the middle pasture. He wanted to take a look at his heifers and steers and see if he could wean and sell some to use cash to buy a bull. He rode into the pasture and started looking the cattle over. He was pleasantly surprised that he had more head ready to sell than he had previously thought. He counted fourteen steers and twelve heifers, and all of them seemed to weigh around seven hundred pounds. At least he thought that was what they would weigh, but he knew he couldn't guess very well. He was pleased with their condition, and hoped they would bring a good price.

He spent the rest of the day working on fences and rode into the barn at dark. He fed and watered Pudge and went to the house to get some supper. He had skipped dinner after the big breakfast he had eaten. He fixed two sandwiches and had chips and pickles with them. He drank two cups of coffee and went back to the barn to brush Pudge. It had been a warm day, but the night air had a chill to it, so he fired up the stove again.

Toby brushed Pudge for over thirty minutes and then sat down on the stool. The full day had caught up with him, and he was still feeling the effects of the illness. He decided to respond to Kali while he was resting.

"I'm not mad," he wrote. "I can't relate to what you went through, so I figure you have to do things in your own time."

He sent the message and leaned back against the wall and closed his eyes. He said a prayer, and when he finished, he kept his eyes closed and fell asleep again.

He didn't wake up until 5:00 a.m. the next day. He woke up and looked at Pudge, who was looking at him, and said, "I might as well rent out the house. I sleep better out here."

Toby got up and went to the house. He took a shower and then fixed breakfast. He tended to the chores at both places and made it to Sunday school and worship service. He saw Kali and Carla walk in. Carla looked at him, but Kali didn't. He blew it off and paid attention in class and to the preacher. He left as soon as the closing prayer was said and went to the steak house to eat a steak, potato, and salad.

He was eating his steak when Hank and Sadie and all the Matthewses walked in. He was sitting where they couldn't see him and he was in his Chevelle, so he didn't figure they recognized it. He didn't want any problems with Carl or Kali, so he finished eating and paid and slipped out. He didn't know Sadie had seen him leave.

Toby drove home and changed clothes and saddled Pudge. He was getting ready to ride out when Hank and Sadie pulled in. He led Pudge over to their car and asked, "What's up?"

Hank said, "Sadie saw you leave the restaurant, and we were wondering if something was wrong since you didn't speak."

Toby hesitated a minute and then said, "No. I just figured it best to not upset Carl and Kali."

"I was afraid it was like that," Sadie said. "You don't ever think you aren't welcome at our home, table, or anything else. No matter who is around."

"Yes, ma'am," Toby replied.

"That settles that," Hank said. "So what are you doing?"

"I am going to round up twenty-six steers and heifers to take to the sale tomorrow so I can go buy a bull."

"You need some help?" Hank asked.

"I wouldn't turn it down," Toby answered.

"I'll be back in a few minutes."

Hank and Sadie pulled away, and Toby rode out to start separating the calves. He had Pudge at a trot and heard his phone ring. He answered it, and it was Sam. She asked what he was doing, and he told her. She hung up without saying anything. He looked at the phone and shook his head and stuck it back in his pocket.

He cut out the first calf and drove it to the makeshift corral in the corner of the pasture. He had three of them cut out and penned when Hank got back.

"I'll work the gate for you," Hank said.

Toby nodded and went after the next calf. He pushed it into the pen, and Hank said, "These calves look very good. I bet they weigh over eight hundred pounds."

"That would help." Toby went and got the next calf, and it tried to be cantankerous. Pudge was ready, and they worked the calf up in picture-perfect form. The calf went into the corral.

Toby looked up and saw Sam riding up. "What are you doing here?"

"Thought I might be of some help," Sam said.

"There's no doubt of that, but what about y'all's cattle?"

"Dad didn't want to work any today."

"Works for me."

Toby and Sam went and got two calves, and as they got them to the corral, Kali and Jessie pulled up in Hank's MULE.

Toby took his hat off and scratched his head and said to himself, "Oh, brother, this can't be good."

32

Toby decided to just ride out and get another calf rather than wait to see if fireworks started.

"Wait for me!" Sam hollered.

Toby acted like he hadn't heard her and let Pudge run a little. He picked a calf and started cutting it out, and Sam got there and tried to pick one out too. They worked the calves toward the pasture, and as they started moving in the direction of the corral, Toby glanced to see what was going on at the corral. He was surprised to see Jessie and Kali sitting on the top rail of the fence. He glanced at Sam. She was looking at the corral, so he focused on the calves. They got them to the gate, and Hank let them in and closed it behind them.

"What are you two up to today?" Toby asked Jessie and Kali.

"Nothing productive, it would appear," Sam interjected.

"We wondered if you needed any more help fixing things up in your house, so we thought we would come and check," Jessie said.

"How is it you just happen to ride the mule over from Hank's place to 'fix up' the house?" Sam asked.

Jessie stuttered for an answer, and Sam said, "You have to be better at making up stories if you are going to try and outwit me, dearie." She rode off to get another calf.

"I best get back to bringing in the calves." Toby tipped his hat and rode off.

Kali said to Jessie, "This is useless. She has his attention and can do things he likes. He won't look my way again. You might have a chance."

"You give up too easy," Jessie said. "That was just the first round."

Toby laughed to himself about what had just happened and noted Sam was quick-witted. He cut out two calves, and Sam got one, and they worked the three to the corral.

"How many more do you have to round up?" Sam hollered.

"Nineteen," Toby responded as he rode out to get others.

"We are going to have to sit here too long to even talk to him," Kali said. "She is working with him. Let's go."

"You go if you want," Jessie said. "I am not leaving. I have decided to get him for myself."

Kali looked at her. "Are you serious?"

"Very," Jessie said. "I told you to stop fooling around, or I wouldn't hold back anymore. You're still doing it. Besides, I'm not losing to Sam Weber."

Kali climbed down. "Well, good-bye, *friend*."

"We are still friends," Jessie said.

Kali looked at her and got in the MULE and left.

Hank hollered to Jessie, "Where is she going?"

"Back to your house," Jessie responded. She jumped down off the fence and walked over to help work the double gate. "I'll help with the gate."

"Sounds good," Hank said. "That will help create a lane to bring them in."

Toby and Sam were bringing four in this time, and Toby was surprised to see Jessie working the gate with Hank. He noticed Kali was gone and wondered what was up.

"Jessie is helping, and the prima donna is gone," Sam said. "Figures."

The two gates worked well penning the four calves. Toby looked at Jessie and said, "Thanks for helping."

Jessie smiled at him, and Sam scoffed as she turned and rode off. Toby followed, and they got four more. Three more trips brought the last eleven in.

Toby dismounted and walked over to Hank. "What do you think?"

"I am surprised," Hank said. "They look much better than what I thought they would."

"I sure hope they bring a good price so I can get the bull and a couple of cows," Toby said.

"What are you planning to do with these cows?" Hank asked.

"I figured I would try to preg check them and see if they are bred and how far along, and then decide my next steps," Toby answered.

"Sounds like a good plan," Sam said.

"Well, I best go get them some feed," Toby said. "I need to look to buy a tractor too so I can feed big round bales. I guess I will stay with small squares for now if I can find some."

"You can bring one of my bales down with my tractor," Hank said.

"Thank you," Toby said. "How much do I need to pay you for it?"

Hank said, "Nothing."

"Jessie and Sam, thank you for your help," Toby said.

"I'll race you back to the barn," Sam said.

"You're welcome," Jessie said. "Can I ride back with you, Toby?"

"I don't guess Pudge would mind having a pretty girl on his back." Toby looked at Sam. "Jessie is saving you from embarrassment."

Sam laughed. "I know Pudge is good, but..."

Hank started the truck and pulled away.

Toby looked at Jessie. "There's a stirrup."

She put her foot in and swung up behind him. He noticed she was real close behind him. He glanced at Sam, and she was glaring at Jessie. He started Pudge out, and Sam bolted on ahead. Pudge didn't want to walk and started to trot, so Toby said, "Hang on. He wants to run."

Pudge pulled up beside Sam's horse and then pulled past, but Sam pulled up on her reins to slow him down. Toby slowed Pudge. "I thought you wanted to race?"

"Not with two on your horse," Sam said. "She might get hurt."

"Yes, I am quite sure you are worried about my health," Jessie said.

Sam changed the subject and asked, "When are you hauling the calves off, Toby?"

"I think I will wait and haul them early Monday so I can keep feed in front of them until then," Toby replied. "I may go ahead and bring the cows up tomorrow and start preg checking them to see if I need to go ahead and take some of that group off as well."

"I will help you haul them off, if you like," Sam said. "I can use our truck and trailer."

Jessie was quiet because she knew she would be back at school.

"I appreciate the offer, but don't y'all still have cattle to work?" Toby asked. "I hate that I haven't been able to help as I promised."

Toby the Rancher

"Yeah, we do, but Dad understands you had the flu," Sam said. "I think he is actually waiting for you to be able to help. He was so impressed with how you handled that wild group of heifers."

Toby laughed. "Just got lucky. Maybe I can get back over this week."

Jessie was feeling awkward, so she said, "I can help tomorrow, Toby, if you need it."

Toby started to speak, but Sam said, "I'm sure you can preg check a cow."

Jessie looked at Sam. "Can you?"

Sam hesitated for a minute and then said, "No."

Jessie laughed. "Sam can't cowboy up."

"Come on, ladies," Toby said. "Quit quibbling with each other. I thought you were friends?"

Neither girl said anything. They rode back into the barnyard. Toby helped Jessie dismount, and then he climbed off. He was leading Pudge to his room when he asked Sam, "Why do you go by Sam all the time? I think Samantha is a pretty name."

"She wanted to be a boy," Jessie said.

Sam looked at Jessie. "I can kick your butt like a boy if you don't shut up. I like being a cowgirl, and Dad started calling me that. I know I am a girl and am pretty, and don't need to use my full name to feel that way."

"Okeydoke," Toby said.

"Sorry," Sam said. "Didn't mean to sound hateful."

Toby smiled. "No problem. Was just curious. You clean up real nice. Saw that last night." At that comment, he saw Jessie's smile disappear, and he knew she didn't like what he had said.

Sam smiled. "Why, thank you, cowboy."

They walked out of the barn, and Sam said, "I better head home and take care of some chores."

"Thanks again," Toby said.

Sam smiled. She loaded her horse and drove off.

Toby looked at Jessie. "You seem to be afoot."

"Yeah," Jessie said. "I hope Kali comes and picks me up."

"I have got some things to do, so take my truck to Hank's and drop it back off when you leave," Toby said.

"I'm not that good with a standard."

"It doesn't have a standard."

Jessie realized he meant the '72, and she burst into a grin. "I will be careful."

Toby smiled and pitched her the keys. He got in his truck and left to go to town.

Jessie took off in the '72. She pulled up to Hank's. Kali saw the truck and walked outside. She saw Jessie driving it and got mad. Jessie got out, and Kali asked, "What are you doing driving that?"

"I had to get here somehow," Jessie said. "Toby had to go to town, so he let me drive it down here."

Kali just turned and went back in the house. Jessie saw Hank out by the barn, so she walked out to visit with him.

Toby went to the feed store and bought a 30 percent protein tub and eight bags of Stocker sweet feed to feed along with the hay. He stopped and got a cup of coffee and a bag of doughnuts to eat on the way back. When he walked out of the store Carl and Drew were getting out of Carl's truck.

"Hey, Carl," Toby said. "How's it going, Drew?"

"I saw you at the dinner last night," Carl said. "Why were you there? You aren't a cattleman."

Drew snickered at what Carl said. Toby just looked at him and walked on to his truck.

Carl was feeling good about his cut, and he and Drew were lingering and watching Toby.

Toby opened his door and stood up over the cab. "For a grown man, you sure act like a big baby all the time. Why don't you grow up and be a man? One thing for sure, I'll be a cattleman before you are, sir." He got into his truck and watched Carl stop grinning and turn and go into the store with his minion following him like a puppy.

"There *is* something wrong with that guy," Toby said to himself. He pulled out and drove home.

He decided to go get Hank's tractor and the bale of hay before he put out some of the feed and the protein tub. As he turned into the drive, he saw Jessie and Kali starting to leave. Jessie stopped beside him and thanked him again for letting her drive the '72. She pulled off. Kali came by and didn't look at him.

It's just as well, the way her Dad is, Toby thought.

Hank had gotten a bale of hay on the loader spike and had it waiting for Toby. He stuck his head out and hollered to Toby, "Let me know if you need anything."

Toby waved and started the tractor and pulled out. He got to his drive as Jessie and Kali were leaving. He waved. Jessie waved back. Kali didn't look or wave.

Toby went and fed the bale of hay, and the calves started eating it like they were starved. He took the tractor back and drove home and back to the corral where the calves were and put the protein tub out and fed three bags of feed. He took care of the rest of the livestock and went in and got a cup of coffee and went back out to spend some time with Pudge.

He talked to Pudge and brushed him as he did. He drank his last sip of coffee, and it was cold, so he said, "Pudge, I am going to have to get me a coffeepot to put out here. I'll be right back. Got to get another cup."

Toby walked out of the barn as a car pulled up into the drive. He couldn't readily identify it with the light shining in his eyes, so he strained to try and make it out. The car stopped. Both doors opened, and two guys got out. He made one out to be Drew, and he saw the cast on the right hand of the other one and realized it was Stone.

Toby didn't say anything; he waited for them to speak.

"You thought you were cute today, didn't you?" Drew said.

"We are going to show you how stupid you are," Stone said.

"Guys, this is not a good idea," Toby said. "This is my land. You will wind up in jail if you start anything. Turn around and leave."

"You won't feel like calling the law when we are through with you," Stone said.

Just then a truck turned into the drive and sped up to where they were. Sam jumped out of the truck and hollered at Stone, "You fool! What are you doing here?"

"Get out of here, Sam!" Stone hollered back. "This is no concern of yours."

Toby wondered how Sam knew what was going on. She walked over beside Toby and stood there. "You will have to beat me up too."

"Sam, it's okay," Toby said. "Step aside so you don't get hurt. Hold my cup for me." He handed her his cup as she stepped back.

Stone didn't like Sam siding with Toby. He started at Toby hard, and Toby readied for whatever Stone brought. Stone stopped and kicked at him. Toby jumped back on his right leg and kicked across his body and caught Stone's leg and spun him sideways. He jumped toward Stone and grabbed his right arm and left shoulder to turn him toward their car.

As Toby turned Stone, Toby saw Drew come toward him with something in his hand. Toby tried to turn to guard against whatever it was, but he was too late, and the bat Drew swung hit Toby's left arm up by his shoulder. It hurt, but Toby shook it off and kicked Drew hard in the groin. Drew dropped like he had been shot. Toby turned back to catch Stone turning around. Toby grabbed him and shoved him down hard on the hood. He had his elbow shoved in Stone's back and was pushing hard.

"You have two choices," Toby said. "Get in your car and leave, or get your tail kicked all over my barnyard. What's it gonna be?" He pushed and dug his elbow into Stone's spine as he was talking.

"I'll leave," Stone said.

Toby let him up but held Stone's arm and shoulder and shoved him to his door. He shoved him in the car. "I don't ever want to see you on my place again." Toby went over and grabbed Drew and lifted him to his feet and shoved him up against the car. "You are lucky. I ought to put you in the hospital for hitting me with a bat."

Toby started to let Drew go, but his anger got him, and he hit Drew in the stomach as hard as he could and then slugged the side of Drew's head by his eye. Toby opened the door, picked Drew up, and shoved him in the car. "Get out of here, but don't mess up my gravel."

Stone started the car and drove slowly until he was out of the drive. Toby watched them leave and then grabbed his left arm and leaned back against the barn and slid down to the ground.

Sam came running over. "Are you okay?"

"My arm is killing me, and I am shot," Toby said. "I just haven't got my strength and stamina back."

"Let me get you in the house." Sam helped him to his feet, but Toby said, "I need to shut the barn down."

Sam helped him walk to the barn, and he said to Pudge, "Sorry, bud. I am dead. I'll see you in the morning." He turned the light off, and they shut the door.

As they walked to the house, Sam said, "It is so cool how you treat Pudge."

"He is my best friend," Toby said.

"I would like to fill that role."

Toby looked at her as they got to the door. "You are starting to make me think that way."

33

Sam got both of them a cup of coffee and walked into the living room. "Take your shirt off, and let's look at your arm."

"It is hurting and kills me to try and move it." Toby took his shirt off. Below his T-shirt was a huge knot, and it was already black-and-blue.

"I think we need to get you to a doctor to check this out," Sam said.

Toby shrugged. "Bad as I hate to, I guess I better." He got ready, and Sam drove him to the hospital.

The ER doctor asked what happened, and Toby said, "Had an accident." They took x-rays, and the doctor came back in and said, "You have a hairline fracture. We will need to cast your arm."

"Is there any way to go without a cast?" Toby asked.

"It is risky to do it," the doctor said, "but you might get by with just keeping it wrapped tight with a small splint on that upper arm."

"Let's try that," Toby said. "I have too much to do to be hindered by a cast."

"I want to reiterate that I don't recommend this procedure," the doctor said.

"I understand and take full responsibility," Toby said.

Toby the Rancher

The doctor smiled. "Typical cowboy. Think you can rub some dirt on it and it will be better."

"That is Toby to a tee," Sam piped in.

They wrapped his arm, and they headed back to Toby's. It was after midnight, and Toby said, "You better be getting home. Your folks will be worried. I do thank you for the help, though."

"I'm a big girl," Sam said. "My parents don't worry about me like that anymore." She walked over to Toby and started to hug and kiss him, but Toby stopped her and asked, "Something is bothering me. How did you know they were coming out here?"

She didn't hesitate to answer, which made Toby feel good. "I had run to town to get some milk and eggs for breakfast for my mom, and I stopped to get a Coke and they were there. They made comments as they were leaving, and I got to thinking about what they said on the way home and figured out they were talking about you."

"I'm glad you did. I didn't realize those two ran together."

"Me either. I'm not sure how they got together other than a hatred for you." Sam smiled as she said that.

Toby looked at her and grinned. "Seems like I have that effect on people."

They kissed, and Sam headed for the door. "I'll talk to you tomorrow." She shut the door and left.

Toby was tired and went to bed without showering. He said his prayer and was asleep shortly after hitting the pillow.

He woke up early, and his arm was hurting. He got up and put ice on it as he made coffee and cooked breakfast. He headed out to do the chores, and his arm definitely hampered his activities. Everything seemed to hurt it. He kept pushing forward and got everything done at both places in time to get ready and make it to Sunday school.

He was sitting by himself and reading some verses when someone sat down right beside him. He looked up and was surprised to see Sam. "Hello. I am glad to see you here."

"I usually don't go anywhere, so I figured I would come with you this morning," Sam said.

Toby smiled. "Good deal."

When class was over and everyone came to the auditorium, Toby and Sam got several looks. Kali burned a hole through Sam with her glare. Sam smiled. "Ouch! That stare singed my hair."

Toby just smiled and didn't comment.

Hank walked over and shook Toby's hand and jerked him some, and Toby winced with his arm. Hank noticed and asked, "What's wrong?"

Not wanting to talk about it, Toby said, "Nothing. Arm is a little sore."

"Stone and Drew attacked him last night, and Drew hit his arm with a bat," Sam blurted out.

Toby gave her a look, and with that, she knew she had messed up.

"Say what?" Hank said. "Where did this happen?"

Toby looked at him and knew Hank wanted answers, so he said, "They came to my place."

"They came on to your place and attacked you?"

Toby just nodded.

Hank asked, "Is your arm okay?"

"It is fractured," Sam said.

"Fractured? Why isn't it casted?"

"He wouldn't let them."

Hank shook his head. "Doesn't surprise me." He went to his seat.

After services, Toby and Sam walked to their trucks.

"You want to eat dinner before you head home?" Toby asked.

"Absolutely!" Sam said as she climbed into her truck.

"Sounds good," Toby said.

They were sitting and talking when the Parker clan walked in.

"You can't seem to get away from them, can you?" Sam said.

"Don't want to," Toby said. "Hank and Sadie are great people."

"Yes, but I can't say that about the Matthews. They are a troubled sort."

Toby thought about what she had said. "I guess that is one way to put it."

They finished eating and got up to leave. Hank hollered at Toby and asked them to come over. Toby and Sam walked over, and Hank said, "Now tell me about last night."

"I don't want to spoil your dinner," Toby said. "We'll talk later."

"Toby, why are you holding your left arm like that?" Sadie asked. "Is it hurting?"

"Some," Toby replied.

"What's wrong?" Sadie asked.

"Drew hit him with a bat last night," Hank said.

"What?" Sadie exclaimed.

"Stone and Drew went out to his place and attacked him," Hank explained.

"I doubt that," Carl piped in. "He probably went after them."

Toby ignored him. He glanced at Kali, and she looked concerned. "Hank, I will talk to you later."

Toby and Sam walked out of the restaurant.

"How did you not respond to that jerk Carl?" Sam asked.

"He isn't worth the effort," Toby said. "I will talk to you later. I need to get home and get started bringing the cows up to preg check." He climbed into his truck and pulled away. He saddled Pudge and got the corral ready and then headed out to the pasture.

He was working to bring the cows in when he looked up and saw a horse and rider coming toward him. He assumed it was Sam but looked again when they got closer and saw it was a man. He strained to try and figure out who it was but couldn't make him out. He kept working the cattle and thought to himself, *Whoever that is sure sits a horse like Tom Gray did.*

Toby continued to move the cattle along. When he looked up, he saw Tom Gray riding through the gate. Toby was shocked. He stopped and waited for Tom to ride up to him. "Hello, Tom. It sure is good to see you. You are looking good."

"It is great to be riding a horse and seeing you too," Tom said.

"You come to visit?"

"Yeah. I wanted to see your place and ride my horse a while."

"That's great," Toby said. "How did you know I was out here?"

"You were riding out as I started up your drive," Tom replied. "What are you doing with these cows?"

"Bringing them in to preg check. I penned those calves yesterday to sell, and if these aren't far enough along, I may sell them too."

"Let's move them along."

Toby and Tom worked and talked as they rode. When they penned the cows, they dismounted, and Toby could tell Tom was still suffering from some paralysis from the stroke. "You want a cup?"

"Love one," Tom said.

They sat and talked for over an hour and were walking outside when Sam came pulling up into the drive. Toby introduced Tom and Sam, and they all went to work cattle. Of the twenty-six cows Toby checked, nineteen of them were better than seven months bred, so he decided to keep them until they calved and try to sell them as pairs. The seven that were less than three months bred were going to the sale barn with the calves.

It was 7:30 p.m. when they finished working the cows. Toby could tell Tom was tired, and Toby's arm was hurting badly, so he decided to go to town and get some burgers.

"Tom, why don't you go in and rest, and I will head to town and get some burgers," Toby said.

"You will do no such thing," Sam said. "I will make supper."

"Are you sure?" Toby asked.

"Positive."

Toby and Tom talked and waited for supper. Sam fixed a Mexican casserole and corn, and they ate until they were nearly sick.

"Young lady, that was one of the best Mexican dishes I have ever had," Tom said.

"Why, thank you, kind sir," Sam replied.

"I agree," Toby said. "It was great."

Sam cleaned up and left, and Toby and Tom were in bed by 10:00 p.m. Toby read the Bible and said his prayer and fell asleep.

He woke up with his arm hurting again. He put ice on his arm and took a pain pill the doctor had given him and started breakfast. He had eggs, bacon, and pancakes ready when Tom woke up at 6:45 a.m. They ate breakfast, and Toby told Tom to take it easy while he went and took care of Hank's place, and then they would start loading and hauling his livestock to the sale barn.

Hank walked into the barn while Toby was feeding. "How is your arm?"

"Hurts but doing okay," Toby replied.

"I like the way you just ignored what Carl said yesterday."

"He's not worth it. I made the mistake of letting him get under my skin when I saw him Saturday."

"Go ahead and use my trailer to haul off your calves today," Hank said. "You can get them in two trips."

"Thank you," Toby said. "I am taking off seven cows too. They are too short bred to do me any good."

"You got them all checked already?"

Toby told him about Tom coming in and about Sam helping too.

Hank was glad to hear Tom was doing well and had come to see Toby. "Let me know if you need anything." He walked out of the barn.

Toby finished his task and then rode Pudge back home to get his truck. He got the trailer, and he and Tom loaded the seven cows first and hauled them to the stockyards and then headed back for a load of calves. They got all the calves hauled in two loads, and they grabbed a burger at the stockyard concession before sitting down to watch the sale.

Toby was pleased that the cows brought $6,300.00 and was hoping the calves did as well. He went to get a cup of coffee, and the heifers were in the ring when he walked back in. The heifers had averaged 825 pounds and brought $1.49 a pound. The steers came in next and weighed in averaging 874 pounds. Toby was afraid they might be a little large to bring a good price per pound.

Hank walked in and sat down by him as the auctioneer started. "They weighed more than I thought."

"Me too," Toby said. "I hope it doesn't hurt me."

The steers hit $1.40 quickly and kept going. They ended at $1.63 a pound, and Toby looked at Tom. "Pinch me to make sure I'm not dreaming. I never dreamed they would do this good."

Hank patted Toby on the back. "Looks like the Toby Parker Beefmaster herd will be starting out good."

Toby laughed. "Thanks. Hank, I would like you to meet Tom Gray."

Hank and Tom shook hands.

"I am going to try and buy a couple of the red angus heifers I saw out there," Hank said.

"We are going to see if we can pick up the check today," Toby said. "See you later."

Toby inquired about the check, and they told him he could pick it up in an hour, so he and Tom went to the store to get some groceries. They swung back by, and the check was ready. Toby hadn't calculated what it would be and was pleasantly surprised when he opened it to see it was $40,005.68. He was ready to head to Weatherford and buy some Beefmaster cattle.

Toby and Tom drove back to Toby's place and kept the trailer so he could pull it to Weatherford. Tom went in to rest. Toby went and got Pudge and rode out to check all the cattle on both places. He talked to Pudge about his plans and what the cows brought. He put Pudge up and was brushing him and talking

Toby the Rancher

to him when the door to his room opened. Sam stepped in and asked, "Where you been all day?"

"Hello to you too," Toby said.

"Sorry," Sam said. "Hello. I came by twice to see if you needed any help."

"Tom helped, and we have been at the sale barn."

"How did you do?"

Toby explained what they had brought and how he was making plans to go to Weatherford to try and buy a bull and some heifers or cows.

"Would you mind if I tagged along?" Sam asked. "I would love to see a registered herd like that."

"Fine with me," Toby said.

They walked to the house, and they saw Tom had dozed off. They sat on the porch talking to let Tom sleep.

"Are you about to get back to full strength?" Sam asked.

"Still running down too quickly but definitely getting better," Toby said.

Toby heard a car. He looked to see Jessie pulling up into the drive.

34

Toby walked off the porch and out to Jessie's car to see what she was doing. She rolled down the window, and he saw Kali was in the car too. Sam was sitting on the porch railing, keeping a close eye on what was going on.

"Hey, girls, what's up?" Toby asked.

"Heading back to school, and thought we should stop by and say good-bye," Jessie replied.

"I figured you went back yesterday," Toby said.

"We both only had one class today, and we decided to skip it and stay home another day," Jessie said. "I was helping my mom do some things to get ready for a festival she is doing."

Toby started to speak, but Jessie continued, "What have you been doing the last couple of days?"

"Working and selling cattle."

"Kali tells me you hurt your arm."

"Well, my arm hurts, but I didn't hurt it."

"Yeah, I heard."

Toby noticed Kali wouldn't even look his way. "She sure seems to be here a lot," Jessie said.

"She has been helping and just dropped by to see how the cattle sold."

Toby the Rancher

"Uh-huh."

Sam was walking off the porch, and Jessie spoke up loudly. "Hi, Sam. You wearing out your welcome?"

"I don't know," Sam said. "Toby, am I?"

Toby didn't like being caught in the middle, and so he said, "You girls be safe, and, Sam, thanks for all the help. I am beat, so I think I will turn in."

All of them left, and Toby went into the house.

Tom was laughing when Toby walked through the door.

"What's so funny?" Toby asked.

"Looks like you got yourself in a female pickle there, bud," Tom replied.

Toby just shook his head and walked into the kitchen. He got a cup of coffee and walked back into the living room. "You want to go to Weatherford with me tomorrow?"

"I would love to," Tom said. "Should be a good trip."

"I plan on leaving by nine in the morning," Toby said. "Hank said he would watch things if we didn't get back and had to spend the night."

They watched some TV and went to bed at around 10:30 p.m. Toby read the Bible for a while and then dozed off.

He was awake by 5:00 a.m., and he started breakfast. He was eager to get things done and hit the road. He was looking forward to seeing the Beefmaster cattle and starting his own herd.

Tom walked in just as Toby got breakfast ready. "This brings back memories. I remember all those breakfasts you helped Cookie with. I can't wait to dig in."

"I wonder how Cookie is doing," Toby said. "I sure hope he is okay."

Tom echoed the statement, and they sat down and ate breakfast. They walked out of the house to do chores, and Tom said, "I think I know what to do with your stock. If you want, I will do it while you go take care of Hank's, and then we can be ready to leave when you want."

"That sounds great," Toby said. He saddled Pudge and rode out to Hank's. He walked to the house when he finished everything and knocked on the door.

Hank answered and said, "Good morning."

"Morning," Toby said. "I have everything taken care of. We are going to try and get away around 9:00."

Sadie walked to the door. "Toby, how is your arm?"

"It is still sore but coming along," Toby said.

"You better not overdo it," Sadie said.

Toby grinned. "Yes, ma'am."

"I'll take care of things while you are gone," Hank said. "Call if you need anything. Drive safely."

"Yes, sir." Toby rode back to his place. He unsaddled Pudge, brushed him, and told him what he was going to do. Toby walked into the house, and Tom was sitting at the table.

"I sure wish I could get my stamina back," Tom said.

"Tom, you have to be patient," Toby said. "You are recovering from a major stroke. You are doing great. Let's get ready and hit the road."

They packed up and were rolling out by 8:50 a.m.

"I need to run to the bank and then we are westbound," Toby said. His phone rang as he pulled out of the bank parking lot, and it was Sam.

"I wish I could go with you guys," Sam said. "I would love to see their place."

"Yeah, I wish you could," Toby said.

"Thanks for asking," Sam said. "I'll meet you at the old station as you head out of town."

Toby realized he had just got hoodwinked. He grinned and asked Tom, "You okay with Sam going with us?"

"I don't mind at all," Tom said. "She seems to really like you."

Toby pulled up, and Sam was standing outside her mom's car with her bag.

"You are a fast packer," Toby said.

Sam laughed. "Yes, I am." She got in, and Tom said, "Good morning, young lady."

"Hi, Tom," Sam said. "Hope you don't mind me tagging along?"

"Not at all. We might have gotten bored talking to each other that long."

"How are you getting away from your ranch so much?" Toby asked.

"Mom told Dad to let me go," Sam replied. "She likes you."

Toby glanced at Tom. Tom was grinning at him. Toby shook his head and pulled onto the road.

They talked as they drove toward the Dallas/Fort Worth Metroplex. They stopped and ate dinner at a Cracker Barrel and then continued on toward Weatherford. They pulled into the ranch at 2:30 p.m. They introduced each other and then walked out to see the bull.

"This place is nice," Sam said.

"Yes, it is," Tom said. "And looking at that group of cows over there, the cattle are as nice."

Toby was walking ahead of them with the owner and didn't hear their conversation. When they reached the corral and the owner went to let the bull out, Toby looked at Tom and Sam. "What do you think?"

"I would love to have a place like this and cattle like that," Sam said.

"I'm hurt," Toby said. "You don't think mine is this nice?"

Sam started stammering and stuttering, and Toby started laughing. "Just kidding." He turned around and said, "Holy smokes, would you look at that?"

A huge bull had walked out of the barn.

"That thing must weigh well over a ton," Tom said.

Three other bulls walked out of doors into individual pens, and then the owner came walking back to where they were admiring the bulls.

"Mr. Ellis, that is the largest bull I have ever seen," Toby said. "What does he weigh?"

"He will go about 2,700 right now," Mr. Ellis replied. "He drops some during the summer."

"And I thought Boss looked good," Toby said.

"Boss is a very good bull," Mr. Ellis said. "I saw him at the stock show." He paused. "The other three bulls are for sale. All have similar genetics, but the far two are out of the big boy there."

Toby looked them over. "What are you asking for them?"

Mr. Ellis said, "I'll take $4,000 for this one and $4,500 for the other two."

"I'll take the one in the third pen."

"Good choice. He would have been the one I would have wanted if I were in your shoes. He will give you a good base to build your herd on."

"Sir, you wouldn't have any heifers or cows for sale that would be separate from his bloodline that I could purchase, would you?" Toby asked.

"I sure do. I wondered why you brought such a big trailer for one bull. How many you looking for?"

"Depends on the price but hoping for at least ten."

"Let's climb in the Ranger and run down the lane and look at the pen we just preg checked," Mr. Ellis said.

They pulled up, and Toby was amazed at how good the heifers looked compared to his. He hoped he could buy some.

"These heifers were all from AI sires and are bred AI, so there would no genetic issues with the bull," Mr. Ellis said. "You would have two totally different generations."

"You said they were preg checked," Toby said. "How far along are they?"

"They are slated to start calving around the first of June."

"How much you asking for them?"

"Three thousand dollars each, unless you take ten. Then it is $2,500 each."

"I would like to buy fourteen of them. I think I can haul that many."

"That sounds good. I am confident you can haul that many. Let's get them rounded up, and you start picking out the ones you want."

Toby picked out what he thought looked like the best fourteen heifers. They got them loaded and were on the road by 5:30 p.m. They would be back at Toby's ranch by 10:00 p.m. if all went well.

"You two have been quiet," Toby said. "Do you have any thoughts?"

"I was totally impressed by the ranch and the cattle," Sam said. "I think you picked some fantastic stock."

"Sam and I talked and agreed," Tom said. "You got some good cattle."

"I guess y'all are okay with heading on back tonight since we are rolling this early?" Toby asked.

"Yes, because you can't leave your cattle in a trailer overnight," Sam said.

"Not a problem," Tom said.

They stopped and ate supper and pulled into Toby's drive at 10:30 p.m. He unloaded the heifers into one pen and the bull into another one and put out some feed to help calm them down. He parked the truck and trailer and went in to check on Pudge while Tom and Sam went on to the house. He talked to Pudge and brushed him for about ten minutes then headed into the house. It was after 11:00 p.m. He walked in and saw Sam in her PJs. "I take it you are spending the night."

"I hope you don't mind," Sam replied.

"Nope. The bed in the other bedroom isn't the best, but hopefully, you can sleep since I'm sure you're tired."

"I am tired. Thanks. See you in the morning." Sam kissed him on the cheek as she walked to the bedroom.

Tom was already in bed, so Toby decided to head in to bed as well. He read the Bible and said his prayer and was asleep by midnight.

He had breakfast fixed when Tom and Sam came walking into the kitchen.

"It smells great," Sam said.

Tom said, "The boy can cook."

Toby smiled, and they sat down and ate. As he finished eating, he said, "Sam, I'm sure you need to get on home, so feel free to take the '72, and you can bring it home later."

Sam grinned. "That will be cool."

She left, and Toby and Tom walked down to look at Toby's new additions to his herd.

"I sure would like to have a few head like that," Tom said. "We live in town, and so that is out of the question."

"Is there not any land to rent outside of town?" Toby asked.

"Nothing I can afford, especially with the hospital and doctor bills."

"That's too bad."

They walked back to the barn and started feeding. They both saddled up to ride and check on the outer pastures on both places. They took Hank's trailer home and took care of the feeding.

Hank walked out. "So you got you some Beefmaster and got back last night, huh?"

"Yeah," Toby said. "I sure hope they turn out."

"I'm sure they will," Hank said. "I plan to come and see them after dinner."

"That would be great. Thanks again for the use of your trailer."

"You are more than welcome."

Sadie stuck her head out the door. "Toby, how is your arm doing?"

"It's getting better," Toby responded.

"Here's an apple pie for you to take home," Sadie said.

He walked up to her and hugged her. "Thank you so much. This will go great with coffee."

They headed back to his house, and Tom asked, "You thinking about your dad?"

Toby the Rancher

Toby looked at him. "Yes. How did you know?"

"I remember you telling Cookie and me about you and your dad eating apple pie and drinking coffee," Tom replied.

Toby smiled. "Yeah, I sure wish he could be here. I think he would like what I'm doing."

Tom smiled. "I know he would. Any dad would like his son taking charge of his life and doing things the way you are."

"Thanks," Toby said.

They went into the house and got a cup of coffee and cut a piece of pie for each. They were enjoying the pie and coffee when Toby said, "Tom, you are more than welcome to put a few head here. I know it is a long ways from your home, but the offer is there if you want to consider it."

Tom thought for a minute. "You know, I might take you up on that. I wouldn't be able to work with them, but it would give me a stake in something."

They went back out, and Toby started working on repairing the shed in the bull's pen. "I like his name. Maximus. I think I'll call him Max."

Tom was helping hold boards and hand Toby what he needed, and he said, "This brings back memories of building a line shack."

Toby laughed. "Yeah. That was fun."

They put the bull in the pen and fed the heifers some hay and then headed to Sam's to get the '72. Ryder walked out of the barn as they pulled in, and waved for them to come to the barn. "Hello, Toby. You about to get back to full strength?"

"Stronger every day," Toby said. "Ryder, this is my friend Tom Gray."

They shook hands, and Ryder asked, "You bout ready to help finish bringing my herd up?"

"Yeah, I think so," Toby said.

Sam came walking out and asked, "How are the new cows doing?"

"Seem okay so far," Toby said.

"Sam said you got some Beefmaster," Ryder said. "I'd like to see them."

"You're welcome to come over anytime," Toby said. "We better get back."

Toby and Tom drove back over and pulled in ahead of Hank. They walked out to look at Max, and Toby glanced toward the pasture and saw two hogs running. "Well, crud." He took off for the barn. Luckily, he hadn't unsaddled Pudge. He tightened the cinch and jumped in the saddle and took off. He didn't want to start seeing hogs showing up again.

Toby spotted the hogs and ran them down and shot them. He rode back up to where Hank and Tom were looking at Max, and Hank asked, "You get them?"

Toby stepped down off Pudge and said, "Yeah. Need to go bring them in."

"Tom and I decided you're heading back to Weatherford tomorrow and buy him some heifers," Hank said.

Toby laughed. "Is that right?" He looked at them and saw they weren't kidding. "I guess I am."

Hank and Tom both laughed then, and Tom asked, "Do you mind?"

"Not at all," Toby said.

Hank left, and Toby and Tom went to get the hogs. They loaded them and took them on to town. They stopped and got a burger and ran into Carla and a couple of her friends.

"Hello, Carla," Toby said.

She looked at him and said, "Hey, Toby."

Toby and Tom sat down, and Carla walked over and said, "They want to meet you." She introduced Toby to her friends, and they walked off, giggling.

"You seem to be a novelty around here," Tom said.

Toby just looked at him and looked back at his menu.

Carla walked back over. "Toby, we are having a backwards dance tomorrow night. Would you go with me?"

Toby looked at her and said, "Thank you, but I don't know how to dance backwards."

"No, silly," Carla said. "It is called that because girls ask the guys to go."

"Oh, I see. Well, I'm not sure I will be back from Weatherford in time to go."

"We can go Friday," Tom said.

Toby looked at him. "Are you sure?"

"Yep," Tom replied.

"Okay," Toby said. He looked at Carla. "I'll go with you."

"Great," Carla said. "I'll pick you up at 6:00."

"Okay. See you then."

Carla turned. The girls were all grinning at her, and they left the café.

Toby looked at Tom. "I'm not sure what that is about. She hasn't spoken to me in a good while."

Tom smiled. "You need to settle down with a good girl and break all these others' hearts."

"Ha, ha," Toby said. "Very funny."

They ate and left the café.

35

Toby decided to take a ride for the rest of the day and look for hogs or hog signs on both places, so he saddled Pudge and rode out. Tom needed to rest, and he decided to stick around the house and barn and call his kids and grandkids. Toby did a lot of thinking while he was riding, and he talked to Pudge as they rode. He didn't spot any hogs but saw areas of rooted dirt and some damage, which made him believe there was more than the two he had just killed. He would need to keep his eyes open and his gun ready in the next few days.

When he got back, he finished things up, and he and Tom went to midweek service at church. They watched some TV when they got back. Toby was up at 5:00 a.m. the next day, and he went and checked on the new cattle and Pudge before starting breakfast. Tom woke up at 6:30 a.m., and they ate breakfast and were out with the livestock by 7:15 a.m.

"You just don't know how good it is to be out doing this again," Tom said. He paused. "Not because of where I am living now but because of the stroke. I didn't know if I would ever sit a horse or feed a cow again."

Toby listened and then responded, "I understand what you are saying. I am glad you were able to come over."

"I'll be coming more since I will have some cattle here."

Toby the Rancher

"I like the sound of that."

They finished the morning chores and went in to drink a cup.

"You feel up to cowboying some today?" Toby asked.

"I would love to cut and drive some cattle for a change," Tom said.

"I think I will call Ryder and see if he wants to try and bring some up today."

Toby got in touch with Ryder, and Ryder was more than ready to try and bring in another couple of pastures. Toby and Tom loaded up their horses and headed over to the Webers'. They unloaded and were saddling up when Sam walked out of the barn, leading her Paint.

"Hello, good-looking, and you too, Toby."

Tom got a big kick out of that, and Toby liked seeing Tom enjoying himself.

"Hello," Toby said. "Isn't there a very pretty girl living here? I haven't seen her yet."

"I'm getting on my horse and getting out of here before sparks fly," Tom said.

Toby laughed and grabbed the saddle horn and swung into the saddle with ease.

"You sure make that look easy," Tom said. "I never could do that."

"Let's go," Toby said.

Sam mounted up, and they rode out. She said as they left the barnyard, "Dad is out there waiting for us. He went to check a fence."

They rode quickly to the pasture, and Ryder had the gate open. Toby nodded as he rode by Ryder and rode in to find the cattle. They were rounding them up in a matter of minutes, and Tom and Toby were working well together. They took the herd of fifty-five cows and moved them straight to the corral at the barn without needing Sam and Ryder.

They penned them, and Ryder said, "You two work well together. Must have ridden together before."

"A little bit," Toby said. "Where is the next pasture?"

"Sam will show you, and me and boys will start working these," Ryder replied.

They had the other sixty head to the pen in short fashion, and Toby was ready to help vaccinate, put in fly tags, and trim hoofs. He was keeping an eye on Tom to make sure he didn't overdo it or get in a situation he couldn't handle.

It flowed fairly well and they were well into the second pen when Toby said, "Ryder, we are going to need to go take care of our stock before dark, and Tom needs to rest."

"Sam told me he had a stroke not too long ago," Ryder responded. "I sure appreciate the help. You available tomorrow?"

Tom walked up as Ryder asked the question.

"Nah, that is why we need to get on back," Toby said. "So we can take care of things since we will be gone to Weatherford tomorrow."

"Plus, Toby has a date tonight," Tom said.

Sam's head jerked around to look at them, but Toby didn't see her as she was down trimming the hooves of a cow.

"Let's load up." Toby walked about halfway back to the pen where they were and hollered, "We'll see y'all later. Bye, Sam."

She didn't acknowledge him, but he figured she didn't hear him. He walked back to the truck, and he and Tom drove home.

Toby tended the livestock and took care of Pudge last. He was brushing him and talking over the day. "You know, buddy, I don't know why I agreed to go tonight. I guess I was hoping it would help relations with Carla's family. I don't need them as enemies. I guess we'll see if it helps. See ya later." He shut the barn up and walked to the house.

He got ready and was drinking a cup with Tom when Carla pulled in. He told Tom, "This seems a little weird. Being picked up by a girl."

Tom laughed. "Now you're getting the name. Backward dance."

Toby grinned and walked out on the porch. He waved to Carla as he walked down the steps. She grinned at him and waved. He opened the door and said, "Hi, Carla."

Toby the Rancher

"You clean up good," she said.

They drove to the school and made small talk on the way. When they walked into the gym, several girls came up to Carla, and she turned aside to talk to them. Toby felt like a fish out of water, being at least seven years older than everyone but the sponsors. He mumbled to himself, "I must have lost my mind."

He walked over by the wall and leaned back against it with his left foot bent up behind him and resting on the wall.

"Hello," someone said.

He turned to see a tall, slender woman about his age, and he said, "How ya doing?"

"From the looks of things, a little better than you."

"Is it that obvious?"

"I'm Gayle Perkins," she said.

Toby stuck out his hand to shake hers. "Toby Parker. Pleased to meet you."

"I teach history and coach girls' basketball."

"What kind of history?"

"American."

"You a chaperone or something?" Toby asked.

"One of the senior class sponsors," Gayle responded. "What are you doing here?"

"Well, it's a long story, but the short of it is, I was asked by Carla Matthews."

"Too much of a gentleman to say no?"

"Nah. Just seemed like the right thing to do at the time."

Gayle laughed. "I better walk around and make sure everyone is being good."

"Okay. It was good to meet you, Ms. Perkins."

"Just call me Gayle."

Toby nodded and tipped his hat to her. Gayle smiled and walked away.

Carla came walking up with three girls in tow. "What was Ms. Perkins wanting?"

"Him," one of the girls said.

◆ 295 ◆

They all giggled, and it made Toby more uncomfortable than he was already. "She was just introducing herself."

"You want to dance?" Carla said.

"I only know a couple of line dances from college," Toby said.

"You can't two-step?"

"Not very well. Can you?"

"Yes."

"This song is good for a line dance."

They all said, "Let's go."

Toby reluctantly followed them onto the floor.

"Start us off," Carla said.

"Oh, brother," Toby muttered. He got the beat of the song and started the dance. He was surprised that he could still remember it and was able to do it pretty good. He was stepping and turning once when Gayle slid in line beside him. The song ended, and Toby wanted off the floor, but as he turned to walk off, four guys fronted him.

"What's up, guys?" Toby asked.

"We don't like you," one of them said.

"Give it some time," Toby responded. "I'll grow on you." He pushed on through them. One of the guys started to grab his arm, but Toby caught his hand before he could. "Unless you want to draw back a nub, I wouldn't do that."

The kid looked shocked and backed away.

"Good move," Toby told him. He walked over to the wall and glanced toward the guys and saw that the girls who had been with Carla were being chastised by them. He surmised the girls were the dates of those guys and didn't like them hanging around him.

"Another reason this was a bad move," he mumbled.

Gayle walked up to Toby. "You handled that well. Thanks."

Toby nodded. "I hope it stays handled."

Carla walked up, and Gayle walked off.

"Well, I see Ms. Perkins can't seem to stay away from you," Carla said.

Toby the Rancher

"She was just thanking me for not causing a scene with those boys," Toby said.

"You moved good out there."

"I doubt that, but thanks."

The next hour or so went without incident, and Carla said, "Some of us want to leave and go eat. You okay with that?"

"Leavin' is good for me," Toby said.

They started toward the door.

Gayle stopped him. "It was good to meet you, Toby. Maybe I'll see you around."

"Yes, ma'am," Toby said. "It was good to meet you. I don't get into town much, but maybe we will."

She smiled. "Good night."

Toby nodded and walked out.

"Well, that was a very obvious come-on," Carla said.

"Oh, bull," Toby said. "Is that all you girls ever think about?"

"We are going to the restaurant where we eat on Sundays," Carla said.

"Okay," Toby said. "They have good food."

They walked into the restaurant as Sam was walking out with her parents. Carla and the others went on to the tables.

"Hey, Toby," Ryder spoke up. "What you doing?"

"Getting a bite to eat." Toby turned to Sam. "Sam, you look nice tonight."

Sam looked at him. "Aren't you complimenting the wrong girl?"

"Don't think so. You are the one I'm looking at."

"Sam, be nice," Sam's mother said.

"Did ya have fun at the kids' dance?" Sam asked.

"I guess that would depend on your definition of fun," Toby said.

"Well, enjoy your meal," Ryder said. "We are heading home."

Carla came walking up and said, "Toby, we decided we don't want to eat. We would rather go the movies."

"I really don't want to go to the movies," Toby said.

◆ 297 ◆

"Uh, how you going to get home?"

"We can take him home," Sam said.

"Are you okay with that?" Carla asked Toby.

"Yeah," Toby said. "That will work, if they don't mind."

"Be happy to," Ryder said.

"All right," Toby said. "Thanks for the invite, Carla. See you later."

As they drove down the highway, Ryder asked, "She was kind of young for you, wasn't she?"

"Yeah, but it wasn't really a date," Toby said. "She asked me to the backward dance. There is more to it than I can discuss, but it wasn't a date."

Sam was looking at him as he talked. He turned to look at her, and she looked puzzled and turned away.

They dropped Toby off without any exchange with Sam. Toby just thanked them for the ride as he got out. Tom was asleep when he got home, so he changed clothes and got a cup of coffee and walked to the barn to see Pudge. He sat and talked over things with Pudge and fell asleep in his chair he had put in the room.

He woke up at 5:30 a.m. and headed to the house to get breakfast. Tom woke up at 6:15 a.m., and they ate breakfast discussing Toby's night and the upcoming trip. They were outside taking care of the chores before 7:00 a.m. and were hooking the trailer to the truck by 9:00 a.m. Since Tom was only looking to buy five heifers, they were taking Toby's twenty-four-foot gooseneck trailer he got with the ranch purchase.

Toby was walking to the pickup when his phone rang. It was Mike Stine asking if Toby was still willing to let him drive his truck to prom. Toby told Mike he could and that he could pick it up on Saturday morning since they figured to be back late tonight.

Toby and Tom locked the front gate and hit the highway heading to Weatherford. They traveled for a hundred miles, and Toby pulled off to get a cup of coffee. They didn't take much time getting back on the road and were running 70 mph down the highway when Toby looked to his left and saw a church van

Toby the Rancher

coming across the median straight for them. He reacted and hit his brakes and veered to his right. The shoulder was narrow and had a drastic drop-off. Toby steered off the road, and the truck rocked hard to the right. At the same time, the van slid sideways into the rear of the truck and the front of the trailer, causing the truck and trailer to roll over three times down the twenty-foot embankment and land on its top.

36

Tom gathered himself together once the vehicle stopped rolling. He was rattled but didn't feel any major pains. He looked to his left, but he couldn't see Toby because the cab was caved in too far. He hollered Toby's name, but no answer came, so he started trying to unbuckle his seat belt. The truck was on its top, so he had a lot of pressure on the belt. He finally got the button pushed and fell into the top of the cab.

The door glass was broken out, so he worked to crawl out of the window. He heard people talking outside as he was crawling out, and then someone grabbed him to help him out. He saw it was a man, but not Toby.

"Is the other guy out?" Tom asked.

"No," the man said. "The cab is crushed on that side, and we can't get to him."

Tom was scared and started to the other side of the truck. When he saw how bad it looked, he dropped to his knees.

"The police should be here shortly, and maybe they will have the Jaws of Life, where they can tell if he is still alive," the man said.

"He was doing this trip for me, and it may have cost him his life," Tom muttered to himself.

There were a couple of guys still trying to find a way to get to Toby, and Tom heard kids crying. He looked up the embankment and saw a group standing around. One of the men by them came down and said, "I am so sorry. I couldn't control the steering. If y'all hadn't turned, we would all probably be dead."

"The one that saved your lives may be dead," Tom said.

"Oh, I pray he's not," the man replied.

Tom paused a minute and then asked, "Are the kids all okay?"

"Yes," the man replied. "Just shook up and a few bumps and bruises."

Sirens were heard in the distance, and everyone started looking down the road for them. Tom asked the two guys still down around Toby's truck if they were hearing anything. Both replied in the negative.

Tom was feeling sick. He was fearing the worst. The state trooper and ambulance pulled up, and the EMTs and trooper started working with the help of some volunteers. They had a Jaws of Life and started tearing the truck apart to find Toby.

Tom tried to get close enough to try and see if he could spot Toby. One of the EMT guys said, "I can see him, and he isn't conscious. I can't tell if he is breathing."

Tom had tears welling up in his eyes. They kept working to try and get Toby out.

"His side of the cab must have hit those boulders as it rolled and that is what crushed it," the trooper said.

There were some big boulders off the side of the road, and as Tom looked around, they were the only ones he could see. *What are the odds*, he thought to himself.

"Let's see if we can get a hold of him to move him some," one of the guys said.

Tom looked around and saw the kids and the guy driving the van sitting in a circle, holding hands and praying. The tears kept coming as he wiped them away.

"I have his arm, and it is cold," one of the guys said. "It doesn't look good."

"You don't know that, young man," Tom said. "He is fighter." He didn't know why he said it. It just came out.

They kept working, and Tom saw them pulling Toby out. Toby's face was covered in blood. They got him out and started working on him.

"I have a very light pulse," one of them said. "He is losing too much blood. He has an artery partially severed in his neck. We need to get him stabilized and slow down the bleeding and get him to the hospital."

They kept working on him as Tom tried to watch and see what they were doing. The trooper was by the truck and said, "This phone is ringing." It was Toby's, and Tom said, "I'll get it." He answered the phone and said, "Toby's phone."

It was Hank. "Hello, Tom. Are y'all on the way?"

Tom proceeded to tell Hank what had happened and what was going on. There was silence on the other end when Tom finished. He waited awhile and then, "Hello? Hank, you there?"

"Yeah, I'm here," Hank replied. "I am on my way. Let me know where they take him."

Tom was glad to hear Hank was coming and told him he would keep him updated. They were loading Toby in the ambulance when Tom got off the phone. He walked to catch up to them and asked, "What hospital we going to?"

"Tyler," the EMT replied. "They may have to Medi Flight him from there."

They let Tom get in the front seat, and they took off toward the hospital. Tom felt numb. He didn't know what to do. Toby was lying in the back almost dead, and he was wondering if he should have stayed to take care of things. He wanted to be with Toby but doubted himself. Toby's phone rang again to break his thought.

"Hello?" he said.

"Who is this?" a female voice asked.

"This is Tom Gray. Who is this?"

"Carla Matthews. Is Toby around? I wanted to thank him for going with me last night."

Tom proceeded to tell Carla what had happened, and just as he finished, he heard one of the EMTs say, "We are losing him. We have to get to the hospital fast for surgery, or he will not make it."

Tom hung up. His eyes were already tearing up from telling Carla about it, and the tears were running down his cheeks now. He couldn't even think straight. He was trying to pray, and his mind kept going back to the wreck and then to Toby. They arrived at the hospital, and the EMTs and hospital personnel worked fast to get Toby out and in the ER.

Tom was in the waiting room, and a nurse came out and said, "They are taking him into surgery." Tom started to follow her when he looked and saw Hank and Sadie walk in.

"You made good time," Tom said.

"Yeah," Hank said. "Our boy is in trouble, so we had to get here."

"They are taking him into surgery," Tom said. "This nurse is going to show us to the waiting room."

They followed her, and Hank asked Tom, "How is he doing?"

"They said if the surgery doesn't get done in time, they could lose him," Tom said. "I hope we made it."

"Oh no!" Sadie exclaimed. "Please, Lord, don't let us lose that boy."

Toby's phone rang, and Tom answered it.

It was Carla. "How is Toby?"

"He is going into surgery," Tom replied. "It is touch and go."

"Who is that?" Hank asked.

"Carla Matthews," Tom said.

Hank turned to Sadie. "Grandma, talk to her."

Tom handed Sadie the phone. "I guess she is your granddaughter."

Sadie took the phone and talked to Carla. They all waited for two hours, but it seemed like twice that long. The doctor came in and asked for Toby's family. Tom and Hank both stood up.

"We were able to repair the artery and stop the bleeding," the doctor said. "He lost so much blood he is still not out of danger.

He also has some swelling around the brain, so we will have to watch that too. We are hoping it is minimal and only a bad concussion. Only time will tell."

"When can we see him?" Hank asked.

The doctor told them it would be a while yet and they would let them know when.

"He made it through the surgery," Hank said. "That is good. Toby is a fighter. If it is up to him, he will whip this thing."

"You are right there," Tom said. "That boy never backs down from anything."

Sadie smiled. "You guys just keep talking. It makes me feel better about him."

Hank's phone rang. "Hello? Hey, darlin'. Yes, he is in bad shape." He paused and listened then said, "It's touch and go for the next few hours. They fixed the artery, but they are afraid his brain is swelling." He paused again and then said, "Don't cry. We will keep you updated." He hung up and looked at Sadie. "Kali is regretting how she has been acting toward Toby lately."

"Poor child just doesn't know how to express herself to him," Sadie said. "Hopefully she will get the chance to."

They sat and waited for about forty-five minutes. Hank got up and walked up and inquired of Toby's status. The lady told him they could go to the ICU to see him.

Tom was surprised. "I guess it didn't dawn on me that he would be in ICU."

"Yeah, I hadn't thought about that either," Hank said.

They made it to the unit, and Hank asked the doctor, "What are the chances of him having any brain damage if he comes out of this and makes it?"

"It is still too early to tell," the doctor responded. "Anything is possible, good or bad, at this point until he shows change."

Sadie gasped. "Oh my. He has so much promise and so much to live for."

"We have to think positively, pray, and remember we are talking about Toby," Hank said. "If it can be beat, he will beat it."

Time went by. Hank, Sadie, and Tom went and got motel rooms and tried to get some rest. Hank checked on Toby's truck and trailer to find out where they were and called his insurance. They went to eat breakfast, and Hank was telling Tom what he had found out about his truck and trailer and the insurance.

"Toby sure caught a break when he met y'all," Tom said. "I am so happy he did."

"We feel the same way about him," Hank said.

They walked into ICU, and the doctor was walking out of Toby's room. Hank approached him and asked, "How is he today, Doc?"

The doctor looked at him and said, "He is still unconscious, but we don't see any swelling of the brain, so that is a plus. His vital signs are slightly better but still in the danger area. We will just have to watch him. If you are people that believe in prayer, offering some up would be good at this point."

Hank and Tom just nodded to the doctor as he walked off. They went into the room, and Sadie started talking to Toby. She sat and talked to him for about fifteen minutes before a nurse came in.

"His vital signs have improved since you all came in," the nurse said. "Keep talking to him."

Hank and Tom joined in the conversation, and Toby had some movement in his fingers.

Suddenly, something dawned on Tom. "Hank, there isn't anyone taking care of Toby's stock. Pudge needs to be taken care of, and so do his new bull and heifers."

Hank looked shocked. "Geez, I had plum forgotten my stock too."

The nurse came in quickly and said, "His vitals just dropped back to where they were when he was brought in. He was improving some."

Tom thought a minute and then whispered to Hank, "He heard me say Pudge hadn't been taken care of, and it made him drop."

Hank looked at Tom. "I bet you are right." He stood up. "Sadie, Tom and I are heading home to do the chores, and then we will be back."

"Okay," she said. "Drive safely."

Tom and Hank headed for home and discussed Toby all the way.

"I need to get Toby's phone charger so I can leave it on," Tom said. "I better turn it on and see if he has any messages." He turned it on, and it showed four messages. He checked them and hung it up, saying, "Oh no, Toby had promised to let a young man drive his truck to prom, and he is thinking he changed his mind."

"Who was it?" Hank asked.

"Mike somebody."

"Mike Stine. I will call him. What is the number?"

Hank called Mike. Mike was very apologetic for the hateful messages he had left on the phone. He understood and wished Toby well.

Hank hung up. "He feels bad. Who were the other messages?"

"Three were him. One was Sam. She sounded mad too."

"We'll call her later." Hank pulled up into his place. He got out and said, "Take my truck, and do Toby's chores, and then we will head back to the hospital."

Tom agreed and drove to Toby's. He saw a truck sitting at the gate, and as he got closer, he recognized it as Sam's. He pulled up, and she was walking back from the house. Tom walked to unlock the gate, and she hollered, "Where is he? Is he with the Matthews girl again?"

Tom looked at her. "You need to calm down before you say something you'll regret."

She looked at him. "What do you mean? Where is his truck? Why isn't he answering his phone?" She aggravated Tom, and so he just blurted out, "He is in the hospital close to death."

"You serious?" Sam asked.

Toby the Rancher

Tom told her the whole story, and about halfway through, she dropped to her knees and buried her head in her hands. Tom tried to console her, and she said, "I am a jerk. I have to go see him." She got up and walked to her truck and drove away.

Tom shook his head and went to feed.

37

Tom brushed and curried Pudge and talked to him about Toby. He noted that Pudge seemed sad when he was told about Toby.

I have never seen a bond so strong between a man and his horse, Tom thought.

It took Tom longer to feed than it did Toby, because he wasn't 100 percent in his mobility yet. Hank was waiting when Tom pulled back into his place.

Hank walked out and said, "I called the hospital, and Toby is about the same. At least he hasn't gotten any worse."

"That is a plus." Tom walked to the passenger side of the truck. He and Hank didn't talk much on the way back.

They walked into the hospital and saw Mike Stine getting on the elevator. He saw Hank and held the door for them.

"Hello, Mike," Hank said.

Mike replied, "Hello, Mr. Parker."

"Mike, this is Tom Gray, Toby's friend," Hank said, "Tom, this is Mike Stine."

Both of them spoke to the other. The elevator stopped, and the door opened. There were three elevator doors, and as they started to step out, Sam walked past them.

"Hi, Sam," Hank spoke.

Sam turned and saw them. "Hi, guys. Any word on Toby?"

"Sadie said he was still the same when I called," Hank said.

"He has to pull through. He just has to."

They all walked toward the waiting room.

"Sam, why don't you and Mike go in first?" Hank said.

Sam was happy to hear Hank say that and started toward the room, with Mike trying to keep up with her. She opened the door and walked in and saw Sadie, Kali, Carla, and Jessie in the room.

"Hello, Sam and Mike," Sadie said, "Come on in. How are you two?"

"Doing well, Mrs. Parker," Mike said. "How is Toby?"

Sam and the three girls were glaring at each other. Sam never dreamed they would be there. She was upset she didn't know about it sooner so she could have been the first one there.

"He is still the same," Sadie replied to Mike. "We thought he was improving, but he slipped back."

"What are the doctors saying?" Sam asked.

"They are saying it is up to how strong Toby is," Jessie said.

Sam glared at her. "You talked to the doctor?"

Jessie didn't look quite as confident as she said, "No, that is what Sadie said."

"That is why I was asking her," Sam replied.

"Girls, this isn't the place," Sadie said. "Why don't you girls go to the waiting room and let Samantha and Mike have some time with Toby? They wouldn't like this many being in here." Sadie was trying to diffuse the situation before it got ugly in the room.

Jessie, Kali, and Carla reluctantly left and went to the waiting room.

When they were gone, Sam asked, "He is going to be okay, isn't he?"

"It is up to Toby and the Lord at this point," Sadie said.

Sam started crying, and Sadie got up to hug her. Mike's eyes filled with tears, and he turned and left the room. He walked into the waiting room, and Hank could tell he was wiping away tears.

Hank walked over and patted Mike on the back. "Thank you for coming. He will thank you himself one day."

Mike didn't know how to act or respond, and he said, "I have to go. Thank you." He walked to the elevator. Carla called after him and said, "See you at the prom." Mike raised his right hand to acknowledge what she had said.

"Hank, let's go see Toby," Tom said.

The two men walked into the room as Sadie said, "I think I saw his hand move."

"I will get the nurse," Sam said.

"Mrs. Parker, are you sure?" Tom asked.

Sadie looked up and said, "I'm positive."

Sam walked out and told the nurse that Toby had moved his hand. The three girls saw her. Sam glanced at them and smiled as she turned to walk back into the room.

Jessie looked at Kali. "Did you see that?"

"I did," Carla replied. "She is a—"

Kali cut her off and said in a stern voice, "Don't worry about her."

Jessie and Carla looked at each other and then back at Kali. None of the girls said any more.

The nurse checked Toby and said, "His vital signs are looking better." As she finalized saying it, Toby's right eye opened some. Sam saw it and screeched, "He's awake."

Her voice made the others jump, and Toby's eye opened wider. The nurse checked his pupil, and he tried to open his left eye. She spoke to him, "Toby, can you hear me?"

Toby nodded, and Sam started crying. She looked at Sadie. She was crying too, and Hank and Tom both had tears in their eyes.

Toby laid there with his eyes open but couldn't focus. He was trying to realize where he was and what had happened.

"I will get the doctor," the nurse said.

She left the room, and Tom walked up closer to the bed. Toby saw him, and tears formed in his eyes. As he was trying to remember what happened, he had just thought of Tom being with him and was afraid he was hurt or dead. Seeing Tom relieved him and caused him to tear up.

Jessie, Carla, and Kali saw the nurse come out of the room and pick up the phone. They wondered what was going on, so Jessie stood up and strolled over by the desk so she could hear.

"Dr. Graves, Mr. Parker has awakened from his coma." She paused.

At this, Jessie's head snapped around. She looked at Kali and Carla and grinned. Kali stood up and rushed over to Jessie.

"Toby is awake," Jessie whispered.

Kali smiled, and then immediately, the smile turned into a frown.

"What's wrong?" Jessie asked.

"Sam is in there, and he will see her first," Kali said.

"Oooohh, yeah," Jessie said.

The nurse hung up and walked back into the room.

"Hey, bud," Tom said. "It is sure good to see you awake."

The corner of Toby's mouth curled up in a smile. He moved his eyes around, trying to see who was there. He saw Sadie, and she said, "Hello, sweetie." He saw Hank, and Hank just grinned real big at him. He moved his eyes on around and spotted Sam.

"Hey, cowboy," Sam said.

Seeing her jogged Toby's memory. He remembered they had not parted on the best of terms, and he was glad to see her.

"Hank, you need to tell the girls that he is waking up," Sadie said.

Hank started to leave the room, but Sam said, "I'll tell them." She started for the door, figuring she could rub it in that she was there when he woke up.

Kali looked up and saw Sam walking toward them. "This should be good," she whispered.

Sam stopped in front of them. "We just wanted to tell you that Toby woke up and looked at each of us." She turned to walk back to the room.

"Then we need to go in since he has already seen your mug," Jessie said.

Sam kept walking like she didn't hear her.

"Can you believe her?" Jessie said. "She acts like she is his family."

"If she has her way, she will be someday," Carla said.

Kali cut her eyes at her sister. "She doesn't have a ring yet. The game is far from over."

"Well, now, it seems Miss Kali is back to her old self," Jessie said.

Kali got up and walked into the room. Jessie wanted to go but figured she would let Kali do her deal.

The door to the room opened. All of them looked to see who was coming in, hoping it was the doctor.

"Kali girl, come here and see Toby," Sadie said.

Kali glared at Sam as she walked toward the bed. She looked at Toby, and their eyes met.

Toby smiled at Kali and nodded. He couldn't figure out how to talk yet. He didn't know what was going on.

"It is good to see you awake," Kali spoke up. "You had us worried."

The doctor walked in, along with two nurses, so everyone left the room while they examined Toby. The doctor checked him out and asked Toby a couple of questions, but Toby couldn't answer.

"Don't be alarmed that you are having trouble speaking," the doctor said. "Your brain needs to start working again, and it will."

In the waiting room, Sadie asked Carla, "Are you ready for your prom tonight?"

"Yeah," Carla replied. "I have to go get my hair done in a couple of hours."

Sam was on the phone talking to her dad, and when she hung up, she said to Tom, "You know he will be wanting to go get your cattle as soon as he can."

"Knowing Toby, I figure you are right," Tom said.

"We will have to make sure he doesn't overdo it," Hank said. "We all know he will try."

"I wish school was already out," Kali said.

"I will help him," Sam said. "Dad has already said I could."

That upset Kali and Jessie, but there wasn't anything either of them could do as they had finals coming up and couldn't miss school.

The doctor and nurses came out of the room, and Sadie, Hank, and Tom went to talk to Toby. Sam followed close behind them. The doctor told them that Toby was on his way back and the talking would come. He would be moved out of ICU and put in a room to be watched for a couple of days.

The four of them walked back into the room, and Carla said, "She is beating you two out of the gate and pulling away before you even hit the home stretch."

"I don't want to cause a scene," Kali said.

"And she would," Jessie said.

Tom walked up to the bed and laid his hand on the rail with his eyes closed. Toby raised his arm and laid his hand on Tom's. Tom opened his eyes and looked at Toby, and Toby strained to say, "Pppuuddggee?"

Tom smiled. "He is good. I curried and brushed him good this morning. You need to get well and get back to him."

Toby smiled and blinked and nodded.

"We are going to go and let you get some rest," Sadie said. "Sam said she will stay here with you."

"I will stay too, and ride back with Sam," Tom said. "I really do appreciate you coming to help."

"No thanks is necessary," Hank said. "This young man is like our grandson, and you are a dear friend of his."

Hank and Sadie left the room, and Kali met them halfway. "Is he okay?"

"Yes," Hank said. "We are going home and will come back tomorrow."

"Can I see him?"

"Yes, of course."

Kali smiled and headed to the room. Jessie and Carla got up and went after her. Kali opened the door and started in the room, and Sam asked, "What do you want?"

Kali just looked at her and walked over to the bed. She smiled at Toby, bent down, and kissed him on the cheek.

Toby was surprised and mustered a "Hi."

Sam was furious, but Tom looked at her and caught her eye and slowly shook his head side to side. She nodded okay and turned away.

Jessie walked into the door just in time to see Kali kiss Toby, and stopped briefly before continuing on. She walked to the other side of the bed and kissed Toby herself. She rose up and looked at Kali as she did. Kali gave her the evil eye, and Jessie grinned at her.

Carla walked over. "I guess you won't be teaching me any more line dances for a while. I'm sure Ms. Perkins will be upset you can't come to the prom."

Toby smiled.

Kali frowned. "Who is Ms. Perkins?"

Sam had turned back around.

"Our teacher and class sponsor," Carla replied.

"How does he know her?" Sam asked.

Jessie smiled. "Down, girl. The man is hurting here."

Sam's nostrils flared, but before she could speak, Tom said, "It is time we all left and let Toby rest. See you tomorrow, buddy." He started ushering them all to the door.

Sam looked back. "Bye, cowboy."

Toby raised his hand in acknowledgment.

While they were waiting for the elevator, Sam asked, "How does he know Ms. Perkins?"

Carla laughed. "I was joking with him. She was at the dance and talked to Toby."

"Did they dance together?" Jessie asked.

"No. It was a joke."

"You gals all need to lighten up, or don't come back," Tom said. "Toby needs rest, not this kind of behavior."

Sam looked at Tom. "You're right. I'm sorry."

The other three didn't respond and just got off the elevator and walked out to their car.

Kali and Jessie didn't talk all the way home, and as Carla got out of the car, she said, "You two need to think about what you are doing. You have been friends too long for this. The bad part about it is Toby isn't doing it. You are." She got out and went into the house.

Kali got out, looked at Jessie without speaking, shut the door, and walked into the house.

Sam drove Tom home, and as he got out of the truck, she said, "I am sorry, Tom."

"Don't worry about it." Tom shut the door and went up on the porch.

Toby laid there thinking about things and prayed and thanked God for protecting Tom and him. He wondered if the people in the van were okay. He thought about Pudge and how he was missing him. He thought about the girls and what each had done. He didn't know what to do about that. He just wanted out of there and back to riding Pudge. He dozed off and slept for a couple of hours. He woke up. The nurse came in, and he tried to speak. "Can I make a call?"

The nurse smiled. "It's good to hear your voice."

He asked her to dial the number for him. She put the phone to his ear.

"Hello?" he heard on the other end.

He said slowly, "Tom, this Toby."

"Man, it is great to hear you," Tom said.

"Did the people in the van get hurt?"

"No, Toby. You saved their lives." Tom's eyes were teary.

"That's good," Toby said. "Pudge okay?"

"Yes."

"Okay. Bye."

"Bye." Tom knew Toby was struggling to talk. Toby wanted to talk more, but it was too hard to talk.

Tom sat down and said to himself, "He is lying in a hospital bed and had nearly died, and he is worrying about the other people." He started crying.

Toby thought about the accident, and tears filled his eyes.

"From what I hear, you are a hero," the nurse said.

Toby shook his head from side to side. She smiled and left the room.

Toby closed his eyes and prayed again. He dozed off and slept for a good while.

Tom walked out to the barn and took care of Pudge. He was in bed himself by 8:00 p.m.

38

Toby awoke while it was still dark. He was achy but knew he couldn't get out of bed. He tried to reposition himself and set off an alert, and the nurse came running into the room. She saw him awake. She fixed the alert and asked, "You just trying to get my attention?"

"Sorry," Toby said. "Trying to adjust in the bed."

"So that is what your voice sounds like," the nurse said. "About like I figured. Deep and manly."

The light was dim, so Toby couldn't see her real good, but he strained to try and make her out. He could tell she was a young lady. "Thank you, ma'am."

"That must be your hat."

He looked over on the table and saw his hat, and it was all bent up. "I sure liked that hat."

The nurse laughed. "Save it as a memento from your brush with death." She started to walk out and stopped and said, "My name is Mindy, and I'll be with you for the next few hours."

It just dawned on Toby that he was in a different room. "When did I move?"

"A couple of hours ago. You slept right through it."

Toby didn't like that feeling. He liked the fact that he was a light sleeper. It had helped when he was on cattle drives. "Okay, thanks."

Tom woke up at 6:30 a.m. and started taking care of the chores. He didn't check the pastures but did everything else. He was on the road by 9:00 a.m. to see Toby.

Sam had gotten up early and pulled into the hospital parking lot at 8:00 a.m. She went to the ICU and found out Toby had changed rooms. She headed to his room and opened the door and walked in as Mindy was laughing. She had come in to check Toby, and he had told her a joke. Sam stopped halfway in the door and listened.

"That must have been a campfire joke," Mindy said.

"Actually, it was," Toby replied. "Good call."

Mindy turned to walk out and saw Sam. She looked back and said, "You have a visitor."

Sam looked at Mindy and walked in. Toby still wasn't talking real clear but said, "Thanks, Mindy."

Sam waited until Mindy was out of the room and said, "On a first-name basis with the pretty young nurse, huh?"

"Their first name is all they offer," Toby said.

"Oh, I see."

Toby thought a minute and said, "I am tired of you acting this way. Lighten up on the jealousy."

Sam felt bad. She didn't want Toby upset at her, and knew he was by saying what he did.

"I will try," she said.

"Do more than try," Toby replied.

They sat and watched TV until Tom walked in, and then they all talked until Toby dozed off for a nap. Mindy came in to check on him, and Sam asked, "Do you visit all the rooms this often or just the ones with good-looking cowboys in them?"

Mindy looked at her. "Are you his girlfriend?"

"No, she isn't," Toby responded.

Sam was surprised Toby was awake and jerked her head to see him looking at her.

"Sam, let's get a cup of coffee," Tom said.

Tom and Sam went out to get some coffee.

"Sam, I know you like Toby, but you are getting dangerously close to hurting your relationship with him," Tom said. "I like you, and hope you don't do that."

"Tom, I know other girls like him, and I am afraid he will like them," Sam said.

"Acting jealous and getting mad won't help," Tom said. "In fact, with Toby, it will hurt. Just be yourself. That is what Toby likes."

"Okay, I will work on it," Sam said. "Thanks for caring and helping."

When Sam and Tom walked out, Mindy said, "That girl had her claws out."

"Yeah," Toby replied. "I'm sorry about that."

"Don't sweat it. Are you from Tyler?"

"Nah. Nacogdoches."

"You're going to have a drive to pick me up for a date, aren't you?"

Toby looked at her.

Mindy was grinning. "Got ya. You don't need more girl problems, do ya?"

Toby chuckled. "Definitely caught me off guard. I seem to have them wherever I go."

Mindy continued checking things and changing IV bags. "Do I take it you don't have a steady girl?"

"You take it right," Toby replied.

"Hmmm," Mindy said. "Well, I'll see you later in my shift."

Mindy walked out of the room about the time Tom and Sam were coming back in.

"Did she say how you were doing?" Tom asked Toby.

"Nah," Toby said. "Just wrote it on the chart for the doctor."

"How are you feeling really?" Sam asked.

"I am very sore, but my head is getting more clear all the time." Toby paused for a minute and then asked, "How is Pudge doing?"

"He is doing fine," Tom said. "Misses you. I feel weird saying that, but it actually looks like he is sad when I mention your name to him."

"I have got to get well and get out of here," Toby said. "I miss him and need to ride."

The talk died off. Tom and Sam sat while Toby dozed off. Tom and Sam left to go get a bite to eat, and while they were gone, Hank, Sadie, Kali, and Jessie came to see Toby. Toby woke up and looked around the room and saw them and smiled. "Hello, folks."

Hank laughed. "I believe the boy is feeling better."

"My head is definitely doing better," Toby said. "I'm still sore, but I figure that is to be expected."

"Kali and Jessie wanted to stop by on their way back to school," Hank said.

Toby looked at Kali. "How are you doing?"

"I'm okay," Kali said. "You need to worry about yourself."

"Have they said when you might get out?" Jessie asked.

Toby the Rancher

Toby was about to speak when the door opened and Mindy walked in. He looked at her and said, "No, but Mindy might be able to tell us something."

"Whoa, I keep getting a lot of attention when I walk in here," Mindy said.

"We are just curious as to when our boy will be able to go home," Sadie said.

Mindy looked at Toby and said, "So this is your family."

Hank spoke before Toby could. "Nah, but we feel like family."

"I work for them on their ranch," Toby said.

"So you really are a cowboy," Mindy said.

"I suppose," Toby said.

Jessie spoke up. "He is in every sense of the word."

Mindy looked at her and asked, "Sister?"

Jessie laughed. "No. *Gooood* friend."

Mindy laughed. "I already met one of those in here today."

Jessie and Kali both looked at Toby, and Kali asked, "Who?"

"Tom and Sam have been here all morning," Toby said.

"Oh, you met Sam," Kali said.

Mindy smiled. "Oh that was her name."

"All right, let's stop this," Hank said. "Sam is just passionate about things."

The door opened, and Tom and Sam walked into the room. Mindy looked up and said, "Hail, hail, the gang's all here."

Toby chuckled.

"Oh, great," Kali said.

Tom walked over and shook Hank's hand and Sam spoke to Sadie. She ignored Kali, Jessie, and Mindy and spoke to Toby. "How are you, cowboy?"

"Just laying here like a cow patty."

Mindy started laughing. "That is one I haven't heard before. So do you live in a bunkhouse on their place?"

"No, he has his own ranch," Sam said.

Mindy looked up at her and then back at Toby. "I thought you said you worked for these folks."

♦ 323 ♦

"I do, but I have my own place too," Toby replied.

"Impressive," Mindy said. "I'd like to see your place."

"You'll have to come down when I get out of here," Toby said.

"I'd like that." Mindy looked up, and all three girls were glaring at her. She mused as she walked to the door, "I will leave you to your entourage. The doctor will be in shortly."

When she left, Jessie asked, "Who the crud is she to ask to come to your ranch?"

Toby just looked at her.

"She probably just hasn't seen a ranch before and is curious," Kali said.

"Oh yeah, I'm sure that's it," Sam said sarcastically. "Jeez!"

Sadie had listened to all that had been said, and she calmly said, "You girls are not acting very ladylike. We are supposed to be here supporting Toby, not trying to cause him grief."

Nobody spoke for nearly an hour.

Hank finally said, "I need a cup of coffee."

"I could sure use one too," Toby said.

"I'll bring you one." Hank started for the door and met the doctor coming in. He stopped to hear what the doctor said.

The doctor checked Toby out and then said, "You are making good progress."

"Any idea when he can go home?" Tom asked.

"If things continue to improve, he should be going home by noon tomorrow," the doctor said.

"Yoohoo!" Toby cheered.

Everyone was cheering, and the doctor said, "Folks, this is a hospital. Please hold it down." He left.

"That is great news," Hank said. "Man, what a roller coaster the last few days have been."

"I will have a good meal for you when you get home tomorrow," Sadie said to Toby.

"I will help Tom with your chores until you can get back out among the livestock," Sam said.

Toby the Rancher

"Well, I guess Kali and I better get on to school," Jessie said.

Toby looked at her and then Kali and said, "Thank you for being here. Please drive safely."

Kali bent down and kissed him on the cheek again.

Jessie just said, "Will do."

Sam didn't like the kiss. "Bye, girls. I'll take care of him."

Kali stopped. "Grandma, didn't you say you were going to take care of Toby when he got home?"

Sadie frowned at her. "If Toby needs it, I will. Give me a hug, and be good."

Kali hugged Sadie, and they left the room.

Sadie was a little perturbed at how things had gone the last couple of days, so she said, "I think Toby is probably needing some rest so he will be ready to leave tomorrow."

"I agree," Tom said. "I will be here to get you tomorrow once I finish feeding."

"Sounds good," Toby said. "Y'all drive safe."

Sam bent down and kissed Toby on the cheek. "Later, cowboy."

Toby nodded at her.

Hank walked over and laid his hand on Toby's shoulder. "You don't know how happy I am you are doing okay. Can't wait until you get home and back to your old self."

"Thank all of you for everything," Toby said. "It means more than you can ever know."

They all left. Toby laid there thinking about how lucky he was to have people like Hank, Sadie, Tom, and Sam in his life. He didn't feel so all alone anymore. He thought about what he needed to do at home and wondered how things were going with his insurance since he needed another truck. He was about to doze off when someone knocked on the door.

"Come on in."

The door opened, and people started streaming into the room. Toby couldn't figure out what was going on.

The first man inside the room said, "Hello, sir."

"Hello," Toby replied. "Can I help you?"

"We are all the passengers of the van you saved by wrecking yourself," the man said. "We wanted to come by and tell you how sorry we are for you being here and thank you for saving our lives."

Toby was blown away. "You don't need to apologize for anything. It was an accident, and I am just glad everyone was okay."

They all talked for a while, and then the first man who had spoken said, "We know it isn't a lot, but we took up a donation for you to help with some of your costs you incur because of the wreck."

"Oh, you didn't need to do that," Toby said.

"We wanted to and wish it was more," the man said.

"I truly do appreciate it," Toby said.

Each one of them shook Toby's hand before they left. Toby had tears in his eyes when they had all gone. He was thankful he had been able to avoid hitting the van head on and possibly have killed some of the good folks he had just met.

Mindy walked in. "I just wanted—" She stopped short when she saw tears in Toby's eyes. "What is wrong?"

Toby reached up and wiped off the tears. "I just met the people from the van that I tried to avoid hitting. They are a great group of people. They even took up a donation for me."

"That was very nice of them. How much did they give you?"

"I don't even know. Would you check?"

Mindy opened the envelope and counted the contents. "There's $5,000 here."

"What?" Toby said. "You have to be kidding."

Mindy smiled. "Nope, not kidding. That should help get you a new truck. I am going off duty, so I will see you in the morning."

"Okay," Toby said. "Have a good evening. Thanks for everything."

Mindy smiled and started for the door. As she opened it, she stopped and said, "Whoa, I almost ran into you."

Toby the Rancher

Toby looked but couldn't see who it was. He heard a voice ask, "Is this Toby Parker's room?" The voice sounded familiar, but he couldn't place it. He heard Mindy say, "Yes, it is. Go on in."

Toby was watching the door, and his mouth dropped open when he saw who walked in.

"Hello, Toby," Chanel Small said as she walked toward the bed.

"Hey, Chanel," Toby replied. "What are you doing here? I mean, how did you know about this?"

Chanel bent down and hugged him. She stood back up and smiled. "I am working for the *Albuquerque Journal* now, and I saw a report come in about an automobile crash in Texas and how the driver was a hero. It intrigued me, so I started reading it, and lo and behold, it was you. I told my editor about you and what you had done in Colorado. He said I could come and see you and maybe do an interview, if you are willing."

"How did you wind up in New Mexico?" Toby asked.

"I really liked the time I spent there when I was there doing the story on you, and had the opportunity to go to work there, so I took it."

"Do you like your job there, and living in Albuquerque?"

"I have a good boss, but I don't really like living there. I would prefer a slower pace in a smaller town. There is too much crime for my liking as well."

"I figured you would like a smaller town better," Toby replied.

"How are you doing?" Chanel asked.

"Doing much better. I get to go home tomorrow. I can't wait."

Toby the Rancher

"That's good news. Knowing you, I can imagine a hospital isn't your cup of tea."

Toby laughed. "Definitely not."

"Where is home these days?" Chanel asked.

Toby told her the story about how he wound up in Nacogdoches and came to have his own place.

"It couldn't happen to a more deserving guy," Chanel said.

They talked some more, and she asked some about the wreck and then, "Do you have a ride home tomorrow?"

"I figure Tom will come and get me," Toby replied.

"I could take you home," Chanel said. "I would like to see your place and add that to the story, if you don't mind."

He smiled. "That would be great."

"It's settled then. I will go get a motel room and be back in the morning so I can take you home when they release you."

"Good night," Toby said as Chanel left the room.

Toby felt good. It was good to see Chanel. She was good people, and he always felt comfortable around her. Not to mention she was very pretty. He stopped thinking about Chanel and called Tom and told him about Chanel and that she would bring him home. Tom was glad he could stay and check the pastures as Toby and Hank both had cattle close to calving.

Toby slept good for being in a hospital and was itching to go home when he woke up. The nurse didn't know when he would get to leave, but she was going off duty.

Mindy came in at 7:10 a.m. "You ready to get out of here?"

"Absolutely," Toby said.

"The doctor should be here to check you by 9:00, at least," Mindy said. "I do plan on coming and seeing your place someday."

"You are welcome anytime," Toby said. "Can you ride a horse?"

"Yes, sir. Been riding since I was six."

"Outstanding."

Mindy finished checking things and started out of the room and met Chanel coming in.

"Are you taking him home?" Mindy asked.

"Yes," Chanel said. "Is he ready to go?"

"Not yet," Mindy said. "Just wondered who was picking him up."

Chanel walked on in. "Good morning," she said to Toby. "How are you today?"

"Morning," Toby replied. "Doing well. Ready to flee this place."

Tom's phone rang, and he answered to hear Sam say, "Tom, this is Sam. I would like to go with you to get Toby."

"Sam, I am not picking him up," Tom replied. "Chanel Small, a girl he met in Grand Junction, Colorado, showed up yesterday and is bringing him home."

There was silence on the phone.

"Hello?" Tom said.

"Yeah, I'm here," Sam said. "I will talk to you later."

"Okay," Tom said. "Bye."

They hung up. Tom mounted up and headed to the south pasture.

Toby had gotten up to go to the restroom, and the phone rang. Chanel answered it. "Toby Parker's room."

"Hello?" Jessie said. "Who is this?"

"Chanel Small. Who am I speaking with?"

"This is Jessie Stoddard. Is Toby available?"

"He is in the bathroom. Just a minute."

Toby came out. "Who is it?"

"Jessie Stoddard," Chanel said.

Toby the Rancher

Toby took the phone. "Hello, Jessie. How are you?"

"Hi, Toby," Jessie said. "You sound good."

"Yep. I am going home today. I feel like I have been off feed for a week, but other than that, I am ready."

"Who is taking you home?" Jessie asked.

"Chanel is taking me home," Toby responded. "She is a friend that I met in Colorado and came to see me in New Mexico."

"That's convenient," Jessie said.

Toby, not realizing her sarcasm, said, "Yeah, it works out well. Tom doesn't have to make the drive."

"Well, take care," Jessie said.

"You too," Toby replied. "Thanks for calling."

When Toby hung up the phone, Chanel asked, "Who was that? A love interest?"

"Nah. Just a friend."

The doctor walked in, and Toby said, "Hello, Doc. Can I leave?"

The doctor smiled. "Let me check you over first." He finished his review and said, "You can go home. You just need to be careful with your neck. You don't want to rip that open."

"I will take it easy," Toby said.

Mindy walked in, and the doctor said, "Nurse, he needs to get checked out."

"I'll get it done," Mindy said. She smiled at Toby. "I could drag my feet and keep you here longer."

"You wouldn't do that, would you?" Toby said.

"I might not see you again," Mindy said.

"I expect you to come and see my place and my horse."

Mindy laughed. "Count on it." She left

"Hmmm," Chanel said. "You seem to have won her over rather quickly."

Toby looked at her. "Jealous?"

Chanel smiled. "Maybe."

He laughed and shook his head. They got his stuff ready to go, and Mindy walked back in, pushing a wheelchair.

◆ 331 ◆

"What is that for?" Toby asked.

"Hospital policy," Mindy said. "Everyone rides a wheelchair out the door."

Toby frowned as he sat down on it. "I expect a smooth ride."

"I'll do my best," Mindy said.

Chanel left to go get the car pulled up, and Mindy started pushing Toby out of the room. As they turned the corner, they nearly ran into Sam.

"I'm glad I got here in time to take you home," Sam said.

"Sam, I already had a ride home," Toby said. "Didn't Tom tell you?"

"He said you might have someone, and I don't see anyone," Sam said. "I know the nurse isn't taking you home."

"Chanel is pulling her truck up to the door."

"Well, okay then. I will just do some shopping since I'm not wanted."

Mindy laughed. "Wow. Can you twist things."

"Kiss my foot," Sam snapped. She turned and went to the stairs and went through the door.

Toby felt bad about what had happened. "Man, I hate she made the trip thinking I needed a ride."

"Toby, you are too nice or a naive one," Mindy said. "She knew you had a ride with a girl, and that is why she came up."

Toby looked at her. "You think so?"

Mindy laughed. "That is part of your charm."

She pushed him inside the elevator, and they rode it down and to the truck. Once he was loaded, Mindy bid him farewell and Chanel started the truck. As they started to pull out, Toby spotted Sam sitting in her truck, watching them, and he figured out that Mindy was right.

Toby and Chanel talked about several things as they rode to Toby's. He showed her Hank and Sadie's as they drove by and then said as she turned up the drive, "I never knew this place could look so good to me."

◆ 332 ◆

Toby the Rancher

"You probably had doubts that you would see it again," Chanel said. "It is a very nice place. You have done well, Mr. Parker."

"It needs a lot of work, but it is home now, and thank you."

Tom was on the porch as they were getting out of the truck. "Hello, young lady."

"Hello, Mr. Gray," Chanel replied. "It *is* good to see you."

"Hey, Tom," Toby said. "Can you show Chanel the other bedroom? I need to see Pudge."

"Sure thing," Tom said. "I will put a pot of coffee on too."

"Thank you," Toby said as he walked toward the barn.

He walked into the barn and opened the door to Pudge's room. Pudge looked and saw Toby and snorted.

Toby smiled. "Hello, buddy. It is sure good to see you. I have missed you."

Pudge moved his head up and down, like he was nodding his head in agreement. Toby grabbed the curry comb and started brushing Pudge. He was telling Pudge what he had been through when Chanel came walking in.

"I remember you," she told Pudge. "Do you remember me?"

Pudge snorted. Toby and Chanel laughed, and Toby said, "I guess you can take that any way you want."

"I know," Chanel said. "I will take it as good."

"I will be back later to see you. I can't ride today, but we may try a slow ride tomorrow."

They walked out of the barn, and they saw Hank and Sadie were pulling up the drive.

Hank got out and said, "It is sure good to see you walking out of that barn again."

"It feels good," Toby said. "Hank and Sadie, this is Chanel Small. She is a friend and reporter. She wrote the story on me in Grand Junction. She heard about the wreck, and her editor let her come down from Albuquerque to follow up."

"It is very nice to meet you," Sadie said. "I read your story, and it was very good."

333

"Thank you," Chanel said. "It is good to meet you too."

Tom came up to them. "I have a pot of coffee ready. Everyone want a cup?"

"Oh yeah," Hank said. "That will go good with the apple pie Sadie made for Toby."

Toby grinned, and Chanel said, "They must know you love apple pie."

"I love the story of Toby and his dad eating apple pie and drinking coffee together," Sadie said.

"Yeah, I feel the same way," Chanel said.

They went inside, ate pie, drank coffee, and laughed and talked for nearly an hour.

Hank and Sadie were getting ready to leave when they heard a vehicle pull into the drive. They all walked to the front porch to see Sam getting out of her truck.

"Hello, Sam," Hank said. "Isn't it good to see Toby back home?"

Sam nodded. "Yeah, it is." She looked at Toby. "How are you feeling?"

"Pretty good, so far," Toby replied.

"I promised to help Tom with the chores, so I thought I'd stop by before I go home and see if anything needs done," Sam said.

"I pretty much have it done today," Tom said. "But I could use some help tomorrow."

"Okay," Sam said. "Well, I'll see y'all later." She turned and started walking back to her truck.

"You might as well have a piece of Sadie's apple pie before you go," Toby said.

Sam stopped and turned around. "Sounds yummy."

"Come on in," Toby said. As Sam started up the porch, he said, "Samantha Weber, this is Chanel Small."

Sam reluctantly shook Chanel's hand and then walked on into the house.

"I am going to check on a cow that was acting strange this morning," Tom said.

"Sick or calving?" Toby asked.

Toby the Rancher

"She is springing heavy, so I figure calving."

"Can we ride in your truck?"

"Sure."

"Let's let Sam eat some pie first," Toby said.

They went in, and Chanel got Sam a piece of pie. Toby started to ask Sam about her coming to the hospital but decided it wasn't worth it. "Sam, how are things going on your ranch?"

"You have your own ranch too?" Chanel asked.

"No, it is my dad's," Sam said. "I work it with him."

"I see," Chanel said.

"I cowboy up every day," Sam said.

Chanel just looked at her and wondered what that meant.

Sam took another bite of pie. "Have you ever ridden a horse?"

"Yes," Chanel said.

"Didn't you ride out to the line shack?" Tom asked Chanel.

"Yeah," she said.

"Line shack?" Sam asked slowly.

"She came down to New Mexico and finished the interview," Toby said. "I was out at the line shack Tom and I had built."

"That was cool," Chanel said. "The setting was great, and the shack was rustic."

"Sounds very cool," Sam said. She finished her pie and said, "Guess I better get home."

They all walked out. As Sam got in the truck, she said, "It's good to see you back home, Toby."

"Thanks," Toby said. "And thanks for stopping by."

Sam left, and Toby said, "Chanel, you can wait in the house. Hopefully we won't be too long."

"Can I go?" Chanel asked.

"Sure," Toby said. "If you want to."

He locked the house, and they loaded up and headed to the pasture. They pulled up into the gate. Toby immediately spotted the cow. She was having trouble. They pulled up beside her, and she got up. She had only one of the calves' feet out and looked like she had been trying.

◆   335   ◆

"Crud," Toby said. "We need the chains and a rope."

"I'll go back and get them," Tom said.

Toby and Chanel got out and watched the cow while Tom went back to the barn. They stood watching her, and she was very irritable. Toby turned to look at the other cows across the pasture. He had his back to the cow when he herd Chanel scream, "Watch out, Toby!"

Toby jerked his head around to see what was happening, and saw the cow charging him. He hurt his neck when he jerked his head around, but he hurt more when he tried to jump out of the way. The cow was bearing down, and it didn't look good for him.

40

Toby was weaker than he thought, and the quick movements were filled with pain. He was bracing himself for the impact of the cow when he heard a whack.

Chanel had tripped over a limb and had reached down and picked it up to carry. When the cow started charging Toby, she moved in toward the cow and swung the limb and hit the cow on the nose. The blow startled the cow, and she stopped and turned around and moved away.

Toby turned when he heard the whack and saw Chanel holding the limb. He looked at the cow and then back to Chanel. "You just saved me a lot of pain. Thank you."

"Are you okay?" Chanel replied.

"Not really. I hurt."

She looked at his neck and saw blood. "Oh no, you're bleeding."

"I knew it hurt."

"Let me look at it." Chanel loosened the bandage and saw that Toby had torn the stitches apart. "You are going to have to go to the hospital. You have torn the stitches. Hopefully, you didn't hurt the artery."

"Great," Toby said. He looked at the cow. "We need to get her taken care of first."

"Toby, you could be bleeding inside your neck," Chanel said.

"I doubt it. I have to take care of my livestock."

"Okay. I'll be quiet."

Toby looked at her and smiled. "I didn't mean to snap. Just frustrated."

"I know," Chanel said. "Don't apologize. I'm learning how to be a rancher."

He leaned up against a tree a ways from the cow and rested and pondered. Chanel looked and saw Tom coming from a distance. "There's Tom. It looks like someone else is in with him."

Tom pulled up, and he and Mike Stine climbed out of the truck.

"This young man came by to see how you were doing and offered to come and help," Tom said.

Toby stood up straight off the tree. "Hello, Mike. I sure am sorry about the truck and prom."

"Hey, don't sweat it," Mike said. "You didn't just forget."

Tom looked at Toby. "You look pale." He then noticed the blood on Toby's bandage. "What happened?"

Chanel explained what had happened, and Tom said, "We need to get you to the hospital."

"We need to take care of the cow first," Toby said.

"Tom, I already tried," Chanel said. "It's no use. We need to help the cow before he will go."

"Stubborn," Tom muttered.

Toby laughed. "Hand me the rope."

"No," Chanel said. "You are not roping that cow."

"That's right," Tom said.

"Well, I'm not letting you get hurt doing it," Toby said.

"I'll help him hold the rope," Mike said.

"There," Tom said. "Problem solved."

Toby hesitated and then said, "All right, but please nobody get hurt. I should be doing it."

"You have to let people help you when they want to," Chanel said.

Toby nodded and started walking toward the cow. Tom got the rope ready. He threw a loop and caught the cow's head on the first throw. Mike moved in quickly to grab the rope and help tie it off on a tree. Toby was making the cow move toward the tree to take up the slack and give her less opportunity to move. They got her close and tied up, and Toby moved in with the calf pulling chains. She was distressed, so she wasn't worried about kicking, and Toby was able to work and try and get the calf coming out as it should.

Chanel was watching Toby's neck. "Toby, don't strain so much. You are causing it to bleed more."

Toby heard her but didn't acknowledge it. He got the calf turned and the legs coming out and then hooked the chains onto the legs. "Mike and Chanel, I need you two to help pull the calf."

All three grabbed a portion of the chains and started pulling. They got the calf pulled out in short fashion. Toby made sure the calf was okay and then took the chains off, and Tom turned the cow loose.

"Let's get back so we can get you some help," Tom told Toby.

"Okay." Toby looked at Chanel. "I wasn't ignoring you. I heard you but needed to get that calf lined up."

"I understood," Chanel said. "Just felt better saying that."

Toby grinned at her and winced. "Crud, that even hurt."

They walked to the truck and drove back to the house. They dropped Mike off.

"I really do appreciate you stopping by and sure thank you for your help," Toby said.

"Glad I was here," Mike replied. "Hope your neck is okay."

Tom pulled away and headed to town to get Toby seen about. Tom and Chanel walked Toby into the ER, and then Tom went to park the truck.

Tom walked back in and was surprised to see that they had already taken Toby back. He was afraid it was worse than they thought. He inquired, and the nurse showed him back to where Toby and Chanel were.

Tom walked in and asked, "How bad is it?"

"We don't know yet," Chanel said.

"I was surprised you got in so quick."

"It was because of the neck and the original injury. They didn't want to take any chances."

"Good deal," Tom said. "You okay, Toby?"

"Yeah," Toby replied. "I'll be okay. Just have to be more careful."

"I can't wait to see that," Chanel said.

"Ha, ha," Toby replied. "Very funny."

Tom laughed and sat down on a chair. The doctor came in, and they tended to Toby's neck and told him he was lucky. It could have been worse. They gave him pretty much the same restrictions he had leaving the hospital.

"He will follow them this time," Chanel said.

"You seem pretty sure of that," Toby said.

"Tom and I will make sure you do."

Tom smiled. "Sounds like Miss Chanel is sticking around awhile. And yes, we will make sure."

Toby looked at the doctor and nurse. "I think I'm outnumbered."

The doctor laughed. "Yeah, and I don't think I would try to go against them."

Everyone laughed, and the doctor and nurse left the room. Toby, along with Tom and Chanel, checked out, and they left the hospital.

"I'm hungry," Toby said. "I want a good steak. I'll buy."

"I'm a little gaunt myself," Tom said.

Chanel said, "Well, I was going to cook, but if you would rather just eat out, I guess it is okay."

Toby started backpedaling and trying to smooth things over by saying, "Oh, I didn't know. I just thought it would be good to eat out. I'm sure what you cook will be just as good."

Chanel started laughing and said, "Gotcha. I was just kidding."

Tom laughed, and Toby said, "I'm going to have to stay on my toes around you, aren't I?"

Chanel smiled. "Tiptoes."

They walked into the restaurant and waited to be seated. They were talking among themselves and not paying any attention to anyone else in the place. The hostess showed them to their table, and as they walked by, someone said, "Lookie, lookie, if it ain't the hero of I-20."

Toby turned to see Harry and Gwen Stuart and Jimbo and Kathy Carter sitting at a table. Toby just smirked at them and walked on toward their table.

"Where's Sam?" Jimbo continued. "She wise up to your game?"

"Who's the jerk?" Chanel asked.

"Just a couple of guys I met at the cattleman's banquet," Toby replied. "Not sure what their beef is with me. I guess they had an unhappy childhood or something."

Tom and Chanel laughed, and Toby never acknowledged the group again. The group got up to leave and Jimbo started walking their way, but Tom held up his hand and said, "You guys need to go ahead and leave. We aren't interested in what you have to say."

Jimbo looked stunned and turned and walked to the door.

Chanel smiled. "Very nice."

"I have always had a distaste for individuals such as them," Tom said.

"So they know Sam?" Chanel asked.

"I think she said they went to school together," Toby said.

"I think they must be jealous of your success," Tom said. "There is no other reason for them to act that way since you haven't had any dealings with them."

Toby just shook his head like he didn't know. A little later, Toby heard a voice say, "Hello, Toby."

He looked up and saw the sheriff. "Hello, Sheriff. Been a while since I've seen you."

", Yeah it has," James replied. "I noticed Jimbo Carter was trying to give you some trouble."

"Yeah, and I have no idea why," Toby said. "I only met him one time before at the cattlemen's banquet, and he was a jerk then too."

"He is a relative of the deputy you had trouble with, so I guess he figures he will make it rough for you," James said.

"I guess that explains it some, but I'd just as soon not ever see him again."

"I doubt you can do that. This ain't that big a town."

"I know. I will try to avoid any trouble with him."

"From what I've seen, that would be to his benefit."

Tom laughed. "I take it you have seen Toby in a scuffle."

"Yessir." James looked at Toby. "By the way, how are you? That was a great thing you did, avoiding that van."

"I'll be okay, but it is going to take a while," Toby said.

"Well, take care," James said as he headed to the door.

"Well, I guess you know now why he is acting like he is," Chanel said. "Although, the curiosity is killing me."

"It's a long story," Toby said.

"I got time, and remember, you do too," Chanel reminded him.

Toby glanced at Tom.

"I think you are hooked," Tom said.

"I'll tell you at home," Toby said.

They finished supper and headed to the ranch. Toby went out to see Pudge. He spent some time with him, talking to him and brushing him good. "Well, Pudge, I guess I better quit stalling and go in and talk to Chanel."

Toby bid Pudge good night and went into the house to face the music. He got a cup of coffee and told Chanel the story about the robbery he had broken up at Hank and Sadie's.

Chanel was amazed. "You just keep amazing me. You know, I have to include this in my story."

"I figured you'd say that. If you still write a story like you did on the first one, I'm okay with it."

"What do you mean?"

"You didn't try to overdramatize it."

"Oh. No, that's not my style."

"Good deal."

They went to the living room to watch TV, and Toby received a text. He looked at it, and it was from Sam.

"So you went out on a date with the reporter, huh?" the message read. "Just a friend, huh?"

"We didn't go on a date," Toby texted back. "The three of us went to eat leaving the hospital. You need to watch who you listen to."

About twenty minutes later, she texted back. "Why were you at the hospital, and why didn't you call me?"

"Sam?" Chanel asked.

Toby looked at her, surprised. "How did you know?"

Chanel smiled. "I figured when those people at the restaurant said what they did and are her friends, they would tell her and try to stir something up."

"Is that women's intuition or the reporter instinct in you?" Tom asked.

She laughed. "Probably both."

Toby replied and told her what had happened. He ended it with, "I honestly didn't think to call anyone."

"Well, all right then," Sam replied.

They watched TV, and Toby headed to bed at 11:00 p.m. He read the Bible, said his prayers, and was asleep at 11:45 p.m.

"I sure wish Toby would find him a girl," Tom said to Chanel. "They all seem to turn cuckoo when they start liking him. You like him?"

Chanel laughed. "Why, am I cuckoo?"

Tom laughed. "No. I think you are good for Toby."

"Well, thank you." Chanel got up. "Think I'll turn in."

"You're dodging the question."

"You noticed, huh?"

"Yeah, and that gives me the answer I wanted."

Chanel smiled and walked to her room.

Tom turned off the lights and went to bed too.

41

Toby was up first. He was still sore and moving slower, but he had breakfast started by 6:00 a.m. He had eggs, bacon, sausage, biscuits, and gravy on the table when Chanel walked into the kitchen.

"The good smell woke me up," she said.

Toby grinned. "I hope it is up to expectations." He poured her a cup of coffee.

Tom walked in. "You will make someone a good wife, Toby."

Toby laughed. "But I don't know how to crochet."

"Better learn," Tom said.

They all laughed and sat down to eat breakfast. They discussed the events of yesterday and what they expected of today. They finished eating. Chanel said she would do the dishes, so Toby headed out to see Pudge. Tom started feeding while Toby brushed Pudge and talked to him about the cow that nearly got him. He sat and enjoyed just being in Pudge's room and thinking about the things they had been through together.

Toby heard a vehicle and walked out of Pudge's room. He saw Hank getting out of his truck.

Hank saw Toby and said, "Good morning. How are you feeling today?"

"Morning," Toby replied. "I'm okay. Just sore."

Chanel came walking up from the house. "He had to go to the emergency room yesterday."

Hank looked at Toby. "What happened, and why didn't someone call us?"

"I apologize, Hank," Toby said. "We had trouble with a cow calving, and my neck wound opened up."

"Mr. Parker, I am sorry," Chanel said. "We should have called."

Hank looked at her. "No, I am the one that needs to apologize. You did what needed to be done."

Tom drove up. "Have another cow calving."

"Hopefully, she won't have any trouble," Toby said. "We can check her in a little bit."

"Tom, is there anything you need help with so Toby will remain at the house?" Hank asked.

Tom laughed. "Nah, but if I have anything come up, I will call you."

"Hank, you might as well come on in for a cup before you leave," Toby said.

"Sounds like a winner," Hank said.

They all walked into the house and sat around the table, talking and drinking coffee.

I am going to have to find me a good apple pie," Toby said. "I miss my pie and coffee."

Hank winked at Chanel. "The bakery in town makes good pies."

Just then there was a knock on the front door.

"I wonder who that is." Toby got up and walked to the front room, and saw Sadie at the door. He opened the door and said, "Hello, Miss Sadie, how are you?"

"I am doing fine, Toby," Sadie said. "But I thought you might want an apple pie while you recoup."

Toby grinned. "Wow, you are a mind reader."

Sadie smiled. "You were wanting one, huh?"

"Most definitely," Toby said as they walked toward the kitchen.

Chanel laughed. "I see now why you winked at me when you said that."

Toby the Rancher

"Oh, I see how it is," Toby said.

"This sure feels good, being around good people that care for each other," Tom said.

"Thank you," Hank said. "We sure have enjoyed having Toby here in Nacogdoches."

They ate a piece of pie, and then Hank and Sadie left. Tom and Toby started for the truck to go check the cow that was calving.

"I would like to go, but I better stay here and do some work before I get fired," Chanel said.

"Understood," Toby said. "Be back in a while."

As Tom and Toby drove through the pasture, Tom said, "I sure do like Chanel. I liked her in New Mexico, but even more now."

Toby just listened.

"She seems levelheaded and not afraid of work," Tom continued.

"Sounds like you are going to ask her out on a date," Toby said.

Tom jerked his head to look at Toby. "What?"

Toby started laughing. "Gotcha."

Tom laughed. "She is good for you."

"She is good people and I like having her around, but I just don't know," Toby said. "I have a lot to weigh out, and right now, getting my health back and this ranch where I want it comes first."

"She could help you with that."

Toby, changing the subject, asked, "How long are you going to stick around? It has been great having you here. As far as I'm concerned, you can stay permanently."

"It is tempting," Tom said. "I love being here and being back to working with cattle and riding horses. Although I moved to be close to my family."

"I know you did. You wouldn't be too far away from here, and you could get away anytime you wanted."

"That is true."

Toby spotted the cow and saw she had already calved. "There she is, and the calf is already standing up. I hope it is a bull."

Tom pulled up and got out to check it.

"Be careful," Toby said. "She may be protective of her calf."

◆ 347 ◆

Tom nodded as he moved toward the calf. It turned, and he could tell it was a bull. He started back to the truck. "It's a bull."

"We can band it when I get back to riding," Toby said. "I'll rope it and band it then."

Tom started back to the house and asked, "If I stayed, how would I make a living?"

"I still plan on going and getting your cows," Toby said. "I just have to get me a truck and trailer. That reminds me, I need to call my insurance and see where things stand."

"That wouldn't bring in any money for a good while."

"Are you honestly considering it? If so, we can discuss how much you need and whether we can do it."

"I would like to kick it around," Tom said. "I want to call the kids first."

"That's understandable," Toby said.

They pulled back up to the barn, and Toby walked to the house to call the insurance company. Toby got off the phone with the insurance agent as Tom walked into the house.

"We can go truck and trailer shopping," Toby said. "I just need to go pick up the check and put it in the bank. I am glad they moved quickly on it. Hank sure helped with that by calling them for me."

"That's great," Tom said. "Can we talk some more about me staying?"

Toby sat back down. "Absolutely."

"Where would I stay?"

"Right where you are now."

"But what about when you get married?"

Toby laughed. "Well, that ain't going to happen anytime soon, and when and if it does, we will deal with it. By that, I mean we will fix your own place."

Tom grinned. "I'm going to make a call."

Toby was excited. He was able to go look for a truck and trailer, even though he would have to have extra money or finance it, and Tom might be moving there. He didn't realize he was grinning

Toby the Rancher

when Chanel walked into the room and asked, "You just swallow the canary? That grin looks mischievous."

Toby laughed. "Nah, just happy with some prospects." He went ahead and told Chanel.

She was happy for him. "I hope Tom can move here. You two make a good team."

"I think it would help him totally recover from his stroke," Toby said. "He seems to be getting better every day he has been here."

"I sent in my story, and my editor loved it," Chanel said. "It will run tomorrow. He even suggested I might want to write a book about Mr. Toby Parker. I told him as much as I would like to, I doubt you would agree to that."

Toby listened and thought a minute. "I sure don't want to cause you any problems, but I'm not sure about the book thing. I kind of like being a simple guy with a low profile."

"I know, but that it part of the lure of the stories and the book. Here is a guy that likes a low profile and his privacy, but he keeps doing all these great things for others."

Toby got embarrassed. He got up and asked, "You want to go truck shopping?"

Chanel smiled because she knew she had embarrassed him. "Definitely."

Tom came walking back in and said, "The kids think it would be good for me to move over here. They said it wasn't too far, and it would give them some place to visit too."

"So are you coming?" Toby said.

"I believe so."

Toby laughed and slapped Tom on the back. "Fantastic. We have enough room here for your kids and grandkids to come and visit anytime."

Chanel was watching Toby and just smiling. Toby's phone started ringing. "Excuse me." He answered the phone as Tom walked to the bathroom. "Hello?"

It turned out it was Carol, Tom's daughter. She told Toby she thought Tom coming there was the best thing for him. Tom had really been depressed since his stroke. She thanked Toby over and over. Toby assured Carol he would look out for Tom and that they were welcome to come and visit anytime. Carol thanked him, and they hung up.

Tom walked in, and Toby asked, "Are y'all ready to go to town?"

Tom and Chanel said they were, and they all headed out the door. They stopped by the insurance office, and Toby picked up his check. He was happy with the settlement for the truck and trailer he had but knew he would need more money for new ones. He knew Hank would let him use his trailers, but he hated to constantly borrow things, since he had his own ranch now. He decided he would just try to finance it with the car dealer rather than going to the bank.

Tom pulled into the Chevrolet dealership, and Toby climbed out of the truck. A salesman met him before he even got both feet on the ground.

"Slow down, bud," Toby said. "I know what I am looking for and will let you know if I need help."

"What is your name?" the salesman asked.

"If I decide to buy one, I will tell you my name." Toby started walking toward the trucks. The salesman looked stunned.

Tom and Chanel were snickering as they followed after Toby.

"I take it you don't like dealing with salesmen," Chanel said.

"Not car salesmen," Toby said. "Too dern pushy for my liking."

"I would never have guessed that," Chanel said sarcastically.

Toby looked at her and smiled, and as he did, he spotted a truck. He headed over to it with a smile on his face. It was a Silverado 3500HD dually, with a Duramax engine and an automatic transmission. It was Mocha Steel metallic in color and had leather interior. He walked around it and looked inside and then at the sticker. "This is the one I want."

"It is a pretty thing and should do the work you need it to do," Tom said.

"I could see myself driving that," Chanel said.

Toby looked at her and grinned. "You'll have to wait your turn." He looked at the truck a little more. "Well, I guess it's time to go see Mr. Pushy."

They walked to the showroom. The salesman met them halfway and asked, "You leaving without giving me a chance?"

"No," Toby said. "I want to try and get together on the Mocha one-ton dually."

"My name is Harry Sims," the salesman said. "What was your name?"

"Toby Parker."

"Toby, what do you like about the truck?"

"Harry, I like the truck and want to try and buy it. It's that simple. What will it take to drive it off today?"

"Come on in, and we'll look at it."

Toby followed Harry in, and when he sat down, he said, "I'll give you $55,000 for the truck."

"I don't know if that will work," Harry said.

"Then go find someone who will know if it will work."

Harry got up and walked out. In a little while, he came back and said, "We can't do it for any less than $59,500."

Toby stood up. "All right, I'll go elsewhere."

"Wait a minute. Will you buy it right now for $55,000?"

"That's what I said."

Chanel and Tom were in the showroom, watching the office, and Chanel said, "Looks like Toby started to leave."

"Yeah," Tom said. "He must have gotten his attention."

Toby bought the truck, and in forty-five minutes, they were leaving. Chanel was riding with Toby, and Tom was following them. Toby pulled into Braum's to get a hamburger. He parked his truck away from everyone else's.

Tom laughed. "I don't blame you."

They walked in and ordered and started to sit down when they saw Sam and her mom.

Sam saw Toby and said, "Hey, cowboy, how are you doing?" Then she saw Chanel, and her smile turned to a frown.

"Hey, Sam," Toby said. "I'm doing okay. Just trying to take it easy."

"I see the reporter is still hanging around," Sam said.

"Yes, I am," Chanel said. "Did you see Toby's new truck?"

Sam looked mad. "No, I haven't." She turned to her mother. "Mother, are you ready to go?" She got up and walked to the door.

Toby watched Sam leave. He shook his head and sat down.

"She sure has a short fuse," Tom said.

"Sorry," Chanel said. "I shouldn't have said anything."

"It's all right," Toby said. "I don't know why she acts like that."

Chanel laughed. "Are you serious?"

"What do you mean?" Toby asked.

"Toby, I love you like my son," Tom interjected. "But you can't be as naive as you act about girls."

Toby got a little upset. "I am not naive."

"You act like you don't know these girls are crazy about you, and you are surprised when they act upset," Tom said.

"I don't try to lead them on."

"You need to let yourself like one and become a couple and relax," Tom said. "You might wind up married."

"That is part of the problem," Toby said. "I don't know how a couple or family is supposed to act. I never had a family until my dad adopted me, and then it was just him and me."

"You will figure it out if you let yourself have feelings."

"You are probably right."

Tom looked at Chanel. "Sorry, Chanel. Kind of a heavy discussion over a hamburger, huh?"

Chanel smiled. "This is a good burger." She didn't want to say anything because she wanted to be the one Toby decided to let himself like. But how to do it? She would have to figure it out while all the girls were doing the same.

They ate. Afterward, Toby and Chanel went to the trailer dealer, and Tom went home to rest. Toby bought a twenty-four-foot cattle trailer, and they put a gooseneck hitch and a wire plug in his truck. It took over two hours, and Toby and Chanel talked about a lot of things and generally got to know each other a lot better.

The truck and trailer were ready. Toby and Chanel loaded up, and they started to pull out on the street. Suddenly, a truck cut them off and nearly caused them to wreck. Toby was hot and decided to see how well the truck would run and pull. He chased the truck down, and as the guy got out of the truck, Toby saw that he recognized him.

42

It was Stone.

Toby's blood started to boil. He opened the door to get out.

Chanel reached over and grabbed his arm. "Toby, you are in no condition to get into a fight with that jerk."

Toby stopped and looked at her. He thought for a minute and then said, "You're right. Plus he isn't worth it." He shut his door, put his truck into gear, and pulled into the road.

"That guy keeps trying to get under my skin," Toby said. "I have already had two incidents with him."

"And no doubt you kicked his tail."

He smiled. "Sort of."

She laughed. "This truck is super nice. You sure you are going to drive it in the pasture around the cows?"

"Nah. I think I will try and find an old one to kick around the pasture with."

They pulled in, and Tom walked out to see the trailer. "Looks like you are all set now."

"All set to head to Weatherford to buy you some cattle," Toby said.

"We don't have to be in a rush."

"Nothing has changed. We were heading there to get some, and just because we had a wreck doesn't mean we don't go."

"But Chanel—" Tom started.

"She can go with us if she likes," Toby interrupted.

"I would like to very much," Chanel said.

"It is settled," Toby said. "We will leave in an hour and drive to Fort Worth and get rooms. We can be out there first thing in the morning, buy the heifers, and be back here in time to feed tomorrow night. I will call Hank."

Chanel and Tom looked at each other as Toby walked up the porch and into the house.

"I guess we better get ready to go," Tom said.

Chanel smiled. "I believe so. I think he must need to do this to feel like he is doing something."

"You are probably right."

Toby called Hank. Hank said he would take care of things in the morning.

Tom and Chanel were packed and ready to go in an hour, as Toby had said. He walked to the barn to talk to Pudge and made sure everything was okay with him, and then he got into the truck and pulled out to shut the gate.

They made good time talking and laughing all the way to Dallas. They got into their rooms, and Toby lay down and said his prayers and fell asleep at around 1:30 a.m.

He was up and had his coffee made by 5:30 a.m. He showered and went out and checked his truck and trailer. Then he knocked on Tom's and Chanel's doors to make sure they were up. Tom was up and ready, but Chanel had just gotten out of the shower. She opened the door with her hair wet and in a robe.

"So that's what you look like without makeup," Toby said.

"I don't wear that much makeup," Chanel blurted back.

He laughed. "Just kidding, but we need to be hitting the road once we eat breakfast."

"Give me 10 minutes."

"Not a problem."

Chanel walked out of the room, and Toby already had the truck running.

He glanced back to see her coming and said to Tom, "Dang, she looks good in those work jeans and shirt."

Tom laughed. "Looks like a rancher."

Chanel had on a long-sleeve plaid work shirt, faded Schmidt jeans, and work boots, and her hair was pulled back in a ponytail through the hole on the back of the ball cap she was wearing. She climbed in and said, "Sorry to keep you waiting, guys."

"It was quite all right," Toby said.

Tom grinned. Chanel looked at Toby with a puzzled look, like she had missed the joke.

"Any preference on where to eat breakfast?" Toby asked.

"A small home-cooking café would be good," Chanel said.

"Kind of like the one I saw you in," Toby said.

She smiled. "Exactly."

"Was that in Grand Junction?" Tom asked.

"Yep," Toby said. "I went in for breakfast after I slept in the fair barn, and she came in for breakfast. I had met her at the hospital the night before."

"I see," Tom said.

"There's a country-looking café," Toby said. "Let's try it."

They went in and got a table and ordered breakfast.

"This is good," Chanel said. "You picked well, Toby."

"It is very good food," he replied.

They finished breakfast and were on the road forty-five minutes later.

Toby's phone rang. "Hello?"

Hank was on the other end. "Toby, you have another calf."

Toby the Rancher

"That's great. No problems, I hope."

"Nope. Everything is good. Y'all about there?"

"Should be there within a half hour."

"Drive safely, and we'll see you when you get back. Sadie wanted to invite y'all over for supper tomorrow night."

Toby answered for all of them. "That would be great. Thank her for us." He hung up and said, "Sadie invited us to supper tomorrow night. She is an excellent cook."

Chanel and Tom were both happy for the invite. They reached the ranch, and Toby turned into the drive.

Mr. Ellis was walking to his barn and saw them turn in. He stopped to greet them. He noticed it was Toby and said, "Nice truck and trailer. Are you okay? I read the story in the paper about your wreck."

Toby was embarrassed. "Yeah, I'm doing okay. Just not able to do all I want yet."

"Be sure to take it easy," Mr. Ellis said. "You have to take care of yourself. It was a great thing you did, both there and in Colorado. I am happy to know you."

Toby was getting red from embarrassment, and Chanel saw it. "Toby hasn't introduced us, I'm Chanel Small."

Mr. Ellis started to shake her hand then realized her name was the one who wrote the story on Toby. He plum forgot to tell her his name and said, "You are the one that wrote the story. You two are friends?"

"Yeah," Toby said. "We met in Colorado."

Mr. Ellis just nodded and looked at Tom. "How are you, Mr. Gray?"

"I'm doing good," Tom said. "I was hoping to buy four or five head of heifers."

"Absolutely. I have some over in this pen."

They walked over with Toby and Chanel trailing. She walked over and bumped shoulders with Toby as they walked. "Turning kind of red there, buddy."

He grinned and looked at her. "Hush up."

Chanel snickered to herself. They looked at the heifers, and Toby commented, "These look even better than the ones I bought."

"These are some of the best we have raised," Mr. Ellis said. "Their bloodline is a newer one, and we haven't had any cows yet, so we don't know how they will be maternally."

"The bloodlines usually prove out what the parents and grandparents are, don't they?" Tom asked.

"Yeah, but the bloodlines combining is sometimes a risk," Mr. Ellis replied. "If you are interested, I would let you have them for $1,800 a piece."

"That is a great price," Tom said. "I would like to have five of them."

"Pick your five," Mr. Ellis said.

Tom looked at Toby. "Which ones do you like?"

Toby pointed out the ones he liked, and Tom took a careful look at each one. While he was looking, Mr. Ellis walked over by Toby and asked, "How is Maximus doing?"

"He has settled in," Toby said. "He sure looks good."

"I hope he is a good one for you," Mr. Ellis said. "There is no reason he shouldn't be."

Tom walked up to them. "I know which ones I want." He handed a slip of paper to Mr. Ellis with the heifers' numbers on it.

"We will get them cut out," Mr. Ellis said.

Toby walked to get his truck and backed the trailer up to load them up. They had them loaded and were on the road back by 10:30 a.m. Toby pushed it to get back and only stopped to get a cup of coffee and a snack. He turned into his drive at 3:00 p.m. They unloaded the heifers and fed and watered them.

Toby walked over to look at Maximus. "Max, I sure am counting on you to make my herd a good one. Don't let me down, buddy."

Chanel had walked up without him knowing it. "He won't let you down."

"I hope not. I am hoping to build a herd like Mr. Ellis has."

"Sounds like a good, reasonable plan. I have no doubt you will make it happen."

Toby the Rancher

"I wish I was as confident as you."

They walked to the barn to see Pudge. Toby brushed one side while Chanel brushed the other, and they both talked to Pudge. Chanel was doing everything right. Toby wondered if it was legit or a ploy to get on his good side. He leaned toward it being legit. She had never done or said anything to make him doubt her intentions.

He decided to give it a shot. "I think I want to try and take a slow ride."

She looked at him. "Are you sure you can keep it slow? You could hurt your neck very easily."

"I promise I will keep it slow. You might need to help me with the saddle."

They worked together, and Toby mounted up and rode through the barn door. He looked back and said, "I will be back in about an hour."

"If you aren't back, we will come looking for you," Chanel said. "You better be safe."

"I will." With that, Toby rode off.

Chanel walked into the house, and Tom said, "Please tell me that wasn't Toby riding out."

"He was," Chanel said. "I couldn't talk him out if it. He swore he would ride slow and be safe."

"He probably will as long as no problem pops up. If it does, he will disregard his neck."

"Yeah, I know. I hope the hour passes quickly."

Toby felt so much at ease with Pudge just walking along. He knew he needed to be safe, so he was letting Pudge set the pace.

He was looking around and enjoying the look of his ranch when he caught a glimpse of something moving in the bushes. He started to spur Pudge and reach for his rifle but remembered he didn't bring it and he was supposed to ride easy. He pulled on the reins to stop Pudge, but he saw the movement again and just had to go check it out. He started Pudge in that direction, walking slowly, looking things over as he closed the gap. When he was about fifty feet away, he caught sight of it and wasn't happy he had forgotten his gun. It was a wolf. Where did it come from, and were there others?

Toby spun Pudge around and spurred him to run to the barn. He was going after his rifle. The wolf saw them and gave chase for a short distance. He gave up. Toby was riding and hoping the wolf was a loner and that it hadn't gotten any of his calves. He needed more guard donkeys. He rode into the barnyard and smoothly swung out of the saddle and onto his feet while Pudge was coming to a stop.

Chanel spotted Toby's actions from the house. "He is already back. Riding too hard, though. Wow, that was impressive, even though he shouldn't have dismounted like that."

Tom walked over to the window to look too. "The boy can ride better than anybody I have ever been around."

Just then they saw Toby come jogging back out of the barn with his rifle in hand. Pudge was standing close to a hitching post Toby had built, and so Toby jumped a foot into it and used it to spring him up on Pudge's back from the rear. They were off, heading back out to the pasture.

Tom and Chanel looked at each other.

"What in the world was that about?" Tom asked.

"I don't know," Chanel said. "But we probably shouldn't just be standing here watching him do fancy mounts and dismounts."

Tom started for the door. "You are right. I'll get the truck."

They got in the truck and started toward the pastures but weren't sure where Toby was. Tom started to say, "Well, I—" when he heard a gunshot.

"That came from the south," Chanel said.

Tom turned and headed that way.

Toby had ridden hard to get back and had his rifle still in his hand. He saw the wolf. He reined Pudge around and pulled the rifle up and dropped the wolf in his tracks. He started Pudge on over in that direction, cautiously looking for possibly more and hoping he didn't see the remains of a calf. He rode up to the wolf and heard Tom's truck coming up behind him.

Here comes a chewing out, Toby thought.

He didn't see any other wolves, and no calf remains were in sight. Of course, that didn't mean it hadn't struck elsewhere. He wasn't worried about the west pasture because of his donkey protection. He dismounted and checked the wolf to make sure it was dead. He rolled it over and saw that it had a litter somewhere.

Tom and Chanel walked up, and Tom said, "Wolves here too?"

"What do you mean?" Chanel asked.

"We dealt with a lot of wolves in New Mexico," Tom answered.

"I killed some on Hank's place a while back, but they aren't supposed to be common around here," Toby said. "This one has a litter somewhere. We need to find her pups and get them to animal control. I just hope we don't find any dead calves."

"Me too, but what was the idea of mounting and dismounting like you did?" Chanel said. "You forget where you have been the last week?"

"I'm sorry," Toby said. "It was just habit when my adrenaline gets pumping."

She asked, "You okay?"

"Feel great. The ride helped."

"In that case, that dismount and mount were cool."

Toby laughed and looked at her.

Tom chuckled. "Where do you reckon the litter is?"

"I don't know," Toby said. "I guess we need to try and see if the tracks come from elsewhere or if they are all confined to this area."

They started walking around and looking for tracks. Chanel heard some dog whimpering. She looked into some bushes and saw six baby wolves. "Here they are guys."

The men walked over, and Tom said, "It's hard to believe those cute things turn into vicious animals."

"Yep," Toby said. "Let's get them in the truck and take them to town."

They loaded the litter up and headed back to the house. Toby tied up Pudge and said, "I'll unsaddle you when we get back."

They headed to town, to the police station. The police took the wolf pups, and Toby was glad they were gone. They got home, and Tom helped him unsaddle Pudge. He brushed and fed and watered his friend. "Thanks for the ride, bud. Best therapy a guy could have."

Chanel fixed supper. They watched TV, and all were in bed by 10:30 p.m.

Toby rolled out of bed early and headed to the kitchen, but he smelled bacon and saw the light on. Chanel already had breakfast going, and when he walked in, she handed him a cup of coffee. "Good morning. Have a seat, and breakfast will be ready shortly."

"Well, good morning, and thank you, ma'am." Toby sat down and started looking at a magazine of Beefmaster cattle. Tom walked in at about 6:00 a.m. and saw that Chanel was cooking. "Man, we need to keep her around, Toby."

Toby looked up from his magazine. "Makes a good cup of coffee."

Toby the Rancher

They ate breakfast, and it was apparent Chanel was a very good cook. Tom and Toby both told her how good her cooking was, and then they headed out to do the chores.

"I am going to ride out," Toby said. "I will call if I see anything I need help with."

"Okay," Tom said. "By the way, when do you think we can put my heifers with Max?"

"I don't see why we can't now," Toby said. "When I get back, we will work them down to him."

Toby could tell Tom was excited to get his heifers bred. As Toby rode out to the pasture, he felt good about being able to have Tom with him. Everything was in order, but they did need to get the wolf buried. He called Tom to see if he could bring a shovel out. Toby waited a while then saw Tom's truck coming. Chanel was driving. She got out, and Toby asked, "You ready to dig a hole?"

"Of course," Chanel said. "You don't need to."

They worked together and got it done, and Chanel headed back while Toby rode on to check one last spot. He rode back into the barnyard about forty-five minutes later. He saw Sam's truck. He dismounted and led Pudge into the barn. Sam and Chanel were arguing, and Tom was watching. Toby listened for a minute and heard Sam say, "You are taking advantage of Toby."

"Toby is a big boy," Chanel replied. "I don't think he lets anyone take advantage of him."

"What is going on here?" Toby asked.

Chanel was surprised to see Toby.

Sam had spotted him after she had spoken. "I am just concerned about you."

"How so?" he asked.

"This reporter has attached to you like a leech and is taking advantage of your hospitality."

Chanel didn't speak because she knew she was not doing anything and knew Toby would take care of it.

◆ 363 ◆

Toby looked angrily at Sam. "What has happened to you? You are not the same person I met a few weeks back. I liked that person. I don't like the change."

Sam got angry and said, "You have been hurt and sick, and I am just trying to not let people take advantage of you. He moved in, and now her. They are mooching."

"Stop!" Toby said. "You are speaking of things you know nothing about. I think it is best you leave until you get your act together."

Sam glared at Chanel then back to Toby and stormed out of the barn.

They stood there silent until she pulled out of the drive, and Toby said, "I apologize for that. She was way out of line."

"I sure didn't mean to cause you any trouble coming here," Chanel said.

"Me either," Tom echoed.

"Both of you need to stop," Toby said. "If I hadn't have wanted you here, you wouldn't still be here. I don't let people run over me."

Tom chuckled. "You can say that again."

"Is everything good around here?" Toby asked.

Tom nodded.

"Let's move your heifers," Toby said.

They got the heifers moved and Max put in with them. They went to the house for dinner.

"I think we need to take something to supper tonight," Chanel said.

"That sounds good," Toby said. "What?"

"I figure a dessert, but I need to go to the store," Chanel said.

Toby handed her a $100 bill. "Will that cover what we need?"

"I believe so, but if not, I will pay the difference," Chanel said. "It's not up to you to feed us."

Chanel left for town, and Tom and Toby went out to clean the barn. The rest of the afternoon was spent cleaning the barn and then going to check on Hank's cattle.

Toby the Rancher

Toby walked into the house at 5:30 p.m. to get ready, and smelled the dessert. "That smells great. What is it?"

"A German chocolate cake," Chanel said.

Tom walked out from his room. "Outstanding. I love them."

"That was my specialty I learned in home ec in school," Chanel said. "I used to cook them and sell them to the café you ate at for extra money."

"I can't wait to try it," Toby said. "I'm going to shower."

They all got ready and headed for the truck at 6:30 p.m. Toby pulled up at the drive at Hank's and noticed there were no other cars there. He parked, and they walked up to the porch and knocked.

As Hank opened the door, Carl's truck started up the drive, followed by Jessie's. Hank stepped out on the porch and shook Tom's and Toby's hand and gave Chanel a hug. He motioned for the others to come on in as he led Chanel toward the kitchen. Sadie was very gracious to Chanel and thanked her for the cake.

Toby was getting a cup of coffee and Chanel and Sadie were talking about the cake when Kali, Jessie, and Carla walked into the kitchen. All three looked at Chanel.

"Who are you?" Jessie asked.

43

Sadie took the lead and said, "Girls, this is Chanel, Toby's friend. She is writing a story about him."

"Why is she here?" Kali asked.

"Because I invited her," Sadie said matter-of-factly.

Kali and Jessie both looked whipped and turned and walked out of the kitchen.

Sadie looked at Chanel. "I am sorry. I'm not sure what came over those girls."

Chanel smiled. "That's okay. I think I know why they did it."

Sadie looked puzzled for a minute and then smiled. "You are probably right."

Toby sipped some coffee. "You two lost me at the bakery."

"It's a girl thing," Sadie said. "You wouldn't understand."

"You are probably right." Toby walked into the living room. He and Carl met eyes but didn't speak. He sat down, and Hank said, "Toby, Tom is telling me he picked up some good heifers."

"I think he may have hit the jackpot," Toby replied. "They look better than mine."

"You must not have picked his out," Carl said.

Tom got angry. "I'm not sure what your deal is, but you are out of line. He did help me pick them out."

"Don't worry about him, Tom," Toby said. "He isn't worth it."

Toby the Rancher

Carl got hot, but Hank gave him a look that told he best let it go. Hank turned to Toby. "Toby, I got a call today from an old friend. He has a ranch of over ten thousand acres in far southwest Texas, and he is needing to round his cattle up and work his three hundred momma cows and the calves. From what he said, they must be scattered over the entire twenty square miles."

"Ten thousand acres doesn't equal twenty square miles," Carl said.

Hank looked at Carl but just went on talking, "He has lost three hands since last year."

"That sounds like quite a job coming up for him," Toby replied.

"Yeah, and he is no spring chicken," Hank said.

Sadie was standing in the kitchen door and asked, "Does any of his family help him?"

"I think his son and granddaughter are helping," Hank said.

"Supper is ready," Sadie said.

They all migrated to the dining room to enjoy the meal. As they were eating and idle chitchat was going on, Toby leaned over and asked Tom, who was seated beside him, "Do you think you could run the place for a while?"

Tom swallowed and looked at him. "Why do you ask?"

"I was thinking I might see if Hank's friend wanted my help," Toby said.

Tom smiled. "I can do it. There isn't anyone better at a drive than you and Pudge."

They finished eating supper, and they had a cup of coffee and a piece of German chocolate cake. Then they all went back to the living room.

Toby walked to the kitchen first and said, "Sadie, that was excellent." He looked at Chanel and smiled. "The cake was too."

Chanel laughed. "Thank you, kind sir."

Toby walked to the living room and asked Hank if he could talk to him on the porch.

Hank followed him out and asked, "What's up?"

367

"I have already talked to Tom, and he has agreed," Toby said. "I was wondering if your friend could use my help."

Hank was speechless for a minute. "Are you serious?"

"Yes. I would like to help if I could."

"What about your neck and strength?"

"I will be okay in a few days. I would watch what I did."

"I will call him. I know he will be excited."

"What is his name?" Toby asked.

"Charlie Young." Hank replied.

The evening ended, and Toby, Tom, and Chanel headed home.

"Any idea how long you will be gone?" Tom asked Toby.

Toby started to respond, but Chanel cut him off. "Gone? Where? Doing what?"

Tom laughed. "I guess she has been left out of the loop. Toby is going to southwest Texas to help on a cattle roundup."

"When was this decided?" Chanel asked.

"Tonight," Toby said.

"What about your neck?"

"I will take it easy, plus it probably would be a few days before I am actually wrangling."

They pulled into the drive, and Toby got out. "I'm going to see Pudge."

Tom and Chanel went into the house. Once inside, Chanel asked Tom, "Why is he going to do this?"

"Hank's friend needs some help, and Toby is the best wrangler I have ever worked with," Tom said.

"I have no doubt he is the best, but he also just nearly died."

"That may be why he feels the need to do this. He may need some time to think things through. He will have plenty of alone time with just him and Pudge."

There was silence for a minute, and then Tom added, "I guess this short-circuits your stay. I'm sorry. I wasn't thinking."

"Nah," Chanel said. "Really, I needed to get back home and back to the office. They have liked what I have done here, but I need to check in. Besides, I have something I am considering that I need to talk to some folks about."

"That sounds intriguing."

Chanel smiled and walked into her room.

Once in the barn, Toby shut the doors behind him as he planned on being there for a while. He started brushing and currying Pudge and telling him about the trip they were getting ready to take. "It will be good to get back to riding and herding cattle every day. Don't you think so, buddy?"

Pudge snorted and stamped his right foreleg in agreement.

Toby sat down, and it wasn't long until he was asleep.

Chanel woke up at around 2:00 a.m. and started to the kitchen to get a drink of water. She walked by Toby's open door and noticed he wasn't in bed and that the bed was made. She looked around for his boots and saw that the front door was unlocked. She put her boots on and headed for the barn. As quietly as she could, she opened the barn door and then the door to Pudge's room, and there was Toby, sleeping away.

She smiled and started to shut the door, but Pudge moved, and Toby woke up and saw Chanel. He motioned her in, and she sat down beside him.

"I am sorry for not telling you about the trip," Toby said. "You can stay here while I'm gone."

"You don't need to apologize," Chanel said. "And I need to get back to Albuquerque, anyway."

They sat there, looking at Pudge, and Toby put his arm around Chanel. They both went to sleep.

Toby woke up at 5:30 a.m. and tried to move and leave Chanel sleeping, but she woke up.

"Let's go in, and I'll start breakfast while you sleep," Toby said.

They went into the house. Chanel lay down on the couch and went back to sleep. Toby cooked breakfast, and Tom walked in as he got it ready.

"Why is she on the couch?" Tom asked.

Toby explained what he had done and how she came out, and Tom said, "I think you need this trip and roundup, my friend."

"I think you might be right," Toby said.

They were just finishing breakfast when Toby's phone rang. He answered it, and it was Hank. Hank had called Charlie, and Charlie was excited to have Toby come down. He had read the story in the paper that Chanel had written. It had been published in nearly every newspaper in Texas, even though she worked for the Albuquerque paper.

Toby hung up. "Chanel, you are famous. Your story was even printed down where Charlie Young lives."

"Are you kidding me?" Chanel replied. "Wow! Toby Parker is a celebrity."

Toby looked at her. "No, he isn't."

Tom laughed. "I believe she is right, Toby. When do you leave?"

"I leave at noon," Toby replied.

"Wow, that is quick," Chanel said.

"Yeah," Toby said. "I better get packed and ready."

"Me too."

"I better get out and get started taking care of things," Tom said.

Toby was packed and had Pudge loaded and was ready to pull out of the drive at 10:00 a.m. He talked to Tom down at the barn and asked, "You sure you are okay with me leaving?"

"Yes," Tom replied. "You need this, and I need to see for myself if I am still capable."

"There's no doubt in my mind you are more than capable."

They shook hands, and Tom started cleaning a stall as Toby walked out. He walked to the house to see Chanel. She met him on the porch. "Are you already leaving?"

"Yeah," Toby said. "Figured I'd get on the road and try to make it down there to be able to start in the morning."

"I'll be leaving shortly after you do. I sure appreciate your hospitality and you letting me do another story on you."

"You make it sound like this is good-bye. I think it is just so long for a while."

Chanel looked at him. "So I am welcome to come back sometime?"

"You better come back, and not in the too-distant future," Toby replied.

Chanel grinned. "You can count in it."

They hugged. She moved to kiss him on the cheek, but he turned so they kissed on the lips. Then he turned and walked off the porch. He got into his truck and put it in gear and waved to her as he pulled away.

Chanel stood and watched him leave. *I have to figure out a way to get closer.*

A little while later, Chanel finished loading her car and was getting ready to leave when Tom came walking up.

"Looks like you are packed up and ready to leave," Tom said.

"Yeah, I have a long drive ahead of me," Chanel said.

"When you coming back?"

"Sooner than later, I hope."

"Good deal," Tom said. "That boy needs you."

They said good-bye, and Chanel left for Albuquerque.

Toby set his cruise and planned to not stop until he was a couple of hundred miles down the road. He hoped to pull into Alpine by 10:00 p.m. and then to find Charlie's ranch. He stopped at 2:30 p.m. to use the restroom and got a burger and coffee. He was back on the road in fifteen minutes.

He finished his burger and fries and called Chanel to see how her trip was going. They talked for about an hour while they drove, and Toby convinced her to stop in Amarillo for the night since she wouldn't get home until well after midnight.

Toby pushed it for the next two hours and then stopped to get fuel and a cup of coffee. He called Tom to see how things went for the day and then pushed on to Alpine. He pulled in at 9:35 p.m. and then started for the ranch. He pulled up into the drive at 10:00 p.m. Charlie walked out to greet him.

Toby got out and stuck out his hand. "Hello, I'm Toby Parker."

Charlie shook his hand. "It's a pleasure to meet you, and thank you for coming. If you want to unload your horse, I will show you where to put him."

The barn looked big, but it was dark, so Toby couldn't tell much about it until he walked in. He stopped inside the door and just looked around. The barn was huge and very nice.

"Wow," Toby said. "What a barn."

Charlie laughed. "Yeah, we kind of overbuilt it."

"The indoor arena is great."

"It comes in handy during bad weather. Gives us something to do."

"It's not getting much use without any hands," someone said behind them.

Toby turned to see a man and young lady behind them. He nodded to them, and Charlie spoke up. "Toby, this is my son Walt and my granddaughter Betsy. They work here along with me."

Toby the Rancher

"Pleased to meet you," Toby said.

"Slave away here is more like it," Walt continued. "This place will just put people in an early grave. It did my mother."

Toby was surprised by the statement.

"That's not what took your mother from us," Charlie said. "She had cancer."

Toby was still puzzled as to why Walt would work there, especially with his daughter if he truly disliked it as he indicated.

"Well, I don't know how one guy is going to help us that much," Walt said.

"Dad, it's better than nothing," Betsy said.

"We'll see." Walt turned and walked out the door.

Betsy looked at Toby. "I hope you are good. Dad will be unmerciful if you aren't." She turned and followed Walt out the door.

Toby slowly turned and looked at Charlie. Charlie shook his head. "I am sorry. I wish I could tell you what was wrong, but I don't know why he has turned like he has."

"All I want to do is ride and round up cattle," Toby said. "Anything else is between y'all. I hope he realizes that."

"I know," Charlie said. "Let me show you to the bunkhouse, and then you can come back and tend your horse."

He showed Toby the bunkhouse. It was very nice and big—and very empty. Charlie went back to the house, and Toby walked back to the barn. It was late, but he wanted to let Pudge get some movement, so he took Pudge and ran him around the arena. He fed him and went to the bunkhouse. He had left his phone there and checked it when he got back. He had two messages. One was from Kali, apologizing for how she had acted last night. The second was from Chanel, hoping Toby had made it safely and telling him good night.

Toby sent a message back to Kali, saying, "Thanks for the apology." To Chanel, he said, "I made it safely. Thanks and good night."

He read his Bible some and said his prayer and was asleep by 12:15 a.m. He was awake at 5:00 a.m. and ate a honey bun that he had picked up since there weren't any groceries in the bunkhouse. There was some coffee but no pot, so he made some cowboy coffee and drank a couple of cups before he went to check on Pudge. He saddled Pudge and rode him around the arena some and then started back to the bunkhouse.

It was 7:10 a.m., and Walt and Betsy were on the porch when Toby came around the corner. He heard Walt say, "If he can't get up early, we sure don't need him."

"I knocked but got no answer," Betsy said.

"Let's get him up now," Walt said.

As they opened the door, Toby asked, "Are you looking for me?"

They both jumped when he spoke, and Walt said, "It's about time you got up."

"I've been up for over two hours waiting on y'all," Toby replied.

Charlie was walking across the barnyard. "It's time to roll. Let's go."

They all walked to the barn, and when they walked in, Charlie said to Toby, "You already have yours saddled. You must have been up early."

"Yes, sir," Toby replied.

Walt grumbled something and started saddling his horse. When they were ready, they rode out, but Toby wondered what the plan was since nothing had been shared with him.

He asked as they rode, "Charlie, what's the plan? I understand you have ten thousand acres and the cattle are fairly scattered."

"Yeah," Charlie said. "I just want to try and bring in the cattle in these two sections ahead before we head out for the south end of the ranch."

"Why don't you just ride and let us do the thinking?" Walt said.

Toby started getting mad but stopped and said, "I can't do the job if I don't know what the job is."

"Understood," Charlie said. "Walt, you and Betsy go left up here, and we'll go right and circle around and meet in the middle with whatever we pick up."

Toby the Rancher

Neither Walt nor Betsy acknowledged Charlie but cut off without a word and left. Toby and Charlie rode on, and Toby was pleased that his neck wasn't hurting at all. They found some cattle and went to work. Charlie was impressed.

After they had gathered thirty head, he turned to Toby and said, "Young man, Hank wasn't exaggerating. You know how to sit a horse and work cattle."

"Thanks," Toby said.

44

Toby and Charlie split up again, and Toby found and brought up eleven more head. He was confident he had rounded up all he had on his side of the pasture.

Charlie brought in three more. "Let's see what Walt and Betsy have, and we can take them up together."

They rode in Walt and Betsy's direction. Toby and Charlie separated some as they rode, and Toby went around a hill and was out of sight from Charlie. He saw a draw in the distance and thought he would see where it led and if Walt, Betsy, or any cattle were there.

He was riding up on the back side to try and get a better vantage point of more area when he spotted Walt. He was riding away from some cattle Toby saw. Toby stopped and was kind of behind a mesquite bush where he couldn't be clearly seen. He thought for a minute about what it meant but decided to just go round them up unless he saw signs of illness or something. He rode up to the cattle, and he saw they all looked healthy and the calves were doing well too. He counted, and there were twenty-two cows and thirteen calves. He was surprised the calves were as big as they were. He guessed each one weighed at least six hundred pounds. Spring calves would only be weighing a couple of hundred.

Toby the Rancher

Toby dismissed any thoughts of wrongdoing and started the cattle toward where he thought Charlie would be. Charlie and the other two were standing and talking as Toby pushed the cows and calves around the knoll. They all had surprised looks on their faces when they saw him and the cattle. Once Toby had them with the rest of the herd, he rode up to Charlie and dismounted.

"Where'd you find them?" Charlie asked.

"Back over that direction," Toby said. "I didn't realize you had calves that large out here this time of year."

"I didn't either," Charlie said. "We must have missed them in the fall."

Toby watched Walt. Walt seemed very nervous and somewhat upset.

"Well, we've got them now," Walt said. "Let's get the herd moving toward the barn and corrals."

Toby spurred Pudge and started for the far side of the cattle, and they worked them toward the corrals. When they had them all in and Toby was off shutting the gate, Betsy rode by and said, "You and that horse sure know what you're doing."

"You can tell this isn't his first rodeo," Charlie agreed. "I am feeling better about this roundup now."

Walt just sat and listened, looking like he had just taken a big bite of lemon. Toby wasn't looking for his praise but thought his demeanor was odd. It had been different ever since he arrived but had taken on an even more sour tone since Toby had brought in the cows and calves that Walt had missed. Was he thinking Toby did it to show him up? Toby shook it off and climbed back on Pudge to ride to the barn.

"Let's get a bite to eat before we start working on them," Charlie said.

"What all are you wanting to do to them?" Toby asked.

"I thought you knew cattle," Walt answered in a gruff tone. "We are going to brand, worm, castrate, and vaccinate."

"I was hoping y'all did things right in south Texas," Toby snapped. With that, he swung off Pudge and walked up the steps to the porch and followed Charlie in the house. Toby glanced back, and he saw Walt and Betsy were talking.

Walt's wife, Gwen, was there and had dinner ready. Charlie introduced her to Toby and then said, "Gwen, you timed that perfectly."

Gwen laughed. "I cheated and sent a text to Betsy to let me know when you would be in."

"Smart thinking," Toby said.

There wasn't much talk during the eating. When they finished, Charlie said, "Let's get at 'em."

Toby stood up. "That was excellent, Gwen. Thank you."

Gwen smiled. "Thank you, and you are very welcome."

Toby walked out, and Gwen looked at her husband and daughter. "That is a fine young man. Betsy, I hope you can find a husband like him one day."

Neither of them said anything, and both got up and headed for the door.

Toby, Charlie, Walt, and Betsy worked cattle the rest of the day and finished right at sunset. They walked to the barn, and Charlie said, "Toby, I know I've said it before, but I'm sure glad you came down. I've never had anyone handle a horse and cattle as well as you do."

Walt got mad. "Well, thanks, Dad. I only know what you taught me, so I guess you aren't very good either."

"Walt, don't get mad," Charlie replied. "I was including myself in that."

"Thanks, Charlie," Toby said. "I enjoy it, and it helps me." He paused for a minute. "I will have to say, although it is none of my business, I have never seen a son disrespect his dad like that. It is disgraceful."

"Don't worry about it," Charlie said.

"Nobody cares what you think," Walt said. "The quicker we can get this roundup over and get you out of here, the better off we will be."

Toby started to get mad but remembered he was there to help Hank's friend and that Charlie had treated him very well. Instead, he said, "I'm going to take care of my horse." He walked off.

Toby spent quite a bit of time with Pudge and then walked to the bunkhouse. He was surprised to see some supper in the microwave with a note from Gwen that it was there. She had also put some groceries in the fridge for him and brought him a coffee pot. He enjoyed the hamburger and fries and drank a pot of coffee before bed. He was tired and sore but happy that he had been able to do what he did today. His neck was doing well. He called Tom and Chanel and told them how things were going and checked on them.

He lay down around 10:30 p.m. He read the Bible, said his prayers, and drifted off at about 11:15 p.m. He was up by 5:30 a.m. and cooking breakfast. He ate and had things cleaned up and his gear ready for a trail drive. He walked out at 6:30 a.m. and headed to the barn. He had Pudge out and saddled, waiting for the others to show.

Charlie came out of the house at 7:15 a.m. and saw Toby all ready to go. "Man, you are going to push us and make us cowboy up."

"I'm just an early riser," Toby replied. "Like to get things going."

Walt and Betsy had walked out.

"Well, whoopee," Walt said. "Aren't we lucky to have you with us?"

Toby ignored him and asked Charlie, "How are we loading up?"

"I have a friend coming over to drive us to where we need to start the roundup," Charlie replied.

"Where's the packhorse?" Toby asked.

"Must be worried about his stomach," Betsy said.

Toby looked at her, and she was smiling. He nodded at her and said, "Nah, but we may get that way before we return."

As he finished speaking, they heard the truck and trailer coming up the road. Toby took Pudge's reins and led him to the side. The truck pulled up and stopped, and Gwen came walking out of the house.

"Your mother going?" Toby asked Betsy.

Walt heard and answered, "Since you showed up we don't have enough room for everyone in the truck. She will drive me and Betsy out."

Toby started to disagree, knowing the crew cab truck would seat at least five, but he decided to let it go. He really didn't want to ride in a truck with Walt, anyway.

They loaded up and headed out. Given the roads and the distance, it was well over an hour until they reached the back side of the ranch where they would start. Toby was kind of surprised they didn't just ride out instead of being hauled out and around. He wished they had ridden out as it would have given him a better feel for the land and terrain, and he would much rather be in a saddle than the backseat of a truck.

They mounted up and Charlie pointed to the east. "Walt and Betsy, you go over that direction, and Toby and I will cover this side. We will meet at the old windmill for camp tonight."

"Hopefully, the cattle agree," Walt said. He and Betsy lit out and left both packhorses with Charlie and Toby.

Toby didn't like it but wasn't in a position to say anything. He started to ride out and heard Charlie grumble, "Dat blame them. They left us both horses."

Toby smiled to himself and led his packhorse out. He was riding and looking for cattle and contemplating how Walt had been acting. He couldn't figure Walt out. Toby was only there to help out, and yet Walt acted like a heel most of the time.

Toby spotted a bunch of cows and started that way. He got them rounded up and started pushing them toward the east and driving them along. He counted thirty-one head, and one yellow ugly-looking bull.

"You ever seen such an ugly bull?" he asked Pudge. "I don't know if it is just the color or the loose skin, but something makes it look bad."

He pushed the cattle along and noticed some movement in some bushes, so he rode over to check it out. It turned out to be another two cows, and there were nine more on the back side of the sand hill. He gathered all of them and moved them along. He came upon fourteen more cattle as he worked a wide path moving the cattle along. He saw Charlie in the distance and moved the herd toward him.

Charlie saw the cattle raising dust and then saw Toby and waved to him. Toby continued to work the herd in that direction until the two groups were merged into one herd. Charlie had rounded up thirty-two cows, and Toby had fifty-six and an ugly bull.

Charlie saw the large number Toby had and said, "Nice job. How many did you have?"

"Fifty-six cows and an ugly bull," Toby replied.

Charlie started laughing and said, "He is that, but you should see the calves he throws."

"Are you serious?" Toby asked.

"Yeah. I nearly sold him, but I had trouble getting him penned up, and his calves started dropping, and they were so good-looking I kept him. They were better than eight hundred pounds at weaning."

"My apologies, Mr. Bull."

Charlie laughed. "I wonder how Walt and Betsy are doing. Up ahead there is the windmill."

They got their herd there and Charlie started camp while Toby rode the herd. They knew they would drift off, so they would have to nighthawk all night, every night until they got them in.

It was getting toward dusk. Toby spotted some dust and pulled his binoculars, and saw it was Walt and Betsy. They didn't appear to have near as many head as Toby and Charlie had put together. They pushed them in, and as they rode up, Charlie rode up too. He asked Betsy since she was closer, "How many you have, girl?"

"Thirty-seven cows and one bull," she replied.

"I sure figured there were more than that down through there," Charlie said.

"How many did you find?" Toby asked.

"Twenty-eight, and the bull," Betsy answered. "Dad didn't have much luck."

Walt had moved in closer. "You got a problem?"

"Nope," Toby said. "Just making conversation."

"Well, don't," Walt said. "She has a boyfriend."

Toby started to say something and caught himself. He looked at Charlie, and Charlie looked perplexed.

"Walt, where do you figure the other 175 are?" Charlie asked. "I sure thought we would have more by now."

"There may not be that many now," Walt said. "Some may have died, and others may have been taken and moved across the border."

"I sure hope that didn't happen," Charlie said. "We need all of them to calve so we can sell them to pay Momma's hospital bill. Otherwise we may have to sell some or all of the ranch."

Walt didn't speak. Toby could see the pain in Charlie's face. He had lost his wife and was worried about losing his ranch that they had built together.

"Charlie, if they are out here, we will find them," Toby said.

Charlie gave a half smile and nodded to Toby.

"What's for supper?" Walt asked.

Toby the Rancher

"Ham hock stew and corn bread," Charlie replied. "Y'all go eat, and I'll watch the herd."

"Nah, you go ahead, Charlie," Toby said. "I will watch while you eat."

"You sure?"

"Absolutely. You cooked it."

Charlie laughed. "Well, I warmed it up, anyway. *Gwen* cooked it."

Toby laughed, and the other three rode toward the fire. He rode and thought about how Charlie had looked and how his voice had quivered. Toby wondered if many of the cattle were being stolen, and would they take them down into Mexico?

His phone started vibrating. It was Tom. They talked for a while, with Toby telling him about the roundup. Tom said everything was good at home. He told Toby to be careful and not to worry about things there. Toby hung up and decided to call Chanel. Something about talking to Tom and thinking about Charlie and how he had looked sad about his wife and ranch made him want to talk to her now, even though he was riding nighthawk at this point.

"Toby, is everything okay?" Chanel asked.

Toby laughed. "Hello to you too."

"I'm sorry. I just didn't figure I would hear from you while you were on the roundup, and I was afraid something had happened."

"Nah. I'm doing good. Neck is healing, and Pudge and I are enjoying the work and time together. I just wanted to call and see how you're doing. Everything okay with your job?"

"Everything is great," Chanel said. "I'm working on a deal that I can't talk about right now, but if it works out, it will be fantastic."

"That sounds great, but sure leaves me hanging with a lot of time to sit here and wonder what you are up to."

"I know, but I can't tell you until I know for sure."

"Okay," Toby said. "Well, take care. I better pay attention to the herd since it is totally dark. I will talk to you later."

"Be careful, and I miss you."

"Same here. I mean, the 'Miss you' part."

She laughed. "I knew what you meant."

They hung up, and Betsy rode up.

"Your turn to go eat," she said.

"Much obliged." Toby rode toward the campfire.

45

Toby rode into camp, and Walt walked away from Charlie, with Charlie watching him and shaking his head. Toby pulled Pudge up short to get a better feel for what was going on. Charlie looked around and saw Toby, and he motioned for Toby to come on in. Toby dismounted and walked Pudge and tied him up and got him some feed. He then walked to the fire, and Charlie greeted him, asking, "Everything going okay?"

"Yeah," Toby replied. "They are peaceful tonight."

Charlie handed him a plate of food. "Eat up. There is plenty."

Toby ate the food and drank a cup of coffee. Walt walked up while he was eating and sat down without saying a word. Toby finished eating and then got up and walked toward Pudge.

"You already fed him once," Walt said. "We can't afford feeding your horse every hour of the day."

Toby walked on without acknowledging Walt's comment. Walt started to repeat himself when Charlie stepped in and said, "Walt! Leave him alone. He isn't doing anything wrong."

Walt didn't like that. He walked over to his horse, mounted up, and rode off into the darkness.

Toby spent some time with Pudge and then walked back to the fire. He got another cup of coffee and asked, "Charlie, have I done something to offend Walt?"

Charlie shook his head. "No, you haven't. He has something eating at him and has for a while."

Toby sat and sipped his coffee and thought about the situation. He was struggling with what he was seeing. He had seen bad relationships all the time he was in foster care, but he didn't believe a son should treat and talk to his dad like Walt was doing to Charlie. He knew he never would have his dad. He shook his head and thought to himself, *I need to stay out off this.*

"How are we running nighthawk?" Toby asked Charlie.

"Which do you want?" Charlie said.

"Whichever you need me to take."

"I appreciate it," Charlie said. "I would figure the last watch."

"Okeydoke," Toby said. He lay back on his saddle and started reading the Bible he had on his phone. He liked it because he could do it without needing a light. He was reading when a text came in. It was from Sam. "I went by your place today, and Tom said you were gone out of town. What's up?"

Toby texted back, saying, "I am on a roundup in southwest Texas."

"Oh," Sam's text read. "Well, have fun."

He sent back, "Thanks."

Toby went back to reading his Bible, and Walt came riding in. Charlie told Walt how the nighthawk would go, and Walt rode back out. He apparently had gone and told Betsy because he came back and laid down on his bedroll.

Toby closed his eyes and tried to go to sleep. He woke up when Betsy came in and also when Walt came in. He got up at 2:30 a.m. and drank some strong coffee still on the coals and rode out to relieve Charlie. He shone his flashlight up in the air to let Charlie know he was coming up, and when he rode up, Charlie said, "You're early. I didn't expect you until about 4:00."

"I'm good," Toby said. "Go ahead and go get you some rest."

Charlie laughed. "I won't argue with you." He turned his horse and headed for camp.

Toby the Rancher

Toby spent the rest of the time riding around the herd and was glad to see daybreak come. He was on the east side and spotted movement in the distance. He pulled his glasses and looked to see if he could tell what it was. He watched and counted six coyotes. He wasn't too worried since they didn't have any calves in the herd, but they could spook the cattle to run in the right situation. He periodically looked over at them until about 8:00 a.m., when Betsy rode up. "Better go get some breakfast. We all slept late."

"Will do." Toby thought to himself on his way in, *How can you sleep late on a cattle roundup and drive? Jeez.*

He rode into camp as Walt rode out. Toby dismounted, and Charlie said, "Good morning. Everything going okay out there?"

"Yeah, just some coyotes on the horizon," Toby replied.

"Hope they don't cause us any trouble," Charlie said. "We decided to have Betsy stay with the herd and keep it moving along, and we will find others and move them into the main herd."

Toby had taken a bite of food that Charlie had handed him, and he was glad he had so he didn't have to speak. He thought that was a bad idea. He wasn't sure she could push the herd. He had figured Charlie would stay with the herd.

"You okay with that?" Charlie asked.

Toby swallowed. "Charlie, it is your herd, and you are free to do it however you choose."

"Walt felt Betsy needed to try, and he said he could go at it alone and I could stay with you since you didn't know the country."

Toby chewed another bite and just nodded an understanding, but he figured Walt had a hand in the setup, and sure enough, he did. Toby finished eating quickly and helped pack things up, and they headed out. They rode by Betsy and the herd and helped her get them moving. They rode on west, and when they reached a ridge, Charlie said, "You go left, and I'll start from here."

Toby nodded and took off. He rode a ways and then said, "Pudge, I am getting some bad feelings about what we are into here. I hope it is just the breakfast working on me, but I'm afraid it's not."

He rode for about thirty minutes before he spotted his first cow. He looked and worked for the next four hours, gathering twenty-two head. He was thinking that they must be really strung out and it was going to take a long time to gather up three hundred cows when he rounded a sand knoll and saw a good number. He worked them into the herd he already had, and it totaled fifty-three cows. He was surprised to see two of them had calves that looked to be about a month old.

Toby decided to work his herd to the main herd so he could be more effective in finding others. He started working them toward the east and where he figured the herd should be. He spotted Charlie with a small herd, and they joined up and pushed them on. They reached a point, and they still hadn't seen the main herd.

"There aren't enough tracks to show the herd has passed," Toby said. "They must be behind or off track."

"Doggone it," Charlie said. "We need to stay on schedule. I guess one of us better ride back and find them and see if Betsy needs help."

Toby knew she needed help. He had noticed she wasn't near as good on a horse as Sam was. Sam could probably have pushed the herd by herself.

As Charlie rode off, Toby spotted some horse tracks. He couldn't figure out why they would be there. "Pudge, my feeling is getting worse all the time."

Toby kept the fifty-three cows he had rounded up and the twenty-two head Charlie had moving forward slowly, waiting on the main herd. Forty-five minutes passed, and still no herd or even any dust in the distance.

Toby was torn. He knew he needed to stay with this group but wondered if there was trouble with the main herd that he needed to help with. He decided to try and call Charlie and hoped it didn't spook the cows if he had it on ring.

Toby the Rancher

Charlie answered and sounded frustrated. As it turned out, the main herd had gotten away from Betsy, and they were trying to round them back up. Charlie asked Toby just to stay with the day's cattle and they would try to bring the herd along. Toby hung up the phone and felt frustrated and, in a sense, helpless. He knew things needed done, but he couldn't do anything but watch seventy-seven head of cattle. He had found a small patch of grass, and the cattle were content to graze it off. He decided to ride a ways in each direction to see if he could spot any more cattle to bring in. He felt if he didn't, this roundup would drag on entirely too long.

Toby found nine more cattle when he went west, and then he drifted off to the east and found a high spot to look from. He spotted Walt, but he only had a handful of cattle. He wasn't pushing them too fast, and Toby noticed Walt was missing cattle as he rode by a draw. He thought maybe it was a different look from Walt's vantage point, so he rode over and rounded up the sixteen head.

He got them back to the herd before Walt even showed up, and when Walt came up out of the swag he was following, Toby waved like he hadn't watched him. Walt didn't wave back, and when he had the thirteen head of cattle he had added to the herd, he rode toward Toby. "Where are Dad and Betsy?"

"Trying to get the main herd rounded up and brought along," Toby replied.

"Why aren't you helping them?" Walt snapped.

Toby fought his anger and calmly replied, "Because Charlie wanted me to keep these together and moving slowly forward."

"I'm going back."

"See ya." Toby just pulled the reins left and turned Pudge to walk around the herd. "Pudge, something is just not right here. Charlie is a class individual, and Walt is an A number-one jerk. My gut tells me he is up to something, but I can't figure out what. We haven't done anything but try to help."

Toby decided he was going to do some more wide sweeps. He didn't find any on the west but rounded up twenty-six on the east. He settled the herd down and kept them moving slowly and did another sweep. He found ten on the west and twenty-three on the east. He could have sworn he saw other riders in the distance but dismissed it, thinking he was just seeing things.

He worked the herd and tried to not have them moving too fast, and then he saw a dust cloud to the south. It took another forty-five minutes before they got the herd to him, and Charlie looked frazzled. He started to speak to Toby, "Well, this is going—"

He stopped and looked around. "Well, I just changed my mind. It looks like there are nearly three hundred head here."

Toby smiled. "I believe there is."

"How in the world?" Charlie asked. "Walt, did you bring in a bunch?"

Walt was looking around and looked like he was sick to his stomach. "Nope. I didn't find hardly any."

"I just kept sweeping to the west and then the east and finding more," Toby said. "I really pulled a good number from the east."

Charlie just sat there in the saddle, smiling and looking over the herd. His smile wilted some as he said, "I am surprised there aren't more calves. I hope we are getting ready to drop a bunch."

"I did figure we would find more calves," Toby replied.

"I guess we will need to preg check them too," Charlie said.

"Probably need to sell a bunch of them," Walt said.

"What good would that do?" Charlie asked. "They wouldn't bring anything, and we would have to use what we got for two cows to buy one back."

There was silence for a while, and then Charlie said, "Let's eat some dinner, and then we can start the herd toward the ranch while one of us scouts out for other strays. There are probably still some others out there."

Walt jumped on it and said, "I will scout. I know the land better."

"Toby has had good results," Charlie said.

"He isn't a part of this ranch. I will do it." Walt rode off.

Toby watched him and shook his head. He didn't realize Betsy was watching him.

"Don't shake your head at my dad," she said.

Toby looked at her and didn't apologize. "I am tired of hearing how I am not a part of this and questioning why I am here."

"Betsy, you are out of line," Charlie said. "Help me get some dinner."

Toby rode herd while they whipped up some grub. Charlie motioned him in, and he rode in for a bite. He was eating, and decided to tell Charlie what he had seen. "Charlie, I have seen horse tracks as I have been doing my sweeps, and I could have sworn I saw some riders."

Charlie looked at him, puzzled. "There shouldn't be anybody out here but us."

"I can't swear to the riders, but the tracks are real," Toby said. He noticed Betsy looked nervous. "You got a boyfriend riding around out here? You seem nervous."

Betsy looked at him. "Go to—!"

Toby laughed, mounted up, and rode out.

46

Toby's neck was bothering him some today. He rubbed it some and made it feel a little better. He wondered if it was just because it was healing. He decided to swing out and see if he could find any more cattle, whether Walt wanted him to or not. He found six more and pushed them back to the herd. He did see more cattle and horse tracks.

Charlie saw him bringing the cattle in. "Where did you get those?"

"Off to the west. I saw more tracks."

"Cattle or horse?"

"Horse. More than a couple."

Charlie scratched his chin. "That has me puzzled."

Walt came riding up, and Charlie asked, "Did you find any more?"

"Nothing," Walt replied.

"See any horse tracks?" Charlie asked.

"What?" Walt asked, disgusted.

"Toby has been seeing extra horse tracks."

Walt looked at Toby. "You trying to stir up Dad?"

"What do you mean?" Toby asked.

"Making up wild stories," Walt said.

Toby the Rancher

Toby started to speak but decided against it. He just frowned at Walt and then at Betsy and rode away, saying, "Let's get 'em moving."

"So he is giving orders now!" Walt said.

"He is right," Charlie said. "Let's get them up and heading toward the barnyard."

They pushed the herd for a while. Toby was keeping his eyes open for strays or outliers. He noticed Charlie was the only other one who seemed to be doing it. He broke off and rode around one knoll and found three cows and a calf, and drove them toward the herd. The other three saw them coming in, and Charlie waved. Betsy rode over to Walt, and they talked. She then rode back to her spot riding drag.

Toby worked his way to her and asked, "You 'bout ready to switch and stop eating dust?"

Betsy looked at him and smiled. "That would be great." She rode back to the east side, and Toby started riding drag.

He got a text from Chanel asking how he was, and he responded that he was doing well. He asked her how her job was going, and she said it was getting exciting. He had no idea what that meant, but he told her he was happy for her. Actually, he wasn't happy, because it meant he wouldn't see her much.

All of a sudden, Toby heard a commotion to his right and looked to see Charlie's horse rearing up. Charlie couldn't hold on and fell off, and he fell right by a gully. When he hit the ground, he fell off in the gully.

Toby spurred Pudge to get over to Charlie. He saw a rattlesnake slithering off but didn't want to risk a shot with the herd. He swung down off Pudge and dropped to his hands and knees to get a good look in the gully. It was over ten feet deep where Charlie had fallen in. Toby saw Charlie's legs but couldn't see his whole body. "Charlie, are you okay?"

Charlie was hurting and found it hard to talk but mustered a response, "I think I broke some bones."

"I'll be down there in a minute." Toby grabbed his rope and tied it on the saddle horn and then around his waist. "Stand here, buddy," he told Pudge. "And don't move so I can check on Charlie."

Toby started climbing down the side of the gully as Betsy rode up and asked, "Is Grandad hurt?"

Toby just nodded as he went on down. Pudge was holding good, and Toby wasn't at all nervous about his rope being tied to Pudge and being suspended as he climbed down. He reached Charlie quickly. "What hurts, Charlie?"

"Dad, you hurt?" Walt hollered from up top.

"Yes, he is," Toby answered.

"I asked Dad," Walt snapped.

Toby ignored him. Charlie was hurting and whispered, "My back and leg and arm are hurting bad."

Toby could tell Charlie's arm was broken just by looking. He tried to look at Charlie's leg. He cut his pants, and the bone was about to puncture the skin.

"Whereabouts does your back hurt?" Toby asked.

From where Charlie pointed, Toby surmised it was his hip. He wondered if Charlie had broken his hip.

"Walt, do you think we can get a life flight helicopter out here pretty quick?" Toby hollered.

"Why?" Walt asked. "What's wrong?"

"He has broken bones, and some are bad."

"Dad, I told you we needed to sell out. This just proves it. If you had listened—"

"Walt, this isn't the time or place," Toby cut him off. "Your dad is hurting down here."

Walt didn't respond. He huffed away like a big kid. Toby waited a minute and hollered, "Walt, you got help on the way yet?"

Walt had walked back up and said, "I'll try to call 911."

Toby worked to try and make Charlie as comfortable as possible without moving him.

Charlie was hurting a lot and grumbling. "I can't even stay on a horse anymore."

"Hey now," Toby said. "A rattler will spook any horse enough to throw their rider."

"So that was what it was," Charlie said.

"I saw one when I got to you," Toby said.

"They are willing but don't know where we are," Walt hollered.

Toby called back up to him. "Can they not target your GPS on your phone? If not, we can build a big campfire for spotting."

Walt didn't respond, so Toby figured he was talking to them. He wiped the sweat from Charlie's forehead that was being caused from the pain.

"They are on their way," Walt called out. "It will be a while from Odessa. That is where they said it would come from."

Toby called back up, "Hopefully, the chopper can cover ground quickly."

"Let's get him out of there," Walt said.

"We don't want to move him," Toby said. "I think his hip is broken. Hey, you may want to push the cattle on up the trail so the chopper doesn't spook and scatter them when it shows up."

Walt didn't like Toby telling him what to do, but it made sense, so he and Betsy started working on it. It seemed like a very long time, but in reality, it was less than forty-five minutes before the helicopter arrived. Walt and Betsy left the herd and rode back. The paramedics worked with Toby to get Charlie out of the gully and into the helicopter.

Charlie was hurting but still had his senses about him. "You three work together to get the herd pushed in."

Toby tipped his hat. "Yes, sir. You don't worry about that."

Walt heard his dad but said, "I'm going with him."

"No," Charlie said. "I'll be fine. We need these cattle in and taken care of."

The chopper took off. Toby gathered his rope up, and he mounted up and headed for the herd. He felt bad for Charlie but in a sense was feeling bad for himself. How would Walt act now that Charlie wasn't around anymore? Toby didn't want to mess with an attitude. He started driving the cattle, and Walt rode up beside him and said, "Betsy and I will work the sides if you can ride drag."

Toby was surprised that Walt actually made sense, and he replied, "I'll push them along as fast as you need."

"Let's make good time but not run them," Walt said.

Toby nodded and started pushing the herd hard as Walt and Betsy rode off in different directions. They continued to drive the cattle until it was dark, and Walt and Betsy made camp while Toby rode nighthawk.

Walt came to relieve Toby, and Toby asked, "Any word on Charlie?"

"He has as you thought—a broken arm, leg, and hip," Walt said. "They don't think he will need surgery, but we'll see."

"I sure hate it," Toby said. "I can tell he loves what he does."

Walt had started to turn away, but he stopped and looked back at Toby for a minute, like he was thinking of something, and then he went on.

Toby ate and then called Hank and told him about Charlie. He called Tom to see how things were going, and also to talk. Then he called Chanel, but she didn't answer. He headed back out to the herd to relieve Walt.

"You didn't need to come back," Walt said. "Betsy can take her turn."

"You two have Charlie on your mind," Toby said. "I don't mind doing this for you."

Walt stuck out his hand to shake Toby's. "Thank you."

Toby shook Walt's hand and wondered as he rode out, *Had Charlie getting hurt changed Walt's attitude that much?*

Toby rode nighthawk and rode around and out at times to check for strays, and he found a high spot he could watch from. He was looking around and noticed what he thought was a fire off in the distance in the east. He pulled his binoculars and

Toby the Rancher

looked out into the darkness and tried to find the glimmer he had spotted. He finally found it. It was a campfire, and there were four cowboys sitting around it. He watched it and pondered for a while. He rode around checking the herd again and then rode back to the high place to check the fire again.

He was watching it and saw another cowboy ride into the dim light. The cowboy dismounted and walked up to the fire, and Toby thought he looked like Walt, but he wasn't getting a good-enough look. He wanted to ride over there but knew he couldn't leave the herd unattended. He watched them, and it looked like they were having a rather heated conversation.

Toby looked back at the cattle. They were starting to mill around more, so he rode down to keep them tight and settle them down. He rode around the herd for the next hour and then rode back up to the high spot. He pulled his binoculars and looked again, and the fire was out. He couldn't see anything in the dark. There was only a crescent moon, and it wasn't giving off much light.

He stayed up there watching the herd and looking all around, straining his eyes, when he saw Walt riding toward him. But Walt was coming from the north side of the herd, and the camp was south. Toby thought it was odd but didn't question him.

"I'll take over nighthawk, and you can go on in," Walt said.

"Are you sure?" Toby asked. "I thought I was doing it all night."

"I can't sleep. Go on in."

"Okay." Toby started toward camp. He looked at his watch and saw it was 2:30 a.m. He saw a couple of cows drifting out, and he rode over to bring them back in. When he rode around a thicket to flank them, he ran smack-dab into trouble.

47

Four riders were waiting as Toby rode around the thicket. All he could see were the outlines of the four riders and their horses, and as far as he knew, they were not supposed to be there. He had his rifle in his hands before he even realized it; he had pulled it from the scabbard. He had dealt with rustlers before, and if this was what the riders were, he was going to be ready.

Toby squeezed Pudge with his knees, and Pudge pulled up and stopped. "What are you guys doing out here?" Toby hollered.

They spun their horses to leave and took off. Toby started to give chase but thought better about it since it was dark. He turned and started toward the campfire that was dimly burning and pondered what to do as he rode. He dismounted and walked to the fire to check the coffee. It was hot, and there was about a half a pot, so he was happy. He sat and drank a cup, looking off into the dark. He was startled from his thoughts when he heard Betsy say, "Man, you must be a thousand miles away the way you are sitting there, staring."

Toby looked back at her. "Sorry, did I wake you?"

"Nah, I just woke up. Not used to having my saddle as my pillow."

He laughed. "It does take some getting used to."

"What were you thinking on?" Betsy asked.

Toby the Rancher

"Just a variety of things. Mainly about Charlie." Toby wasn't lying, because he was wondering how all this was going to work out for Charlie.

"I know. He and Dad have different ideas about things, and it is putting stress on both of them."

"I don't know the history, but this is Charlie's life, so I guess I can see his side better from my viewpoint."

"I suppose," Betsy said. "But Dad seems adamant that they need to sell out."

Toby took a drink of coffee and then refilled his cup. After a while, he asked, "Did your dad get some sleep before he came out?"

"No, he left to join you about the time I laid down. I was asleep pretty quick too."

Now Toby knew it was Walt he had seen at the campfire. What was going on? Who were these guys? Why did Charlie not know about them? Toby finished his cup of coffee and mounted back up and rode out. Even though it was dark, he was going to try and find the four riders and see what he could find out.

He didn't like the thoughts he was having about Walt and what he was trying to do to Charlie. Toby hoped he was wrong, but too many things were starting to add up. He had Pudge walking slowly so he didn't step in a hole or on a rock and hurt himself, plus he was hoping to find them without them knowing he was there. He traveled in the direction he had seen the fire and was surprised to see they had started another one. It made it easy to slip up on them as they were blinded by the firelight and couldn't see into the dark.

Toby took his rifle. He left Pudge and started sneaking toward the camp. He was trying to stay away from the horses so they didn't spook. He was able to stay behind some mesquite bushes and then he crab walked a ways to get close enough to listen.

He heard one them say, "We need to go back and get the cows cut out and moving to the trailer."

"Walt said that guy was nosy and might try to stick his nose in," another said. "He was right there."

◆ 399 ◆

"Well, I figure if he does, we can break his nose," another said.

Toby had heard enough. He stood up and cocked his rifle as he walked into camp. The four guys started to scramble to their feet, and one of them fell all over himself as he tried to get up too fast.

"You boys just stay where you are." Toby started to walk in but heard a horse riding up, so he stopped and stayed in the darkness.

Walt came riding up, and swung down off his horse before it actually came to a stop. "What are you doing? Where are the cattle?"

The men looked at Walt as he was talking but then turned back toward Toby's direction. Walt looked that way too and asked, "What are you looking at?"

Toby walked into the firelight, and Walt's mouth fell open from shock.

"Hello, Walt," Toby said.

Walt got over his shock. "What are you doing here?"

"The better question is what are *you* doing here?" Toby replied. "You are stealing your dad's cattle. Is that what you are doing?"

"They're partly mine too," Walt said.

Toby smiled. "That just makes it even more stupid."

"I'm not stupid!" Walt snapped.

"What you are doing is," Toby replied. "I can't even start to imagine what would make you think what you are doing is okay in any book."

One of the four guys asked, "Can we sit down, and will you take the gun off of us?"

Toby glanced down at the rifle and decided it wasn't needed. "Sure."

They sat down. Walt walked over by them. He poured a cup of coffee and sat down.

"I'm waiting," Toby said.

"Waiting for what?" Walt asked.

Toby was getting mad. "Your foolish excuse for why you are stealing your dad's and your own cattle."

Toby the Rancher

Walt sat for a minute and then started in, "I'm not stealing them. I've had these guys sifting them off and selling them for me. I have the money in an account. Dad won't lose any money."

Toby thought for a minute and then asked, "You sold all the calves, didn't you?"

"Yes. I thought if Dad felt like we were going over a year and a half without calves, he would decide to sell out."

"Why? Why do you dislike your dad so?"

"I love my dad," Walt snapped back quickly. "I just hate ranching."

"But your dad loves it," Toby said. "Why would you take that away from him at this point in his life? It would break him."

"He would have more money than he could spend."

"I'm not talking about money. I'm talking about his spirit. If you love him, why did you not just sell out to him and move on?"

There was a long silence, and then Walt started talking again. "It's a long story."

"I need to hear it, or I'm calling the law," Toby said.

One of the guys asked, "Calling the law for what?"

"Guys, this is illegal, even if he does own part interest," Toby said.

Walt spoke up. "I had an older brother. He loved ranching, just like Dad. I was more like Mom and didn't particularly care for life on the ranch. We tolerated it but wanted other things. I got in trouble when I was sixteen, and my brother knew the guy that I damaged his property, so Mom wanted him to go talk to the guy and get me out of trouble. Tony didn't want to. He wanted to let me have to take any punishment that I was due. Mom wanted me home before Dad found out, and she and Tony argued, and he left mad. He was driving to get me, and a drunk driver crossed over the centerline and hit Tony head-on and killed him instantly."

Walt paused. "He was only twenty years old and very athletic and strong. He reminded me of you. He was my big brother, and I knew I could never live up to him. Mom and I were devastated because we both felt it was our fault, and we never lost that feeling. Dad nearly lost it. He had so many plans for his ranch with Tony, and to be fair, me too. I didn't want it, but he did. Mom begged me to stay on and do the ranching with Dad to help with the loss of Tony. I felt like it was my duty, but I have never liked it, and as Dad has gotten older and Mom passed away, I decided I wanted a different life for all of us. Dad disagreed, so I came up with this plan to convince him it was time give it up."

"I am sorry about your brother and you having to do something your whole life you didn't want to," Toby said. "But this is still as wrong as can be."

There was a long silence, and then Walt said, "I'll tell Dad, and we'll decide what is best together."

One of the guys asked, "Did your dad find out about you being in trouble and that Tony was coming to help?"

Walt shook his head. "No. He never knew, and still doesn't to this day."

"I am going back to the herd," Toby said. "Walt, I trust you will do the right thing with these guys and Charlie."

He mounted up and rode back to the herd. He rode nighthawk the rest of the night, and when morning came, he started pushing the herd by himself. Pudge was on the ball, and he and Toby had the herd moving good when Walt and Betsy caught up and joined them. They didn't talk but drove the cows hard all day long and made it into the corrals just after dark. They got the cows penned, and Toby told them he would put some hay out if they wanted to go on to the barn. He finished and walked into the bunkhouse at 8:30 p.m.

Betsy brought him some supper shortly thereafter. He ate, and as he finished, his phone rang.

48

"Hello?" Toby answered the phone without looking at it.

"Hello, Toby," Hank said on the other end.

"Hey, Hank, how ya doing?"

"I'm doing well. How are you? How is the roundup going?"

Toby proceeded to tell Hank that they had the cattle up and in the corrals. As Toby talked, he was trying to decide whether he should tell Hank about the deal with Walt or not. He wouldn't even think of it, if Charlie wasn't such a good friend and now injured.

"Man, y'all must have pushed them," Hank said. "How are you holding up? How is your neck?"

"I'm good," Toby replied. "Getting my strength back."

"Good deal. I talked to Charlie. He seems to be in good spirits, considering his injuries and pain. He sure sings your praises."

Toby decided he needed to talk to Hank about Walt. "Hank, I debated discussing this with you but have decided since you and Charlie are such good friends, I need to fill you in."

Hank could tell the concern in Toby's voice and said, "This sounds serious. What's up, son?"

Toby started slowly but went through the entire story all the way up to getting the cattle in the corral. Hank was silent through the story and didn't speak for a while after Toby finished.

Toby was wondering if he had screwed up when Hank finally broke the silence. "Toby, I'm glad you told me, and I am even more glad that you are there helping. What do you think needs to happen?"

Toby hesitated but then said, "Hank, I don't really know. I don't know Charlie well enough to know how he would take it all."

"He will be hurt, but he is strong," Hank said. "He has dealt with a lot of heartache with the loss of Tony and Claire, his wife. He needs to be told."

"I was hoping Walt would man up and do it. I think it would serve him better."

"Yeah, but he hasn't seemed to man up to anything, from the way I see it. I am having a hard time grasping how a son could do that to his dad. I mean, I couldn't even justify that if Charlie was a low-life individual. I don't get along with Carl, but I could never see him doing something that evil, and he is my son-in-law." There was a pause, and then Hank said, "I'll quit venting. How are you going to handle it?"

"I think I'll talk to Walt and give him a chance to tell his dad, before I do it," Toby said.

"You be careful," Hank said. "If he would do that, he might try anything."

"I will. How are things there?"

"Things are good. Tom is doing well."

"Is Miss Sadie doing well?"

Hank laughed. "She is still in charge."

They both laughed and said their good-byes and hung up.

Toby sat and drank a couple of cups of coffee while he pondered what to do and how to do it. He decided to call Chanel and see how she was doing. He woke her up, so he apologized and ended the call with, "I'm sorry. I hope you can go back to sleep. Good night." He didn't give her a chance to speak, hoping she could go right back to sleep if he didn't get her involved in a conversation.

Toby headed for the shower and bed, realizing he could use some good sleep too. He crawled into bed at 10:30 p.m., read the Bible, and said his prayer. He was asleep by 11:15 p.m.

The next day, he was awake and on the front porch drinking coffee at 5:00 a.m. He had several thoughts running through his mind. He was thinking of Charlie, Walt, Tom, and Chanel. He hadn't ever missed a girl like he was missing Chanel at this point. He sat pondering things a while longer and then said as he got up from the chair, "I'll read Walt this morning and let that help me decide my course of action."

Toby ate a quick breakfast and then headed to the barn to see Pudge. He fed and watered him and brushed him down before saddling up. He had Pudge saddled and was leading him out of the barn when Walt walked up.

"Mornin', Walt," Toby said.

"Yeah, good morning," Walt replied. "Toby, Betsy and I are going to go to the hospital to see Dad. We'll have to wait to work any cattle."

"I understand, but I may try to start working some while you're gone."

"By yourself?"

"It will be slow, but it will give us a jump on tomorrow."

"Okay." Walt turned to walk off.

"Walt, I have to ask," Toby continued. "What are you going to tell your dad about your deception?"

Walt stopped but didn't turn around. "Just let me deal with it, will you?"

"I wish I could do that," Toby said. "But since I found out about it, I have a responsibility."

Walt kept his back to Toby. "I will tell him, but it is on you if it kills him."

"He is stronger than that," Toby said.

Walt walked away. Toby climbed on Pudge and rode toward the far corral.

◆ 405 ◆

Toby worked cattle all day long. He didn't stop for lunch and made good progress in spite of doing it himself. When it started getting dark, he shut down for the day and started feeding. He finished feeding after dark and then brushed and fed Pudge before taking a slow walk to the bunkhouse. He put a pot of coffee on and plopped down in the easy chair. He was as tired as he could remember ever being but was very happy with what he had accomplished for the day. He wondered if he was so tired because of the wreck or just the fact he had done a lot today.

His phone ringing woke him up. He looked at the clock, and he saw he had been asleep for about an hour. He answered it, and Hank was on the other end.

"You sound groggy," Hank said. "Did I wake you up?"

"I was tired from working cattle all day," Toby replied. "And I guess I dozed off waiting for the coffee to brew."

"Who helped you?"

"No one."

"No wonder you're tired," Hank said. "And if I am right, you probably worked more than just a few head, if I know you."

Toby chuckled. "I made a good dent in it."

"That's great," Hank said. "Hey, I am heading your way. I should be in around 2:00. I got a call from Charlie, and he was so down in the mouth I felt I needed to come."

"So I take it Walt talked to him?"

"Yeah. It broke Charlie's heart worse than I thought it would."

"I'm sorry, Hank," Toby said. "I should have stayed out of it, and he wouldn't have known."

"Don't you ever think that," Hank said. "You did right, and he needed to know. He will make it through."

"Are you coming to the ranch or the hospital?"

"To the ranch tonight. I will go to the hospital in the morning."

"Okay," Toby said. "See you when you get here. Drive safe."

They hung up.

Toby sat there, running everything over in his mind. Should he have just let it go? Hank said no, but he still wondered. He got up, poured himself a cup of coffee, and started some supper. He guessed it was because he had taken a nap, but he had a hankering for breakfast, so he cooked himself some eggs, bacon, biscuits, and gravy. He enjoyed every bite of it.

Toby had just finished the dishes when his phone rang. He reached and answered it, and it was Chanel.

"I didn't wake you, did I?" she asked.

"Nope," Toby replied. "Just got through doing the dishes."

"A man after my own heart."

They talked for about twenty minutes, just on things in general, and then said their good-byes.

Toby sat and drank another cup of coffee and considered how the morrow would go. He dozed off on the couch and woke up when he heard a truck pull up. He looked at his watch and saw it was 2:05 a.m. He walked over and opened the door.

Hank walked in. "You didn't need to wait up."

"I fell asleep on the couch and woke up when I heard you pull up," Toby said.

Hank got settled in, and they both went to bed, figuring anything else could wait till morning.

Toby was up and had breakfast started when Hank got up. Toby got breakfast ready, and Hank walked in and sat down.

"Sleep well?" Toby asked.

"Yeah," Hank said. "I used to be able to drive like that easier than I can now."

Toby smiled. "Aw, you are still a spring chicken."

Hank laughed. "Thanks, but my bones and muscles would tend to disagree."

Toby laughed. "You heading to the hospital?"

"Yeah," Hank replied. "I figure I'll get on over there and see how things are."

"I haven't heard a peep from Walt, so I guess I will just keep working cattle today," Toby said.

Hank thanked Toby. They finished eating, and they went their separate ways.

◆ 107 ◆

Toby started working cattle again. Things went smoothly, and he made very good progress by midday. He stopped briefly and had a bite to eat. He started back and worked three cows he had caught in the lane, and then he went to pen up three more. He got three going in the lane and was waiting to shut the gate when he heard a deep bawl. He turned his head to see a bull rushing him.

Toby jumped sideways to avoid the bull, and the bull hit the gate and broke one of the boards. He grabbed the fence to try and swing and jump out of the corral. He had forgotten he had brought Pudge into the corral earlier to cut some cows and had left him in there. Just as he swung over the top rail, he heard a collision behind him. He jerked around to see that Pudge had run headlong into the bull with his chest and had knocked it off its feet. Pudge stood over the bull, and the bull scrambled to its feet and headed for the far side of the corral.

Toby climbed the fence and took Pudge's reins. "Thank you, buddy. You saved me again."

"That horse never ceases to amaze me," someone said.

Toby looked to see Hank walking up. "I didn't know you were back."

"I just pulled up and saw the bull charge at you," Hank said. "I couldn't do anything but was sure glad to see Pudge take care of the bull. He is the best horse I have ever seen."

"Yes, he is. I wouldn't take a million dollars for him." Toby petted Pudge and kind of hugged his neck, and then he turned back to Hank. "How is Charlie?"

"He is struggling," Hank replied. "He is concerned that the ranch will fall apart while he is laid up. He is hurt about Walt but really hopes he comes around. I don't expect him to, but I may be wrong. I hope I am."

Toby thought about what Hank said and started working the cattle he had in the lane. Hank watched him and asked, "What can I do to help with these three?"

Toby the Rancher

"If you can worm them, I will do the rest," Toby said. "What options do you see Charlie having?"

Hank walked up to start giving the lead cow wormer. "That is why I came back early. I need to talk to you."

Toby stopped what he was doing and looked at Hank. "About?"

49

Toby could tell Hank wasn't really liking what he was fixing to say.

Hank slowly began to speak. "Toby, I know what I am about to ask goes well beyond the norm and is asking a lot of you." He paused to inject a cow with wormer, and Toby figured he knew what was coming.

Hank finished with the cow and continued, "Charlie isn't going be able to work his ranch a good long while, and it appears that Walt isn't an option to step up. I was wondering if you would be willing to stay on here and work and run the ranch until Charlie is ready, or makes a decision of what to do."

It was what Toby had expected, and he had mixed emotions about the request. He finished with the cow he was preg checking and wrote down the number and how long she was bred. Once he was done, he looked at Hank and asked, "How long do you think it would be?"

"I'm afraid it may be six months or longer," Hank said.

Toby let another cow in and started working on her while he was thinking on what Hank had asked and said. Could and would Tom be able to handle his place for that long? Did he even want to do this? Chanel popped in his mind. He had never missed a girl like he was missing her. If he stayed there, he sure

Toby the Rancher

couldn't go see her. Would she lose interest? His mind went back to his ranch and his cattle.

Then he thought about Pudge. He was glad he was with him. He needed to talk it over with Pudge and really think it through.

Toby finished preg checking the cow he was working on. He looked at Hank and said, "Hank, I need some time to think this through. I mean, I have come to like Charlie and sure want to see him do well, but staying here and leaving my place for even six months is hard to comprehend on the spur of the moment. Are there not any other options, like trying to hire a good foreman? Or offering someone some stock to run the place?"

"Unfortunately, Walt has done a good job of bleeding the ranch dry to the point of Charlie actually having to consider selling out," Hank said. "He just wants to do it on his terms, which means have the stock primed and ready, and he knows they're not right now. I understand you need some time. When do you think you could give us an answer?"

Toby heard the "Us" and knew Hank and Charlie had discussed it, and maybe it shouldn't have, but that added pressure to the situation. He sure didn't want to affect Charlie's physical health or, for that matter, his financial health. What a pickle he was in, and it was none of his doing this time. He kind of smiled to himself as he let the last cow out. He looked at Hank. "I'm going to feed and call it a day, and then make some calls."

"Sounds good," Hank said. "Need any help?"

"Nah," Toby said. "I can get it."

Hank walked to the bunkhouse, and Toby headed to the barn, leading Pudge. He put Pudge in the stall and said, "We have a tough decision to make, Pudge ole buddy. I wish you could tell me your thoughts."

Pudge snorted, and Toby laughed. "I guess you miss your room."

Pudge stomped his foot and raised his head up and down. Toby laughed and went to get the tractor. When he finished feeding, he sat down and talked to Pudge a little more, just to help himself work it out in his mind. He left the barn and walked

♦ 111 ♦

to the bunkhouse. Hank had started some supper. Hank said he had it, so Toby called Tom to talk to him.

Tom was shocked at first, but after the initial shock of the question of whether he could take care of the place or not, he realized Toby wouldn't ask if it wasn't something he felt was totally necessary. He realized from Toby's tone and what Toby was saying that Toby was very concerned about what he was considering doing. After they had discussed things and how things were going at both their locations, Tom said, "Toby, I know this is hard for you. You just got your own place and were looking forward to making it go, and now you are torn trying to accommodate Hank and his friend. I will do my best to take care of your place and cattle if you decide to stay over there."

"I never had a doubt," Toby replied. "Just wondered if you thought your health was good enough."

"Speaking of health, how is your neck doing?" Tom asked.

"It's good as new. No problems."

"Good deal. Have you talked to Chanel lately?"

"We have been missing each other. I sure have been thinking about her and missing her. I know that sounds weird to say."

Tom laughed. "It doesn't sound weird at all. It just seems weird to you, because you never have let yourself feel like that about a girl."

Toby was quiet for a minute. "I guess you know me better than anyone."

"We spent a lot of time around the campfires."

"Yep."

They talked a while longer and then ended the call. Hank hollered that supper was ready, so Toby went to eat. They discussed the situation as they ate, and as Toby finished, he said, "I am going to call Chanel. She may not have an opinion, but I need to see if she does."

He dialed her number, and it went straight to voice mail. He left a message that he wanted to talk to her and would call back later. Hank and Toby watched TV until 10:00 p.m. Toby tried to call Chanel again, but she had very bad reception and they couldn't hear each other, so they hung up. He sent her a text and said he was trying to talk to her to discuss an important matter. He waited for a response, and finally, an hour later, he received a text. She responded that she was on the road and the area she was in didn't carry her cell provider and her signal was either no service or one bar.

Toby didn't respond. He sat and wondered why she would go on the road like that without letting him know she was going. Maybe he had read her signals wrong and she didn't have the same feelings he had for her. He became mad at himself that he had allowed himself to fall for a girl, only to have it go like this. He had let his guard down against his better judgment, and now he was left feeling like an idiot.

Hank was already asleep, so Toby read the Bible and prayed. He went out on the porch and looked at the stars for well over an hour. He was disappointed and somewhat hurt and angry at himself. He vowed to never make the same mistake. He didn't care if he lived as a bachelor all his life.

He went to bed and finally fell asleep at around 3:00 a.m. He woke up at 5:30 a.m. and started breakfast. Hank got up just before 6:00 a.m. and walked over to get a cup of coffee.

"Morning, Hank," Toby said.

"Good morning," Hank replied.

"I'll stay and take care of the ranch."

Hank was taking a sip of coffee, and he looked up. "Are you sure?"

"Yeah. I would like to build out a stall for Pudge so he will feel more at home. He is my family."

Hank smiled. "I know how you feel about him, and I don't see any problem with doing that. It will always be usable even after you come home."

Toby nodded and handed Hank a plate of food. They ate breakfast, and Toby headed to the barn as Hank headed out to the hospital. Toby went and told Pudge they would be staying.

He told Pudge about his stall Toby would build out for him like home. He finished saddling Pudge and rode out to check things around the corrals. He started cutting cows out and penning them so he could start working them and try to get to a hundred worked by the end of the day. It was slower and difficult by himself, but at this point, there were no other alternatives.

He worked straight up until 2:00 p.m. and emptied the pen of the first bunch he had penned. He rode Pudge to the bunkhouse to eat a sandwich and drink a couple of cups of coffee. He was finishing his second cup when he heard a vehicle pulling up into the drive. He figured it was Hank, and got his hat and gloves and started out the door to go cut out more cows. He was surprised when he walked out on the porch and saw it was Betsy who had pulled up.

She got out of her truck and walked over to the porch. "I was at the hospital, and Hank and Gramps said you were working the cattle by yourself, so I thought I would come and see if I could help."

Toby was relieved. "I appreciate it. I can use the help."

"My boyfriend is on his way too."

"Does he know cattle?"

"He has helped us some. He is good at anything he does."

Toby smiled. "I hope that is not just affection talking, but if he can help, I am glad to have him. What's his name?"

"His name is Tommy Smith. Why do you ask?"

Toby laughed. "I just wanted to know what to call him."

Betsy was embarrassed and didn't respond. She just turned away and started walking back to her truck.

"Don't leave mad," Toby hollered.

"I'm not," Betsy said. "I'm just getting my gloves."

They were penning up more cows when Tommy pulled up. Toby looked toward the barn and did a double take to see the vehicle he was driving. It was a small weird-looking pickup. He looked back at the cows as two of them were being rowdy and not wanting to cooperate. Pudge handled them well, but the cows didn't like it. Toby got them in, and Betsy shut the gate as Tommy came walking up.

Toby was dismounting and sizing him up as he walked up. Tommy was kind of frail, to Toby's thinking. He didn't look like he had done too many tough jobs.

Betsy climbed the fence and hugged Tommy. She looked back at Toby and said, "Toby, this is Tommy Smith, my boyfriend. Tommy, this is Toby…I can't remember your last name."

"Parker. Good to meet you, Tommy. If you don't mind me asking, what is that you are driving?"

Tommy grinned. "That is an Isuzu Pup. A very economical vehicle."

Toby smiled. "Good to know it has something going for it."

"It is a classic," Betsy chimed in.

Toby laughed. "When does it become a full-grown dog?"

Betsy and Tommy both glared at him, and Toby just said, "Let's get started. Tommy, what can you do?"

"I can get them in the lane for you," Tommy replied.

"All right, sounds good," Toby said. He turned to Betsy. "Betsy, can you worm them?"

Betsy nodded, still mad at Toby for making fun of Tommy's vehicle.

Toby let the first cow in and went to work. Betsy wormed the cow, and they had her ready to go out quickly. They worked off the first five cattle. Tommy was trying to get more cows in the lane, and Toby was trying to watch while he was working on a cow. He could tell Tommy didn't know what he was doing. Toby felt he was responsible for what was going on. He was struggling to work the cattle while trying to keep an eye on Tommy—and also Betsy, for that matter. He heard a vehicle pull up and looked to see who it was, and just as he did, he heard a scream.

50

Toby jerked his head back around and saw that one of the cantankerous cows had gotten Tommy down. The cow was trying to mash Tommy into the ground with her head. Betsy was just screaming.

Toby grabbed the top rail of the six-foot corral fence and cleared the fence with ease as he swung over it. He ran to Tommy yelling at the cow. It didn't faze her, so he reacted without thinking and grabbed her by the nose and top knot and twisted. He bulldogged her and then hollered for Betsy to come check on Tommy while he was holding the cow down by keeping her head twisted back. Tommy was trying to get to his feet when Betsy got there. She helped him out of the corral.

Toby got ready to jump up and let the cow go. Luckily, she didn't want any part of him when she got up and ran to the other side of the corral.

Hank came running up as Betsy and Tommy were walking out and checked on Tommy as he watched Toby to make sure he didn't get hurt letting the cow loose. "Are you okay, young man?"

Tommy shook his head. "Just scared and bumps and bruises."

"You are lucky you had Toby here," Hank said. "I don't know of anyone else that could have gotten you out of that situation as quickly and unharmed."

Toby hopped back over the fence and walked over to Tommy. "Tommy, are you okay? She didn't step on you, did she?"

Tommy looked up sheepishly and nodded. "Nah, I'm okay. Thanks for your help."

"I'm just sorry it happened and glad you are okay." Toby walked on around the corral to get Pudge and use him to cut the cow and pen her up.

After Toby walked off, Betsy said, "That's odd."

"What's that?" Hank asked.

"He didn't even acknowledge what he did," she said. "Usually guys will want to brag about something like that, and that was definitely worth bragging about."

Hank smiled. "Not Toby. He knows what he can do, and doesn't need to brag about it. Now that you mention it, I've never seen anyone clear a six-foot fence so easily."

"Even though I was fighting off the cow, I noticed him come flying over the fence," Tommy said.

They all laughed.

"You want me to help you to the house, son?" Hank asked.

Tommy straightened up. "I'm okay. Toby needs my help, and I am going to help him."

Hank chuckled. "Sounds good. I will change my clothes and be back down in a minute to help."

Toby looked and saw Tommy climbing the fence to get back into the corral. He smiled and said to himself, "He's a lot tougher than I gave him credit for."

Tommy glanced over at Toby. Toby tipped his hat to him, and Tommy grinned big and gave a brief wave back. They got going again and knocked out a good number for the rest of the afternoon. Betsy left about thirty minutes before they quit to go get some pizzas for supper.

When they shut down the cattle working, Toby rode Pudge up. He brushed, fed, and watered Pudge before he went to feed. Betsy returned with the pizza, and Toby finished feeding. They were waiting on Toby to get to the bunkhouse before they started. Hank blessed the food, and they all dug in, hungry from the afternoon's activities. They talked about the day, and then as they were cutting the pie that Hank had bought, Toby said, "About two more days with some help, and we should be done."

"That will be a relief to Charlie," Hank responded.

"How was Charlie today?" Toby asked.

"His spirits lifted a lot when he heard you were going to stay and run his ranch for him."

Toby didn't reply. He was doing it, but with mixed feelings and disappointment that things didn't work out with Chanel.

"What do you mean Toby is going to run the ranch?" Betsy asked. She looked at Toby. "Don't you have your own place to run?"

"I have a friend tending to mine," Toby replied.

"I still don't understand," Betsy replied. "Why isn't Dad going to run the ranch?"

"Betsy, that would be best taken up with your dad," Hank said. "He hasn't been to see your grandpa since the first day y'all got back from the roundup."

Betsy looked stunned. She got up from the table and walked outside. Tommy got up and followed her out. Toby and Hank looked at each other but didn't speak. They sat and ate their pie and drank their coffee.

Tommy and Betsy walked back in, and Hank said, "I cut you a piece of pie. It's pretty good for a bought pie. Better give it a try."

Tommy smiled. "I believe I will."

Betsy stood there for a while and then asked, "Is this why you came here, Toby? To root Dad out and take over yourself?"

Toby got mad but didn't let himself snap back. He took his time to speak.

It was Hank who spoke up. "Betsy, girl, you are out of line. You have no right to accuse Toby of that. For that matter, you don't have any right to accuse him of anything. He came over here because I asked him to. Because your grandpa needed help. He has agreed to stay on because I asked him to. He has his own place that he would love to get back to but is putting his life on hold to help your family out."

Toby hadn't seen Hank that mad in a long time, if ever. He glanced at Betsy and saw her attitude and demeanor had definitely changed.

"I'm sorry," Betsy said. "I know he came to help. I don't understand why Dad isn't being allowed to run the ranch, though."

Toby cut his eyes to Tommy to see how he was acting. Tommy was looking a little upset. Toby watched him to see what his next reaction would be when Hank responded.

"Charlie would love nothing more than to have Walt run things," Hank said. "He has worked and planned on that for the last twenty-five years. Unfortunately, your dad hasn't been back to hospital since the first day, and you see he hasn't showed up around here. Things had to move forward, because livestock don't wait on people to be fickle."

Toby was curious of Tommy's change in facial expression.

"So you mean Walt is not going to get his part of the ranch?" Tommy asked.

Hank turned slowly to look at Tommy and calculated what Tommy had said. "Young man, I don't think anyone said anything about Walt being cut out of anything. Besides that, what business is that of yours?"

Tommy was embarrassed, but he had brought it on himself with his question.

Hank continued, "Are you dating this young lady for her inheritance?"

Tommy looked like the cat that swallowed the canary.

Toby couldn't help but chime in. "So that is why you came out to help, and stayed after getting knocked down."

"No, it isn't," Tommy blurted back. "I like Betsy."

Betsy looked at him. "*Like?*"

"I-I-I mean, love," Tommy stammered.

"Leave!" Betsy cried out.

Tommy tried to reach out and touch her and say something, but she pulled away. "Now!"

Tommy kind of glanced at Hank and Toby then turned and walked to the door.

Once he was out, Hank said, "Betsy, I am sorry."

"It's okay," Betsy said with tears in her eyes. "What about Dad?"

Toby could see that Betsy thought the world of her dad and it was hurting her that he was not doing as he should.

"Betsy, I think it would be good for you to go talk to your dad," Toby said. "Maybe he can explain."

Betsy kind of shook her head. She got her stuff and walked to the door.

"Drive safely," Hank said.

She nodded as she shut the door behind her.

Hank and Toby stood there for a while, and when they heard her truck, Hank said, "She is in the dark, and that is not a good place to be. Hopefully, Walt will come clean with her."

Toby nodded. "Yep." He started cleaning up the dishes. As he finished, he said, "This thing looks like it is going to be constant trouble with their family."

"Yeah, and I am sorry I put you right in the middle of it," Hank said.

"Don't worry about that," Toby said. "I just hate it for them. Charlie is a good man. I don't mind helping him out."

Toby sat down with a cup of coffee and caught himself thinking about Chanel. He wondered why she had seemed to lose interest. He thought the times they had spent together were good and fun and that they had both grown in affection for each other.

Hank spoke something, but Toby's mind was not on what he said, so he repeated it. "I said I guess Tom is doing okay with your place."

Toby brought himself back to the present. "Huh? Oh, yeah. He seems to be doing well and enjoying it when we talk."

Hank laughed. "You tired or thinking about someone else?"

Toby was a little embarrassed. "A little of both. I think I'll walk out and see Pudge."

As Toby reached the door, Hank said, "Toby, you know you saved that boy from bad injury, or even saved his life today. I know you don't care for any credit, but you need to realize what you did wasn't just run of the mill."

Toby had stopped to listen. He nodded and walked on out the door.

"Hello, Pudge ole buddy," Toby said as he walked into the barn.

Pudge snorted and shook his head. Toby sat and petted Pudge's head and talked over things that had happened with him.

Hank heard a phone ringing and saw that Toby had left his phone on the coffee table. Hank answered it, and it was Chanel.

"Hello," Chanel said. "I was trying to get Toby Parker."

Hank laughed. "This is his phone, but this is Hank Parker."

"Oh, hello, Hank. This is Chanel."

"Yeah, I saw your name on the phone when I answered it. Toby is out in the barn checking on Pudge."

"I missed his calls last night, and I wanted to see what he was needing."

"I'll tell him you called when he gets in."

"Thank you," Chanel said.

Toby dozed off, leaning back against the stall wall. He had done that so many times since he was eighteen it almost seemed as natural as lying in bed.

Hank gave up on Toby and went to bed.

Toby woke up at around 2:30 a.m. and headed to the house to crawl in bed for a couple of hours. He woke up at 5:00 a.m. and started breakfast. Hank got up at 6:00 a.m. Toby had Hank's breakfast on the table but was out in the barn saddling Pudge for the day. He headed for the corral and started penning cattle. He wanted to get finished by tomorrow evening if everything went smoothly.

Hank walked down before he left for the hospital. "You got started early."

"Yeah," Toby said. "I didn't figure I would have any help, and I need to get done by tomorrow. Some of the few calves need to go to market to help buy more hay and feed."

"Sounds like you have a plan," Hank said. "I will tell Charlie. He will be happy."

Toby was preg checking a cow and nodded to what Hank had said. Hank started to walk off and then stopped. "Oh yeah. Did you notice you had a phone call last night?"

"No," Toby said. "Who called? Tom okay?"

"Chanel called. She said she had missed your call and was calling back."

"Okay, thanks."

"That girl has it bad for you, son," Hank said as he walked off.

Toby hesitated and thought about what Hank had said. He wondered why Hank would say that. He decided to forget about it and pay attention to what he was doing. He stayed at it for the next three hours and was in the middle of preg checking another cow when his phone rang. He couldn't answer it with both hands occupied, so he just ignored it.

The cow was bred and was carrying twins. That piqued Toby's interest. He made sure he got the cow's number written down and noted that she would have twins. He had forgotten his phone had rung.

He heard a vehicle and saw Betsy pulling up. Toby took a break and walked to the bunkhouse for a cup of coffee. He met Betsy on the way. "Good morning. You doing okay today?"

"The morning is nearly gone," Betsy replied. "Sorry I'm late."

Toby stopped and looked at her. "Are you okay?"

She kind of smiled. "I am okay. Thanks for asking."

"Let me drink a cup, and we'll get started back."

"Okay. I will go down and get ready."

Toby drank his coffee and started to walk off the porch, and remembered his phone had rung. He reached for it just as it started to ring again, and he answered it. "Hello?"

"Hey, Toby," Hank said. "Walt just came to see his dad. I'm hoping for good things from him."

"That is good news," Toby said. "That will have to help Charlie. Betsy just showed up, so I should be able to get more done this afternoon."

"Sounds good," Hank said. "I'll be back to help some in a couple of hours. You two be careful."

They hung up, and Toby headed for the corral. They worked a lot of cattle through before Hank got back. He changed and walked down to help. Toby's phone buzzed as he was moving cattle into the working lane. He grabbed it out of his pocket and flipped it to Hank. "Would you answer that for me?"

Hank answered it. "Toby Parker's phone."

It was Chanel. "You still answering Toby's phone?"

"Yes, ma'am," Hank said. "He is in the cattle pen."

"I tried to call this morning too."

"I am sorry about last night. He fell asleep in the barn. He is working hard here."

"He always works hard," Chanel said. "I called Tom, and he said Toby seemed upset with me. Do you know what he is upset about?"

"No, ma'am," Hank said. "I sure don't."

"Well, okay. Thank you."

Toby was working on a cow, and Hank said to him, "That was Chanel."

"Okay." Toby wondered what was up with her. No call that she was going on a trip, and now she was calling him right and left. He shook his head and focused back on what he was doing.

They worked the rest of the day, and Toby fed while Betsy and Hank went to fix supper. Toby walked into the bunkhouse and said, "Man, it sure smells good."

"Miss Betsy is quite the cook," Hank said. "She will make someone a good wife. Can ride and rope and cook. And easy on the eyes too."

Betsy was embarrassed, and blushed. Hank and Toby laughed.

"He is good at embarrassing people with praise, Betsy," Toby said.

They all sat down to eat. As they ate, they heard a vehicle pull up. They heard footsteps on the porch. The door opened, and Walt walked in.

"Hello, Walt," Hank greeted him.

Walt nodded. "Hello, folks."

"What's going on?" Hank asked.

Walt started in, "As you know, I talked to Dad today. I apologized for everything I've done over the years. When all of this came down like it did, and Dad getting hurt, it made me do some soul-searching. It opened my eyes. I was eaten up with my own

Toby the Rancher

guilt about Tony, and I let it control me and my actions for all these years. Toby, I owe you a debt of gratitude. You helped me come to my senses."

Toby nodded. "You're welcome."

"I'm sure that made your dad happy," Hank said.

Walt was getting ready to speak when they heard another vehicle pull in. Walt looked out and said, "I don't recognize the car. Looks like a female."

Betsy walked over to see if it was one of her friends. "Nobody I know."

"I guess we'll wait and see," Hank said.

There was a knock on the door, and Walt opened it to show Chanel.

Toby was so shocked he couldn't even speak.

"Hello, Chanel," Hank said. "This is a pleasant surprise."

Chanel was looking at Toby. "Hello, Hank. Thank you." She stopped looking at Toby and looked at Walt and Betsy and introduced herself.

Toby had gotten up and walked toward her. She looked back at him and said, "I figured if we couldn't connect on the phone, I would just come down here. Tom told me how to get here. It is a ways from everything."

They all laughed, and Toby said, "Let's step outside so we can talk."

Once he and Chanel were on the porch, Chanel asked, "What were you wanting to discuss with me?"

"I was trying to contact you to see what you thought about me staying here and running this ranch for a few months since the owner got hurt," Toby replied.

"Oh, I see," Chanel said. "I'm glad I came then."

"When I saw that you had taken a trip without telling me and I couldn't seem to talk to you, I told them I would stay and help out," Toby continued. "Tom can tend my place for a few months. You seem to be focused on your career, so it is probably good timing for me."

◆ 125 ◆

Chanel's smile left her face. She looked sick to her stomach. Toby looked at her, and neither said anything for a good while. He finally spoke and asked, "So I guess your new job opportunity came through for you?"

She was looking at the porch. "I thought it did, but…"

"What does that mean? Are you moving?"

"It is all up in the air now, so it probably won't happen. I'll stay in Albuquerque."

"The trip wasn't a good one, huh?" Toby said.

"The one earlier was," Chanel said. "This one isn't."

Just then the door opened, and Betsy said, "When you get through, can you come in, Toby?"

He nodded, and she closed the door.

"Is she why you are staying here?" Chanel asked.

Toby looked at Chanel and smirked. "Not hardly. There was only one girl I was interested in, and apparently, that isn't working." He turned to walk to the door. As he walked in, Hank said, "Toby, Walt has some news for you."

Chanel stayed out on the porch. She was wondering how everything could go wrong in a couple of days. Who was the girl Toby was talking about? Sam? Kali? She sat down on the steps and took a deep breath to keep from crying.

Toby was frustrated and wasn't sure he wanted to hear what Walt had to say, but he looked at Walt and asked, "What's the news?"

"Dad and I have talked, and as I said earlier, my whole focus has changed," Walt said. "I am going to run the ranch until Dad gets back on his feet, and then we will decide together what to do. Either keep it going or make changes. Toby, I know you had committed to stay here and take care of things, and I do appreciate it, but this is my responsibility, and I aim to live up to it."

Toby couldn't believe his ears. He felt like a load had just been lifted off his shoulders. He stuck out his hand. "Walt, that *is* great news. I know your dad has to be excited, and don't worry about me. I have a place to go back to and take care of." He looked at Hank, and Hank was grinning from ear to ear.

"I figured that would please you," Hank said. "I can't tell you how thankful I am for all you have done."

"I second that," Walt said.

"I think you have someone waiting on the porch," Hank reminded Toby.

"Oh, yeah." Toby turned and walked out.

Chanel was walking to her car.

"Where you going?" he asked her.

She stopped but didn't turn around. "I'm going home."

"Can we talk first?" Toby asked.

Chanel turned around. "I suppose, but it is getting late."

"We have room here, if you want to stay the night."

"Thanks. We'll see."

"I just got some good news," Toby said. "I am going home. Walt is going to run this ranch."

Chanel started smiling. He looked at her and said, "You seem happier than I am."

"You have no idea."

"Why is that?"

Chanel started to speak but then remembered what Toby had said about the girl whom he cared for, and stopped short.

Toby saw the change. "What's wrong?"

"I have some news about my job," Chanel said. "But whoever the girl is you were referring to might not like my news."

He shook his head. "What? That makes no sense. *You* are the girl I was talking about."

♦ 127 ♦

Chanel started to grin. "Oh, Toby, that is the best news I have ever heard."

They hugged and kissed. Toby realized it was the first time he had really kissed her.

"Now what about your job?" he asked.

"I quit the paper," she replied. "I have a publisher to back me, and I am going to write a book. Provided the subject doesn't say no."

"That is a change, but a good one," Toby said. "What is the book about?"

Chanel looked at him. "You."

"Huh?"

"They want me to write a book about Toby Parker."

"You may have a hard time making that book not be boring," Toby said.

"Hardly," Chanel responded.

He laughed. "You still in Albuquerque?"

She smiled. "Nacogdoches Texas."

He was stunned. "Say what? Are you serious?"

Chanel smiled, nodding.

"That is great," Toby said.

They hugged and kissed again. Toby stepped back and took a deep breath. "Wow, how things can change in a just a few minutes. I can't believe how well everything is working out for me. I am going home, and the girl or woman I have fallen for is going to be living there too."

He took her by the hand and went in to tell Hank. They all talked until midnight, and they decided Toby and Chanel would stay and help Walt and Betsy finish the cattle tomorrow and then they would head home.

Toby lay down in bed and said his prayer, thanking God for the way everything had worked out. He was so happy he was having trouble going to sleep. For the first time since his dad had passed away, Toby didn't feel alone anymore. He had someone whom he wanted to share his life with. That was very unique for him. He had this feeling only one other time, and that was the day Jeb Parker had adopted Toby.

Toby jumped out of bed and headed to the barn to talk to Pudge. Pudge and Toby were going home, and for the first time, Toby felt he knew his place and lot in life.